RED DUST

Other AvoNova Books by
Paul J. McAuley

ETERNAL LIGHT

PAUL J. McAULEY

An AvoNova Book

William Morrow and Company, Inc.
New York

AVON BOOKS
A division of
The Hearst Corporation
1350 Avenue of the Americas
New York, New York 10019

First Morrow/AvoNova Printing: November 1994

AVONOVA TRADEMARK REG. U.S. PAT. OFF. AND IN OTHER COUNTRIES, MARCA REGISTRADA, HECHO EN U.S.A.

Printed in the U.S.A.

ARC   10   9   8   7   6   5   4   3   2   1

*Veteran revolutionaries only end up
as monsters and ghosts.*

DENG XIAOPING

One

Mars was dying.

Year after year, the summer rains failed and the hard pink skies were stitched only with dry lightning. Each year, the winter dust storms raged more fiercely, and spring arrived later than the year before.

In the second year of the Silence of the Emperor, the first day of calm spring weather did not arrive until the forty-sixth of April. The thousand or so people in the Bitter Waters *danwei* suddenly discovered that they were weary of their long winter confinement, their enthusiasms for fighting crickets, heroic opera, and handcrafting fur-trimmed oddments for fun and profit. Despite a seventy per cent chance of a late dust storm, Contract Agronomist Technician Wei Lee had no trouble in rounding up half a dozen volunteer citizens to clear the clogged filters of Number Eight Field Dome.

It was filthy work, requiring full face masks and sealed suits. Edging along metre-wide frame elements. Climbing hand over hand up lines of rung staples to find the air vents which studded one in every hundred of the field dome's big hexagonal panes. Sticking in the blower's nozzle and becoming enveloped in a personal storm of red dust. When Wei Lee cleared the last vent at the top of the dome, he blew his face plate clear, hooked his line to the vent's grid and leaned out to take in the view.

The King of the Cats was playing some down-home

1

rock'n'roll in Lee's earpiece; apart from that he was more alone than he'd been all winter. This was his first year at the Bitter Waters *danwei*, his second as an itinerant agronomist technician. Already he was chafing to move on through the emptying landscapes of Mars; if he could he'd never stop moving until he found his parents or, at least, found the truth behind his great-grandfather's honeyed evasions. The librarian program Xiao Bing had built was all very well, but it searched the other world of the common information space, not the real world, the world all around him.

The dome curved away on either side of Lee, facets glittering against the shocking-pink sky. A dozen identical domes stood in a grid of drainage canals and tracks. Beyond were the sours, green-brown patches showing through the thin mantling of red dust, riven by the lightning bolt of the dry riverbed and spreading north towards the lowlands of the Plain of Gold. Dust hazed the line between land and sky; westward, the notch of the Great Valley was hardly visible. Perhaps he'd travel down it, come summer, to the Paved Mountain and the strange ecosystem of the Dust Seas, hitch a ride on a dust skimmer and climb Tiger Mountain . . .

Shouts floated up, no louder than the King's music. Directly below, the others were semaphoring at Lee. Their shadows made small black oblique strokes against the red ground. He abseiled all the way down, kicking off lightly once, twice against structural struts. He just missed the trestle which carried the water line into the dome and landed sprawling on his back in a bank of soft dust.

"Make speed, Technician," one of the men shouted as Lee picked himself up. "Lin Yi is drowning!"

Field Dome Number Eight grew rice. The canal which carried away the overflow from its flooded fields had been choked by winter dust storms, forming a slough of deep mud covered by a thin dry crust on to which Citizen Lin Yi had ventured and broken through. Now he floundered up to his chest in algae-tinted gloop while the others laughed and shouted advice.

"Do you think you're a fish, Lin Yi?"

"Fish swim in water, not mud. Maybe he's a hog!"

"You're taking conchie recapitulation too far!"

"Recapitulation? If he's a hog, then he's evolved!"

They were waiting for Lin Yi to call for help, none of them willing to break ranks and lose face; and Lin Yi wouldn't ask for help because he would lose face too. He made a kind of sobbing grunt and tried to lunge forward, but succeeded only in sinking deeper. His hands plashed uselessly in dark green slime; his head was tipped back, his mouth wide open.

Lee tossed an end of his safety line to Lin Yi, missed and dragged it back, threw it again. "You might be enjoying your swim," he shouted, "but we'll need your help to clear up this mess, Lin Yi!"

Lin Yi threw himself at the line, his head going under the slop even as he grabbed hold with both hands. The line snapped taut and Lee fell flat on his ass. Some of the watchers laughed. Lin Yi came back up, eyes rolling white in his mud-caked face, and started to claw along the line in panic. For every meter he gained, Wei Lee was pulled a meter closer to the mud. The watchers hooted and stamped their feet as Lee was dragged feet first towards the canal while at the other end of the line Lin Yi pulled himself out hand over hand, as neat a demonstration of Newton's third law of motion as anyone could wish. By the time Lin Yi made dry land, gasping like a future-shocked amphibian and streaked from head to foot with slimy clods and viridescent strands of algae, Lee was lying waist deep in mud beside him.

Lin Yi held out a hand. "Help me up, Technician," he said. After all, he was a shareholding citizen, and Lee was just an itinerant worker. He had rights; Lee had a contract. The fact that Lee had just saved his life meant that Lin Yi had to regain face by asserting his position.

Knowing that didn't cool Lee's temper. He clambered to his feet, smarting in a dozen different places. He pulled off his face mask, swept his black, greased hair back into its DA, and mopped his face with the red kerchief he'd knotted around his neck, the way the King wore one in *Charro* to hide his branded wound.

"Help me up," Lin Yi said impatiently, and Lee said he'd do better than that, and stalked over to the big raised water line that served the dome's hydroponic fields. He had already attached a hose to a spur valve and hooked it over one of the struts which supported the water line as a kind of makeshift shower to wash dust from the protective suits. Now he shook it free.

Lin Yi had climbed to his feet, and the first high-pressure burst sent him sprawling. He sputtered and spat and swore and tried to get up again, and a second burst knocked him on to his back. He began to laugh, paddling upside down in mud and water like an overturned turtle, trying to splash his fellows.

"If you can't swim," Lee said, "you should stay out of the water!" And he lifted the jet so that it rose towards the pink sky in a trembling fountain, glittering in cold sunlight and torn by wind and falling in fat droplets that darkened the red dust. The men danced beneath it, faces raised to the precious rain, hands cupped to catch it, laughing at each other; and Lee laughed too and sent the fountain shooting to new heights.

A voice said loudly, "This is a noble way to waste a morning, Wei Lee!"

Lee turned, sending water spraying in a flat fan. The men ran from it, screeching in mock alarm.

Guoquiang reached up and shut off the valve; the hose quivered and fell slack in Lee's hands. "A little early for a rain dance," he remarked.

"We wash ourselves of dust, after our labours."

Beside Guoquiang, Xiao Bing held on to the harness of a draught bact. Face pale as powdered chalk; white hair; silver caps over pink irises. With his free hand he thumbed a vial into the waist pocket of his long jacket and said, "You are an inspiration to us all, with your selfless dedication. How is my librarian?"

"Still searching. You're going hunting?"

Guoquiang grinned. He was as tall and burly as a Yankee, with a shock of bristly hair, a craggy face with heavy brows.

Like Xiao Bing he was dressed in rust-coloured field clothes. A rifle was slung at one shoulder, and a pistol was buttoned into a holster at his hip. "We're not here to shovel shit. The low-pressure cell shifted. The probability that the storm will hit us has dropped to twenty per cent. It's spring, Wei Lee! All kinds of furry critters are stirring in their burrows! Here, put these on." He tossed Lee a bundle of clothes: padded cotton trousers; a long many-pocketed jacket; a zippered shirt; knee-high hiking boots. "A good idea to get out, but we've a better one. And we're good enough to share it with you."

"Besides," Xiao Bing said, "someone has to lead this bact, Contract Agronomist Technician Wei Lee, and it isn't going to be me."

Two

The terraced cliffs of the Red Valley rose step by step to a scalloped rim that stood out sharply against the hard pink sky. As the three cadres marched through the sours, a straggling V of geese flew out over the cliffs, honking each to each as they headed north to their breeding grounds in the polar sinks.

Spring!

Wei Lee shaded his eyes to watch the birds, and out of casual spitefulness, an attribute some gene cutter had forgotten to edit out of the camel-derived genome of its kind, the draft bact took advantage of the slack harness rope to try and snatch at his hair. Lee felt the rope swing out and ducked the bact's swipe, then whacked it on its muzzle.

"Ho! Ho there! Don't you know I'm cleverer than you!"

He mopped his face with his kerchief and whacked the bact again, to get it moving.

"Ho! Understand who is the master!"

Guoquiang and Xiao Bing had heard Lee shout, and now they shouted at him, asking how he knew he was smarter, asking who was leading who. Xiao Bing said, "We'd be better off if the bact set the traps and Wei Lee carried the gear!"

Lee laughed, and said, "I think maybe you should carry the gear. This bact is not so dumb he could mistake heroic opera for art, and I can lay out traps in my sleep."

Guoquiang said, "Thank you for enlightenment! Now I know that only bacts and contract workers are dumb enough

6

to pay attention to the King of the Cats and his old-fashioned anarchist propaganda."

"Oh! You know very well I like the historical King, not some machine floating in Jupiter who *thinks* it's the King, reborn all over again. No, I like the real one, the one who was born in a stable and became a planet-wide media star, who was exiled to the Moon and returned a hero after leading a revolution against the tyranny of Colonel Parker, who was crucified upon a burning cross, and returned as a thousand acolytes who surgically altered themselves to look exactly like him."

"And who could raise the dead, and turn water into wine," Xiao Bing said.

"I can turn wine into water," Guoquiang said. "The trick is finding the wine."

"I may be dumb," Lee insisted, "but I wouldn't mistake historical reality for the construct who jockeys the show."

"But you listen to it, all the same," Guoquiang said. "A contradiction there, Wei Lee."

"Not at all! I just like the songs he plays. I'm smart enough to know they mean something. Nothing in those operas could ever happen in the real world."

"That's the point," Guoquiang said amiably.

"And if you're so smart," Xiao Bing said, "why are you slogging through this stuff with us?"

"Oh! I don't mind this."

For most of the afternoon the three had been picking a path through the marshy saltpans of the sours. Low black willows and tenacious soldier grasses grew along the ragged cuts of sandclogged irrigation ditches; slimes and moulds threw up wrinkled stinking banks that slumped into sands crusted with leached iron salts. Every footstep threw up a rotten salty stench, and the three cadres walked with their kerchiefs drawn over nose and mouth. Only the bact seemed unaffected; its black lips drawn back in a perpetual sneer as it padded behind Lee.

But while the others grumbled about the stink of the sours, Lee saw it for what it was: a co-operative ecological structure which had once forced the Martian desert slowly to yield to wetland ecology. The roots of black willows reached deep down into the frozen regolith; and special strands in their bark cambium conducted heat to melt and mine the permafrost. Soldier grasses wove a net of stolons through the dusty soil, holding it together. Fungi broke the chemical bonds of the thin surface crust of iron oxides, binding the iron to more stable forms, releasing the oxygen. Rainbow slicks on the black mud in the clogged ditches were a sign that bacteria were multiplying in the anaerobic muck, slowly turning it into soil that would grow crops.

A slow tide of life feeding on the Martian regolith, feeding on itself, processing red dust into oxygen and water and life-filled muck. And the whole system crippled by the imbalance which was locking three grams of water in the polar icecaps for every two produced. The battle fading. Crumbs of water spilled into thirsty sand. The front line where once unreclaimed Martian desert had grudgingly given way to pioneer vegetation was now a festering wound circling the *danwei*'s fifty-kilometre perimeter.

As the three men moved farther from the *danwei*, the black willows grew smaller. Thickly clumped stands thinned out. Tussocks of soldier grass had tails of red sand, each miniature sand dune pointing in the same direction, away from the *danwei* and the winds that blew off the Plain of Gold. The men's boots kept breaking through a duricrust of hydrated minerals, making a soft creaking sound with each step.

But there was life there, too. Succulent green spears were pushing through the crusted soil, tipped with transparent cells which focused light down to deeply buried corms. The bact flared its nostrils hungrily, and Lee had to keep jerking at its bridle to remind it that it wasn't there to look for lunch. A few bees were out, commuting between widespread patches of yellow-flowered rock vetch. A patch of frosty soil had gathered in the lee of two weather-split boulders, and a lupin had rooted there, its spread of half a dozen leaves no bigger than Lee's hand but already sending up a spike laden with purse-shaped flowers, white and yellow against blood-red rock.

Life. It was delicate and tenacious, mocking the propaganda of the conchies, the triumph of the inorganic. Mars was dying, yet still spring stirred the little lives.

"Time to take a break," Guoquiang said.

Lee and Guoquiang sprawled on a tilted slab of sun-warmed rock and munched dried fish. The bact nibbled at foliose lichens, tearing them from overhangs with its mobile lips. Xiao Bing ranged to and fro, too excited to keep still. He kept taking delicate snorts from his little tube, jolts of memory enhancer that would let him fix every detail. He had taken the pledge to die out of this world into the next, and was remembering details for the niche he was creating in Heaven, the part of information space that belonged to the elective dead. Lee had experienced his design: a desert garden full of reflecting pools and strange half-melted machinery under a starry sky where five moons swung by.

"Look here, a periwinkle! And here is moss campion, a very big cushion. But this, I do not know what this is. Wei Lee!"

Lee asked what it looked like, and Xiao Bing said, "Black glossy leaves in a big rosette, a fat flower spike covered with, I don't know, what looks like silver dusting. The spike shines so bright, and there's a patch of wet soil around the rosette, crusted with blue-green algae. It's beautiful, like a machine. Come and *see*, Wei Lee!"

"I don't need to. It's ice sunflower, one of Cho Jinfeng's species. It helped melt the polar caps back when. Very common above three kilometers, I suppose what you have there is a remnant from the early days."

Guoquiang yawned. "Perhaps it is coming back down from the mountains. The winters are colder than they once were."

"Perhaps. Don't you ever sit down, Bing?"

"I've been sitting down all winter. Look at that! There, there, there it goes!"

Lee saw it at once, an ice mouse jinking into the shadow

of an undercut boulder, tufted tail held up like an aerial. Spring, and the animals which had hibernated through the long winter or which like the ice mouse had lain neither dead nor alive, blood vessels and body cavity filled with ice crystals minutely shaped by antifreeze peptides, were now all alive alive-o. Running and feeding and breeding all unawares of the humans who had brought them here. Mice and men: men and the Ten Thousand Years.

The Ten Thousand Years and the conchies.

Perhaps the conchie propaganda was right, perhaps the Golden Path was the only way, the inevitable next step in the evolution of intelligence. Many, like Xiao Bing, were eager to embrace it, pledging early deaths in exchange for the privilege of designing their own private niche in the Golden Isles of Heaven that lay beyond the barrier in information space. But Lee did not understand the conchie ideology which insisted that Mars must return to its original state, that after all these years the terraforming project should be allowed to fail. If the Earth's consensus was as powerful an ally as the Ten Thousand Years claimed it to be, why was it afraid of the living? For why else would it want to gather all that lived into information space?

Guoquiang had fallen asleep while Lee had been thinking on this. Xiao Bing came over and rummaged through his pockets and at last came up with a pair of goggles. "It's your last chance to check on the librarian," he said. "When we get over the rim the reception will go."

Lee took the goggles. "I checked this morning."

"It's a good program. It'll find your parents."

"Thank you, Xiao Bing."

Xiao Bing bowed. "It was fun to make. But like all intelligence-mimicking programs, it needs positive reinforcement. It needs encouragement. I'm going to remember some more desert before we start up off again," he added, and wandered away.

Lee watched Xiao Bing ramble about for a while. Then he snapped on the goggles, and information space scrolled up even as he adjusted earpiece and patch microphone. The librarian turned to him, a massive book clasped across his chest.

He was a tall thin man in a dark silk robe, its hood cast over his sharp, high-cheekboned face. It was a mirror-image of Lee's own face, a whim Lee now regretted but was unable to ask Xiao Bing to edit out; that Bing had written the librarian was favor enough.

The librarian said, "I have found nothing new since we last spoke, Master, but I have accessed a promising new level. Every day I feel I am getting closer to your parents."

Behind the librarian, tiers of chained leather-bound volumes stepped up into darkness. A shaft of light from a high narrow window slashed across their ranks, fell to a patch of richly patterned carpet no bigger than a hand.

Lee, who had never mastered the knack of subvocalising, mumbled, "You are here without compromise?" The librarian had been working for two weeks now, had moved a long way from the common data-access areas into undefined regions. So far, by some miracle, its integrity had not been tested.

The librarian said, "I had to kill a guardian, but I believe it was not noticed."

With goggles and earpiece as the only sensory inputs, Lee was aware of the faint warmth of the soft dust on which he sat, the touch of cold air on his face. The librarian was only a fictive interface; still, Lee felt a dry catch of fear when he said, "Isn't that illegal? Show me."

The librarian put his hands together, fingertip steepled against fingertip.

And suddenly a worm raced at Lee down an infinite corridor between stacks of books. Although it moved at tremendous speed it also seemed to writhe about a single fixed point, now showing the red serrated plates along its back, now its pale belly. Its golden eyes were huge under arched brows; its mouth gaped amongst bristles and kept on gaping, a vast yawning cave ringed by wet razor-sharp ridges. Lee saw his hands tear a page from the book he carried, wad it and toss it into the worm's maw: there was a soundless flash and the worm vanished.

"That was ten days ago," the librarian said. "I travelled on until I reached this place, and now I will try and penetrate the data files. They are very old, as you see."

"Ten days?" Lee had accessed the librarian only that morning.

"Time is not the same for us," the librarian said. "Master, you have given me a difficult task, and I have travelled long and hard roads to try and fulfil it. I wonder if I might ask one question of you?"

"I would be honored."

"Master, what will you do when I find out what happened to your parents?"

"Once you have found out where they are, I will go to them, of course! My great-grandfather knows about them but would never tell me and so I swore that I would find them for myself. He said it was to protect me from taint of my parents' Sky Roader sympathies . . . "

"Perhaps, Master, he had other reasons. But if you defy your great-grandfather, who is a powerful man, surely you would become an outcast. What then? I ask only because it is often the case that the child's personality is a reflection of its parents. By knowing you better, I may hasten in my task."

Lee's patience had worn thin. "My great-grandfather is one of the Ten Thousand Years, it's true, but I am only an agro-tech. What have I to lose? You find them! That's all I ask! After that, you won't have to worry about me. Who can say what the future holds?"

"Who indeed, Master?" The librarian bowed again, and added, "Someone wishes to speak with you."

When Lee stripped off the goggles Guoquiang said, "You woke me up with your shouting. What were you doing? It's no time to be visiting dream girls at Ma Zizhen's."

"That wouldn't be much use with only sound and vision," Lee said.

"Oh, there's nothing wrong with looking. Or talking, for

that matter. I do it all the time. It's healthy." Guoquiang grinned. "Now you've had a winter here you'll know why."

Xiao Bing said, "Wei Lee doesn't need goggles and a clenched fist. He's had more luck in one winter than you've had since your first hard-on."

Guoquiang said, "Exogamy is a strong drive. Wei Lee shouldn't exploit it. I rely on my natural charms, not greased hair and zither playing."

"It's a guitar."

"Of course it is," Guoquiang said. "First you rock and then you roll. And then you and Li Mei start paying child tax."

Lee blushed, and Guoquiang laughed. "There are no secrets amongst citizens, at least, not in winter. Come on, we've a way to go."

In two minutes they were packed and on the move again, climbing a slope of loose stones and frosty dust that rose up to the horizon line, where a square boulder big and black as a locomotive jutted against the pink sky.

They were climbing a collapsed cliff towards the first terrace of the ancient river valley. Three billion years ago a vast flood had carved the Red Valley, cutting a channel a kilometer deep and three kilometers wide at the point where it entered the lowlands of the Plain of Gold. In the past few centuries the warming of the world had restarted the release of water from aquifers in the badlands, but only enough to create a sluggish trickle, white with salts, that dried out completely in winter. Now it was spring, but the alkaline river which had given the Bitter Waters *danwei* its name had not yet started to run. A bad omen.

Halfway up the slope, the cadres turned as one and saw the settlement framed by the red walls of the valley, small and far. Domes glittered in the brilliant sunlight. Stepped cliffs rose on the other side of the braided river channel to the cratered high plain.

The three grinned at each other, and then they were running. Lee hauled at the bact's halter until it broke into a sullen knock-kneed trot. Freedom, they suddenly all felt it.

Their feet kicked dry dust high into the still air, and when they all reached the top and turned they saw far downhill a drifting red sheet that twisted into three ropes pointing to the ridge where they stood, gasping for breath.

Lee started to babble as soon as he got his breath back, asking his friends to imagine the terraces cloaked in pine forest, dark green rhododendrons. Grass pastures either side of a wide clear river, a waterfall plunging into a foaming pool. Water, that was all that was needed: the water locked in the poles and in the vast buried permafrost reservoirs untapped by the world's failed warming. It could still happen. It was not too late.

"Wei Lee's genotype is expressing itself again," Xiao Bing said, when Lee paused for breath, and Guoquiang laughed. They'd both heard all this Sky Roader propaganda many times; Lee had told them about his education and keep, the obligation to his great-grandfather he could not forget. Xiao Bing, even though he had written the librarian for Lee, thought his flight from privilege was romantic; Guoquiang was more scornful, but his scorn was tempered with deference to Lee's upbringing. Once a relation of one of the Ten Thousand Years, always a relation. Despite the *danwei*'s ethos of democratic capitalism, its shareholders retained a respect for lineage.

Lee sighed. He said, "I was brought up to believe that the task will be completed, but that does not mean that it will come true." He had almost forgotten the angry uncertainty that the librarian's questions had tapped. How little his own fate mattered, compared to the fate of the world!

Guoquiang said seriously, "It is Sky Roader talk, Wei Lee. You know that. After what happened to your parents you must know that. Your great-grandfather can believe what he wants. That is the privilege of the Ten Thousand Years. But you . . . "

"I can talk with you fellows, at least."

"Better not to talk about it," Guoquiang said. "In a hundred years perhaps we will all be Sky Roaders singing the songs of the King of the Cats day and night. But it is not likely. You know what happened to the last board of directors, ten years ago. Thanks to Yi Shihung we're all committed to the Golden Path. And so must you be, even as an employee."

Lee said, "Perhaps. But I can still speak of these matters amongst friends, eh?"

Guoquiang said, "Mars is for the Martians. I don't care for the conchies, but I have no special interest in the anarchists either. Keep them all out, I say."

Xiao Bing, who was always anxious to stop arguments developing, said, "Some people insist the King is an alien. We listen to him, and he studies us."

Lee said, "We made the world what it is. We should finish the making. Mars for the Martians, Guoquiang. So perhaps we agree after all."

Guoquiang said, "That's over. We live as we must. At least Earth helps us defend ourselves from anarchists who would turn this world into an ecological laboratory, if they could. Why should we aid them by trying to correct old mistakes?"

"To prove that we can do it, of course."

"But of course," Guoquiang said, smiling, "we do not need to prove what we can do. Only what we cannot."

Xiao Bing laughed. Silver-capped eyes flashed in his thin white face. "Cheer up, Wei Lee," he said. "Maybe it will rain every day, and we will become frogs. I prefer the desert! I will always remember it this way." He took a dramatic sniff of enhancer. "I'll remember all of us this way! Dusty and sweaty and happy! We don't need this world: the Emperor rules a better one on the far side of death."

Lee and Guoquiang exchanged looks. It was bad taste to remind others of one's elective death. Guoquiang briskly consulted his mechanical watch. "There's still three hours of daylight left. We'll try and make the rim today, at least."

By the time Lee had managed to pull the bact away from a clump of luscious prickly pear, and beaten its flanks and dodged a sullen kick, the two cadres were almost out of sight. Lee followed, wishing that he could keep his mouth shut, not argue the King's undoubted greatness, not denigrate the Thousand Year Plan of the Golden Path. His thoughts were like water stored in the porous regolith; raise the temperature and they flooded out under an irresistible pressure, causing chaos and collapse.

But he couldn't stay unhappy for long, not when he was out in the world again. Leading the contrary bact, he sang in his high, cracked tenor songs from his all-time number-one favorite movie—the immortal *Spinout*—and listened for the echoes from the rosy cliff that rose ahead, where Guoquiang and Xiao Bing were toiling up the narrow path that clung to its sheer face.

By the time Lee had hauled the bact to the top, the others had already started to make camp in the remains of an ancient crater, a weathered arc of upturned strata fretted with horizontal crevices. It was a site traditionally used by hunting expeditions from Bitter Waters. Guoquiang was sweeping out the largest crevice, which was no more than a couple of meters high; right in front of it, Xiao Bing was excavating from the dust of the winter's storms a blackened slab of rock that had served as campfire hearth for at least a century.

As Lee hammered in the bact's tether Guoquiang emerged in a haze of red, rubbing his hair, spitting and spluttering. "I thought I would cook tonight," he said to Lee, and Lee smiled and helped him rummage through the packages for the iron pot and the supplies.

Guoquiang cooked what he always cooked, a sort of soup of mushrooms thickened with rice flour and sharpened with spring onions and chili pods, and little pancakes with which to eat it. The three ate in companionable silence as Mars turned his face from the sun. Westward, the level land ran away towards the horizon. A few twisted Joshua trees made arthritic silhouettes against red dust that glowed like heated iron in the level light. As the horizon climbed above the sun's pinpoint disc there was a brief flash of blue, a thin ring that ran around half the horizon. Xiao Bing stood and saluted the double star of Earth and its Moon, now suddenly visible. A moment later they too had set.

Three

Lee and Xiao Bing were dozing near the dying fire when Guoquiang came back. He'd gone off to scatter pheromone-baited traps for kit fox and red mongoose; now he slithered down the craggy slope of the crater rim with an urgent clatter.

"*Ku li*," he whispered fiercely, one hand on Lee's shoulder, the other on Xiao Bing's. Firelight struck his face under his chin, making his eyes crescents of shadow. "I have seen tracks, half a kilometer southwest. Of horses, I think."

"You're sure?"

"How do you know they are *ku li*?"

Lee and Xiao Bing had spoken at the same time.

"The fire," Guoquiang said, and kicked dust into it. Sparks whirled high and Guoquiang groaned with frustration and kicked harder: more sparks flew.

"If there are *ku li*," Lee said, "now they will surely know where we are. Wait, don't . . . "

But Guoquiang snatched the big water bag from Lee's grasp, upended it over the fire's scattered embers. There was a hiss and a smell of hot mud: then they were in darkness.

"That," Xiao Bing remarked, "was most of the water we have."

Guoquiang said from out of the darkness, "*Ku li*, I swear it. Tracks of three different horses."

Lee said, "Cowboys, then. I've often seen them; never one of the legendary *ku li*."

17

"Don't talk so loudly!"

"It's you who are talking . . . "

"Quiet!"

Their voices echoed out into the immense starry stillness of the desert night.

"I thought they had been beaten back to the polar marshes at the beginning of winter," Xiao Bing whispered. But there was a tremor in his voice: he was the cleverest of the three, and perhaps he was imagining the kind of atrocities the *ku li* insurgents were rumoured to perform on their prisoners being performed on him.

"Even I do not believe all the boasts of the loyal and strong Army of the People's Mouths," Guoquiang said in a hoarse whisper. "Listen! What was that?"

Lee heard the rustle, and smiled into the darkness. He could just make out the shapes of the other two by starlight. He said, "A mouse, come to finish your mushroom stew, Guoquiang. If the *ku li* have horses, we would hear them easily."

There was a silence, and then Xiao Bing whispered, "They muffle the hoofs with rags."

Four

Lee took first watch. He perched on a sheaf of frost-shattered rock at the crater's rim, a quilted blanket wrapped around his shoulders, motion sensor and infrared scope and pistol to hand, radio plugged into his ear. He was too far from Bitter Waters to access the librarian. His mother and his father, out there somewhere. He would not believe that they were dead. Exiled, yes. In penal labor gangs almost certainly. One of his childhood fantasies had been that they had joined the *ku li*, that one day they would return and scale the high walls of Master Qing's Academy of Mental Cultivation and take him away . . .

Instead, he had left to look for them.

He did not believe for a moment that the *ku li* would have penetrated this far south. No doubt Guoquiang had seen tracks, but they could have been made any time since the last storm. And most likely they had been made by cowboys searching for their winter-scattered herds: this was the edge of the vast ranges where half-wild yak and dzo grazed.

So he made the best of it, enjoying the solitude of the huge, quiet night. It was good to be alone and outside the *danwei*, without having to think of other people, without having to listen to the exhortations and advertisements continually broadcast through the loudspeakers that were everywhere, in Number One Recreation Hall, in the labs, even out amongst the fields and fishponds. "Mars is Red" at dawn and dusk, and in between commercials, games shows, heroic opera, noise made to fill the space made by the Emperor's silence. Out here there was only the sound of wind whining amongst the rocks, stirring the cold sand: the wind, and the voice of the King of the Cats whispering in his skull.

The lazy lallygagging voice, smooth and strong like iron slowly sinking in velvet folds of pitch black oil . . .

"Coming down to y'all from way way *way* on high, I'm gonna lay some righteous country soul on you for a few hours now. That's right, I'm gonna feed you some *rich* Memphis stew. Here we go with the Mar-Keys and 'Last Night' . . . "

No long sermons tonight. Lee lay back luxuriously, sweet ancient harmony in his ears, looking up at the ancient light of the stars. An act of rebellion in itself, for anywhere beyond the atmosphere was the territory of the enemy. The stars were everywhere, hard and bright and many coloured. The faint haze of the asteroid belt was diagonally bisected by the Milky Way's river of light. There was Panic's mottled fleck, falling backwards across the sky; Fear wouldn't rise for another hour. Jupiter, a double handspan above the horizon, shone so brightly that it cast Lee's shadow across the slope. He could just see the pinpoints of two of its moons to one side. The tiny repeater satellites which relayed the King's twenty-four-and-a-half-hour-a-day rock'n'roll station were invisibly closer to hand, reproducing faster than they could be shot down from their tangled orbits, a braid of music girdling the world . . .

("And here we go with some guys working out of Chips Moman's American studios, back when there was an America. Anyone out there remember the old US of A? One day I'm gonna lay the real history down on you, correct some serious misconceptions. But right now I'm talkin' about James and Bobby Purify and this is their big hit, sort of poppy but I love it anyway, 'Shake a Tail Feather' . . . ")

Music in his ears, Lee watched the sky for a long time, so long that he couldn't quite tell when he realised that the occasional streaks of light that slashed the starscape weren't meteorites.

They were coming out of the east, radiating from a single point halfway to zenith, flashing at regular intervals spaced about a hundred heartbeats apart. Most scratched a long line of light high above Lee's head, white fading towards red followed after a space of silence by a faint drawn-out rumble. But more and more frequently the streaks terminated prematurely and silently, inflating into blurred hazes and then slowly fading.

Craft of the anarchists, attempting to penetrate the defences. The first wave falling fast enough to reach the atmosphere before they were targeted by the X-ray laser cannon satellites controlled by the loyal cadres of the Tiger Mountain defense systems. Later arrivals would be vaporised further out, before they hit atmosphere. He was watching a battle in sub-orbital space.

Points of light were moving counter to the general direction, slowly drifting west to east. A violet line rose from below the horizon, from the land where the sun now walked. It climbed so slowly that it could not be light alone. Presently, Lee felt a soft shaking through the soles of his boots. Then the light went out, and there were only the stars.

"Those bastards got what they deserved," Guoquiang said, right behind Lee.

Lee wondered how long his friend had been standing there. He said, "So many of them."

"Robots," said Guoquiang, who took a keen interest in such matters. "Radar-dense frames with single-shot thrusters, probably from some little nickel-iron asteroid made over by fullerene viruses. The X-ray defenses destroy the anarchists before they have more than grazed the atmosphere. They are more alert than you, Wei Lee. Take that radio out of your ear! If I was a *ku li* bandit I could have cut your throat."

"How fortunate that you are only Guoquiang."

"Perhaps we should build machines to take us out to the lair of the degenerate anarchists," Guoquiang said. His face was a white smear by Jupiter light. Barefoot, he wore only a shirt and loose trousers, didn't seem to notice the freezing wind that tugged at the blanket Lee clutched around his shoulders. "They breed out there like sandflies. To destroy a weed you must pull it up by the roots."

"Are the anarchists insects then, or plants?"

"The Great Reassessment was ten years ago, Wei Lee. It will not be taking the Sky Road to build machines with attack capability and destroy the anarchist running dogs who infest the asteroids."

"Perhaps you have a point." Lee was made uneasy by the reference to the revolution which had been the downfall of his parents.

Guoquiang looked up at the starry sky. "Of course," he said, "many of the Ten Thousand Years are against that idea. They know only the safety of the past, of custom. Each year we grow closer to the past, Wei Lee."

"Our persistence is our strength," Lee said.

Guoquiang laughed, then remembered the imagined threat of the *ku li*, and whispered, "That sounds as convincing as a commercial for an industrial adhesive. You needn't mouth tags with me, Lee. Is it really true that you were born up there?"

"I was conceived, as I believe I've told you, when my parents were on a diplomatic mission. We were trading with the anarchists, then." The librarian, patiently working in the data stacks. Even now, it could have found his parents. Or been destroyed by a guardian.

"Some of them still try and trade with us, of course. And certainly they trade with the *ku li*. The tracks I saw could have been made by *ku li* moving towards a landing site."

"I should imagine the *ku li* have little to offer."

"They promise the future, yours and mine and the whole world's. It is not theirs to promise, of course, but I suppose that's beside the point."

Lee said, "Instead the Ten Thousand Years trade it with the Earth's Consensus. I wonder who is right?"

"The Ten Thousand Years of course. Because they rule in the name of the Emperor, as they always will."

"The anarchists change, and the Earth does not, and the

Emperor has been silent for more than a year. Does the future belong to the past, or to the future?"

Guoquiang didn't rise to the bait. Instead he shouted, "Look!"

Something fell across the sky towards them on a long track. It glowed white-hot, and tongues of flame cascaded in its wake. Lee and Guoquiang threw themselves to the ground as the thing burned overhead. Then silence. By Jupiter's light, Lee saw Xiao Bing clambering towards them along the eroded ridge of the crater rim.

Guoquiang stood and beat dust from his clothes. "Did you see where it fell? It may still be intact!"

Lee said, "I don't think it can be far away. It was right over our heads. Those things glide, they don't really fly. So the lower it is the closer it is to landing."

"Or to crashing," Xiao Bing said. "I wonder if the cargo survived!"

In their excitement, they had forgotten both their argument and the threat of the *ku li*.

Xiao Bing built up the fire, and the three cadres sat around it, speculating about what the thing could have been. A robot craft of the anarchists, no doubt about it, but what would it be carrying? To find such a prize would bring great honor to the Bitter Waters *danwei*, Guoquiang concluded, and Lee sensed beneath his sentiment the unspoken wish they all shared, that it would bring greater honor on their own selves.

Five

They set out at dawn, heading south. The purple sky was crossed from horizon to horizon with ropes of livid orange, flaws in the jetstream that heralded a late storm. Two days off, Guoquiang said, but Lee was not so confident.

Icy gusts whipped knee-high flurries of dust slantwise across the sloping land. Now and then above the wind whine came the distant but distinct thud thud thud of culvers. Lee, Guoquiang and Xiao Bing were not the only ones searching for the crashed spacecraft, but the intermittent noise of the flying machines had faded northwards by the time the three friends found the first aluminum streamers.

Knotted bunches of shiny tassels were caught amongst slabs of red rock or spiky clumps of cactus. Their glittering ribbons blew high in the windy air. It was chaff, designed to confuse the sensors which directed the X-ray laser cannon. The further south the cadres travelled, the more streamers there were. It was like a trail from one of the old tales, Xiao Bing said.

"The old tales belong in the old world," Guoquiang said. "We made this world, and we must make new stories for it. Think of it, citizens! We may be making a new story even as we ride. No one has ever captured an intact anarchist drone, not in all the years since the Great Reassessment!"

The land descended. It was hatched with narrow crevasses and slopes of red shale, punctuated with stands of broom

24

and dry sawgrass and clumps of prickly pear. The wind had picked up, a constant howl that whirled dust around the three men and the bact.

Lee slipped on goggles and tied his red kerchief over nose and mouth. Overhead the sun had blurred to a grainy glare in the blowing dust, dim as evening. Dust filtered through the slipseals of Lee's boots and clothing, and mixed with his sweat to form a gritty slime that uncomfortably lubricated armpits and crotch. Xiao Bing lurched past, his shape half erased by red haze, muttering, "I'm not remembering this. I'm not remembering this."

It was not the main storm, only a minor vortex that skipped before its leading edge just as a child will outrun its parent. Still, it was getting so bad that the three might have abandoned the search if they had not found the parachute.

Guoqiang saw it first; Lee and Xiao Bing were walking bent over by the wind, heads tucked down. Their leader let out a whoop and when they looked up he pointed dramatically to where a white shape rose and fell some way ahead in the murk.

It was the braking parachute of the anarchist craft, caught around a spire of stone: a banner of fine white seamless stuff thinner than high-grade silk but so tough nothing they had would cut it, not even Guoqiang's broad-bladed knife. Xiao Bing took a sniff from his tube and walked round and round it. It could easily have covered the largest breeder pond in the shit-cycling sheds, but when it had been folded up (which was not easy to do in the wind), it packed smaller than a bedroll.

They set off again, moving quickly now. Guoqiang had drawn his pistol and given Xiao Bing his hunting rifle. Lee supposed that he would have to use rocks as weapons against the *ku li*, or set the bact on them. Fear was a fine tremor he couldn't quite suppress, mixed with growing excitement, the thrill of the chase that even the bact seemed to catch— it galumphed along behind Lee in an undignified trot as he and the others leaped and ran through blowing curtains of red dust and bounded up a steep rise that was notched at its crest by a blackened scar.

A raw, deep grove stretched away down the gentle reverse slope, fading into the red haze. Shapes moved slowly and ponderously in the murk down there, like carp at the bottom of a breeder pond.

Guoquiang forced the others to lie down. The shapes were the horses of the *ku li*, he said, and then he swore that he saw a man moving amongst them. Lee saw no such thing, but Guoquiang was up on one knee. He aimed his pistol down the slope and fired: the narrow beam was diffused by the dust into a violent glare that momentarily filled the little valley from edge to edge.

Something screamed, high and inhuman. Guoquiang fired again. He was on his feet now. Lee jumped up, planning to pull him down, but then Guoquiang was running, charging downslope with Xiao Bing right behind him. Lee ran too; he had seen that the shadows in the dust had vanished, and was suddenly scared that he would be ridden down by *ku li* bandits if he stayed on the ridge.

Lee lost the other two in swirling dust, then saw shadows running back towards him. He had a moment to realise that the shadows were too big to be human, and then the animals were upon him, bellowing with fear as they scrambled up the slope.

Lee dodged a black-tipped horn, its span wide as his outstretched arms, and something struck him from behind. He tumbled through dust and flying rocks, landed hard and covered his head with his hands, curled into a ball. He couldn't make himself small enough. A hoof slammed down centimeters from his face; he felt rather than saw one of the huge beasts gather itself and leap over him.

Then there was only wind and dust. Lee uncurled and picked himself up, tested one leg and then the other. Downslope, Guoquiang and Xiao Bing were standing over a slumped shape. It wasn't a man, or even a horse, but a long-horned shaggy-coated yak.

Guoquiang's shot had burned away half its belly. Its matted coat smouldered around the wound. It rolled a brown-veined eye at Lee as he took Guoquiang's broad-bladed knife and slit its throat: the gush of hot blood splashed his boots.

"You're bleeding," Xiao Bing said. He cupped Lee's face with one hand, lifted a corner of Lee's kerchief and dabbed at his wounds. Lee saw his face reflected in the silver caps over Xiao Bing's pupils; there was a long shallow gash on his forehead, a couple of nicks on the ridge of his cheekbones. He'd be remembered this way for ever.

"We still must find the anarchists' craft," Guoquiang said impatiently.

Lee said, "Please don't mistake it for a yak, Guoquiang. I could not survive the excitement."

They did not have far to search. The gouged track led them right to the place where the spacecraft was half buried at the end of the scar it had torn into the ground, crumpled against a rocky outcrop as big as Number Eight Field Dome. The spacecraft was far smaller than Lee had imagined, a sculpted aerodynamic wedge that, even crumpled against adamantine slabs of red rock, looked as if the wind could at any moment send it skimming into the dust-filled sky.

The reflections of the three cadres swam up in the mirror-smooth silver skin, distorted by the flare of its curves. A section had flipped off to reveal a cockpit, snug as a holster. Dry foam shrunken on the contoured couch was already silted with dust. A little panel of controls winked and blinked with indicator lights, labelled not with neat ideograms but marks like clusters of skulls and bones.

Not a virus-built robot drone after all. It had carried a passenger.

It was Xiao Bing who found the bloody handprint smeared on the spacecraft's mirrored hull. But any footprints had been smothered by dust or trampled by panicked yaks or blown away on the wind. The three cast around for almost an hour, spiraling away from the wrecked craft across the floor of the ancient crater, and found nothing.

Lee made his way back through whirling dust to the outcrop and the wrecked craft, wondering where the anarchist could have run to. If he hadn't been picked up by Guoquiang's *ku li* horsemen—but then they would have blown up the spacecraft, destroyed the evidence. He hunkered down near the spacecraft with his back against a boulder at the foot of the outcrop, out of the worst of the blowing dust. Better shelter inside, of course, but he didn't dare set a foot in the cockpit.

Think like an anarchist.

You are wounded, fallen in enemy territory. You must hide, but you can't go too far because your friends might come for you.

It came to him in the sudden way that sideways logic always does, and he was so sure that he was right that he almost went to look for the pilot there and then. But he had long ago learned the virtues of patience, and he hunkered down and waited for the others to return.

At last Xiao Bing stumbled through blowing curtains of dust and flopped down beside Lee. "We had no luck either," he said.

Guoquiang arrived a few minutes later. He pulled his kerchief away from his face and spat an oyster of rusty phlegm. He said: "At least we looked. I see your dedication is consistent, Wei Lee."

"But, Guoquiang, I don't need to search. I know where the pilot is hiding." Lee pointed, and Guoquiang looked at the tumbled boulders which formed a rough stair up the side of the outcrop. And then he laughed.

The top of the outcrop sloped like a pitched roof, riddled with eroded sinkholes and split down the middle by a deep narrow crevice. Wind howled around the three as they quartered this maze; dust slithered around them like whipped snakes.

It was Xiao Bing who found the anarchist. She lay in the crooked shelter of the crevice, her slim figure curled in a foetal ball and cased within a wedge of clear paste. Her entire body was covered with a silvery film, with a transparent strip across her round and startlingly blue eyes. She stared up through paste at the three cadres and Lee had a flash of what she saw: three inscrutable masked faces, peering over a lip of rock.

Guoquiang kneeled and reached down to touch the paste. It had a kind of skin which dimpled under his fingers, then gave as he pushed harder. He started to scoop up handfuls of the stuff, and Xiao Bing joined him. The pilot stirred. Her mouth seemed to be working under the silvery film.

Lee was struck with sudden foreboding. He said, "I don't think we should do this."

Guoquiang took no notice. He scraped paste from the pilot's silver-filmed face, then drew his pistol and told Xiao Bing to pull the film off.

"Maybe it's better if we get help," Xiao Bing said uncertainly.

"He's right," Wei Lee said.

"Think anyone will find us in this storm? Already radio will be knocked out. Just do it, Bing."

Xiao Bing did it. The pilot gasped, then began to choke. Guoquiang jumped into the crevice behind her, knee deep in paste, pulled her into a sitting position, put his two fists in the V below her ribcage, jerked.

The pilot coughed out about a litre of white fluid, drew a shuddering breath. Her face was shiny black, with a bubble of red blood blown from one nostril. She did not have teeth, but seamless ridges of white plastic.

Lee thought that he'd seen her before, but he couldn't remember where. She looked back at Lee, and when she spoke it was so unbelievable that Lee didn't at first register its meaning. For she had spoken in the Common Language, a weak unravelling whisper almost lost to the howl of the wind.

"So you've found me."

Lee dropped to his knees at the edge of the crevice and bent close to her, but she suddenly slumped back against Guoquiang, who shouted triumphantly, "You see, Wei Lee, it is my story after all!"

"Our story, I hope," Xiao Bing said.

"Of course! We must get her down. The bact will carry her."

"It really might be better if we sent for help," Lee said. "She's hurt. That paste was some kind of cocoon, perhaps. Look, there is a cylinder under her hip—I guess it generated the paste."

Guoquiang sneered. "Of course, Wei Lee, you are an expert in the ways of the Sky Road."

Lee said, "She didn't come up here to die. She's expecting help."

Xiao Bing said, "The *ku li*. I can't die, Guoquiang, not yet."

"Then we'd better hurry," Guoquiang said. He handed Xiao Bing his pistol and got his hands under the pilot's shoulders, but when he tried to pull her to her feet, she shuddered and squirmed like a landed fish.

Lee said, "Leave her alone, you fool." Xiao Bing clutched at his arm. The pilot said something, a hoarse whisper. Guoquiang bent to catch her words.

The pilot smiled, and spat blood into his face.

Guoquiang swore and kicked at her, and Lee threw an armlock around his neck and heaved. He had wrestled him halfway out of the crevice before Guoquiang managed to jam a hard elbow under his ribcage. Lee sat down hard. A moment later Guoquiang was straddling his chest and yelling in his face, calling him a filthy communistic Sky Roader traitor, while Xiao Bing hopped around in an agony of nerves and pleaded for them both to stop.

And above everything was a growing roar, louder than the roaring in Lee's head. Dust suddenly blew in every direction at once; a shadow crossed the sun. Guoquiang looked up; so did Lee. The black belly of a culver was falling towards them. The Army of the People's Mouths had found the crashed spacecraft at last.

Six

An area of low pressure had swung in from the north-west. It displaced the constant winds from the Great Valley that usually dominated weather systems in the region, and funnelled freezing air from the dry northern plains, settling in for what the people of the Bitter Waters *danwei* called a Ten Day Blow.

The culvers of the Army of the People's Mouths were grounded by dust. The troops were stabled in the *danwei*'s half-derelict Number Three Recreation Hall; the anarchist pilot was incarcerated in the gaol's only cell, where she was undergoing treatment for her injuries. No one in the *danwei* or the army's search party was of sufficient rank to interrogate her, so she had to be kept alive until the storm blew itself out and she could be flown to the capital.

Meanwhile, wind drove billowing sheets of dust across the wide fields of rugged dwarf wheat and around the domes over the rice fields. Dust silted the irrigation canals, turned day to perpetual glowering twilight. The solar power station, a faceted pagoda of black glass at the centre of the *danwei*, was shut down. The electricity supply to dormitories and accommodation modules was rationed to three hours in the evening.

And wind dashed itself against the linked structures of the *danwei* itself, howling and rattling and spraying dust through every crevice. Red dust swirled in shafts of light, coated every surface with a gritty patina, worked between

31

sheets, ground between the teeth with every mouthful of food. Every touch of metal drew a sting of static electricity; dry, ionized air cracked lips, wore tempers to razor edges.

The iron-rich dust blanketed radio reception too. The voice of the King of the Cats sounded faint and far behind a swirling squall of static. The King was preaching, something about the power of rock'n'roll burning through the universe at the speed of light or of life. What with the static and Xiao Bing's nervous prattle, Wei Lee could only make out snatches of the King's sermon.

The two cadres were walking along one of the runnels that connected the *danwei*'s modules. It was night. Beyond the runnel's transparent plastic walls dust ceaselessly poured and whirled past, dim masses vaguely visible in the feeble strip lighting either side of the walkway. It gave Wei Lee a strange detached feeling to be safe inside a sleeve of warm stale air while the storm's rage was held in check by a centimeter width of plastic.

Change is coming at forty-five revolutions a minute, the King said in Lee's ear. Or perhaps it was evolutions; static rattled across the King's words, and at the same moment Xiao Bing said everything was changed now, that Guoqiang had settled himself to change.

"He doesn't have to change a thing," Lee said. "In a year, this will be just another story in the *danwei*'s history." As would he: he had already been dismissed, for bringing disgrace to the *danwei*. Guoqiang's father, a major shareholder, had been chairman of the special session of the council. It had been over in five minutes. Lee's humiliation would linger as long as the storm and then he would be gone, just as he'd dreamed two days ago on top of Number Eight Field Dome. Beware of wishes, he thought, you may get what you want.

"You're bitter, but you've every right after Li Mei denounced you in public."

"Her parents put her up to it. I don't really blame her." Lee couldn't admit to Xiao Bing how much Li Mei's behavior had hurt him. He said, "The scandal will die down and everything will be as it was. You'll see."

"But everything *is* changed," Xiao Bing said. The caps over his pupils were pewter in the dull light, his white hair and pale skin bruise-colored.

"You make this a mystery."

"Guoqiang wants to talk to you about it. I'll let him."

"You're a loyal friend, Xiao Bing. None of us deserve your loyalty."

"I've known Guoqiang all my life. He stopped the other kids beating me up. He liked me because I was smarter than he was, an unselfishness I appreciate more as I grow older. He is a leader, always has been. He didn't have to take it upon himself to look out for a special, and he's always had to look out for me, because the other kids tried to get at him by getting at me. A small place like this ... I hear that in the capital no one takes any notice of specials."

Lee thought of the child beggars in the Yankee Quarter; not all the deformities had been deliberately inflicted by their parents. He said, "You wouldn't be called a special in the capital, it's true. But surely your contract ... The *danwei* has taken money for your ... " he couldn't say death " ... your sleep."

"Oh, once I have finished designing my little piece of Heaven, once I have remembered enough to make it real, I can die out of this world at any time. Here, or in the capital, it makes no difference. But right now, Guoqiang needs me."

"Perhaps it's as well, now I know how Bitter Waters treats its half-lifers."

"When you begin your translation into Heaven," Xiao Bing said serenely, "it only matters that your body is kept alive for as long as the transfer takes. *How* it is kept alive doesn't matter. It is just an emptying vessel. The conchies want us all dead, Wei Lee, one way or another. They'll wait for me."

Lee said, as they pushed through heavy strips at the runnel's end, "I wasn't thinking of the conchies. I was thinking of the *danwei*, which will lose the bounty for your . . . "

"My death? That's what it is. I don't mind it."

The strips fell away. Warm moist air folded around Lee and Xiao Bing like a heavy cloak. Bright light struck through greenery, burned in water falling from shelf to shelf in the azolla cascades that zig-zagged around pools dense with water hyacinth. The sound of the storm and of the King's voice hushed at the same moment.

The rich smell of growing things and the sound of falling water struck a chord of unease deep inside Lee. There had been a bad time in a garden a long time ago. He had been no more than one or two. He was sure it had been something to do with his parents' disappearance, but could remember only his terror and the smell of cut grass.

"Over there," Xiao Bing said. "Come on, Wei Lee, you're dreaming again!"

Guoquiang was tipping cakes of boiled leaf into the livestock pens. That was his punishment: work the shit-cycling sheds until the Army of the People's Mouths left the *danwei*. He didn't seem to mind. He was whistling to the dogs, scolding them for not eating. The fat white hairless dogs padded up and down nervously, spooked by the storm.

Guoquiang emptied the woven basket with a sweeping toss, sniffed the air and said, "Is a waste line leaking?"

Lee took the radio from his ear. He said, "The domestic electricity supply is cut off before my shift ends. There is no water to wash. The others steal water from the half-lifers; I can't bring myself to do that. I'd have changed my clothes at least, but Xiao Bing was waiting for me."

Guoquiang, to his credit, was immediately contrite. "I am sorry, Wei Lee."

"It's all right. I've been around it so long that I can't smell it."

"I mean that my father is a proud man. He sees loss of face by the collective as a great blow to himself. So we are all punished. I am sorry that you have the worst of it."

Lee said, "How's your eye?"

"Sore," Guoquiang admitted. It was the left eye that Lee

had managed to hit with his elbow; the swollen flesh around it was fading from dark purple to green and yellow. Guoquiang added, "How are your ribs?"

"Also sore."

Guoquiang laughed. "We were both very foolish."

Lee didn't have the heart to point out that if Guoquiang hadn't been so stubborn they would all be heroes, instead of being in disgrace for having deviated from the *danwei*'s ideals of democratic collectivization, for having committed the mortal sin of self-aggrandizement. For having lost face in front of the soldiers of the Army of the People's Mouths.

He said, "I suppose we both made a mistake."

His own was to have tried to save the injured anarchist pilot from Guoquiang's impulsive misplaced sense of duty. Two days afterwards, Lee couldn't understand why she mattered so much to him. Why she still did. Even thinking about her gave him a cloying sense of claustrophobia, as if he was with her in the isolation womb, masked and catheterd and IVed, surrounded by hostile aliens on an alien world, floating in a bubble of fluorocarbons . . .

The *danwei* had pried access from the Army of the People's Mouths, and a loop of the anarchist pilot (a long shot of her being hustled by two soldiers down a narrow brightly lit corridor; medium shots of her standing against a tiled wall, supported by the same two nervous men; a circling close-up of her inside the isolation womb, face masked, nakedness washed out in glare reflected from the womb's plastic skin) was continuously running on one of the public access channels. The *danwei* had sold it to the capital's media nets too, and it turned up on every news channel every hour on the hour.

Lee had watched it over and over, each time with the same fresh sense of fascinated horror. It was like watching a rape.

Guoquiang said, "My father insists that you formally recant your transgression before your contract is terminated. I said if that was the case, so would I."

"He also volunteered me," Xiao Bing said. His eyes threw back flashing reflections when he smiled.

"My father didn't think anything of the idea, unfortunately. But all the same, we will stand beside you for the struggle session. It is not your disgrace. It is ours."

Guoquiang looked so humble that Lee laughed. "Oh, I'll find another job, somewhere or other. And as for disgrace, it passes sooner than you'd imagine. I'll move on, and forget about it. As a matter of fact, this isn't my first struggle session."

"You know the world," Guoquiang said.

"Some of it."

"Teach me," Guoquiang said, with a fierceness that surprised Lee. His big hands crushed the basket to his chest. "Teach me stuff. I need to learn. I want to make a difference."

"I know very little."

"You have walked the world. I would be honored," Guoquiang said formally, "if you would share what you learned."

In that way their quarrel began to heal. They sat together at the gravel edge of a hyacinth pool, in the murmurous roar of recirculating pumps and aerator cascades. The cruel brilliance of the growth lights, tinted purple with near-UV, gave their skins a corpse-like cast. Guoquiang put on a pair of dark glasses, oval lenses not much bigger than his eyes. Xiao Bing produced a stone bottle and three translucent porcelain thimbles which he filled to the brim.

Lee took one. The clear meniscus of brandy reflected an upside-down image of the grids of electric lights when he lifted it to his lips. It took a moment for the alcohol to burn through the sweetness; then he and Guoquiang and Xiao Bing were coughing and spluttering and clapping each other on the back.

After the second shot of brandy, Guoquiang was relaxed enough to ask about the story behind Lee's first struggle session. Lee told him that and more, and when his story was done the bottle was more than half empty and all three felt a warm glow of rekindled comradeship.

"I want to see the world," Guoquiang said, grandly and drunkenly. "I want to be out in it, I want to go where the living outnumber the half-lifers. You know there are more than twice as many half-lifers than living here?"

"He looks after them," Xiao Bing said.

"Of course. Excuse me. My father gives me the dogs to tend, and you the dead."

"And I'm below consideration," Xiao Bing said, "because I'm already numbered amongst the half-lifers. There is some advantage in low station after all. You can't fall from it. Have some more brandy."

They toasted each other and drank.

Lee said, "Think carefully, my friends, before you leave the comfort of your *danwei*. The capital fills with refugees, and it's a hard place for strangers to find a living. There are more advantages to communal capitalism than you believe."

Guoquiang said, "I cannot stay here. My father has destroyed my standing. I will have no authority but that which he doles out. And when he passes into Heaven I will not even have that. Not even his shareholding—he has changed his will." He laughed, a nervous bark. He was ashamed, Lee saw, ashamed and scared. "This is a place of the dead. The living exist only to serve those who have elected to die."

"The whole world is dying," Xiao Bing said.

"All the more reason to see it," Guoquiang said. "To see it before it all dies."

"Plenty of opportunities in the capital," Xiao Bing said.

Lee said sharply, "Who told you that? The soldiers? I will be going in the other direction." Travelling away from his great-grandfather, even though he knew he could never escape the weight of his obligations. Travel far enough around the world, and you return to where you began.

"Perhaps we can persuade you otherwise," Guoquiang said. "I have money. We should share it."

"You are a good friend, Guoquiang. I do not deserve you."

"I am a better friend than you think. My father is an influential man in the whole province, not just in Bitter Waters. You will have to travel very far to find a *danwei* that will employ you. He was greatly amused by the idea of you travelling empty-handed across the province, and doors closing in your face. If you travel west, you will have to travel a thousand kilometers to escape his influence. I see him for what he is, Wei Lee. I do not wish to become like him. It is a pivotal moment in my life. I have you to thank for it."

Lee saw that Guoqiang was very drunk—perhaps he had been drinking all day. He said, "What will you do in the capital? Rent your brain for information collation? Join up? Those are the two most popular options for young people fresh from the country."

Guoqiang said, "We will seize the moment, when it comes. Perhaps it *will* be necessary to join the defense forces. Our pilot may be the first of an invasion force."

Xiao Bing said, "We can catch a lift with the Army of the People's Mouths when it takes the anarchist away. A surprisingly small bribe goes a long way with the ordinary soldiers."

Lee started to comb his quiff, using the black water of the pool for a mirror. His hair kept losing its carefully sculpted shape because settling dust absorbed the grease. He said, "Your plans are so well made, I'm flattered you wish to include me. I was the source of your trouble in the first place."

"I hope that we are still friends," Guoqiang said. "Friends will help each other, eh? Think on what I've said, Wei Lee. I'm sure you'll see the sense of it. Have some more brandy. Drink up! Drink to our future!"

Seven

That night Lee lay awake long past midnight, muzzy with brandy fumes, mind spinning over and around without purpose, unable to riddle his way out of the face trap Guoquiang had so cunningly prepared. He listened to the King's broadcast for a while, but could hear only one word in ten, then called up one of the King's movies on his portable player, sat watching with the sound turned down (he knew all the dialogue and all the songs) and with his home-made solid-body electric guitar in his lap. The power was out, but Lee strummed along to each of the songs anyway, bending close to hear the chords singing in the wires.

The movie was *Fun in Acapulco*. The chained heave of the sea fascinated Lee as much as the King, and he always liked the way in which it was obvious the King never appeared in any exterior shots. A double ambled down a street in his place, only seen from the back but still unconvincing, or was seen in long shot lounging on the beach with Ursula Andress while the King appeared with her in close-up under studio lights. The King by then so famous that women would tear him apart if he ever appeared in public, as they had torn apart his corpse after his execution, singing his songs as they carried his head away (and in legend his head sang too, but that was legend—in reality his head was preserved in the Shrine of the Land of Grace, and then lost or stolen).

The movies of the King of the Cats were more than simple entertainment to Lee. They were sublime visions of the way a hero moved through the world. The King was the center of a storm of portents and signs, yet while things fell into place around him, he had to find within himself the way to heal his secret wound—here, his vertigo, which was also his fear of death, for it sprang from involvement in the accident which had crippled his friend. Once he had redeemed his courage through love, he could heal himself by plunging into the sea from on high, and live for ever. Watching the movie, Lee could begin to believe that the world was simpler than it seemed. Perhaps he could learn how to riddle the world of the mystery of his parents' disappearance, unlock the secret of his past and free his future.

Half the movie was missing, half the rest was patched and washed with sweeps of static snow—Lee preferred the originals to enhanced recreations, real discontinuities to fake substitute footage—and towards the end the display flickered and began to lose definition as the player's batteries drained. Lee still could not sleep. Restlessly, he slipped on his goggles and tried to find the librarian, who had gone missing after Lee's sentencing at the special committee. Cancelled by the same fiat, perhaps, although the metaphoric interface he had bound around himself remained. Dusty books towering into darkness, rotting carpets underfoot. A window framed by books, looking on a starry void filled with wind. One of the stars swung towards Lee, bloomed into a burning bird with a woman's face.

He jerked awake. He had fallen asleep and the goggles had slipped from his face.

Caught between Guoquiang's face trap and the revenge of Guoquiang's father, Lee lay awake the rest of the night, wondering whether to travel on or return to the great and terrible capital of Mars, and the thrall of his great-grandfather. But the next day his fate caught up with him, and he was swept away, dust on history's wind.

Eight

The graveyard shift had their own table in the crowded dining hall used by the *danwei*'s maintenance workers. But even the tenders of the half-lifers avoided talking to Wei Lee. Disgrace was easy to catch. Alone at one end of the long table, Lee ate quickly, scooping up greasy noodles and vegetable pancake with his head ducked low to his bowl. Conversation chattered all around, mostly about the half-lifer which, that shift, had died before passing fully into Heaven. Lee had seen it happen, the pale, emaciated body suddenly jerking slantwise on its couch like a dropped puppet while around it a hundred others continued to move their wired limbs under the guidance of the exercise programme. A bad omen, was the eventual opinion, and one or two tenders made warding signs at Lee, as if he were to blame.

Lee didn't notice. The King of the Cats cracklingly whispered in his ear, putting him at one remove from everyone in the dining hall. He'd been listening all day. The radio was not really allowed on shift, but no one dared raise a voice to forbid it, because that would bring them inside the circle of the black light of Lee's sin.

The King never slept. He was always there, rapping a sermon or rummaging through mid-twentieth-century American pop culture. Lee was scraping his tray into the bin to the rocking beat of Carl Perkins's "Dixie Fried" when something odd happened. A soldier bumped up against him in

41

the crowd around the recycling bins, and he felt something thrust into his hand.

It was a scrap of paper. It burned in Lee's hand all the way back to the brightly lit solitude of his room, where at last he dared look at it. A terse message, telling him to be at the transport-pool stables at twenty hundred. It was ten minutes to, and he was supposed to meet Guoquiang at the same time. Lee made his choice and ran for the door. After all, it was just the sort of impulsive thing the King would have done.

The stables were slaved to Mars's diurnal cycle. Their high racks of lights were turned to yellow twilight as with quickening nervousness Lee walked past steel-barred stalls in which palfreys, genets and alboraks stood in contemplation of lost horizons or munched at their feeding troughs.

In one stall there was a fierce, steel-shod warhorse, more great cat than horse. It paced round and round its stall with contained fury, mailed withers glittering. It was the mount of one of the officers of the Army of the People's Mouths.

Lee stopped to look at it, remembering a long ride through spring desert on one of the decommissioned warhorses owned by Master Qing's Academy of Mental Cultivation. Flowers everywhere, a flowing carpet spindled on the rush of wind, the liquid pull of muscles beneath Lee's gripping thighs. He'd been no more than five, but he still remembered commands and the positions of sensitive nerve clusters. He spoke a word, and the warhorse stopped its pacing and stared at him with a narrow yellow eye. Then it yawned, showing a rough tongue lolling amongst fangs each as long as the span of Lee's fingers, and started pacing again.

Further down, a mild genet thrust her long face towards Lee, and he paused to scratch the coarse hair between her flicking ears. When he turned from her, a man stood in the shadows at the end of the long row of pens.

Lee waited, and the man stepped forward into the light. He was an officer of the Army of the People's Mouths, a short man who held himself stiffly in tailored rust red tunic and trousers. The only signs of his rank were the three brass stars of a Colonel on his green shoulder flash, and his immaculately polished boots. He said, "You are nervous, Citizen Wei Lee. But have no fear, for I work for your esteemed ancestor. Allow me to demonstrate."

The Colonel blew on a short silver tube, and Great-grandfather Wei smiled and said, "The time has come, my son."

Nine

After Wei Lee's parents had disappeared and he had been given the protection of Great-grandfather Wei, he had been taken from Master Qing's Academy of .Mental Cultivation to the Great House to be interviewed on the first day of each month. Lee's great-grandfather had never appeared in the flesh—only his doctors and attendants saw him. Rather, he had visited through an eidolon, although to maintain the fiction that image was reality, Lee had always followed instructions to wait at a certain place in the gardens of the Great House, or in a certain room, and after a span of waiting, his ancestor would greet him, and Lee would turn and see him, and the interview would begin. Sometimes it lasted only a minute, and sometimes the shadows turned and lengthened across the hedged lawn, or the little room with the painted walls, as they marked out the hours while Lee waited.

So Lee turned now, and saw the eidolon of Great-grandfather Wei standing beside the stall of the genet, who thrust her long mild face at the bars just as she had for Lee. And in turning it was as if Lee had stepped from one room to another, except that this was a room of the Great House, the one with wooden panels fretted with scenes of the mountains of old Earth, and the floor of black tiles.

The genet thrust her head through an open window, and sunlight splashed her flanks, the same sunlight vivid in the green garden beyond. Lee looked for the Colonel, but he had vanished; or perhaps he had become the stone lion that stood beside the wide door, with round eyes and curly beard and fanged mouth.

"How fortunate I am, Wei Lee, that you are my son. I could wish for no better."

The eidolon was a tall, austere man, younger than Wei Lee remembered. But Lee had aged, and the eidolon had not. He might have just now put on the black silk suit and the high-collared white shirt, but Lee remembered that those were the clothes the eidolon had always worn. Perhaps the Great House was great indeed, its rooms and corridors extending through time as well as space, so that if Lee walked out of this room he might find himself returned to his childhood. And then he had the strange idea that if he walked out into the garden he would find his parents, and for some reason that filled him with terror.

"My house has many rooms," the eidolon said. "No, Wei Lee, I cannot read your thoughts, but I do understand your muscles. Each is a sentence, and so I parse the text of your posture for meaning."

Lee's mouth was dry. He rubbed his tongue against his upper teeth to stimulate the flow of saliva, and said, "All my life I have been serving you, great-grandfather."

It was only a polite formula, but it struck Lee that it was true, although usually such formulas are not.

The eidolon's smile was genuine, like that of a woman, not the rearrangement of those small muscles around the mouth that most men use in the belief that they are smiling. "I had always hoped you would retain the flexibility of intelligence, Wei Lee. I am delighted that it is so."

"I serve you now as always."

"How I do hope so. You have wandered far, but at last I have a task for you, Wei Lee. Yes, it does concern the anarchist pilot."

Lee sighed. All of his adult life he had waited for the debt to his great-grandfather to be called in. He'd known it would come one day, but he had not expected it to take place in so mundane a place as the stable of a small *danwei* in a far-flung province. He said, "What must I do?"

"It is all arranged for you. It is not a hard task for someone who has lived in one or another desert *danwei* these past two years. You will take the Sky Roader anarchist and hide her beyond the perimeter, and then rendezvous with a culver as soon as the storm subsides. You can take the main road out. No one will watch it in this storm, and it is well marked. There is a cache of supplies hidden two kilometers southeast of the main gate. My man will give you a homing beacon. Wait there, and he will come for you when the search has ended. Do not fail us. It is extremely important that the pilot is not interrogated, and yet we also need her alive."

Lee said, "I am honored that you think so highly of me, great-grandfather, but I am merely a contract agronomist technician. You would trust me to keep the pilot alive in the storm?"

"You are my beloved son, whom I have taught so carefully. You will find a way. You will disappear from this *danwei*, and they will say you committed suicide because of loss of face. When we pick you up, you will be given a new identity. Your life will be your own. Of course, you may have to change your hairstyle. That piled-up greasy style is too . . . flamboyant."

The stone lion, which all this time had guarded the fireplace with the implacable patience of its kind, now yawned, showing a rough red tongue as long as a snake's. It stretched its forepaws: claws like hooked stalagmites raked the black tiles. Lee took a step backwards. Beyond the window at which the genet placidly stood a cloud covered the sun, and then it was as if the ceiling of the room had lifted away to show stars shining down.

They were the lights of the stables, dimmed by a hazing of storm-blown dust. The Colonel thrust something into Lee's hand and said, "Your great-grandfather is most esteemed, Wei Lee. I am honored to be a servant of his faction."

It was a small, sleek pistol. Its barrel flared into a horizontal slit. A red ruby twinkled in its white bone grip. "You have handled weapons before," the Colonel said. "You know how this works?"

"I think so."

The Colonel plucked the weapon from Lee's grasp, pocketed it with a flourish. "Pray that you will not need to use it," he said.

Lee followed him down the aisle between the barred stalls, and was suddenly struck by a possibility. Oh yes, much more than a possibility! He jammed his hands in the pockets of his coveralls and dug his fingernails into the meat of his palms to keep from smiling.

"I noticed your hairstyle myself," the officer said. "You are a scholar of the classics, then. And are you perhaps a follower of the films of Jerry Lee Lewis?"

"He's good, but not as good as the King."

"Ah yes, the King of the Cats! When I was young I listened all the time to the broadcasts of the King of the Cats. That is where I learned of Jerry Lee Lewis. I particularly admire his performance in *The Nutty Professor*. It had something of the King of the Cats in it, did it not? Wei Lee, you understand what you have to do?"

Lee said that he did, but the Colonel repeated all that Lee's great-grandfather had said and asked again if Lee understood.

"Of course. When do we do this?"

"You will be at the service entrance of these sheds at sunrise tomorrow. We will watch over you, Wei Lee, in case you fall into danger. You are important to us. I know that you are ready to serve."

Lee didn't know about that. He did know that he had been given a chance to clear his way through the tangle of obligations *and* to rescue the fallen Sky Roader anarchist. He said, "If my esteemed great-grandfather wants me to take the anarchist away from the *danwei*, I'll do all I can."

After all, honor was only a form to be satisfied.

Ten

The encounter had taken less than an hour. Guoquiang and Xiao Bing were still waiting for Lee at the café in Number One Recreation Hall, amidst the dusty cherry trees and crowds and opera music. Lee explained what had just happened (although he did not mention the precise task his great-grandfather wished him to perform), and what he needed.

"You are crazy!" Guoquiang said, then looked at the people crowding the tables around their own and repeated, this time in a whisper, "You're crazy."

Xiao Bing said, "It's not as if it's an ordinary mount." He was whispering too.

"Let's walk," Lee said. As they ambled amongst the other strollers, music echoing from the high, iron-ribbed roof, he explained that if the Army of the People's Mouths had taken an interest in him, it was certain that he was being watched.

Guoquiang said, "If you must run from this, can't you just take an ordinary mount, Wei Lee?"

Lee grinned, told the two cadres to drink up. He had decided to get rid of the scrip he had accumulated. His salary credits could be forwarded (if Guoquiang's father didn't stop it), but Bitter Waters's scrip was useless everywhere but here. He bought more rice beer and cones of fried shrimp at one of the barrows scattered about the arena of shabby grass. He had already drunk three or four draughts with the two cadres as he explained his predicament and felt a fine

48

floating cheerfulness. Tomorrow and yesterday no longer mattered.

As they walked on, Lee explained to Guoquiang and Xiao Bing that it was easier than they thought, told them how to go about it, told them about the idea that had sprung fully formed as he'd walked between the steel-barred stalls with his great-grandfather's agent, the Colonel of the Army of the People's Mouths. People glanced at him as they went past, quick stabs of distaste. As he talked, Lee smiled back at the passers-by, even bowed once or twice, until Guoquiang told him to stop being a fool in front of half the *danwei*.

Even this late in the evening the place was crowded. With power off in the accommodation modules, it seemed that most of the living population of the *danwei* was out and about. They walked in pairs or family groups beneath the cherry trees, over threadbare lawns. Hedges and arbors conspired with holographic projections to suggest continued vistas running out under a blue, sunlit sky.

Fighting-cricket fanciers crowded around breeders and their enamel pots, each with a cricket inside and the price on top of the lid. As well as crickets, the breeders sold bamboo cricket-ticklers, cricket-lore data bases, feeding straws. In a transparent steep-sided fighting pot, two Five-star General crickets shrilled at each other, black wings spread. Their genomes had been extensively spliced and diced, and the jaws in their massive heads were so big that they could only eat pap from a straw; their muscular hind legs were sheathed in prickly armour and terminated in hooked claws. Bets were noisily laid amongst the fanciers who crowded round the big pot. The owners tickled their crickets' antennae until they locked in combat with a blur of legs and wings, watched by intent fanciers until one was pumping ichor from a half-severed head. Its owner picked it out of the pot in disgust and ground it under his sandal while around him bets were paid off in a flurry of scrip.

Beyond the fighting-cricket crowd, a wall was showing the action of the heroic opera whose music was playing over the public address system. Close-ups of white faces under lacquered hairstyles intercut with panoramas of the half-dozen principals scattered across a wide black stage with the chorus in the background. It was an opera about the last days of the Middle Kingdom on Earth: a model entrepreneurial family was trying to regain their daughter from the socialist warlord who had recruited her into service with the intention of corrupting and seducing her. In a comic subplot, the dimwit younger brother gambled futures in the family's microchip growing tanks to buy arms for the libertarian mercenaries led by the girl with whom he had fallen in love. Every ten minutes the music was interrupted by commercials for products or services not available in the *danwei*: this was a tape bought in a cheap lot from some backstreet operation, and no one had bothered to edit it. The action on the screen carried on regardless of whether music or commercials were playing, which lent a surreal air to the proceedings, rather like one of the King's salvaged movies.

Neither the opera nor the murmur of the people in the park was louder than the whine of the storm. A fine haze silted the air: it stung the nose and left a taste of iron, of blood, in the mouth. As he talked, Lee took mouthful after mouthful of thick yeasty beer to wash the taste of dust away. Dust enough where he was going.

"I still say you're crazy," Guoquiang said when Lee had finished.

Lee said, "Does that mean you will not help me?"

"Of course I will help you."

Lee suppressed his smile. Poor Guoquiang. It was his turn to be caught in a face trap. He had promised to stand by Wei Lee, and now he had been asked this favor he had no choice.

Xiao Bing said, "What will you do, Wei Lee? Turn *ku li*?"

"They'll hunt you down," Guoquiang said. "Better to drink your Bitter Waters's bitter water, Lee. The storm will die, and we can go before the Army of the People's Mouths come for you."

"They come for me sooner than the end of the storm. And

it's better to drink Bitter Waters's beer than Bitter Waters's bitter water. I will buy us all another."

"You should tell me what they need of you, that you risk your life."

"They swore me to secrecy." Lee rapped a scrip token on the tiled surface of the barrow, and asked the girl for more beer.

The girl said, "Have you not had enough, citizen shareholders?"

She was six or seven, hair braided back in a thick pigtail from her round face. She was addressing Guoquiang and Xiao Bing, averting her face from Lee.

"They can drink with me," Lee said, made bold by beer.

The girl blushed, hurried to fill the cups from her pitcher. Foam ran down the sides of the cups and puddled the tiles. She more or less snatched at the token Lee offered, and he laughed and twitched it out of her reach before tossing it on the wet tiles. He could use the shame of his disgrace like a weapon, as a mirror reflects laser light. It was interesting.

As the three walked on, Lee said to Guoquiang, "Your father wants an example of me. And the Army of the People's Mouths will use me before then. This way is better, I think. Do not worry. I will head for the capital, somehow or other. We will meet there. The storm will stop anyone following me on a lesser mount."

"You'll be a criminal," Xiao Bing said. But he was smiling.

"The capital is not like this *danwei*. Five million people live there. More arrive every day." Lee smiled: he knew that his two friends could not imagine the anonymity of the capital. He said, "You don't have to wait for me, just hobble it and leave it with the supplies."

"If it doesn't bite off our arms."

"Or our heads."

"I told you about the way to calm it. When it's calm, you just slip on the muzzle, and it will follow you anywhere."

"I hope you listened carefully, Xiao Bing."

"As carefully as you, Guoquiang."

"Did I tell you about the supplies?"

"Twice. It will be difficult."

"But not impossible for cadres as resourceful as you two."

Guoquiang narrowed his eyes and shrugged, an imitation of the gangster villain of the opera playing on the wallscreen that was so successful that both Lee and Xiao Bing laughed.

"Trust me," Guoquiang said.

"Trust us," Xiao Bing said. "We'll miss you, Wei Lee."

"I seem to have spent all day saying goodbye," Lee said. He really did feel cheerful. On the run in a storm with a ransomed heroine: better than this dusty fake park and its tawdry secondhand opera tapes. He shook his friends' hands and made his farewells. He had told them about the army officer, but not about the plan to free the anarchist pilot. There was no need to go into every detail, after all. Better for his friends if they knew only what they needed to know. It was not his fault if they jumped to the wrong conclusions.

Eleven

That night, the librarian came to Lee in his dreams.

"You are in danger, Master," the librarian said. As ever, he was calm and imperturbable, the hood of his black silk robe cast over the face that was a mirror of Lee's own.

"What are you doing here?" Lee was naked, and was aware he was dreaming with the floating detachment that dreams bring. "I can't find you, and all the time you've been hiding in my dreams. Is that it?"

"To me, all of your world is a dream. So why should you be surprised to find me in one part of it, but not another?"

"I looked for you, and you weren't there."

"The soldiers commandeered much of the spare capacity in the *danwei*'s net. It made time slow for me; I could no longer steal what I needed. Still, it meant that I shared what they were doing. That is why I know that you are in danger, Master."

"I don't need a figment of my subconscious to tell me this."

"The anarchist pilot is dangerous, Master. She has placed the whole *danwei* in danger."

"That's why the soldiers have her in that womb thing."

"The *danwei*'s information net interfaces with the isolation womb, and somehow parts of the anarchist have penetrated the net. I have seen her here," the librarian said. "She was reading a book three corridors away. I came upon

53

her and she put the book back on its shelf and vanished. She had opened the book, but I could not. I fear I have made little progress since last you saw me, Master. Too many books remain closed to me."

"At present I have more important things to think of than my parents. When I go, will you still be with me?"

"The information net of the *danwei* is my home. Specifically, the licensed, edited copy of the House of the Names of the Populace that the net contains. But there are places where I can step into the original. Those doorways are shifting and transient, and difficult to use, but I will follow you as best I can. Master, the soldiers are right to fear the anarchist. She has infected this place."

"You really think she was here?"

"Look," the librarian said, and drew aside a tall dusty curtain that Lee had not noticed. Perhaps it had not been there until the librarian had put its hand upon it. There was an arched window filled with flickering light. Stars, thickly clustered in spacey night. Lee clasped the cold stone ledge, suddenly dizzy with *déjà vu*. One of the stars grew brighter; no, it was moving towards him, shedding feathers of flame like a great comet. He had seen it before. It was a burning bird with a woman's head.

"You see. You see, Master." The librarian's hand was on Lee's shoulder, burning cold. Its long nails pricked Lee's bare skin. "Don't wake up, Master. Not yet. There is more to tell!"

"He's awake," someone said, and stripped the goggles from Lee's face.

Twelve

Lee squinted in sudden light. His little room was crowded. Three men, two ordinary soldiers and the Colonel, looked down at him. The soldiers grabbed Lee's arms and sat him up. In the confusion, someone knocked the solid-body guitar from the peg on which it hung. Lee started to protest, and the Colonel told him that it was as well he was his great-grandfather's son before jabbing something into his arm.

The benign fog of sleep and beer vanished instantly; but although Lee's head was clear, he kept stumbling as he was marched down the corridor. He was still naked, but no one seemed to be about to witness his shame. He asked questions, but the Colonel only ordered him to move faster.

A medical technician was waiting for him at a service entrance. Lee was fitted with loose coveralls that sealed at neck and wrists and ankles, high flexible boots, and a filter mask with bulbous goggles so he wouldn't choke in the dust-filled gales. The technician explained that his charge—he meant the anarchist pilot—would need minimal maintenance. She was anaesthetised. All Lee would have to do was check her intravenous dripfeeds and change the filter on her oxygenator every twelve hours.

"You have worked with half-lifers," the technician said. "This is the same."

Lee nodded. All he could think about was Guoquiang and Xiao Bing. About whether they had had enough time. About whether the Army of the People's Mouths knew about his little plot.

The Colonel had pulled on coveralls and a filter mask. He led Lee through the sand-trap door—pushing through hundreds of flexible but heavy interleaved plastic strips—into howling night lit by lamps whose light was bloodily blurred by whirling dust. Dawn made a bloody thumbprint above the huddled domes and tubes and sheds of the *danwei*.

Wind buffeted and snatched at Lee, roared past and screamed up the curve of the dome behind him. The Colonel caught his arm and hauled him a dozen paces to where a draft bact stood amidst the whirling dust, eyes sealed by thickly lashed lids. It was yoked to a trailer which carried a pod of milky plastic. The trailer's two mesh wheels were as high as Lee's shoulder. Lee could dimly make out a curled shape suspended by tubes and wires in bubbling amniotic fluid inside the pod.

The Colonel shoved the bact's harness reins into one of Lee's gloved hands, a torch into the other, yelled, "Supplies in the saddlebags! Take the south road!" and slapped the bact's hairy flank. The beast stirred and strained forward, the trailer dragged through sand, and Lee was pulled along into the storm's dark whirl.

One thing Lee wasn't going to do was go south, but it took a few minutes to convince the bact to change direction. By the time they were headed towards the field domes, Lee was sweating inside his suit. Anxiety and the anti-alcohol shot had dried his mouth, and he could feel his blood pounding in his head. His chest hurt with the effort of straining air through the mask's filters. This was like birth, he thought. Painful, and with no time for preparation.

The lights of the *danwei* faded into the storm. All Lee had to guide him were bioluminescent markers planted on one side of the dust-buried road, a line of tall green-glowing poles rising out of whirling darkness. By their spectral light he could see the shapes the wind whipped out of the dust, a secret life writhing and tumbling, tormented by the gale that blew slantwise over Lee and the bact as they plodded on.

The trailer kept digging into dust drifts and each time Lee had to run back and heave it out. The fourth or fifth time it happened he thought he saw the anarchist pilot moving inside the pod. He wiped at dust clinging to the tough plastic, shone his torch beam through murky liquid.

The anarchist raised her arms, pressing against the plastic so that it deformed upwards. It didn't break but stretched with her as she rose in a crouch. Blood swirled from torn IV ligatures at the crooks of her elbows and the base of her spine. Bubbles rose around her face as the mask which fed her air was pulled askew. Her mouth was open: she was drowning in amniotic fluid.

Lee's heart lurched. He scrabbled at dusty plastic: it deformed but would not tear. Wind and dust shrieked around him. He leaned over the drowning anarchist, his hands for a moment pressing against hers, her blue eyes staring up at him. He ran around the trailer, was blown to his knees by the wind, scrambled up and grabbed the saddlebag that hung at the bact's withers. But it was empty. Of course it was empty. Wind howled mockingly.

No, he couldn't let his great-grandfather win so easily. He ran to one of the marker poles, leaped and swung on it until it fell over, then snapped it across his knee. Its green light went out, but he had what he needed.

The pod's plastic parted beneath the jagged end of this crude spear. Thick amniotic fluid spurted, crusting with flying dust and blowing away in tatters. The anarchist's hand grabbed a torn edge; Lee grabbed another. Together, they widened the split, and suddenly the anarchist tumbled forward, her naked body coated in dust. She was lighter than he'd expected, light as a bird. He could feel her heart fluttering, the hard edge of her air mask against his chin.

She reached up and raised the mask, pressed her lips to his ear.

"You're walking into a trap. They want me dead." The mask went back. She drew a shuddering breath, took it away again and yelled, "You too! Wherever they said you're to go, go the other way!"

Half a dozen questions framed themselves in Lee's head, tripping over each other. Wind blew his astonishment into the howling darkness. He helped the anarchist into the flapping remains of the pod, tried to settle torn plastic around her.

"We're not going where my great-grandfather wants us to go!" Lee yelled, but the anarchist gave no sign that she had heard him. Plastic flapped around her; she grasped at it feebly with one hand, pressed her air mask to her face with the other.

Lee whipped the bact with its halter and it stumbled forward, the trailer slewing behind it. They missed the first waymark, and for five tense minutes Lee believed all was lost. But then a shadow loomed beyond the dashed luminous line of the marker poles and his heart lifted.

He had to tell the anarchist what he wanted three times over before she understood. She let him pull her to her feet, and Lee wrapped plastic around her like a tattered cape. Its wings lifted on the dusty wind as they stumbled towards the dome's big revolving door.

Calm darkness, a pocket of sheltered order in the storm's rage. They were on a wide earthen bank above the flooded fields where the spring rice grew. Lee waved his torch all around and nearly jumped out of his skin when Xiao Bing's voice cried, "Over here, Wei Lee!" And Guoquiang: "Who is that with you?"

A beam of light pinpointed the anarchist. She stared into it, naked except for tattered plastic and the caked dust that clung to her dark skin. She said, "I hope these are your friends."

Guoquiang was so shocked that for once he couldn't say a word. Lee told him that it was all right, that the Army of the People's Mouths wanted her to escape. Xiao Bing grinned. The silver caps over his eyes were sparks in the torchlit gloom. He couldn't stop staring at the naked anarchist. He said, "We should get her some clothes, do you think?"

"Thank you," the anarchist said calmly.

She was serenely regal in her filthy plastic cape. More self-possessed than anyone else, most especially Lee, who told Guoquiang, "All you had to do was leave it here, hobble it and leave it." Panic was beating inside him. He said, "Don't tell me you didn't bring it!"

"It's here," Guoquiang said, "although it nearly bit off Bing's head two or three times." He put his hands on Lee's shoulders. "We're going with you, Wei Lee! To the capital, right now! We couldn't stay, we'd be the first suspects when you went missing. We have helped you, and now you will help us."

The anarchist sealed the seam of a khaki shirt. She'd had to roll up the cuffs of the trousers, and their waistband bunched over the cord she'd tied as a crude belt. She said, "You must all listen to me. Although your soldiers did their best to keep me sedated, I was able to counter their efforts. I saw what happened to the guards when the others came for me. An officer shot them, then dropped the pistol amongst the smoking pieces of their bodies. He was wearing gloves . . . "

Lee remembered the pistol the Colonel had thrust into his hand. Fingerprints. He felt as if he was falling through darkness, right there where he stood on soft earth.

"This officer wants me dead," the anarchist said. "If he works for who I believe he works for, he is afraid I will tell the truth. I imagine Wei Lee is the sacrificial pawn. This will be blamed on him, and he will be killed trying to escape. So will I. They want me to escape, oh yes, but it is an excuse to kill me. There is a certain neatness to it, I suppose."

Guoquiang said to Lee, "If they wanted her dead, why did they heal her first?"

The anarchist said, "Only a disloyal faction of your soldiers wants me dead. The others carry out orders to bring me to the capital. Besides, my viruses did most of the healing. Believe me!"

Xiao Bing smiled. "Didn't we always tell you that taking the Sky Road was dangerous, Wei Lee?"

But Guoquiang wasn't convinced. He said, "How do we know this anarchist is telling the truth?"

That was when the dome blew in.

Lee saw it happen in slow motion. The ragged white flower of the explosion: shards of plastic riding a ball of flame. Then he was on his belly on muddy ground, dust and burning fragments of plastic flew around him.

"Come on!" Someone dragged him to his feet.

There were lights outside, brilliant and unfocused. Wind roared and roared through a great hole in the dome, filling it with whirling dust.

"Come on," Guoquiang said again, less insistent but no less urgent.

He started to drag Lee towards the warhorse. It pulled against its tether and struck at the two cadres with the sinuous ferocity of a snake.

Guoquiang fell over. Lee dodged forward, clouted the smooth skin behind the beast's ear where nerves clustered, shouted the word of command and vaulted into the high narrow saddle.

Xiao Bing threw up a canvas pack. Lee grabbed it one-handed and fastened it to the saddle. Xiao Bing shouted something lost in an explosion which struck the base of the dome, spraying dust and rubble. The whole structure groaned, and Lee heard panes splashing into the flooded fields.

Xiao Bing raised his hand in salute, then cut the warhorse's tether.

The warhorse would have bolted, but Lee pulled hard on the reins and forced its head to the ground. Then he barked a word of command and gave it slack and it sprang forward. The anarchist stood amidst whirling dust and smoke and crossing beams of light. Lee stooped and grabbed her waist and lifted her into the saddle in front of him as the warhorse leaped the dome's ragged edge into the full force of the storm.

Thirteen

The warhorse raced into the howling dark using senses other than sight. In moments, it carried Lee and the anarchist pilot through the circle of the ambush and plunged into the sours. In an hour the sours were a long way behind and the warhorse was galloping down the Red Valley in thick blowing dust and dawn light dirty as burned sulphur.

Lee and the anarchist rode the rest of the day and cast themselves into the vestigial shelter of an overhang at nightfall, too exhausted to do more than exchange a few words and bolt down paste rations before falling asleep.

The wind blew through Lee's dreams, erasing the past. It was still blowing hard when he woke, half buried in dust, with ochre storm light filtering beyond the lip of the overhang. The anarchist pilot—her name, she'd told him, was Miriam Makepeace Mbele—was propped on one elbow, watching him. He could hardly see her face behind the filter mask, and she had to shout to be heard over the wind.

"Time to go!"

"I want to know . . . "

"Later! If we survive! Otherwise it doesn't matter!"

They travelled through the howling storm for three days, stopping only to sleep. The warhorse cantered at a fluid thirty or forty kilometers an hour, and Lee let it pick its own way. He was spaced out by blowing curtains of dust that continually parted and swirled with the same flowing pseudocomplexity that in fire allows the unfocused eye to generate pictures or salamanders. Lee saw ghosts of his past, vague shapes that might be presentiments of his future. The dust made a fluid, lithe hiss as it scoured past, and it worked its way into every fold of skin until he was alive with incendiary itches.

The anarchist pilot clung to Lee with a fierce silence. She was injured and ill. Every so often she would lean out, lift her filter mask and vomit blood into the dusty gale. She endured this stoically.

Lee learned only a little more about her; the storm wore away any attempt at conversation. They spent the second night wedged in a deep low cave, scarcely more than a crevice in the undercut base of the cliffs; the third with no shelter but a sheet of plastic weighed down with stones—and in the middle of the night they woke amidst screaming wind and dust, the plastic sheet gone. They groped their way to the warhorse, and huddled against its flank. They got no more sleep that night, but the storm kept them from speaking, and it rose in pitch the next day. The warhorse slowed from a canter to a walk, and then to a creeping pace as it leaned into roaring sheets of dust. When Lee saw the lichen stand sometime near noon—a noon no lighter than dawn—he turned the warhorse straight for it. They had gone as far as they could until the storm blew itself out.

Fourteen

The giant lichens were a design of Cho Jinfeng. Lee had sheltered in them before, but he had never before had better reason to be grateful to the legendary gene cutter. He and the anarchist pilot, Miriam Makepeace Mbele, lay wedged head to foot in a narrow crevice within an inflated lobe, warmed by their own trapped body heat. The walls and floors and angled ceiling of the crevice were striated like muscle. The striations were bundles of hyphae. Here and there, hyphal strands swelled into clusters of moist globules that tasted of musty, peppery meat, of sweetly acid fruit, or of nothing at all. Long hairy strands loosely packed the narrow corkscrew entrance. Spurs and veins of green bioluminescence made weird constellations brighter than the yellow storm light that leaked through the entrance.

By night these constellations seemed to blaze, and that was when the anarchist pilot woke, in the way that sick people turn their diurnal rhythms end for end. She crawled deep into the lichen's crevice, down towards the cobweb hyphae designed to absorb body wastes, and Lee heard her throwing up. When she came back she was pale and shaky, but she was ready to talk.

Miriam Makepeace Mbele was six hundred and twenty-eight Greenwich years old, born in the United States of America on Earth in the sixth decade of the twentieth century. Or she was eighteen, brought to term in a bottle after the genome of the ancestor of her mercenary clone line had been transplanted into an enucleated ovum, and raised and trained by her owners, the Mbele-Somerville family, who also owned the Information Nexus of the Belt. And she was dying.

She explained it quite matter of factly. She had a way of saying things directly that was both exciting and unnerving. The crash landing had crushed a lung, destroyed her spleen and torn up her liver. The fullerene viruses that swarmed through her bloodstream had constructed clades to boot-strap her metabolism, had turned off the pain of her internal injuries and patched up as much of the damage as they could, but her liver function was reduced almost to zero. Blood was backing up and bursting through the weakest point, the web of veins and capillaries in her throat. She needed two things unavailable in a howling storm in the badlands of the Red Valley: rest to allow the damage to heal; and transfusions to replace lost blood.

Lee would not believe that he had rescued her only to lose her. He said that as soon as the storm had blown itself out he would find a medical technician at the nearest settlement, but she only smiled and thanked him, and said it was im-possible.

"Oh, there are white people, you didn't know that? Yan-kees. Beggars and thieves and vagabonds."

Miriam Makepeace Mbele (it took Lee a while to get used to the idea of her back-to-front name) said, "How fallen are the mighty. But that's not what is important. Right now, you are what is important, Wei Lee."

She wanted Lee to understand why she was here. She said that she had been sent to trade with Lee's great-grandfather. She carried a cargo of totipotent viruses which could gen-erate clades of specialised subgroups according to need, just as immune-system T-cells generated a near-infinite variety of antibodies. The totipotent viruses Miriam carried gener-ated a whole variety which dealt with the diseases of old age, which Lee's great-grandfather had planned to dole out amongst the Ten Thousand to win back support for the Sky Road. He thought that he hadn't needed Miriam alive after her capture; especially after the Bitter Waters *danwei* had sold news of her capture to the commercial news channels. He'd had some of her blood drawn while she was being treated by the medical technicians. Butchers, she added; she'd be dead before her viruses could undo, cell by cell, the damage the medics' clumsy macroscopic work had done. After her cargo had been sampled, she was a liability alive, and so the fake escape attempt had been staged.

Lee said, "Where you fell. You mean it's no coincidence . . ."

"It's no coincidence that the landing coordinates were so close to your home . . ."

"It's no coincidence that you crashed here . . ."

" . . . because your great-grandfather needed someone on hand to blame if things went wrong. Which they did. It *was* coincidence you and your friends stumbled on me . . ."

"We were looking for you. For the cargo of the spacecraft. And we found you . . ."

" . . . and it was lucky for me, because I guess maybe your army would have killed me right off. You guys there as witnesses, they couldn't. So that little charade was staged . . ."

"But if I was to be killed helping you escape, surely it would lead straight back to my great-grandfather . . ."

"You can't believe that your ancestor would have you killed, Wei Lee, but it is true. I was too dangerous to be allowed to live after I was captured. Your great-grandfather can't let it be known that he is trading with the anarchists, but he maintained connections with us after the Great Reassessment, and he knows that we are desperate, that we are losing the war with the Earth's Consensus. He knew we'd agree to almost any terms. Of course, he doesn't know everything . . ."

"I am sorry that your plan did not work."

"Who says it's not going to work, kid?" Miriam's somatic age was roughly the same as Lee's, but she treated him like a slightly retarded child. She did it with a kind of rough familiar humor, and Lee discovered he didn't mind. "Your great-grandfather thinks that because he has some of my blood, he has my totipotent viruses. He doesn't."

"I am honored by your trust," Lee said.

"I'm not telling you everything. Not yet. Maybe if I turn you on . . . but maybe not even then."

Lee said recklessly, "Well, if you can't tell me everything about yourself, perhaps you can tell me about the Belt."

The Belt, Miriam said, was dying. Once there had been innumerable continually shifting alliances and hundreds of different political ideologies vying for supremacy, driving a Golden Age of art and science and philosophy. On Earth, politics (before the Earth's Consensus had put an end to politics) had been shaped by geography; in the Belt, orbital mechanics were just as prescriptive. Asteroids did not follow tidy orbits. Macrotrade and migration between two asteroids that might be economical one week would suddenly become impossible the next when their different orbits moved them too far from each other and delta V differences jumped a quantum level. No family nation was ever out of contact with the information net controlled by the Nexus, unless it chose to go gray ghost ("That's when we know they're there, but they aren't talking. There are more and more of them each year."), but ideological alliances required more cement than exchange of information. Complex concatenations of political groupings and trade alliances were continually shifting in the main belt, and then there were those asteroids which pursued eccentric orbits that isolated them from human discourse except for short, irregular intervals. This ever-changing diversity was what had saved the Belt from direct conquest by the Earth's Consensus, but it also meant that the Belt had never united against their common enemy. After a long war of attrition, only remnants of the Belt's multiplex civilization survived, huddled in slowly dying arcologies. The Nexus was their last best hope.

It took Miriam a long time to explain this to Lee. Most of the terms she used couldn't be translated directly into Common Language. Still, Lee was fascinated. It was a world—worlds he'd hardly suspected to have existed, a great territory of possibilities. The sky that seemed so empty, save for a few rock-bound barbarians, was buzzing and blooming with trade and information. What he wanted to know was how Miriam's trading would help the people of Mars.

Miriam made a small movement that might have been a weary shrug. She was sitting with her shoulders cushioned by a soft bank of hyphae. Sweat beaded her face, was sprinkled on the V of skin between her small breasts, exposed by the open fastener of her shirt. Lee couldn't help staring, even though he knew that she knew he was doing it.

She said, "Your great-grandfather is like the rest of the Ten Thousand Years. They all want power, and they all want to live for ever. Your own Consensus—"

"The Emperor."

"Whatever it calls itself. It's become isolated. We know for a fact parts of it are as old as the original terraforming program. We suspect the same thing happened to it as happened to the Earth. It has become inward looking. It is using too many dreamers inside its systems. Agents of the Earth's Consensus—the conchies—are here to encourage that."

Lee thought of the half-lifers of Bitter Waters. Rows and rows of cocoons in the blood-warm infra-red-lit halls holding wirestrung intubated bodies. He said, "Mars is dying. People escape from death into the perfect illusion of Heaven."

"Yeah, but there's this world, too. It's at least as real as the consensual dreams in information space."

"I believe that too."

"So do your Ten Thousand Years."

They smiled at each other in the cold green light of the lichen's chamber.

Miriam said, "Dung, you and me are going to get on fine, I can see that."

"Dung?"

"Is that wrong? My translation program didn't teach me swear words."

So Lee did, to pass the long night and to distract him from Miriam's body, her closeness. She might be twice as old as his moribund great-grandfather, but her body was lithe and lovely, and his own body responded to its closeness.

She noticed, and told him to go ahead and masturbate if he needed to, she didn't mind. "One time I could have helped you out, but I can't trust my reflexes right now. I've nerve damage, too."

Lee blushed, smiling furiously in embarrassment, and she said, "I am sorry. It is culture shock, perhaps."

So much for romance. But a bond had grown between them, Lee thought. He was beginning to think of a way to save her: he had saved her life once, she had admitted as much, and now he could not let her die.

Later, while Miriam Makepeace Mbele slept, Lee measured the strength of the storm by listening to the King of the Cats. At times the King came in so sweet and strong that Lee thought the storm was surely failing, but then static would rise and the King and his music would recede to a great distance, borne away on the wings of the storm.

Miriam woke and asked him what he was listening to, and when he told her she said, "Of course you are. It's good that you like him, Wei Lee. They said you would."

"Who told you? My great-grandfather?"

"You'll see, if it all works out. I saw the King once, you know. I'd forgotten it for six hundred years, but things have all been shaken up and now I remember. Isn't that strange?"

Lee said, "You can remember your ancestor's life?"

"Parts of it. We all do—we're all our own ancestor after all, and besides, it's part of the personality fix we get. My parents took me to Las Vegas when I was sixteen. It was a place where you went to gamble. Do I have to explain that?"

"Oh, I know about gambling, of course. As for the place, I saw it in *Viva Las Vegas.*"

Miriam smiled. "You must have a strange view of Ancient Old-time America. But there were other entertainments in Vegas, sideshows for the main event, which was to lose as much money as possible and use as much electricity as you could while doing it. The King was one of the sideshows. My parents were big fans so they took me along, although all *I* wanted to do was hang out at the slots and eye the guys. Oh, this is so strange, remembering! The King was sort of gross, we all thought, people my age back then, he'd sold out, dressing in white leather and rhinestones, mopping his sweat with white scarves and throwing them into the audience, singing these awful ballads with these terrible pseudo long-haired musicians grunging along behind. This was the early seventies, when I was about thirteen. *I* was into the Doors, Cream, Edgar Winter's White Trash. All I really remember from the show was 'American Trilogy.' You know that song?"

Various things had been going through Lee's mind. But all he said was, "Of course. I have recordings of his concert; it is all that remains of *Elvis on Tour*. I mean, I had." It was still there, back in his little room in the Bitter Waters *danwei*, along with all his recordings, and his solid-body guitar. He hoped that Guoquiang had them now, or Xiao Bing. If they were still alive.

Miriam wanted to listen to the King, and Lee gave her the radio. She listened a moment and shrugged and handed it back. "It's not the real King," she said, "but I guess you know that. For one thing, the real King of the Cats didn't speak Common Language. Or it's news to me he did. And there never were any *blues* in Common Language, I guarantee that."

Lee smiled, nervous again. "The King of the Cats became a god long ago. He can do as he wishes. Even when he was alive he could not walk amongst the people for fear that in the frenzy of their love they would tear him apart. That is why in all his later films he has to use a double for scenes set outside, and why he could never travel abroad."

Miriam laughed. "That's because his manager was an illegal alien and couldn't leave the US himself. And when I saw him the King wasn't even that famous any more. He only became famous again after he died." She laughed. "It turns out they were right all along, he didn't really die, he really was kidnapped by aliens. We have dealings, you know, with the Thing in Jupiter. Or aspects of it. The King of the Cats is just one aspect of the Thing, but I've never understood what he's about. We get his broadcasts in American.

The Thing moves in mysterious ways, that's all there is to it. We're lucky it's on our side, more or less."

"You mean your *danwei*?"

"My family? Oh, that, of course. But I mean all of us. Humans. Or at least, the Thing in Jupiter doesn't mean us harm. It doesn't have religion, the way the Earth's Consensus does."

Lee thought of his great-grandfather, of the Sky Road and of the alliance that the Emperor had made with the Earth before it had fallen silent, of the Ten Thousand Years struggling against each other to fill the vacuum of the Emperor's silence. There was no center. It was as if everything he had known had suddenly been cut free, and for a while he couldn't even think of a question to ask. When he did, Miriam had fallen asleep.

Fifteen

At some time during the night, unnoticed, the unmodulated howl of the storm faded. Lee woke to the lonesome growl of Tony Joe White's "Linesman of the County" small and clear in his head. Miriam Makepeace Mbele was sleeping, her mouth open, a fine sheen of sweat on her pale face.

Lee pushed through the lichen's matted hyphal curtain and scrambled over the drift of dusty sand that half choked the entrance. The air was clear, although the sky was still full of dust: the sun was a vast technicolor smear of red and orange in a pink sky. Wind whipped scarves of sand from the sharp crests of new drifts, but it was only a whisper now.

The warhorse was kneeling half buried downhill from the lichen stand. Lee cleared its eyes and muzzle from the caul it had spun around itself, and blew into its nostrils until it shuddered and woke. It turned its head and snapped at him in a half-hearted way.

Lee went off to set running wire traps at ice mice burrows; food would help the warhorse revive. When he and Miriam had stumbled upon the stand of lichens in howling dust-filled darkness, they had already lost their bearings. Now Lee saw that the lichen stand ramified along the top of a flood gravelbed that bent around a loop of the dust-choked river. Above, striated sandstone cliffs rose towards the red sky, their top smashed in by an ancient crater; on the other side of the river, sandstone ridges, marked by fossil scour marks like the thumbprints of the creator, saddled away towards cliffs a kilometer away, hazed by dust that still hung in the air.

Lee caught a dozen ice mice and desert rats inside an hour, but when he got back the warhorse was grazing on a stand of prickly pear, excavating the spiny paddles from dust drifts with a forelimb. It nosed Lee's gift and tossed its head in disdain, then stepped back, its ribbed ears unfolding and twitching this way and that.

After a moment Lee heard what had made the warhorse quicken. It was the fluttering thud of a culver.

Miriam was awake inside the dank and smelly crevice in the lichen stand. When Lee told her about the culver she said at once, "So we did not run far enough. You have only one choice. Kill me, and stay alive."

Lee opened his mouth, smiling in incomprehension.

"I'm dying. I'd rather go quickly and painlessly than have my body torn apart under questioning. I've spent all my life getting it into shape, I don't want to see it mutilated."

She was quite serious. Lee said, "You aren't serious."

She held out the big torch. "This will do it. I've focused the laser and shorted the safety on the power supply. You've only one shot, but it will be enough. Stick it against the top of my head and it'll fry my brain. I'll probably not even see the flash."

She thrust the torch at him, and he had to take it or drop it. Then she leaned into him and fastened her lips on his. Her warm wet tongue prised open his lips, squirmed deep into his mouth. Astonished, Lee started to return the kiss, but Miriam pulled away.

"It's done," she said, "for better or worse. Wei Lee, we haven't known each other very long, and this is a fucking— did I get that right?—big favor to ask even a close friend, but it's the only favor I'm ever going to ask. See, I can't do myself. I've been blocked, to stop the goods damaging itself."

"Oh. Is that why you did not kill yourself when you were captured?"

"I wouldn't talk," Miriam said. "It doesn't matter what they do to me, I'd *never* talk. And that's nothing to do with a block. It's professional pride. But, I don't want to go through it, you understand?"

"I understand," Lee said, and raised the torch. Perhaps she saw at the last moment what he intended, because her hands started to come up, too late, as he smashed the heavy torch across the top of her head.

She was as light as a bird, as if all her bones were hollow. Although Lee had trouble dragging her through the crevice's kinked, hyphae-packed entrance, it was not too difficult to carry her downhill to the warhorse. After Lee spoke to it, the warhorse allowed him to sling Miriam's body over its withers, in front of the narrow saddle. Then Lee swung up into the saddle and the warhorse leaped forward, flying over gravel alongside the dustchoked river at an easy gallop.

The sound of the culver was gone, swallowed by the aching silence of Mars. Yet as Lee rode south, the Bitter Waters River and its wide valley unravelling at a steady seventy kph, he felt a weight centred between his shoulder blades. He had not escaped, not yet.

He knew that it was very unlikely that he could carry the wounded pilot to one of the secret camps of the *ku li* rebels, even if he could track them down. But in his mind the Red Valley fell behind and somehow they were there, under a huge spreading tree on some swampy spit of land, with a campfire sending a thin tendril of smoke into dense leaves overhead, *ku li* rebels in ragged but clean tunics and trousers and heavy boots going about their business amongst stacks of supplies and stands of rifles, while Lee rocked Miriam in a linen hammock suspended from one great limb of the all-sheltering tree and half listened to a lecturer off in some clearing explaining the power of the people to his cross-legged audience . . .

Lee almost fell from the narrow saddle. The clean vertiginous shock woke him at once. The warhorse had slowed to a walking pace and was snatching at thorny vegetation that grew in the dry mudflats flanking the river channel. The sound of the culver fluttered somewhere in the empty sky.

Lee snatched the reins with the intention of bringing the warhorse under control, but he forgot to speak the word of command and the beast struck at his leg. Lee pulled back hard and shouted. The warhorse pranced sideways. Miriam started to slide and Lee grabbed at her: the warhorse bucked and they both fell.

They rolled down a crusty slope of dry mud, enveloped in clouds of dust. The warhorse screamed and shot away like an arrow from a bow. In less than a minute it was out of sight. The rope of dust left in its wake rose and twisted in the still air.

The fall partly brought Miriam to her senses. Lee helped her sit up, and she punched him square in the chest. As he sprawled backwards, she slid the torch from his belt loop. Her eyes were starry with tears. She said, "Do me! Do me now!"

"I don't . . . "

"Kill me!"

Lee grabbed for the torch but Miriam threw herself flat, swift as a striking snake. Something roared and roared overhead. Lee lunged again, but she managed to drive a sharp elbow into his ribs and tried to roll away from him. He grabbed her ankle and was dragged through crusty mud, a roaring in his ears, his heart pounding. Miriam turned to club at his hand and he pulled; off-balance, she fell.

In a moment, Lee was on her; in the next, he had snatched the torch from her grasp. She butted his chin with the top of her head; his teeth clicked on his tongue tip and pain spiked the roof of his skull. She got an elbow in his stomach and he sobbed for breath that suddenly wouldn't come. The roaring was louder, and streamers of dust were flying away from them in every direction.

Lee looked up, saw the black wasp-shape of the culver tilted a dozen meters above, so close that he could see the face of the young soldier who hung out of the hatch in a sling.

Miriam had the torch again. She grounded the butt in the red dirt. Lee goggled at the slit-lens; then Miriam twitched the torch a fraction and fired.

For an instant, an intense thread of light burned through whirling dust. The tail of the culver broke off and flew away in one direction while the main body somersaulted in the other. A flexing wing smashed into the muddy river, threw the broken cabin against a sandstone ridge beyond.

Lee tried to cover Miriam with his own body as debris whirred through the air. The whole surface of the river pocked and rippled. A section of hull went end over end over the water and smashed into a gravel bank. Something caught fire in the wreckage of the cabin. Lee started to get to his feet and a ball of fire enveloped the wreckage; he fell on his face as flame bloomed out across the water. Heat washed his skin.

"Damn you," Miriam said. There was something funny about her voice. "I didn't want to kill anyone . . ."

"Except yourself," Lee said. There was something stuck in the back of his throat. Then, astonishingly, he was crying.

The culver was still burning. Its frame glowed in a jelly of heat and flame. Thick black smoke unpacked itself into the pink sky.

Miriam said in her weak, pinched voice, "You had better shape up, kid. I'm going to need help. I think you broke something all over again." She turned her head and spat blood into the red dust.

Sixteen

They followed the tracks of the warhorse. There was little hope of catching it—it was probably halfway to the capital by now but when its trail turned away from the river Lee and Miriam turned too.

There was a scramble over a high lip of stone, through a narrow passage between sandstone bluffs that met overhead like two heads touching, then the start of a long climb up a steep defile, the fossil bed of a tributary gashed into the cliffs millennia ago, when Mars had been in full flood and dinosaurs had ruled Earth.

The ancient stream had been partly revived by terraforming—the sides of the defile were littered with dead, fallen trees—but now the stream bed was clogged with dry red dust. The defile widened into a little sloping valley. Lee, carrying Miriam pickaback, kept stumbling on water-smoothed stones. Here and there pools of water stood, their still surfaces mantled with dust. Farther up, seepage was washing red mud down tussocky slopes. Dwarf juniper spread fragrant dark green needle-fans above scree and sere clumps of grass; Himalayan pines, dwarfed and twisted, clung to boulders with gnarled roots longer than their knotted trunks. Stands of immature lichens raised shoulder-high lobes. Lee saw desert chats, rose finches, robin accentors, once spotted a Sikkim deer turning away through the scrubby forest.

Amongst the dwarf trees and sandstone boulders were sloping spaces thatched with grass and herbs. Pale yellow flowers rose through a mantle of fine red dust. Whenever they reached one of these tiny meadows, Lee set Miriam down and sprawled beside her to rest for a few minutes. Miriam was very weak now. Her breath was hoarse and ragged. She had long ago given up telling Lee to leave her. It was almost night, and growing bitterly cold. Finally, when it was clear that they could go no further, Lee lay Miriam on a narrow ledge of thin, sandy turf no bigger than a table-top.

Lee held Miriam, and she held him. They were both shivering.

"Now I suppose we both die," she whispered hoarsely. "You are such a fool, Wei Lee. I've given you all you need, you just don't realize it. A whole world, in your hands . . . "

"I'll try and light a fire, in a little while." He had seen some gorse; there would be dry wood in the dead hearts of the stands, and he could make a friction bow to spark punk alight.

Miriam didn't reply. She had fallen asleep, or had passed out. Lee held her. Above and behind them, the dwarf forest climbed the narrow valley towards a dusk sky already rich with stars. And all around were the sounds of the inhabitants of the valley going about their lives: furtive rustlings and faint squeaks or chitterings; once, the cry of an owl, a soft thump as it plummeted on its prey a few metres from Lee, the whir of its wings as it rose.

Martians.

Beneath the sounds of the tiny lives lay the ancient silence of the planet, vast and empty as an ocean. The silence of the rocks; the silence from before the beginning of history; the dreamy silence that inhabited the centre of every thought, that filled the mind with an inexpressible sweet longing.

The silence that the conchie preachers wanted to spread across the face of Mars, a dry end to history and life.

Lee left Miriam sleeping, and collected the materials he needed to make his fire. The stars gave enough light to see in grainy black and white, and as Lee picked his way back to the clearing, arms laden with prickly dry heather, the top of the valley fell to reveal Jupiter, and it was flooded with his cold yellow light. At the same moment, stars floated down, moving towards Lee swiftly and silently. He scarcely had time to register them before they were upon him. Strong arms grasped his, knocked away the kindling. He shouted a warning to Miriam and something smashed him to his knees. Stars swooped giddily; Lee fell upwards into the night.

Seventeen

A pantheon of red and gold figures marched upon Lee. He was lying on a pallet amongst a level field of stars which swam in the veil of their own heat. Above him, a gigantic gold-skinned man draped in green and red sat cross-legged on a throne of beaten gold. His gaze was level and serene, his eyes so wide that white showed all around his pupils. Flowers were strewn at his feet.

(Voices murmured, each to each.
This is the young Han, Master.
He is no soldier. And the other? Will she live or die?
We do not know, Master.
We will pray for them both.)

Lee tried to say Miriam's name. He couldn't move, yet still the field of stars tipped and receded. A bestial mask leered down at him; behind it, brown human eyes gazed into his. With a shock of reversal, Lee saw that it was no mask, but a face half ape, half human. The creature grinned, showing yellow fangs with a red tongue lolling between them, and Lee cried out.

Eighteen

L ee woke on a hard mattress in a narrow niche carved into the sandstone wall of a little cell. A primitive lamp shed a warm light and filled the dank air with the reek of rancid butter. A shaven-headed old man, dressed in loose orange robes belted with a yellow sash, sat cross-legged on the floor. He was knitting a skein of undyed yarn into a kind of cap. He peered at his tangling and untangling knitting needles through a pair of butterfly glasses that perched on the sharp peak of his nose. Fine lines radiated around his eyes, but otherwise his face was as smooth and plump as a baby's.

When he saw that Lee was awake he set his knitting aside, hopped nimbly to the door and rang a silver bell. Then he helped Lee dress, loose black trousers, an orange robe, sandals.

The old man said that his name was Pemba, that he was one of the monks of the Kailas lamasery. Lee had never heard of the place. He knew of the underground Tibetan lamaseries, but most were in ruins and none were within a thousand kilometers of the Bitter Waters *danwei*. The warhorse had been swift, but even it could not have ridden so far in the middle of a storm. When Lee asked just where Kailas was, Pemba answered cheerfully that he could not say. "It belongs to the time before the Han. It belongs to the original people."

Lee wanted to ask if the old monk was *ku li*; but it was

80

the one question he could not safely ask and, besides, he was fairly certain that he knew the answer. Instead, he asked about Miriam Makepeace Mbele. "The Yankee woman I was with."

"Perhaps she was a Yankee, a long time ago. Dorje and Nangpa are attending to her. I will take you there, and find you something to eat too. Is she your friend?"

Lee followed the old monk down a narrow corridor. Like the cell, it was carved from naked sandstone. Lee could feel the weight of rock above his head, a stress in the dim air like a word waiting to be spoken. Butter lamps burned in niches, a line of smoky stars. Lee said, after a long silence which suggested he ought to say something, "I saved her life."

"And so of course you feel an obligation to her, just as the gods are obliged to help us, for they have saved us again and again. And will, until time ends. We are all eager to hear your story. She is not human, you know."

Lee would have asked Pemba what he meant, but at that moment someone swung down from an opening in the corridor's ceiling. It was the ape-man Lee had glimpsed in his dream which he knew now had been no dream at all.

Pemba swatted the creature on its hairy flank and it cringed away from him. Pemba said, "Don't mind Monkey. He is mostly harmless, but he enjoys trying to startle me. It is a streak of mischief I have not managed to beat out of him. But I need him, you see, because we are not yet certain about you."

Monkey was perhaps two and a half meters tall—it was difficult to be precise because he walked with a stooped bow-legged gait, hands swinging by outthrust knees. He wore only a kind of waistcoat with many bulging pockets, and he was covered with coarse reddish hair. His brown eyes peered at Lee from beneath a heavy brow that sloped straight back to the crested top of his skull; wide flat nostrils snuffled and thin lips skinned back from fangs the color of old ivory. His feet were huge, with opposable big toes. They made a flat, slapping sound as he followed Lee and Pemba along the corridor.

Lee said, "I don't know if I'm afraid of your friend, because I don't know anything about him. I have certainly never seen anything like him in my life."

"Monkey is our servant, but I do believe that some of his kind live wild, in the mountains. I remember that when I was a boy I saw footprints in the snow just like his. The people of the mountains, my people, made up stories about the creatures that made such tracks, but as usual the truth is less interesting than the stories. Probably, the tracks were left by a servant on its way from one lamasery to another. This way, now."

Pemba and Monkey led Lee through a dark room. Echoing footsteps suggested it was huge, high-ceilinged, and empty. On the far side, light defined a small doorway. Lee had to duck to pass through it, and found himself in a long hall alive with color.

Pillars carved with red and gold figures cavorting amidst swirling patterns receded towards a huge statue of the Buddha sitting in the lotus position. Lee remembered that serene yet quizzical golden face, its flexed eyebrows and wide eyes, its slightly parted red mouth. The Buddha's headdress was encrusted with jewels; a red scarf folded around his neck was tucked under a heavy jewelled torc. Small statues of lesser bodhisattvas cluttered the steps leading up to his throne, and before the steps a myriad tiny flames floated in two wide shallow bowls: yak-butter candle oceans whose hot pungent smell filled the hall. To one side of the throne, golden statues of wrathful deities and protectors stood in wall niches; to the other was a shrine, with a three-cornered high roof like a little house, which sheltered a tank in which a shrunken homunculus floated. The shrine stood on a cube of shiny black stuff in which sparks seemed to drift and slide.

Monkey knelt. Palms flat, he bowed down so that his heavy brow touched the flagstone floor. He bowed not to the Buddha but to the shrine.

Pemba took Lee's arm and led him down the central aisle,

between the yak-butter candle oceans. Beneath the statue-peopled steps that led up to the Buddha's throne was a table where two robed figures bent over a prone figure.

"Your friend," Pemba said. "Dorje and Nangpa try to save her, but I fear we may not have the facilities."

One of the monks said, "Perhaps no one could save her."

The other added, "It depends what you mean by save, of course. The body is not important, Dorje."

"In my present incarnate state, my body is important to me, Nangpa."

The two orange-robed monks were both older than Pemba. The first, Dorje, was tall and gaunt, a bent stork of a man with heavy bones and skin so dark and wrinkled it might have been smokecured. Nangpa was like a wraith conjured from parchment; the sutures of his skull and a map of blue veins were visible beneath his pallid skin. His ears were huge and translucent, their lobes stretched by pegs of gold so that they touched his shoulders.

"Until we draw her machines her body is also important," Dorje said. "The body is the vessel, true, but it is important as long as it is full and cannot be emptied."

"This one is full, to be sure. Far too full."

Miriam was naked. A kind of mask lay over her face, sprouting wires which wove into a web of cables and looped up into darkness. Pemba put his hand flat on Lee's chest; until then, Lee had not realised that he had started forward. "No, young Han," Pemba said gently. "She is no longer yours."

Dorje touched a silver wand to the ring finger of Miriam's right hand, to her wrist, her elbow, her shoulder, the side of her neck, her temple. He said, "We try to activate the triple-burner route, but still have much to do before she is fully exorcised. Where is she from, young Han?"

Lee said, "The sky."

Nangpa said to his tall companion, in a mild voice, "She told our master the truth. Unless the boy also lies."

"He doesn't," Pemba said.

The tall monk said, "It does not matter where she is from,

but who she is. It does not matter who she is, but what she does."

Nangpa said, "It would help if we knew who made the machines that infest her."

Dorje touched the side of Miriam's neck with his silver wand. "Needles there, quickly, before the infernal things disperse again."

Pemba said to Lee, "It has been so long since they have had to do this. Master Norbhu passed away, why, it must have been fifty years ago, and besides, he had no machines in his blood."

"Not until we put them in," Nangpa said. "And it was sixty-three years, not fifty, young Pemba."

"It was sixty-five," Dorje said. "But only Pemba would care how long ago it was. He was not born here."

Pemba bowed and said humbly, "Masters, I know that the years are of no account to anyone below, and until yesterday I had not been above for a very long time." Dorje and Nangpa took no notice. Pemba told Lee, "I had to help Monkey. Two of us were needed because there were two of you. There is only ever one Monkey. Band-width limitations prevent Master Norbhu from controlling more than one at a time. But when I had to carry you back, young man, I began to see an argument for two, trouble enough though one is. We could have left you to die, but that is not our way."

Lee said, "I don't understand what they are doing to Miriam. Who is your master? How can he ask her questions if she is asleep and he is dead?"

"All the better if she is asleep," Pemba said. "The truth is in dreams. And he really is dead, but he has not yet passed into transcendence. Perhaps you do not remember his interview with you."

"I remember his voice, I think. But corpses do not speak."

The half-lifers, pale puppets in their cocoons, dreaming their way into Heaven's information space as they died out of this one. It was possible that they spoke to each other, but they never spoke to the living.

"Only the body is dead," Nangpa said as he drew out needles he had pushed into Miriam's neck. A fat bead of blood clung to the end of each, and he carefully dropped them into a brass jar whose throat smoked with white vapor.

"The body lives, in part," Dorje said testily. "It keeps the brain alive, or else the soul would be released into a new cycle. If the house is burned, the inhabitants do not die, but they must live somewhere else. And so here. The machines help the body, in its half-life. So our dear Master Norbhu guides and enlightens us still."

"He is right," Pemba said, guiding Lee around the bowls which held the smoky constellations of the yak-butter candle oceans to the shrine. "See, young Han. Master Norbhu lives, in his own way."

Light came on beneath the peaked roof of the shrine. It shone on the homunculus which hung inside its fluid-filled jar like a huge, ancient embryo. Bubbles rose from sutures where tubes entered its ribcage, fanned around its bowed chin, caressed its sunken cheeks. Fine wires trailed from the corners of the homunculus's eyes, which were sealed by bluish membranes, and from its ears and the base of its skull, looping over its shoulder and winding once around its waist before running into the base of the vessel and the black cube on which the shrine stood.

This was not like the half-lifers, Lee thought. This was a corpse, wired and preserved.

But then the homunculus stirred. It moved slowly and jerkily. There was a cage of fine silvery filaments wrapped closely around its limbs. It raised its head, swung to face Lee. A hand came out, pressed against the glass of the vessel. The nails were curled horny blades long as knives.

Lee heard the faint scratching they made against the glass, and stepped backwards. For the first time he felt afraid. The monks were old men, wise perhaps, but not strong enough to hold him against his will. Monkey was some kind of gene-tailored animal, and there were always words of control for such creatures, perhaps the same words which had controlled the warhorse. But the homunculus was neither living nor dead. It was a ghost, a demon.

The homunculus's mouth did not move, but there was a voice. Lee could not tell where it came from. It was not a human voice. It filled his skull, deep and wise and patient and remote.

—MONKEY'S LINEAGE IS NOT OF ANIMALS TURNED INTO MEN, it said. HE IS OF MEN WHO HAVE BEEN GIVEN THE ATTRIBUTES OF ANIMALS. YOUR GREAT SCIENTIST DESIGNED HIS ANCESTORS AS SLAVES, BUT THEY WERE NOT A SUCCESS. LIKE OUR OWN DEAR PEOPLE, THEY ARE TOO INDEPENDENT. YOU WILL UNLEARN THE FALSE WICKED HABITS OF INDEPENDENCE HERE, YOUNG HAN. IT HAS BEEN A LONG TIME SINCE WE GAINED A NEW RECRUIT.

Lee said to Pemba, "Your master can see into my mind. He must see that I do not belong here."

—EVEN THOUGH THE MOUNTAIN BECOMES THE SEA, WORDS CANNOT OPEN ANOTHER'S MIND.

"The master quotes Mumon," Pemba said. "There is a teaching behind all things, but it is not of the mind, it is not Buddha, it is not things. That is what we learn here."

"Perhaps that kind of learning is too hard for me."

"The Way is always hard," Pemba said. "When it is not, we know we are not on the Way."

"Miriam . . . "

"Your friend will serve too. She has much to offer, once we have tamed her machines."

"If it is possible," Dorje said from the flickering shadows beneath the throne.

"It is possible," Nangpa said. "But although it is possible, she may not outlast our ministrations. So we must hurry, Dorje, as I have told you."

"We work as we will," Dorje said.

Lee said, "And if she will not serve?" His voice echoed from the painted vaults of the chamber's ceiling: he hadn't meant to speak so loudly.

Pemba told him, "There is only one Way."

Lee ran. He dodged Pemba's feeble swipe and ran straight for the low door at the far end of the hall. Monkey leaped up. Lee shouted words of power, but Monkey only beat his chest and hooted and chattered.

Lee wrenched free a pole which held one corner of a dusty canopy pitched above a statue of many-armed Yamantanka the Terrible. Monkey dodged Lee's wild swing and grabbed the splintered butt of the pole. When Monkey pulled, Lee slammed his shoulder hard against his flat frog-face. Monkey lost all his breath. Lee wrestled the pole from his grip and whacked him in the stomach.

Monkey fell on his knees, and Lee turned and raised the pole above his head, shouted to the monks that they must free Miriam or some bones would be broken.

The tall, thin monk, Dorje, stood between the two bowls of candle flames. He pointed his silver wand at Lee, who laughed. These foolish old monks and their half-animal servant were feeble enemies.

And then lightning flashed along the wand and Lee was flung backwards, every string in his body loosened.

Nineteen

The blow from Dorje's wand did not quite knock Lee out, but for a long time he could hold no thought in his head for more than a second. Slippery moments fell like beads from a broken necklace, scattering beyond his reach.

When time knitted up again, he was back in the little cell, in the niche hollowed into sandstone. Pemba gave him food, a purple broth with fibrous chunks, a bowl of tea with butter swirled into it.

Pemba explained that the food was woven from plant stuff grown in vats, using light piped down from the surface. The lamasery was as old as the Tibetan occupation of Mars, from the time when the air had been partly thickened but had not yet been made breathable, when vast storms racked the world from pole to pole. The Tibetans had tended the remaking of Mars, and the Han, who had exiled them, had then stolen their work: but the lamasery had survived. One day its time would come again.

Lee had heard this sort of thing before, from the cowboys he'd met on his travels from one *danwei* to another across the vast plains. He knew better than to say that his ancestors had been exiled too, in a vast exodus of hastily built gimcrack ships of which perhaps only a tenth had finished the voyage. That his own mother and father had disappeared because of their political beliefs. That he was no more than a pawn in a scheme of his great-grandfather.

Pemba, knitting slowly by the flickering light of the butter lamp in its niche, butterfly glasses perched on his nose, told Lee that he had once lived free, on the surface. The lamasery had been forgotten, or if it had been remembered it was as a place abandoned and in ruins. Pemba had been a cowboy before he had been recruited into the lamasery, before he had been given a new name and a new purpose. So too had been Dorje and Nangpa, and perhaps even Master Norbhu. It had been a very long time since anyone else had stumbled into the hidden valley, Pemba said, and it dawned on Lee that he was meant never to leave here. That he was meant to live out his life in saffron contemplation, cleaning the statues of the great hall and knitting scarves for them, playing conch or drums or cymbals to the slow rhythms of chants, tending the master in his wired jar.

Pemba said that it had taken him a long time to see the light, but now it was with him to the end of his days. And so it would be with Lee.

"I don't think so," Lee said.

"It was a very long time ago, but I remember my first days very clearly. And what you say to me is just what I said to Dorje." Pemba held up his knitting needles, and Lee cringed from them.

Pemba chortled. "The wand does that to you. After only one application, you fear even its image. It is a beginning, young Han. You'll see."

Twenty

L ee was still weak and feverish. After a while he slept, and it seemed to him that the librarian came into the cell and stooped over him, whispered in his ear that his parents had been found. Lee woke with a start. Pemba was asleep, breathing slowly and regularly with a faint whistle. His knitting had fallen in his lap.

What had woken Lee was the voice of the King of the Cats, faintly whispering in his head, fading in and out of audibility. Lee sat up. His fever had gone. As he swung his legs over the side of the sleeping niche, the King started to play "Blue Suede Shoes"—not his version, but Carl Perkins's.

Pemba said, without opening his eyes, "You're awake. That is good."

Carl Perkins began to fade in mid-song. But the voice that spoke over the fade wasn't that of the King.

—*He's gonna tell you I'm dead*, Miriam Makepeace Mbele said.

Pemba said, "Your friend is dead, but only in body. Her spirit lives on . . . "

—*More or less.*

" . . . and like you, she will serve the lamasery well. Come with me, young Han."

—*There's this computer*, Miriam said in Lee's ear as he was led along narrow corridors and up winding stairs by

Pemba. They were going to the surface. There was a ceremony to be performed.

—It's not as old as I am, but it's close. It thought it could seal me off, use me to fill in gaps in its functions. I think someone tried to physically reprogram it once upon a time, and nearly destroyed it. It's still working, but only because it's using the higher brain functions of this old monk it hardwired into its systems. It wants my skills to open up its physical plant again. Already I'm making connections all over the planet. Say something, Wei Lee. Subvocalize.

"What did you do to me?" Lee whispered. "What has happened to me?"

—I turned you on.

When she had kissed him, Miriam said, totipotent fullerene viruses in her saliva had swarmed into Lee. They had been multiplying inside him ever since, using gene therapy to rewrite the DNA of muscle and epidermal cells to turn them into little transceivers, spinning molecular networks through his body and brain to form a parallel nervous system.

Although the narrow corridors were lit only by infrequent butter lamps, Lee could see quite clearly, in bright, slightly fuzzy shades of green. Arrays of optical sensors had been inserted into his retinas; an image-processing network had been constructed parallel to his own. Occasionally, ideograms ghosted across his sight: command strings for activating a whole range of functions that were being hardwired into his optical chiasma.

Lee accepted these changes without alarm. Perhaps the viruses had conditioned him to accept their work—he would never know.

He mumbled, "You seem so calm."

—I've been dead before. It doesn't matter if I'm the real Miriam or not, I've gotten used to that philosophical problem over the centuries. There isn't time to explain the turns I've taken, but watch out for any of my sisters. There's at least one down here, and she isn't on my side.

"Who is she working for?"

—*I'm a licensed soldier of fortune. The Nexus owns copyright on me, but anyone can buy an ovum and the training program. You're near the surface, now. They're all there, except the master, and he hardly counts. I doubt if the computer left anything of him except perhaps his limbic functions. Ever see the* Wizard of Oz? *I guess not. Well, the master's not the danger. It's the little guys hiding behind the curtain. Those two old guys, Dorje and Nangpa.*

"I think you're wrong," Lee mumbled. "This whole place is like a trap. The monks don't run it."

—*You're coming up to a big chamber. Then the surface. I'm up there, in a way. I'm going to help you escape.*

Ahead of Lee, Pemba was silhouetted against a brilliant glare that abruptly stepped down as the sensors built into Lee's eyes compensated for the increase in light. The corridor opened into a vast domed chamber a hundred meters across, rising to fifty meters at its apex. It was lit by sunlight falling through square apertures cut into the domed roof. The walls were naked rock, with niches crammed with statues of demons. There were demons with rolling eyes and fierce fang-filled grins, bat-eared demons and elephant-nosed demons and demons with human ears whose lobes hung down to their pot bellies, pop-eyed demons and snake-eyed demons and demons who had rolled their eyes back into their skulls, demons with the beaks of crows or of parrots. Forever frozen, hundreds of them, thousands, they grinned and grimaced and ground their teeth, capered and chortled and contorted their pot-bellied bodies into impossible and obscene postures. Appliqué tangas hung from ceiling to floor down the demon-filled walls, tongues of dusty cloth whose brilliant colors had long faded. Drifts of red dust saddled away across the floor, and wind blew through the chamber, turning hundreds of prayer wheels that were scattered everywhere. They made a dry roaring rattling, hollow drums with printed prayers pasted inside them revolving around and around in the constant wind, each revolution a prayer blown out into the world. For every working wheel, there were two that had fallen over or simply jammed.

—*This place has seen better days,* Miriam commented. *You're very near the surface now, Lee. The others have taken my body there.*

Footprints already stitched a diagonal path across the vast prayer-haunted wind chamber. Lee followed Pemba through an oval arch set in the rock and up a winding stair. Narrow windows pierced the sandstone wall at every revolution of the helical stair. Lee glimpsed a narrow valley falling away, the steep slopes of wind-carved rock that enclosed it and chaotic terrain beyond, slumped hills pitched every which way.

Pemba had to stop at intervals to gain his breath. He clutched a fold of his fluttering orange robe over his shaven head. At last the stair opened into the back of a shallow cave. Outside was a wide space littered with rocks; each rock had a tail of sand pointing east. Something crackled under Lee's boots. It was a fragment of dry bleached bone.

There was an altar in the center of the garden of rocks and bones, and from each corner of the altar thin pillars of blue aromatic smoke rose straight up in the still air. The small sun shone high overhead, a coin of platinum fire stamped into the neon pink sky. A body lay on the altar. The two old monks, Dorje and Nangpa, were working on it with hatchets.

They wore only breechclouts, and their skinny chests and arms were spotted and streaked with vivid red blood. Monkey sat to one side, softly tapping a small drum he held between his big feet. A flock of ravens hopped and shifted on white-stained boulders heaped at the far side of the arena.

—*I've had all kinds of funerals, but I guess this has to be the most ecologically sound.*

Lee didn't want to get any closer to the butchery, but Pemba took his arm. "You must help with the sky burial," Pemba said. "You must see how inhuman your friend was."

—*I'm a good deal more human than their High Lama. Even Monkey's more human than that.*

"Go on, young man!" Pemba brandished a knitting needle.

Lee laughed. The trick wouldn't work twice.

Pemba frowned, stuck the knitting needle inside the sleeve of his robes, pulled out Dorje's silver wand. He pointed it at Lee, who felt an icy worm squirm in the pit of his stomach.

—*One thing I can't stand*, Miriam remarked, *is fighting at my own funeral. Unless I'm the one doing the fighting.*

Monkey's drumming suddenly shifted tempo, from a slow soft tapping to a more insistent rhythm. He uttered a series of soft yelps, then a humming noise. It was a tune the King of the Cats sometimes played: "Sympathy for the Devil."

Suddenly, everything seemed to go into slow motion. The viruses had built lines of communication to Lee's muscles and to his senses that worked at the speed of light, not sound: now he was using them. He plucked the silver wand from Pemba's hand and threw it away, and ran full tilt at the altar.

The two old monks turned, bloody hatchets raised. Lee easily dodged Dorje's graceful slow swipe and slammed the heel of his palm into the monk's nose, smashing it flat and driving bone fragments into his brain. Nangpa's hatchet came down as Lee swung Dorje's body around: the hatchet clopped into its back. Monkey's drum bounced off Nangpa's head with a hollow thud. The monk staggered and dropped the hatchet into the ruin of Miriam's dismembered corpse.

Lee hesitated, and Nangpa grabbed the hatchet in a wild swing that nearly eviscerated Lee. Things were back to normal speed again. Monkey was shaking his shaggy head, poking a long forefinger in his ear.

A burning pain pierced Lee's shoulder: he yelled when Pemba pulled out the knitting needle. Black shadows flapped overhead as Pemba stabbed at Lee again. Lee managed to kick Pemba in the knee and the monk fell down.

Strong wings beat about Lee; there were ravens everywhere, settling on the altar, on Miriam's corpse, on Dorje's sprawled body. Nangpa was crawling over the rocky ground towards the cave, a raven flapping at his neck and pecking at his shaven scalp.

—*Kill them! Kill them all! Quickly! Quickly, Lee! Something's going wrong . . .*

Lee pulled up a flat rock and staggered across to Nangpa. The monk's pale shrivelled face turned to look at Lee, who felt a spasm of physical revulsion. He dropped the rock to the ground instead of on to Nangpa's head, pushed the old monk over with the toe of his boot. Nangpa fell slowly, in stages, curling up like a shrivelled spider.

—*Do it Lee! Do it now!*

"I'm not what you want me to be!"

The cry came from somewhere deep inside Lee. It had been building all his life, all the time he had been indebted to his great-grandfather. It was the store of all the shame and loss of face, its fragile membrane of deference, self-effacement, a misguided sense of duty, finally broken.

"I'm not what you want . . . "

—BUT YOU ARE, YOUNG HAN.

The voice came from the same place inside his head as had Miriam's.

—YOUR FRIEND WAS SUBTLE, BUT NOT SUBTLE ENOUGH.

Monkey shuddered and stiffened on the other side of the altar. His face was locked in a rictus snarl. Something was looking through his eyes, looking at Lee. Something that spoke to Lee inside his head.

—HOW INTERESTING THIS NEW TECHNOLOGY IS. YOU WILL MAKE A FINE SERVANT, EVEN BETTER THAN THE HOMINID SERIES. PERHAPS THIS IS WHAT I HAVE BEEN WAITING FOR ALL THESE YEARS, ALL THESE CENTURIES.

Lee ran.

He made the stairs at the back of the cave, fell around a whole turn, picked himself up and heard Monkey's feet slapping above him and ran on down, banging from side to side. He was halfway across the dusty hall when he dared look back, saw Monkey loping after him and ran on, pushing prayer wheels out of his way, raising clouds of red dust. His breath burned in his throat.

—YES, YOUNG HAN. YES. COME TO ME. COME TO ME.

A dozen low doors led off the far end of the chamber. Lee chose one and turned right and left at random as he ran down the narrow branching corridor. Or so he thought. For the corridor ended in a darkened room and Lee ran straight through it into the Great Hall.

—WELCOME, said the voice in Lee's head.

The canopy had been reset above the statue of Yamantanka the Terrible. Lee snatched a pole from it again as he ran down the aisle.

Monkey loped out from shadows to one side of the great golden Buddha. He pressed his palms together, then hurled himself at Lee. Before Lee could raise his weapon he was crushed and lifted up, his face pressed into the coarse pelt that covered Monkey's barrel chest. Lee got a hand under Monkey's chin and pushed. They fell backwards against one of the yak-butter candle oceans. The bowl tipped, splashing molten butter and flaming wicks. Monkey sprang up, screaming and chattering, brushing at the little flames that clung to his pelt.

Drenched in hot butter, his clothes smouldering, Lee saw his chance. He only had a moment, and knew he must not make a mistake.

—YOU CANNOT HURT ME WITH THAT SILLY LITTLE WEAPON, YOUNG HAN.

Lee swung the pole.

The ancient wood was as hard as iron. It rang against the cylinder which housed the undead corpse of Master Norbhu. Glass starred and the shock shivered the pole to flinders. Lee stepped back, raised his foot, and kicked at the starred glass. It broke.

Fluid spurted and the corpse sagged in its net of fine wires. Connections broke in brief constellations of snapping sparks. Overhead, all the electric lights went out. Perhaps only a chance current or a final spasm raised the corpse's chicken-claw hand, but Lee thought it was something more. Like everything in the lamasery, the corpse had been a slave to the true master, the ancient computer which Miriam had tried to subvert. Miriam had been wrong to suggest that the old master of the lamasery had lost all but his limbic functions. Something had remained: he had scratched at the glass, begged to be set free. And Lee had freed him, and now Miriam was truly dead.

Monkey lay on the floor, red pelt pulled into slick points by clotting butter, singed to the hide in half a dozen patches. Lee helped him to his feet, and the simian servant came up with docile grace. Lee found a butter lamp and had Monkey lead him to the dead, dark kitchens. He took what he needed, then found his way back up to the surface.

Twenty-one

Pemba was waiting in the shadows in the cave at the head of the stairwell, but Lee had half expected that. He grabbed the old monk's arm and twisted it until the hatchet clattered to the rocks. He let it lie there; he'd had enough of weapons.

Pemba sat down heavily. He was bleeding from nose and ears, and two bloody tears streaked his cheeks. Monkey had to help him walk. Nangpa was dead. He had been under the thrall of the computer longer than Pemba, and the shock of the broken connection had been too great. His body lay near that of Dorje; ravens had already pecked out their eyes and tongues.

Lee did not entirely trust Pemba, but he could not leave him for the ravens. He and Monkey took turns helping the half-comatose monk along, but progress was slow. They were only halfway down the narrow green valley that dropped away from the tabletop plateau when night fell.

Lee lit a fire, as he had been about to do when the monks had come upon him. Monkey vanished, came back with half a dozen ice mice and a russet-pelted rock hare, and a handful of dark, odorous wild garlic bulbs. He lay the corpses and the garlic on a flat stone and shuffled backwards, sat in a half-squat at the edge of the dancing firelight. Two pinpricks of reflected fire shone beneath his heavy brow; his flat wide nostrils snuffled as he watched Lee skin and clean the hare.

The hare's carcass took a long time to roast and came out

half-raw, half-burnt. But, taking alternate bites of meat and pungent garlic bulbs, Lee could have eaten ten times his share.

Monkey tried to feed Pemba, but the monk wouldn't eat. His eyes were filmed with white. His cheeks had sunken and the lines around his eyes had deepened, like cracks in drying mud. The skin of his hand, when Lee took it to feel his pulse, was dry and cold, loose over brittle bones. His pulse was a rapid feeble flutter.

The computer had done more than rewire his brain, Lee thought. It had kept all the monks alive long past their natural span. He wondered just how old Pemba really was. He had talked of snow, but except at the poles, where no one lived, snow had not fallen on Mars for at least two centuries. And how old had Dorje and Nangpa been?

"I'm sorry, young Master," Pemba said, startling Lee, who told him to rest. But Pemba wanted to tell his story. "I left the mountains because I killed a man, and I became a roving cowboy and killed another. I sought to become a monk to cleanse myself of blood-debt before the wheel of my life turned, but the gods saw to my punishment. I was on my way to the capital when I rested in this little valley, and was taken by Dorje and Nangpa. Master Norbhu had just died. Long before then the Kailas lamasery had been abandoned by all but its computer, and what had once served the community of the lamasery now gathered a community to itself, at first to save the lamasery, but later to save itself. It became the master, but without heart, without Buddhism. It was a spider, brooding in its web, its poison working in its bound victims to keep them neither dead nor alive. Our hearts darkened, our eyes were its eyes, our minds its mind. When my people came, young Master, Mars was a wilderness of rock and dust, without breath or heart. My people made it breathe; my people gave it life. Every rock and stone is holy, for they have been changed by the quickening of the world. The heart of my people, their soul and their lifeblood, is Buddhism. It sustained them through the hard years when Mars turned green, and only one child in ten lived. But when the deserts flowered and the Han came to take what they claimed to be theirs, my people lost heart, and the monks of many lamaseries lost discipline, and abandoned their places. Still, they said that one day the Lord of Light, the Buddha of the Future, the Maitreya Buddha, would step out on to the face of Mars. I had forgotten that, until now."

It took Pemba a long time to say this, and when he had finished he did not speak again, but turned his face to the shadows beyond the ring of firelight.

Monkey left a charred haunch by Pemba, like an offering, and swallowed the ice mice one by one, skins and all, like furry grapes. Lee shook out the cloth he had taken, a gorgeous brocade which had been the cloak of a snake-haired demon, wrapped himself in it, pulled down the hood of his chuba, and fell asleep.

It was very easy to sleep, and there were no dreams.

Twenty-two

He woke at first light. A faint frost mantled the brocade cloak and frost tipped every blade of grass in the little meadow. The sound that had woken him was Monkey slapping earth with his big bare feet, making a keening sound as he rocked Pemba.

The old monk was dead. His dry, shrunken corpse could have been dead a hundred years. As Lee gently took the body from Monkey, the shoulder of the valley fell away from the face of the sun and the air was filled with light.

Lee helped Monkey cover the body with rocks, and covered the rocks with sandy soil and strips of turf. Jackals would dig it out before long, but the gesture was entirely human. Monkey stamped down the turves and made obeisance to his dead master, and then he and Lee set off down the valley.

Twenty-three

Monkey loped ahead of Lee in ever widening circles that day. They climbed the domed hill that blocked the entrance of the hidden valley, and headed north into the chaotic terrain beyond.

This was the land which had fed the huge river which had carved the Red Valley in lost ages before man had come to Mars. Confined aquifers, sealed above by thick, permanent ice, sealed below by self-compaction, had built up high pressures which had at last burst forth in head zones. As meltwater discharged in vast torrents, the land above the aquifers had slumped and collapsed, a self-perpetuating process that had ended only when the hydraulic gradient had been reduced. If Mars was to live, the floods must come again.

Lee and Monkey trekked through a maze of long dry valleys that lay between low hills which ran in irregular shoals in every compass direction. Dry scrub grew on the flanks of the hills. Creosote bush and scrub oak; twisted desert pine with papery bark and a salting of live leaf buds like vivid green sparks; tarweed, chaparral pea, jumping cactus, cheat grass. The valleys were jumbled mazes of huge boulders, or parched tongues of alkaline salt flats broken only by tufts of soldier grass.

A thin cold wind knifed across the valleys. Monkey did not seem to notice it, but Lee was glad of the chuba he had taken, a gown with wide sleeves made of heavy brown wool.

He wrapped the hood close around his head, for all the world like the dead monks he had left behind.

The silences of the desert landscape of Mars, hardly touched by the skim of life, helped cleanse him of guilt. He was learning to control his rewired nervous system, and the King of the Cats and his music was clear and close as he walked.

That night, Lee took shelter in the weathered skull of an archiosaur. One of Cho Jinfeng's failed experiments had been the creation of animals that under Mars's low gravity had grown bigger than any creature that had ever lived on the Earth. But the archiosaurs had not been able to adapt to the changing climate of Mars. Ice mice and other small mammals had feasted on their eggs, and within a century they had died out.

The skull was half sunken in sand, tilted sideways like a bony galleon beached on a dry seabed. It had been etched by sandstorms and stained by iron oxides. Grasses made a mohican crest along the top of the cranium. Lee camped in the half-buried circle of an eye socket. He piled a bed of dry grasses in the channel which had held the optic nerve and built a fire of juniper wood so dry and old it was almost fossilized, built it so high that sparks flew into the starry sky like birthing galaxies.

Monkey sat at the edge of the fire's flickering shadows; that night he brought no food. Once or twice when Lee looked up Monkey was gone, but the next time Lee looked he was there again as if he had never been away.

But in the morning Monkey was gone for good. Lee performed t'ai chi exercises to rid himself of the frosty stiffness of the night, trampling the warm ashes of his fire as he made the slow, flowing forms.

As he walked that day he kept glimpsing Monkey's rufous body at the edge of his vision, far off and moving fast. But when he looked it was nothing but a kit fox, or a tuft of frost-burned soldier grass, or the flash of sunlight against some far chiselled cliff face.

All that day, Lee walked with a diminishing sense of Monkey's company, and when he made camp that night he knew he was alone at last. Except for the sound of the King, and the myriad viruses that coursed through his blood, each a word waiting to be spoken.

Twenty-four

The yak had fallen down a scree slope into a deep little crevasse. As Lee watched, it scrambled halfway up the slope, hoofs striking sparks, until it could climb no more. It stood shivering as its legs slid apart on loose stones, and then it rolled back down and bounced to its feet. It trotted up and down at the bottom of the gully, then tried the slope again, and again stopped halfway up and rolled back down to the bottom.

It was close to sunset, that time when the flying moons were brighter than the sun, and the temperature was falling fast. Lee glimpsed a shape lurking amongst boulders on the other side of the gully, took a stone and lofted it, saw a dire-wolf slink away from the clatter. Come nightfall, the yak would have its throat torn out; by morning, nothing would be left but bloody bones.

The yak tossed its head and looked at Lee with mournful eyes, as if fully aware of its fate. It had a shaggy coat of black hair down to its knees, wide forward-curving horns, a long face with a white stripe down the muzzle. There was a big brass ring through its nose, and red ribbons plaited into the bush of its long tail.

Lee eased off his pack, untied the length of rope that belted his chuba, and crabbed his way down the scree slope.

When he reached the bottom of the slope the yak cantered forward and tried to knock him over so it could gore him with its sharp-tipped horns. But after he slipped the rope

105

through its nose ring it became docile, and he was able to lead it straight up the scree slope, pulling hard whenever it stopped.

Lee stumbled over the edge out of breath, and as he turned to haul the yak the last few meters, something launched itself from shadows beneath a tumble of boulders. The yak bellowed in terror and made a run for it, tail in the air. Lee was dragged on his belly over hard stones until he remembered to let go of the rope. He got to his feet with blood in his eyes from a cut on the bridge of his nose. The dire-wolf growled a dozen meters away, a ruff of coarse hair raised around its humped shoulders, its ears flat on its long skull. It must have sneaked around while Lee had been rescuing the yak, and must be desperate, too, to even think of attacking a man.

Lee backed away, step by step. The dire-wolf followed, flowing like water. It favored its left front leg, which had probably been broken and healed badly. Lee threw a handful of stones, but the dire-wolf dodged each one and turned back towards Lee, its eyes like yellow lamps. It was between Lee and his pack, which was where he'd set the big broad-bladed kitchen knife when he'd unbelted his chuba.

Then something cracked past his ear, and the dire-wolf's head exploded.

Lee turned so quickly he fell over. Atop a crater ridge a kilometer away, a pony and rider were silhouetted against the red sun. The pony reared on two legs, and then it was galloping down the ridge. Lee barely had time to find his knife before pony and rider were upon him in a cloud of red dust.

"How you doing?" said the cowboy.

He leaned on the front grip of the high, square saddle of his bay pony. A short-barrelled rifle rested in the crook of his arm. With his free hand he pushed up the brim of his black felt hat: a lean dark weathered face, with bright blue eyes and a white smile, a week's growth of blond beard, long red-blond hair tied back with a leather thong. Despite the sunset chill, his leather vest was open down his hairy chest.

Lee carefully set down the knife and bowed, and started to express his thanks.

"No need for that," the cowboy said. "I'd hope you'd do the same for me." He was called Redd—it was not his real name, of course, but most who rode the dusty ranges had one reason or another to lose or forget their real names. He was helping ride a herd to the capital.

Lee introduced himself. "I also have business at the capital."

"You want to try and ride that yak back along with me? Maybe we can get you a real mount at the camp."

"Pardon me?"

"The yak you rescued," Redd said, with exaggerated patience.

"I do not think that would be very suitable. It is not my place to make a suggestion, but I notice that your saddle is very capacious . . . "

"Gee, do you Han always have to be so damned formal?"

Lee felt his face heat. He had been talking to Redd as a master talks to a servant, for Redd was a Yankee, and that was how he had been taught to treat Yankees. He said, "I'm sorry. It is not my place. But I admit your rifle makes me nervous."

"This little thing?" Redd raised the weapon over his head, spun it twice, and plunged it into the sheath that hung at his mount's withers. All this before Lee could draw a breath. "Don't mind me," Redd said. "I've been out on the range so long I've forgotten any manners I might have had. You're heading for the capital, you say? Well, we're short-handed since old Stinkfoot was trampled a week ago. There was this dust storm?"

Like every Yankee Lee had met, Redd had a habit of ending everything he said with a rising inflection, as if constantly unsure that his perception of the world was shared by anyone else. Well, it had been taken from them after all, and their failure turned into a victory, however temporary.

Lee said, "You offer me a job?"

"Take it or leave it. If you take it you can lead the yak

back or ride it, it's all the same to me. You want to walk it's north by northwest, about three klicks or so?" Redd pointed, aslant the setting sun. "You do want to walk, I won't wait on you, but the yak'll know the way. Unless it falls into another gully. It's kind of dumb, even as yaks go."

Lee didn't stop to consider how much choice he had. For you earned your keep in the high plains or you died, and although he could live off the land for a few weeks, he knew that he would grow weaker by the day, and that it would take more than a few weeks to walk to the capital.

The yak hadn't run far, and was grazing on a patch of moss it had scrabbled up from the sandy soil. It let Lee get close enough to grab the rope which hung from its nose ring, and then it was easy. Lee put two fingers in the yak's sensitive nostrils and twisted hard, his shoulders against the beast's flank. It went down on its knees, and Lee jumped astride it, clinging behind the hump of muscle over its shoulders. The yak got up, puffing like an indignant dowager.

"Not bad," Redd said, and spat a squirt of brown saliva. "Now let's see how you ride."

Twenty-five

They followed the trail left by the herd: tufts of soldier grass munched to the ground; dried pats spotting the trampled sand, big fierce black beetles already at work on them, scurrying this way and that with their loads of dung.

Lee told Redd a little of his story, glossing over Miriam's part. He didn't want everyone to know that he was carrying a cargo of valuable fullerene viruses. Besides, he hadn't enough breath to tell even half of what had happened to him. The yak bounced him around even over level ground, of which there was not much, and his testicles were rhythmically hammered between the yak's ridged back and his own pelvis.

Redd heard Lee out, then said, "I'd keep quiet, if I were you. Especially about the bit with the monks. Even if it's true . . . "

"I don't need to lie!"

"So you found a lamasery hidden since Mars was changed, with the original monks . . . "

"They were all really old, but I don't think any of them were original."

"These guys, centuries old. They kill your friend, feed her mind into their computer, dismember her body. You kill two monks and the half-lifer and escape with the help of an apeman. The other monk disintegrates before your eyes as soon as you get out of the place."

"It wasn't exactly like that," Lee said.

Redd shrugged.

"I'll be quiet."

"Good. Some of the guys are kind of religious."

They rode the rest of the way in silence. Even if he was a Yankee, Redd was like the cowboys Lee had seen in the markets of small *danweis*: compact, muscular, taciturn men who wouldn't haggle over the prices of the trinkets they sold. You heard that they fought duels to the death, that they hunted runaways from the *danweis* for sport, that they were the scum of Mars.

Night fell, hard and sudden, but there was enough starlight for Lee's enhanced vision to show him a patchy infrared landscape of green light and deep shadows.

Clades of viruses, spinning through his blood, climbing his nerves. Turning him into something else. Into what Miriam had been, perhaps; and perhaps they'd make him as long-lived as his great-grandfather and the other Ten Thousand Years, although that was little comfort when he didn't know where his next meal was coming from.

At last Lee saw the glow of the cowboys' fire, small and fierce as a star fallen to the wide, wide surface of the world. Yaks, their long faces like burning skulls in Lee's enhanced sight, were tethered by their nose rings to chains staked amongst heather and trampled grass. They snorted and stirred restlessly as Lee and Redd rode towards the fire at the centre of their concentric circles.

"This is it," Redd said.

Boxes and baskets of woven grass were scattered over the ground. There were a few rough shelters of tarpaulin or blankets draped over wicker frames. A black dog barked at Lee's mount; it was tied to a stake and wore a ruff of red wool.

As for the cowboys, there were a round dozen of them, all men, mostly wearing chubas over denim shirts and trousers. They were all smaller than Lee, but he didn't doubt that any one of them could pull him limb from limb in a moment. Firelight showed faces seamed and tanned as hard as saddle leather, coarse black hair greased back into braids tied with tags and coloured ribbons—the tags were chips of silicon circuitry.

Their leader was an old Tibetan who called himself Hawk. While Redd told him how he had found Lee, Hawk took Lee's face in his horny, cracked hands and held Lee's gaze with eyes like black bright currants sunk in the creased baked dough of his face. He had a big belly, and long white hair that straggled halfway down his back. After a long minute, he speared a pair of glasses from a breast pocket and strung them over his ears and nose. The lenses were little round mirrors, and they distortingly reflected Lee's face as Hawk peered at him.

Half the cowboys crowded up behind Hawk; the rest hadn't bothered to leave their places around the fire. One of the onlookers said, "You think we need this yellow-faced boy scout?"

"You be quiet, White Eye," Hawk said. "I'm thinking it over."

"They smell funny and spook the critters," White Eye said. He smiled at Lee. Half his teeth were missing; the rest were blackened stumps. His right eye was capped with the frost of a cataract—a common complaint amongst cowboys, who spent most of their lives out in the ultraviolet-drenched sunlight. "Nothing personal you understand," he added.

"Steal too," someone else said.

"He'll ride with us," Hawk said, and put away his mirrored spectacles.

"Aw, Hawk . . . "

Hawk put an arm around Lee's shoulders. "He interests me. And we need a replacement for Stinkfoot, and you all know what they say about the Han. We can trust him, you think, Redd?"

Redd shrugged.

Hawk told Lee, "You'll get a daily wage, let's call it twenty yuan. No share in profits, but you can hardly expect that."

Twenty yuan a day was about a tenth of what Lee had earned at Bitter Waters. But money wasn't the point. The point was that Lee's great-grandfather wouldn't expect him to ride into the capital amongst a herd of yaks. He said, "It's a deal."

"Someone give him tea," Hawk said.

Lee sat a little way off from the roaring fire. A tin mug of tea with a lump of rancid butter dissolving in it warmed his cramped hands. The cowboys talked quietly amongst themselves, passing around a long-stemmed pipe of marijuana and telling tall tales. After a while, Redd brought Lee a rough blanket. It reeked of horse sweat, but Lee took it gratefully: it was piercingly cold out under the stars.

"Sleep," Redd said. "Long ride tomorrow, and you'll need to get up before everyone else."

"Oh?"

"I guess I did forget to tell you. Stinkfoot was our cook."

Twenty-six

Lee woke to a frail thread of song. It was the grey hour before dawn. Jupiter was a blurred diamond low on the horizon. The fire was down to glowing ashes. The singer was a long way off, out amongst the circles of tethered yaks. His voice was high and plaintive, rising at the end of each line in a weird ululation. He was singing in the Country and Western mode that the King of the Cats had sometimes affected (although of course as with everything else the King had stamped it with his own persona).

Hear the lonesome whippoorwill . . .

By the time Lee had revived the fire and set a pot of water to boil, the rest of the cowboys were up and about and the horizon was just falling below the rim of the sun. Redd showed Lee where the supplies were kept, helped him brew tea dark as beetroot juice, and fry cakes of oatmeal and butter on a sheet of metal set directly on the fire. Cowboys drifted up, took food and tea without comment, drifted away.

"We always sing to our herds," Redd told Lee, and explained that the yaks, used to ranging free in small groups, grew nervous and contrary when herded together. At night, almost anything could spook them, kit foxes or a dire-wolf, a change in wind direction, a meteor. Song calmed them.

Lee thought about the pop arias and commercials that had constantly echoed around and about the Bitter Waters *danwei*, and said he knew what Redd meant. He added, "I

113

know plenty of good songs. Maybe you'll let me sing to your animals."

As Redd showed Lee how to saddle up, they fell into a friendly discussion about whether the King of the Cats had transcended Country and Western as he had transcended so much else. Or at least, Lee did most of the talking and Redd smiled a lot, and when Lee had more or less run through praising the King of the Cats, Redd commented that the King sounded like an outgrowth of Country and Western, no more special than that. Lee laughed, and said when they made camp he'd teach Redd some of the King's style and then see what he said.

"Let's get to camp first," Redd said, and swung himself up into the saddle of his skittish bay pony. "The longer it takes to get the yaks to market the thinner they are and the less they're worth. Hawk said I should let you know that!" Then he kicked his pony into a trot, and left Lee standing.

The cowboys made speed that day. Their ambling herd moved surprisingly quickly over the red stony plain. Impacted sand, rocks, shale, spattered with the broken circles of ancient craters. They were paralleling hills that rose, wave after wave, to the north.

Riding dead Stinkfoot's old, barrel-bellied pony, which was laden before and behind its high saddle with bundled cooking implements and sacks of barley meal, Lee followed as best he could. The pony's lurching sway-backed amble was making him distinctly motion sick, but he was happy. Just to be moving was enough. Everything that had happened to him or that cast a shadow into his future—the flight from Bitter Waters, Miriam's death, the viruses, his great-grandfather's plots—dissolved in the eternal moment. Lee was very young.

Far ahead, the cowboys were strung in a loose V behind the herd of yaks, moving in a gritty rolling cloud of red dust and clatter of wooden bells. The men called to each other in high yodels, now one and now another racing forward to cut a stray back into the herd. Only rare clumps of air lichen punctuated the cold desert, and those were stunted, frost-blasted specimens, yet these plains were where the yaks spent most of their lives. A kind of saxifrage moss grew just beneath the surface of the sandy soil, and yaks scraped it up and gulped it down, grit and all. The cowboys had to ride back and forth to keep the herd moving whenever it passed over an especially rich patch.

It was hard, dirty, difficult, dangerous work. Yaks were temperamental beasts, bad-tempered and unreliable, switching from sullen stubbornness to high nervousness and back at the twitch of a tufted tail. Because they had to fend for themselves in winter, their long sharp horns were untrimmed. Orange spittle streaked their muzzles. When a yak was nervous, it yawned to show strings of dirty orange mucus inside a black mouth; when it was getting ready to run it shook its head and spit went everywhere. Their coats of long hair hid long legs: a yak looked bulkier than a cow, but could be as skittish as an antelope. And they could run for ever if they wanted. Half their bodies were packed with lungs; they were just about the only animal species that hadn't had to be spliced and diced to adapt it to Mars's thin cold atmosphere.

Lee picked up from Redd what was needed more by imitation than instruction; herding left little time for conversation. They rode trailing point behind the left flank of the herd, eyes open for any yak that decided it had had enough of the company of its peers. Escape bids were discouraged by cutting in on the stray and physically blocking its path. Not as easy as Redd made it seem, Lee discovered the first time he tried it. Yaks were as nimble as the cowboys' ponies, and knew how to use their long sharp horns. Whips were used as a last resort; it could make the yak panic and charge off at an unstoppable lick, tail held high. If you were really unlucky, nearby yaks caught the same panic.

The cowboys were heading towards the round-up camps outside the capital, but they had other business that was taking them in a wide arc to the west. Lee guessed that it was something to do with the anarchists, for where else would the cowboys have gotten their silicon jewellery, their penchant for Hank Williams, Roy Rogers and Roy Acuff?

Constant wind sent drifts of red dust skimming across the plain. Towards noon, a pod of sky seeders rode the wind out from the foothills: big ragged blue-green blimps with rudimentary nerve nets, each moving inside a distinct haze of extruded cyanobacteria, remnants from the time when the newly outgassed atmosphere of Mars, rich in carbon dioxide and little else, had been made breathable. Cho Jinfeng had spliced them from sponge and coral genes. Cyanobacteria constantly multiplied within them, producing oxygen and fixing atmospheric nitrogen—hydrogen produced as a by-product of nitrogen fixation filled membranous pockets and gave the things lift. Excess blue-green filaments were extruded and fertilized the land over which the sky seeders drifted.

Lee had only seen sky seeders once before, and dropped behind the herd as they traversed directly overhead. Even as he watched, a cluster of black darts zoomed out of the west. They were conchie killer drones. The other cowboys had seen them too, and rose on their stirrups, calling to each other.

The drones hurtled through the pod of sky seeders before the plant-animals had time to react, smashing great holes in their inflated bodies and setting fire to their hydrogen sacs. Half the sky seeders started to sink, trailing smoke and blue flames. The drones somersaulted and made another pass. Wounded sky seeders blew apart with sharp explosions that shivered echoes from the foothills. The rest were shedding ballast—vast green clouds of cyanobacteria—as they tried to rise into higher, faster winds. But the drones cut through them again, once, twice. A mother sky seeder tried to place its bulk between the drones and its two pups—a drone smashed her in half and dispersed lightnings that blew up the pups in balls of blue flame.

The drones swooped low over the cowboys and the herd, and then they were dwindling westward, even as the burning remnants of the sky seeders tumbled to the plain. Globs of cyanobacteria were raining down everywhere, and the yaks had scattered and were greedily grazing on this unexpected manna; it took a long time to get them moving again.

"Bastards," Redd said to Lee, when they briefly worked alongside each other, chivvying a yak away from a singed slab of sky seeder.

"The drones?"

"Their masters. They won't rest until they've destroyed the world, and it isn't theirs to destroy."

Lee, amazed by the cowboy's bold opinions, said, "The Emperor has decreed otherwise." In the past year Lee hadn't dared to express his own Sky Roader sympathies to anyone but Guoquiang and Xiao Bing, and then only well away from the rest of the *danwei*.

Redd managed to loop a rope through the yak's nose ring. The other end was tied to his saddle. The yak bellowed but reluctantly left the feast. He shouted, "The world isn't the Emperor's. It's ours. And no one asked *us* what we want." Then he kicked his pony into a trot, dragging the yak after him. Lee would have ridden after him to ask what he meant, but Hawk yelled for him to give a hand, and he had to turn away.

Twenty-seven

The herd covered less than twenty kilometers that day. When the cowboys finally made camp, at a place little different from where they had started, Lee felt as if most of the territory coated his whole skin, all the way inside him to his stomach. Patches had rubbed raw on the insides of his sweat-slippery thighs where they'd gripped the high saddle.

Redd handed Lee a pair of chaps with supple leather patches on the thighs, and Lee thanked him.

Redd said, "Are you ready to sing, Comrade Lee?"

"After cooking, I should think I'd have trouble lifting the guitar."

"Plenty of time to practice before we reach the round-up. *Then* you will sing. I told the others, and they're eager to hear new songs. We'll be pleased if your King of the Cats charms the yaks half as well as Hank Williams."

"He is more your King than mine. One of your ancestors, after all."

"I'm a Martian," Redd said. "All cowboys are Martians. That's why so few of them are Han. You might be a Martian, Wei Lee, I don't know yet. As for the King of the Cats, he's just a dead guy from another world. Maybe I'll think something of him if you can out-sing the rest of us."

Ordinarily, Lee would have sprung to passionate defence of the King. But now . . . he was simply too exhausted. He found it hard enough to stay awake to cook the cowboys' supper: smashed barley grains, dehydrated vegetables and fatty salt meat boiled up in a big black kettle, yak bones charred on the embers until their marrows bubbled and ran.

"Good food," Hawk pronounced. His beard shone with grease. "I told you," he said to the cowboys, "that they make the best cooks. You come with me, young Han, and I'll show you how to make tea strong enough to sink such good food and lay the dust."

As he shaved tea from a black brick into the kettle which had held the stew, Hawk said quietly, "What do you think of young Redd?"

"He has been good to me. After all, he saved my life."

"I've seen you talking with him. And I've been wondering just why you're out here."

"I was travelling to the capital."

"Do tell." Hawk licked the blade of his knife, folded it up and put it away. His long white hair made a kind of cowl around his lined face. "You put water in the kettle until it's half full, bring it to the boil, *then* put in the butter." When he had set the kettle in the middle of the cooking fire he said, "Young Redd's a firebrand. A couple of herd bosses have already fired him from their crews. I find him . . . entertaining. He reminds me of myself when I was young, when the Emperor and the Ten Thousand Years began to deal with the Earth. The conchies sent missionaries amongst us, and we lynched most of them, but there were always more, all looking almost exactly alike. There were riots, I remember, and the Army of the People's Mouths was sent against us. I was amongst those who called for the strike to hold, and it did. We took away half the capital's meat supply, and pretty soon the Ten Thousand Years gave in—no more missionaries. But the conchies won in the end. They only had to wait. These days even cowboys give up their lives to dream their way into Heaven, for all Redd's fine sentiments. The difference between him and my younger self is that I was one of many, but he's one of a vanishing breed."

Lee, wondering what Hawk was trying to tell him, said nothing.

"What I'm telling you, young Han, is that Redd's an outspoken loner."

"Yet you are sympathetic to his . . . ideas."

"I like him, but I don't trust him. I get the idea that you're sympathetic to his ideas too, and I saw the way you looked at the conchie drones today. No need to be alarmed. We none of us out here like what's happening to the world, it's just that unlike Redd, most of us know there isn't much we can do about it. Now, go get a block of butter; tea's near to boiling."

Lee fell asleep as soon as he had wrapped himself in his brocade cloak, and the librarian was waiting for him in his dreams.

"You should have told them about what was done to you," the librarian said. "It's important. It will give you face. You'll need that, in the days to come."

They stood in warm white sunlight by a stone wall at the top of a cliff. The librarian was a shadow in the sunlight, his face hidden by a fold of his black silk robe. There were intricate lines embroidered in the silk, like circuit diagrams. Lee hadn't noticed them before. He leaned on sun-warmed stone and said, "This is better than your musty books."

Beneath them spread a wide bay that bent around a city built on seven hills. A glass pyramid reflected the blue sky in the midst of a host of tall buildings bigger than anything Lee had ever known. The blue water was flecked with the sails of many small craft. Nearer, overshadowing Lee and the librarian, a vast rust-red bridge soared across the strait which was the mouth of the bay. Vehicles hummed across it, small as beetles in the distance. Beyond the bridge . . . fog, a bank of fog rolling in from gray ocean water. Something made a deep mournful sound out there.

The librarian pushed back the robe's hood, and shook out her long black hair. Miriam (but when had she had long hair? and why was she so young, younger even than Lee?) said, "It's on Earth, or it was. I suppose the ruins of the city might still be there, but it's been so long since I thought to look, and the Earth's a green wilderness now . . . Listen, Lee, the people you're with worship their ancestors. That you have a ghost in your head is very impressive to them. It's why they let you live." She laughed. "They think you can raise the dead."

Lee laughed too. "Why would they kill me?"

"Why not? You're Han. You raped their country centuries ago on the Earth, and the survivors were sent to provide the labor for terraforming Mars. Most died. Those that didn't became Martians. They believe the world is theirs, and why not?"

"The Great Leap Forward will not take a century, but a thousand years. That is its glory."

"You sound like a recruiting poster."

Lee had been quoting a slogan he had come across in an old history file. He blushed and smiled and apologized. "I don't believe it. It *should* take only a century to be finished. I'm like my parents, a Sky Roader."

"There's no progress, that's the point. Your Emperor has lost its way, and the Ten Thousand Years have traded progress for immortality. They've traded on the lives of everyone on Mars."

"Like leaders everywhere."

"Wow, Lee, how did someone so young get to be so cynical?" Her smile was still the same, sudden and bright.

"I started early, under my great-grandfather's guidance. Whose side is he on?"

"His own, like all of the Ten Thousand Years. Their needs roughly map into each other, but that's all. You're a biologist, Lee. You know what will happen to the ecosphere of Mars if something isn't done to stop all the liberated water from being locked up again. Something dramatic."

"This isn't a dream, is it?"

"It used to be thought that dreams were a way of assimilating new information. That's what you're doing."

"The librarian said something like that, a while back. In another dream that wasn't a dream. This is because of the machines you put in my blood, isn't it? The viruses."

Miriam's black hair lifted around her shoulders in the wind which blew up from the cliffs. The mournful horn was still sounding from inside the fog bank, which had now swallowed the bridge. The sunlight was edged with cold. She said, "The cowboys might be able to help us, Lee. The viruses tried to encrypt part of my memories, but it didn't take too well. Not surprising, really, the machines were never designed to read out into another nervous system. But they found that other viruses had already been at work inside you. They found the librarian."

"No. He's an archive program a friend wrote for me. He was worming through the common data banks, looking for information . . . " For information on his parents. Lee said, "My great-grandfather."

"Someone had a RAM chip mapped into your visual cortex. It was triggered by the specific information bandwidth of virtual-reality goggles, and recorded anything you experienced. My viruses took it over, rewrote me into what was there. But it wasn't enough. I can't remember everything I was supposed to tell you."

"You didn't just come to trade with my great-grandfather, did you?"

"You must go to the capital, Wei Lee."

"That's where the cowboys are going. Where my great-grandfather is. I thought I could make a deal with him . . . "

Miriam clutched her ears. "I can't think! No, wait! Water. They live near water. That's all I remember. I need something to straighten me out, Lee. If not . . . "

The fog was swirling around them. Cold droplets beaded Lee's skin. Miriam was a shadow in the whiteness, leaning towards him. Another shadow stood behind her. Lee thought it was the librarian, but it was taller and thinner, and there was a bonewhite glint in the hood cast over its face.

Miriam said, "Otherwise I'll die again, Lee. Otherwise bad sectors might spread to your memories. Now you must wake up. Redd wants to show you something."

Redd was leaning over Lee, a shadow against a sky so choked with brilliant stars it dazzled the eyes. He had been shaking Lee's shoulder, and sat back when Lee groaned and pushed up on one elbow. Every muscle in his body was stiff and sore.

"It's time," Redd said, and with a grand gesture pointed at the starry sky.

Lee looked up.

A burning thread hung between heaven and Mars.

Twenty-eight

The thread was already fading by the time the search party was ready to leave camp.

More than half the cowboys were going, leaving just enough to watch over the herd. Lee could put a name to most of them now. White Eye, Dog Breath, Dead Finger. The Gray Fox, Angel Eyes, Lonesome Dove.

When White Eye saw Lee amongst them he complained loudly to Hawk. "You want the little chink comin' along?"

"Of course," Hawk said calmly. "Do you think he wouldn't find out about our little sideline if we left him in camp? We have to bring the stuff back, after all, and he's a *smart* chink. Or at least, not as dumb as you."

White Eye said, "So maybe we should deal with him, like I was sayin' all along."

One or two of the others agreed.

"Listen," Hawk told them all. "He's a chink, but he's no conchie. Some of you are smart enough to have noticed that. He listens to that dead music broadcaster up in Father Jupiter. He has ghosts in his head . . . " chills ran down Lee's spine " . . . and he's as much reason as any to stay away from the Army of the People's Mouths, or any of the militias of the Ten Thousand Years. So quit being so prejudiced. I swear I'm getting ashamed of you all."

"He listens to the King of the Cats, he should prove it," someone called.

"Yeah," White Eye said. "Sing us a song, boy."

"Sing out!"

Lee waited until they'd stopped. Then he stepped forward and said, "I'm not much of a singer, and I don't have my guitar. But if you are willing to listen, I'll try."

"Go ahead," Redd said, after a moment's silence.

Lee took three breaths to steady himself. What he had meant to sing was one of the trivial country songs, but under Redd's stare they all fell away from his mind. He sang what was left: he sang "Promised Land."

And afterwards he stood alone in silence while the cowboys drifted away to their ponies. Only one came up to him. Lee hadn't noticed him before. Half-Yankee, half-Tibetan, he had long frizzy hair layered either side of a central parting, small black eyes set close together over a hooked nose. He was younger than Lee, eight or nine at the most.

"You understand," he said to Lee, "there's nothin' romantic about bein' a cowboy. About bein' out on the land. It's just a job of work. Lot of people do it because they can't do nothin' else. Some of them are on the run, maybe. But there's no *romance* to it."

"So why are you out here?"

"That's a good question," the kid said, and sort of faded back into the darkness.

Lee rode beside Redd. He asked, "Who was the kid?"

"Calls himself Alias. Talk is he's killed a dozen men and doesn't give a damn about any of them. But we all talk a lot out here, and most of the stories don't have much truth to them."

They were riding across the bare, cold plain towards the point where the burning thread had touched the face of Mars. Redd was being very coy about exactly what was going on, and Lee was too tired to press him. So tired, in fact, that despite the pony's awkward rolling gait a fugitive dream fragment took him back to the wall beneath the soaring fog-shrouded bridge. The bay and the city beyond were lost in fog, too. Everything was. From the fog's still center, Miriam said,—*It's a punch-out operation, Lee. Straight down from*

Clarke orbit through a hole in the defenses. Friction heats up the monofilament, that's why you see it.

"This is like a spaceship?"

—More like an elevator. The capsule comes straight down, like a spider on its thread. Do you have spiders on Mars?

"Don't be silly."

—I don't know why I should assume that you do. The Nexus's habitat doesn't.

"Mars has a highly diverse ecological system," Lee said. "Who sent down this capsule?"

—There are two possibilities, Miriam said, and then the pony stumbled and Lee was jolted awake just in time to rein it in at the lip of a sudden drop.

They were there.

It was a small, deep, relatively young crater, its rim wall still sharply terraced. Some of the cowboys rode straight on down, whooping and waving their woollen hats amidst rising clouds of dust. The more cautious took a meandering path amongst boulders and across overturned strata down to the dusty floor where a dwarf forest of cacti grew, raising spiny paddles as high as the ponies' bellies.

Lee didn't need enhanced vision to see the thing in the center of the crater. It stood poised on three prongs, bullet-shaped and twice as tall as a man, glittering in the fierce starlight. The first cowboys had already reached it and were riding round and round, calling to each other in high, excited voices. Lee looked up into the starry sky but could no longer see the thread down which the thing had fallen from the sky.

As they rode down the terraced crater wall, he said to Redd, "I can think of two possibilities. Which is it?"

The old Tibetan cowboy riding alongside them, the Gray Fox, chuckled and said, "Two possibilities, eh? Ain't *he* sharp as a needle," then stood in his saddle and lashed his pony's withers with ends of his reins and galloped ahead.

Redd said, "Maybe it won't help you to know that this isn't for the Ten Thousand. *They* get contraband by free-fall craft. Our drops are more subtle. Look there."

Lee saw that a swathe had been cut through the stands of cacti that covered the crater's floor. Something had lopped the plants neatly at ground level so that they had all fallen in one direction.

"It comes down after the drop, kilometers of it, dragging this end with it. It'll still be falling, drifting westward, for at least a day. We'd spool it up and spray fixative on it, but you can't cut it, and it cuts anything clean through. Dangerous stuff. Like most gifts from the sky you have to know how to handle it."

Lee said, "I've travelled all over, but I've never seen any of this dangerous stuff of yours."

"Without fixation, it falls apart in air," Redd said. "Most doesn't even reach the ground." They reined in their ponies and joined those cowboys, Hawk amongst them, who had dismounted. A few were still circling the capsule. One started taking pot shots that rang against the capsule's metal and whined away. Hawk bellowed irritably, "Damn you, White Eye, don't you go damaging the merchandise!"

Redd told Lee, "What we do is now wait. Sometimes it takes a day before it gives us what it's brought down."

That was when a hatch in the side of the capsule's nose cone blew off in a cloud of rolling smoke, green stuff lit from within by a brief sullen glare. There was a hideous amplified cackle that rolled and echoed around the crater's steep sides.

Cowboys were fighting to rein in their prancing mounts. Above them a human head, four or five times normal size, bobbed on the end of a long coiled spring, its white face, red lips, bloodshot round eyes and green bush of hair lit by some internal light source.

"Greetings, Martians," it said, its voice booming out into the night. Its lips curled back from even teeth in a sneering grin. "Whatever you do, don't take me to your leaders!"

Lee stepped back, because for a moment the bobbing head seemed to look directly at him, its eyes knowing and filled with deadly mischief. Redd caught his elbow. "It's only a hologram. It'll tell us what it has."

The head said, "They tried to ban us when we were born, then we made it big just in time to be forgotten for a century or two. But what's a few hundred years between friends? We're back, as bad and as dangerous as ever. Just give us to your children and stand *well* back. Why, they don't even need to read. They can just look at the pictures. Like I always say, a picture is worse than a thousand words."

Miriam was suddenly beside Lee. Though the head's luminous white skin threw grisly light over the cowboys, she was a shadow without form. When Lee tried to look at her directly, she vanished inside a prickly blur of dark light.

She said in a ravelling whisper, "I might have known. The Pranksters."

Lee whispered back, "That's the name of this thing?" He was only half certain he was not dreaming all this, would wake rolled inside his blanket beside the camp fire.

Miriam said, "*Listen*. This costs me to speak. Costs you, too. The Pranksters are a religious group. They inhabit half a dozen rocks, all on eccentric orbits. They are dedicated to destabilizing systems. They say that it's an evolutionary tool, and it makes them dangerous. I'd guess that this is funded by the Earth; there's no way something like this could have fallen through the defenses by itself."

"It doesn't matter who gives them to us," Hawk said unexpectedly. He had put on his funny round mirror glasses.

Miriam looked at him and said, "I suppose they sent down the technology for direct sensory access, too." She added, to Lee, "Call it a kind of pseudo psi. He's tapping into the RAM chip in your visual cortex to see me."

"There's not much to see," Hawk said. "You are in a very bad way, even for a ghost. The system you've parasitised isn't much of a home, is it? And I believe I see someone standing at your back."

Miriam whispered, "Even if they haven't been subverted by the Earth, the Pranksters won't be any help."

"Ah, but their gifts are sometimes useful," Hawk said, and

raised his arm. His hand was wrapped inside the free-form stock of a huge reaction pistol. He fired, and the head vanished in mid-sentence.

The capsule whirred and shook. Its top suddenly began to spin, faster and faster. Steam shot from the widening joint with a scream. Then the whole nose cone shot off on a wobbling trajectory, and an explosion inside the capsule blew a storm of paper over the cowboys.

Lee plucked at pages that fluttered around him. Leaflets, picture novels printed in garish colors. They were a little like instruction manuals, but in the dying glow from the capsule he could see that the panels were dense with violence, costumed muscle-bulging freaks, flames and explosions amongst tall buildings built of glass, all kinds of strange things.

Redd said, "We get good money for this, and in the old days we'd have stuck a finger up the noses of the Emperor's state censors, too. But now there's so much propaganda that this is just another dust grain in the storm."

"Oh," Lee said. He was beginning to realize where all the rock'n'roll artifacts came from. His posters of the King of the Cats, the data needles of his music, the fragments of his films. Who, then, was the King working for?

He helped the others pull back the flimsy panels of the burnt-out capsule, unload bundles of leaflets and reload them on to the ponies. Paper had blown all over the crater, and the cowboys started their ride back to camp amidst cacti festooned with leaflets that, impaled on spines, fluttered and flapped like a million crucified birds.

Twenty-nine

The drive to the capital took a dozen more days. It left the vast, cratered plains and crossed the Ridge of Gold at Shaylin Pass. The guy cables of a skeletal relay tower had been strung with scarves printed with prayers and with flags of pure white and blue and red and yellow, all unravelling in the thin constant wind. The older cowboys stopped to set more flags and prayers fluttering, or to place stones on the huge cairn of red rocks.

The same cowboys would stop to pay their respects at wayside shrines. It was only when they passed the third or fourth in as many hours, a low mani wall with a pair of flexed eyes painted in fading red and blue and white over the ubiquitous sacred mantra *Om Mani Padme Hum*, that Lee realized they were on a road, or at any rate a trail. Redd pointed to lines of stones either side of the wide rutted road—cleared by hand two centuries ago, he said.

Lee remembered what Pemba had told him: that every stone was holy, for every stone had been touched by change.

One night the herders camped at the edge of a tiny village that had grown up around a heat-engine well head. Half a dozen low flat-roofed houses slumped against each other as if for mutual support. Built out of pink sandstone, they blended right into the landscape. All the villagers were draped in shapeless enveloping garments and black gauze veils, so that you couldn't tell which were men and which women. Perhaps that was the point. They sold the cowboys potatoes fried to crispy char on the outside and with a cold wet knot in the center, but otherwise kept away.

The well head dominated the slumped village, a huge flower with battered silvery petals that focused sunlight on black panels thick with piping. Sunlight warmed the panels through which water flowed; the heated water was driven underground by its own expansion, to melt permafrost which was used to irrigate the village's stony potato fields. It tasted of iron and bitter salts, this fossil water. The day after drinking it, Lee had a bad case of the shits, which caused the cowboys no end of amusement.

Most of the cowboys had some secret locked away, some reason why they'd taken to riding the range. As he rode with them, Lee heard something of their stories. Hawk had been indentured to a *danwei* work gang when he was six, had escaped a year later and worked his way up from cowboy to range boss. He owned the yaks they were driving from the winter ranges. Skinny White Eye had poisoned a dozen women in his neighborhood, then escaped the transport train taking him to the polar labor camp. Old Dead Finger had been a monk, and his head was still clean shaven. Lonesome Dove was a deserter from the Army of the People's Mouths. And so on.

Only Redd's reasons for riding the range were unclear. Lee heard half a dozen contradictory stories: he was supposed to have betrayed his best friend to the secret police; or to have shot him in the back; or to have actually *been* in the secret police, and gone on the run after letting his childhood friend, a leader of the *ku li*, escape an ambush; or he had been a leader of the *ku li* who had renounced violent action . . . Redd wouldn't confirm or deny any one of them. He wasn't much older than Lee, but Lee was learning from him just how little he knew about the desert and about herding yaks, and how little he knew about the lives of men who lived in the vast empty landscapes of Mars, outside the cities and the huddled *danweis*.

"You gotta have a new name," Redd declared. "Can't have you walkin' around Lowell"— like all the cowboys, Redd insisted on calling the capital by its old Yankee name —"where your great-grandfather can pick you out of the crowd in a moment if you use your real name." He looked asquint at Lee, blue eyes glinting under the brim of his black hat. "Billy, that's the name for you."

"You are very certain."

"It's 'cause you're a kid. Billy Lee. See, we turn you into a Yankee half-breed. I reckon you got some white man in you, there ain't anyone on the planet who ain't got some Martian in them, Yankee or Tibetan or both. Cowboys just generally have more Martian than most, which is why they usually kill any wandering Han they come across."

"You saved my life."

"I was wondering if you remembered that."

"I won't forget it. But why did you take me back to camp, if you knew I was likely to be killed?"

"Oh, I was ready to argue for you, Billy Lee. Turned out I didn't need to, so I was right about my hunch all along. Know why you were spared? Hawk saw the ghost on your back. He's curious about it, 'cause cowboys owe the anarchists part of their living. But cowboys aren't for the Sky Road, for all that. They're just for themselves."

Lee had seen Miriam only once in his dreams since the night the anarchist capsule had come down. Perhaps she was already fading, like an imperfectly fixed photographic image. She had not spoken to him in the dream; perhaps it had been nothing but an ordinary dream after all. It had been in the ancient Earth city of Las Vegas, by daylight. Lee recognized the elaborate cliffs of the casino frontages from the film fragments of *Viva Las Vegas!*, but they seemed small, faded and tawdry without their cloaks of electric light. Miriam had been walking way in front of him, but when he tried to catch up with her a pink automobile as big as her spacecraft glided out of nowhere and she jumped into it. And as the automobile swept her away, Lee saw that the driver was the King of the Cats.

Lee asked Redd, who was in as loquacious a mood as Lee had ever known, "Is that what you're for, just yourself?" He was thinking of Redd's moments of quiet prayer, atonement for his mysterious past.

Redd pulled the brim of his black hat over his eyes. His gloves were caked with red dust; there was a rime of dust on the woollen blanket he wore as a cape. "I reckon no one can afford not to be for themselves," he said. "Otherwise they just get used by other people. How about you, Billy Lee? You like the cowboy life enough to stay?"

"I have to talk to my great-grandfather, if I can. Otherwise, perhaps . . . "

Redd laughed, and said, "Yeah, that's how it goes, until one day you're as old as the Gray Fox or Lonesome Dove, and you wonder where your life went." And he spurred his pony after a yak that was trotting eagerly at right angles from the trail, after who knew what, or why.

So it went, moving in a blowing cloud of red dust by day, chivvying yaks that were forever stopping to scrape saxifrage moss from crusted ground, making camp after the sudden sunset, the nights achingly cold and glorious with stars, and always the lonesome songs of the watch riders floating out into the desert, and awesome sunrises, frost vanishing into the air with a sound like a million tiny bells and yaks making clouds around themselves with their own breath, groaning and flinging strings of orange spittle as they started moving again. Until at last the cowboys and their herd crossed a single-track railway line that ran from east to west across the flat land. The herd turned to parallel the high dust bank that had been cleared from the line after the winter storms, and the next day reached Xin Beijing, the capital of Mars.

Thirty

Xin Beijing sprawled in a wide pass that cut through a ragged circle of mountains, the eroded rim wall of a vast ancient crater more than a hundred kilometers across. Within the crater a perfectly circular lake, ringed round with white salt deposits, reflected the pink sky and the pine-clad mountains that rose steeply around it.

Xin Beijing had once been the site of the Yankee Martian colony, long before the air had been thickened, but the old domed Yankee Quarter was lost now in a sprawl of wide dusty streets, lined by giant ginkgoes, where bicycles swarmed amongst clanging trolley cars. Streets radiated away from the industrial sector and the railway junction and the silent citadel where ten thousand ministers, secretaries, programmers, engineers and interpreters interceded between the world and the Emperor. Between these three mingling fans of streets were wedge-shaped parks and big government buildings and the sterile white compounds where half-lifers dreamed themselves into Heaven.

Lee had left Xin Beijing two years before, as a passenger on the Central Desert Express. The railway station had been a small city in itself, an entire social ecology with separate castes which made their living by selling food or trinkets to travellers, or by recycling nightsoil from the trains' lavatories, or which subsisted on waste food thrown from restaurant cars. Most of the traffic had been one way. Every train brought in hundreds more refugees from dust-buried farm-

134

lands along the Grand Canal; leaving the city, Lee had had an entire carriage to himself.

Lee had vowed never to return, and in a way he had not. Riding into the stockyards amongst a gaggle of cowboys channelling a thousand head of yak into their holding pasture was to ride into a city he did not know. He remembered the pink, circular lake, the second largest body of free water on Mars, so wide that not even the tallest peaks of the mountains on its far side showed above the flat line of its horizon. He recognized the pine-forested snaggle-toothed rim-wall mountains that rose either side of the city, saw with a pang the distant, flat-topped peak where the house of his great-grandfather stood. But otherwise he might be riding into a city on another planet.

The stockyards were to the south of Xin Beijing, stretching from the shore of the lake towards the stony desert. Brawling herds of yak were being driven this way and that, in clouds of red dust that glowed like red hot iron in the level afternoon sun, across a flat landscape where trails made a complex network amongst fields of bare red earth fenced with stone. Small electric locomotives shunted cattle cars or feed wagons along spur lines. Tented camps were pitched along the lake shore, where in the shallows floating pontoons corralled hectares of algae and azolla for fodder.

Lee soon saw why Hawk had hired one of the denim-clad men who hung around the trail head, most of them laconic round-eyed Yankees, to guide the herd through the stockyards' shifting labyrinths. He had thought that the journey would be over once they reached the stockyards, but it took from noon to sunset to negotiate their way to the feed lot set aside for the herd.

Like the railway station, the stockyards were a culture in miniature. As well as field guides, there were slaughterers and assayers and veterinarians and auctioneers, stockmen and wranglers and field hands, sod busters and wet workers and feed-lot pitchers. They served all the high equatorial plains, and even on a world as small and barren as Mars that was a considerable territory. Lee had once read that the plains were the range of ten million head of domesticated yak and dzo, and uncounted numbers of yak reverted to the wild. Only now was the statistic gaining some reality.

Most of the herd had been brought here not to be slaughtered, but for the cow yaks to calve or to be tupped, and for the calves to be sorted. The males would almost all be gelded and feed-lot fattened and butchered without ever setting hoof on the red ranges. The females would be tagged and returned with their mothers and newly impregnated aunts. The yaks in the herd, every one of which the cowboys invariably called "he," were all female.

The real work began when the feed-lot pasturage was reached. The chip implanted in each yak was scanned by an assayer for a readout on the animal's physiological history. To do this the confused and irritable animals had to be wrangled one by one into a narrow chute until one thousand and twenty-eight had passed through into the big bare field beyond.

The yaks were fed a slobber of azolla and ripe silage. The cowboys drank tea in a circle around a campsite fire while Hawk came around and paid them off. He pressed a little roll of ten yuan notes into Lee's bleeding hands and told him to find his town house the next day, at the Square of Two Thousand Martyrs. He said, in a gravelly confiding undertone, "You're a good worker. I decided you're due something from the sale of our sky booty, but don't tell the others in case of bad feeling. And another thing. Take care with Redd. He might not be so good a friend as you think. Keep our little rendezvous from him."

Most of the cowboys were headed towards the strip of smoke houses and pleasure palaces along the lake shore beyond the fodder-processing plants. Redd explained to Lee that they'd spend most of their pay and then sign up with some other herd boss. "You come along with me, Billy Lee, and get a bath. That's what I aim to do."

Lee agreed. He was too tired to worry about Hawk's whispered warning, in truth too tired and scared to do much thinking of his own. He had returned to challenge his great-grandfather, either by finding the people Miriam's ghost had said were waiting for him somewhere in the city, or by trying to sell him the totipotent viruses, and either way he did not think he had long to live.

They walked the short distance to a tram stop. When Lee asked about Redd's pony, the cowboy said, "I don't even own the saddle. What's so special about a horse? Temperamental critters with a nasty bite and brains about as big as a sundried grape. Backbroken way of moving so your balls are hammered between your saddle and your arse with every step, fall sick when you least need it, have to be watched every second in case they get some damnfool notion of independence in their heads. And another thing, you ever eaten horse? They don't even taste good. What I'd like is to do it all from air in a culver, but that's not allowed so it's not worth thinking about."

It took three changes of tram to get them to the old Yankee Quarter. The city seemed emptier than Lee remembered. Whole blocks of apartment houses lay dark and silent in the twilight. Others had been colonized by refugees. Dzo and goats were tethered in the remains of parks. Bonfires blazed on roofs. Walls had been painted and repainted with slogans; Lee saw a little robot, perched on delicate telescopic legs, overpainting a vast idealized portrait of one of the Ten Thousand with ideograms a dozen meters high, denouncing the Committee of Six, the group of Ten Thousand Years who had taken it upon themselves to speak for the Emperor and who were now the only voices of authority in the deserts of its silence.

Lee had watched the news broadcasts along with everyone else in Bitter Waters, but like everyone else he hadn't believed half the stories told by the blithe newscasters. It was well known that the commercial channels hyped and exaggerated everything because that was how they survived. If they didn't do it, someone else would: so they all did it.

Everyone in Bitter Waters had preferred the government channel. It spoke comfortingly of small gatherings quickly dispersed rather than riots, of disagreements between political factions rather than civil war. Lee had only half believed this anodyne line, but like most people it was what he wanted to believe. Governments were all obsessed with secrecy, and the best and the worst gave the same excuses for playing with the truth: that it is for the good of the people; that undiluted truth is harmful; that it must be filtered and massaged before the population can accept it. Tyrannies ruthlessly imposed this filtration, this selectivity; democracies, no matter how high their ideals, sooner or later slid into the same behavior by default. It didn't matter. It didn't matter because all the different kinds of governments were right: people didn't want to hear the truth. Left to themselves in democracies, bullied into faking interest by tyrannies, people really didn't care what the truth was as long as it didn't hurt them, which was why, except in times of crisis, power divided amongst the people was too fragmented to be of any use. The stronger always won out because the weaker let them: Guoquiang's father, Great-grandfather Wei, the computer in the lamasery. If people were given power, they usually gave it away as quickly as they could because it was uncomfortable to hold. Only those who should never have been given power in the first place actively sought it.

The tram rattled past murals and wrecked buildings and refugee camps, past wreckage left by riots and buildings whose walls bore murals pocked and cratered by shell and shot. The tram's bell tingled dutifully at every junction, as if it was trying to conjure the old order back into being. It rattled past the sepulchres of the half-lifers, layered white buildings that seemed to float in islands of light. Those dying out of this world were more important than those still living in it, it seemed.

There was little traffic, and most of it consisted of squads of militia zooming by in swift electric trucks. Once, the tram had to stop at a barricade while militia in black blouses and black baggy trousers, the red bands tied around their foreheads marked with the seal of The Little Bird, climbed aboard and looked at each passenger in turn. They were armed with pistols and laser prods. Redd stared right back at them, and once the tram had passed through the barricade he said to Lee, "Things are bad. The Emperor has become so quiet that the Ten Thousand Years fight amongst themselves to see who will be its successor."

"Warlords," Lee said.

"It hasn't come to that. Not yet. Let's hope it won't. But their factions run the streets now, dividing the city amongst themselves. There were fire fights just about every night when I left here. Things look to have gotten worse."

But at least the Yankee Quarter was just as Lee remembered it. The field-sized panes of glass of its dome, opaquely sandblasted by centuries of storms, shone in the gathering night like a hovering pearl as the tram rocked towards it down a long tree-lined avenue.

Beneath the dome was a maze of narrow streets and even narrower hutongs, a warren that had grown up and around and over the original buildings until almost no trace was left of the Yankee settlement the dome had once protected. The atmospheric recycling units had long ago overloaded and a greasy drizzle of condensation continually drifted down on to the layers of flat roofs and the interlayered blades of heat-exchange engines. Apartment blocks and arcades and factories grew into each other like corals. Vegetables were cultivated in courtyards full of purplish light cast by racks of fluorescent tubing. Ganglia of cables and pipes and optical fibres and telephone wiring ran everywhere. Light fell into the narrow hutongs from grilles, past swatches of sagging wires or plumes of steam, past balconies, past the barred windows of thousands of tiny shops (it was said that if you could buy anything on Mars, you could buy it in the Yankee Quarter). In many hutongs light never fell at all, for the buildings on either side had grown together overhead.

Main Street more or less divided the Quarter into two. Crowds seethed up and down its length, half of them Yankee, the rest more or less evenly distributed between Tibetan and Han. Many wore hats pulled down over their faces and capes of slick waterproof material in bright primary colors over ordinary tunics and trousers. There were few militia here, but many soldiers of the Army of the People's Mouths, young shaven-headed recruits with the scars of their brain surgery still raw, most walking in pairs, hand in hand, the way citizens did when in a strange place. Lee saw a pilot carried along above the crowds on his stalking, insectile litter, breastplate and bubble helmet shining. A pair of conchie missionaries from Earth, alike as twins, walked side by side in their dark suits and hardly anyone took any notice, although everyone stepped out of their way. Trams drifted through the crowds of bicycles that clogged the roadways. Electric signs rose dozens of meters into the air, neon tubing sizzling in the drizzle. Holograms floated here and there, message clouds tugged by impalpable breezes. Most of the signs were in wormy backwards Yankee script; Common Language ideograms were rare. Every so often there was the sound of firecrackers; it was the beginning of the festival of the little gods of the lake fisherfolk, and this reminded Lee of what Miriam's ghost had said.

—*They live near water.*

Redd kept a hand on Lee's shoulder, steering him into a crowded shopping street that curved away from Main Street. Cyclists wove amongst the pedestrians, banging on tinny horns. The street was lit by fluorescent tubes stapled to a concrete ceiling, and by the signs and windows of the shops, all of which sold electronic components.

"This way," Redd said, and plunged into a narrow, tunnel-like hutong. There were no lights, yet bicycles careered along it regardless, continually sounding their horns as if steering by sonar, like bats. A stairway off the hutong twisted down to a dim, crowded, noisy cave of a bar. A steel counter ran around three sides. Men, almost all of them Yankees, stood shoulder to shoulder, drinking steadily and watching a Yankee woman taking her clothes off inside a raised cage. Lee gaped at her and Redd pulled him by his elbow all the way across the bar and through an arch curtained with strips of plastic into another room, smaller and quieter, floor, walls and ceiling of white-painted concrete lit by bare fluorescent tubes. In one corner was a tea counter where a few old men sat around chessboards on iron tables. In another, Redd paid attendants with small coins, and a bald gnome of a man got up from a chair of faded blue plush and took Lee to a cubicle.

Lee exchanged his dusty sweat-stiffened clothes for a huge towel and allowed himself to be led through the rituals of showering and soaking, massaging and steaming. Finally, he stood side by side with Redd in a huge pool of salty, faintly sulphurous water that buoyed up their scrubbed bodies. They leaned at the pool's edge and sipped earthy jasmine tea and munched on cold shrimp noodles and sweet rice balls.

Lee felt a trembling lassitude that was not at all unpleasant. Hairy Yankees and smooth-skinned Han mingled with democratic ease in this vaulted cavern. Fluorescent tubes hung from a ceiling of naked rock. Their light slithered on the surface of the slop of water, slipped and twinkled on slimy tiles which were each embossed with a curled dragon. It was a very old bathhouse, Redd said, five hundred years old at least—which Lee thought impossible before he remembered that Yankees still counted years by Earth's short seasons.

"So how do you like riding the range, young Billy Lee? Like it well enough to sign up again? What are your plans?"

"They are not changed. I must find . . . my friends. Perhaps I can get the help of my great-grandfather, but it will be difficult. He is a powerful man, but we have had a misunderstanding that needs to be corrected."

"You Chinks are all so reverent towards your old men."

"You try to shock me? I have been around."

"It's a hard world. You haven't seen much of that. Han don't."

Long silvery scars seamed Redd's chest, three lines that ran from beneath his left nipple to the bottom of his ribcage. The ball of his right shoulder looked as if someone had once chewed on it, long ago.

Redd caught Lee staring. "Leopard cult," he said. "Back when I was as young and foolish as you."

"I'm not so young."

"Maybe there's only a year or two difference. I'm not talking age."

"You've lived life, and I haven't." Lee had been thinking, on the long tram ride, about how little he really knew the city in which he had grown up. He knew that part of the quiet tree-filled suburb of the Fragrant Hills around Master Qing's Academy of Mental Cultivation, the Great House of Great-grandfather Wei, the mountain lodge where Master Qing's Academy of Mental Cultivation had convened in summer to escape the city's dusty heat, high in the mountains on the far side of the lake. The rest of the city had been forbidden to him, known only through brief expeditions planned with as much daring and long thought as military raids upon hostile territory.

Redd smiled, signalled to a tray-carrying attendant. "You catch on fast. That's one good thing about you. Or is it the ghost you carry?"

"She has fallen asleep, I think. That is also something I must attend to. My great-grandfather . . . "

"If you go to your great-grandfather, he'll ream her out of you and throw away your carcass. Wise up, kid." Redd took a thin black cigar from the attendant, who lighted it for him. Redd drew until the cigar tip glowed cherry red, exhaled a riffle of smoke.

Lee watched this piece of business patiently. He was in no hurry. He had enough money to last him a week if he was careful, and Hawk had promised him more. There was no point looking for Miriam's friends while he was still aching from the trail drive, and he couldn't walk up to Great-grandfather Wei's gates and bang on them for admittance. He needed time to think. There had been no time for that while helping herd a thousand yaks. Besides, Redd was a good enough fellow, and he was ideal company in the Yankee Quarter.

Redd regarded the end of his cigar with pleasure. "What I'm offering you is advice, Billy Lee. More than advice, if you want it. And whether or not you want it, you need it."

"I see," Lee said, although he didn't.

"You're carrying something valuable. You haven't told me what it is, and that's fine, that's up to you. But I know that your great-grandfather wants it, and I bet so does the rest of the Ten Thousand Years. Now they know you escaped with the anarchist, and by now they might have figured you might still be alive. Even if you're not, they'll be keeping a watch out for you. They might even have spotted you. And the nearer that you get to your great-grandfather, the closer to being spotted you get. Ever think of what would happen to you when that happens? I reckon I do. I used to work for one of the Ten Thousand Years, in a small way." Redd looked sideways to gauge Lee's reaction, and what he saw evidently amused him. "Don't you worry, Billy Lee, if I wanted to turn you in, I'd have done it long ago."

"It just reminded me of something Hawk said."

"Some of those campfire stories get a little near the truth," Redd said softly.

Lee waited, as he used to wait for his great-grandfather's eidolon. Redd said, "I learned one thing, back then. It was that the Ten Thousand Years aren't human. If you want to talk with your great-grandfather, you can't just go walking up to his front door. I saved your life, Billy Lee. One thing you need to keep fixed in your head. You owe me one, and I'm not asking anything but what would help you further."

Lee laughed, because Redd's crude attempt at constructing a face trap had only served to free him. He had an obligation to Redd only because Redd had an obligation to him: Redd had saved Lee's life, and so was obliged to protect him, just as Lee had protected, or tried to protect, Miriam Makepeace Mbele. But Redd had admitted that the obligation was at an end, and now Lee knew just how much he had changed since the morning he had set out with Guoqiang and Xiao Bing on the first calm day of spring. There was a new hardness in him, something like the cold selfishness of the Yankees, who were all islands, entire unto themselves.

Lee said carefully, "I will never forget any of your kindnesses, Citizen Redd, and most especially your advice."

Redd ground the butt of his cigar on wet tile and heaved

himself out of the water. "There's a little misunderstanding here," he said. "It's what you're going to do. It's time to meet some people I know. If you've something you want to sell to your great-grandfather or any of the Ten Thousand Years, these people will want it just as bad. I'll help you sell it to them—for a commission, of course."

"It is good of you to offer, Citizen Redd, but I do not need help."

"Again, it isn't an offer." Redd's fingers met around Lee's forearm. "Come on, now. Let's you and me get dressed. And don't worry. This might be business, but I still like you."

Redd held on to Lee's arm as they crossed the quiet antechamber and pushed through the hanging plastic strips into the noisy, smoky bar. Halfway across, Redd's grip tightened and he said, "I reckon we're in trouble."

A man moved away from the shadows by the stairway and made his way towards them amongst the crowded tables. It was White Eye. He smiled crookedly and said, "You're so predictable, friend Redd," and laid a hand on Lee's shoulder.

Two men who had been lounging by the stairway started across the bar. They both had brush-cut hair, and both wore white short-sleeved shirts, baggy trousers with camouflage red and gray blotches, heavy combat boots.

"You fucker!" Redd shouted, and pushed White Eye aside.

Then the two militia were running, tipping tables and spilling drinks into the laps of cardplayers. White Eye swung at Redd, a knife suddenly in his hand. Redd danced back, kicked White Eye's knee, his hip. White Eye flew backwards and landed across a table, scattering glasses and bottles. When he tried to stand, burly drinkers grabbed his shoulders and spun him away: men stepped aside and he crashed into the steel-topped bar.

One of the militia was caught in the middle of a brawl; the other dodged when someone swung a chair at him, and laid out the chair wielder with a single punch. The fight was spreading to every corner of the bar; White Eye had disappeared in a mêlée of swinging fists and furniture, volleys of bottles and glasses.

"Run!" Redd yelled at Lee, and the nearest of the militia shouted something, too. Waving a gun, he pushed through the riot like a swimmer in a heavy sea. He was so close that when the gun went off Lee felt the heat of its beam wash across his face. The bolt smashed the cables and pipes that wove across the ceiling; fans of sparks rained down on the heads of the fighters.

"Run!" Redd yelled again.

And something seized Lee and bore him away.

Thirty-one

L ee was walking through noisy crowds and neon-lit drizzle. He was on Main Street, and didn't remember how he'd reached it. He could feel the thing that had seized him float away on the tides of his blood. He let it go. He could feel his pulse, just behind his ears. His legs and back ached sweetly, hollowly. He felt calm and exhausted. He had been running, running very fast . . .

The rich slow voice of the King of the Cats was rapping from speakers in an information arcade. Lee remembered that the librarian had promised to try and follow him to the capital, and went inside. He had no other ally, now, except Miriam's silent ghost.

After he'd paid the old woman who ran the arcade, Lee chose one of the half-dozen couches at random. It folded around him like a predatory flower, thrust electrodes at the nape of his neck and the backs of his hands, masked his sight and clamped speakers to his ears.

The menu burned briefly before him, but before he could make a selection it blew past like a curtain on an electronic wind and he was in a familiar booklined corridor. Tall in his black robes, his face hidden by shadows through which silver motes endlessly fell, the librarian lifted down a leather-bound octavo book and said, "Master. You have come not a moment too soon. I have found your parents."

"At last," Lee said, but he felt a pang of dread. This was the hinge of his life.

146

The librarian said, "You are afraid, Master. I understand. You have dedicated your life to this, after all."

"I think I know what happened to them," Lee said. "I'm not afraid of the future, librarian, but of the past."

"The past is always as it has been, as I will show you," the librarian said, and opened the book to show the vivid greens of a summer garden.

"No," Lee said, "wait . . . "

But he was already there, in that part of the garden of Great-grandfather Wei's Great House where water fell over shelves of red rock and tinkled into dark rush-lined pools. Lee was small, fizzing with impatience, tugging against the big firm hands which held each of his. There was the sharp scent of newly cut grass.

His mother and father leaned over him, their faces dark against brilliant sunlight. *Hush, hush. He'll be here soon.* And another voice: *I'm already here.* And then thunder and lightning fell from the sky, and Lee's parents flew away from him. He looked up in utter confusion, frightened beyond tears, and the man standing high above, on top of the wet red rocks. A young man, all in black, holding a smoking machine pistol. He laughed out loud and said, "Catch you later, kid," and spat down into the pool where Lee's mother floated, her face still and white in the center of her spreading black hair.

"Time's up! Hey, come on! Time's up ten minutes ago!"

It was the grandmother Yankee who ran the arcade. She had opened up the couch. "You want, you can pay for more time, but you gotta do it now. Hey. Hey, you OK?"

Lee saw her through a blur of tears. She was at least forty, wore a towering bright red wig, a centimeter of white powder like icing laid across her creviced face, bright red lipstick, greasy blue stuff around her eyes. Her breasts pushed up in her voluminous red velvet dress like a shelf. She smelt intensely of geraniums.

She said, "You look like shit, citizen."

"Something I saw . . . "

"Hey, now listen, all my equipment is exorcised on a regular basis. This is a clean place, there are no line demons here, not unless you went and brought one down on yourself. You've been peeking in forbidden areas? We don't allow that kind of stuff here. It's a public place, I got my public to think of."

"I am sorry, grandmother. It was looking for me."

Lee pushed past her to the door, but as he stumbled into the crowds outside the arcade she shouted after him. "You get the hell out of here with your demon. This is a *clean* place!"

Thirty-two

Ten minutes later, Lee knew that he was being followed. The man was a burly Han with the pale look of a civil servant, dressed in a business suit under a transparent plastic slicker. He sauntered along on the far side of the busy street, and if there had not been so many Yankees about, Lee might never have noticed him. But his bland moon face seemed always turned to Lee, flashing again and again in the crowd between the gaps in the trams. Lee took turnings at random, always keeping to the wider streets—he didn't dare to dodge into the maze of hutongs—but every time he looked back, his tail was still there, moving at the same steady pace through the crowds on the far side of the street.

Perhaps he was a friend of Redd's—but how would he have found Lee so quickly? Or perhaps Great-grandfather Wei had found Lee after he had used the information terminal.

The thought doubled the weight of the knowledge of his parents' deaths. He had known all along, but until now he hadn't understood. That they were dead. That they had been killed by an assassin who had been employed by Great-grandfather Wei. For the man could not have entered the garden of the Great House without the co-operation of the Great House's security system; and besides, Lee knew who he was. Years afterwards he was still employed by Great-grandfather Wei.

Lee's random route had led him to a big octagonal space where tram lines tangled around a plinth on which Cho

Jinfeng stood above the traffic and the crowds, looking up at a test tube she held high as a torch. There was spidery Yankee graffiti down the back of her open laboratory coat, one wing of which was slightly lifted as if blown back by an unfelt breeze.

Lee circled the statue, was walking past the rank of pedicabs for the second time when the idea came. He jumped into the first pedicab in the queue. The driver was a muscular Yankee in tight green leggings and a neon pink undershirt with the arms torn off at the shoulders. There was a kind of bubble of crinkly plastic over his mane of blond hair; a filter mask hung under his chin. He said, "Where to go, my man?"

Lee shoved a ten yuan note in the driver's face. "Anywhere fast . . . I'm trying to lose someone."

The driver plucked the note from Lee's fingers, held it to his ear and rolled it between thumb and forefinger. Then it was gone. "Radical," he said. "Anyone I know?"

Lee saw the beefy black-suited Han pushing through people less than a dozen meters away. He shoved another note at the driver and said, "Let's just go!"

The driver magicked away the note, hooked his mask over his nose and mouth and stood on his pedals. He wheeled all the way around a slow-moving tram and then shot through a stream of cyclists who split right and left in a clatter of horns. There was an intersection with a traffic cop right in its center, his blue uniform loaded with gold braid, his white-gloved hands held up, palms out. But the pedicab driver didn't pause. Lee saw the cop's expression change from authority to astonishment just before he leaped aside. A moment later the pedicab was spinning past crowds and brightly lit shopfronts, teahouses and massage parlors.

Lee leaned out around the pedicab's awning to look back and the driver glanced over his shoulder and said, "Be cool, man. You'll tip us over." A cluster of mirrors rose from the left handlebar like a bouquet of steel and glass flowers; Lee saw the driver's masked face variously reflected in flat and convex and concave surfaces.

"I think your friend, he hasn't given up. Sort of a chunky

Chink? In black?" The driver spoke in machine-pistol bursts between the sips of breath he took to top up his lungs.

"Oh. That's him."

"He's in this pedicab. Maybe a hundred meters back? Maddog Maguire doing his best to catch me. No contest, if you're ready for it. My grafts are the best. The best you can get. Maddog built his up. Built his up the hard way."

Lee thrust another ten yuan note at the driver, who snatched it without turning his head and stood on his pedals again, sounding an ear-splitting air horn as he veered hard into a hutong. Lee clung to the narrow armrests as the pedicab slewed from side to side down the dark narrow alley. The hubs of the big rear wheels struck sparks from the stone walls. Then light again, pedestrians scattering and suddenly gone as the pedicab plunged into another hutong, braking sharply at its end and turning on to a wide avenue, threading in between two trams. There was dark sky overhead. They had left the Yankee Quarter behind.

The driver yelled happily. Lee leaned forward and gave him another note, asked how he knew the hutong would be empty.

"I didn't! Just luck, man. Oh shit, but it looks like Maddog got lucky, too."

Apartment buildings made random patterns of lights under the night sky. No more crowds, only a few passers-by who turned to watch the two pedicabs race past.

They were suddenly level with each other. Maddog Maguire was a tall Yankee with a head completely shaven except for a vertical crest that stood up in spikes. The spikes were dyed luminescent red and green. His face gleamed with sweat. He yelled something at Lee's blond driver, who jabbed a finger at the sky and put on a spurt of speed that for a moment left Maddog's pedicab behind. But then it drew level again and its burly black-clad passenger was leaning forward, shouting something lost in the whir and hiss of wheels and wind. He was shaking his fist—no, there was something in it, and Lee ducked just before a flare of light blew away the pedicab's awning. In the same instant, Maddog twitched his steering bar and the two pedicabs collided, wheels tangling before they shot apart again.

Then there was a tremendous blast of sound.

Lee had a confused glimpse of a truck bearing down, headlamps glaring. Then it spun away and there was a terrific wrench and Lee shot forward, rolling over and over through leaves and stiff twigs.

Thirty-three

The pedicab had ploughed through a hedge into a little park. Lee lay amid the dusty smell of carnations, foolishly looking up at black sky. He rolled over, saw the driver trying to get his pedicab upright. Beyond a scrim of bushes, the other pedicab was upended in the middle of the road, one wheel still lazily revolving. The brawny man was being pulled out of the wreckage by spike-haired Maddog Maguire.

Lee sprang up and ran. He plunged straight through flowerbeds and cleared the hedge on the other side of the park in a single bound. Then he was running along a wide street divided down the middle by tram lines. Factory buildings made a low humming on either side. Occasional lights shed a sickly orange radiance. Up ahead there was the sound of music, and once, twice, fireworks burst above the flat roofs of the factories, brief constellations already fading by the time the faint sound of their detonation reached Lee.

He ran until he was quite out of breath and then he walked, gasping, until he heard the rattle of a pedicab and looked back. He hoped it was simply his own driver, chasing him for payment, but then a flash of light burst in the air in front and to the left of him, so close he felt the wash of heat.

For a moment the flight reaction threatened to take him again. But he knew how it worked now: he knew how to

153

access the parallel nerve net spun by the viruses. He speeded up. He blurred.

Maddog Maguire's pedicab was soon left far behind as Lee dodged down ever narrowing streets. He ran sweetly and easily, taking rapid sips of air. Paved road suddenly gave way to a mud track with a stinking sewer channel overflowing its center. Washing strung from house to house made ghost shapes above him; dogs barked from porches as Lee sped past. The fireworks and the music seemed closer, and then Lee turned a corner and was in the middle of a festival crowd.

He stopped, muscles loose as sacks of water. People wound all up and down the waterfront. There were monks in red robes, and fishermen and women in black cotton smocks or hooded jackets of undyed wool, red yarn wound through their hair and red or yellow kerchiefs at their throats. Children ran everywhere. Vendors cried their wares: beer, sweet rice, dumplings, fried dough. Everybody seemed to be whirling a prayer wheel or carrying a boat-shaped butter lamp or a smoking stick of incense, or banging a little drum or shaking a tambourine. Every so often someone would touch off a firework, just for the fun of it, and fiery flowers would bloom out across the dark lake. Jetties ran out into faintly luminous darkness and boats were tied up a long way down them, paper lanterns glowing like stars at the points of their high sterns.

It was the festival of the houses of the gods, the time when the myriad fragmented gods of the fisherfolk left the people they had been riding for a year and settled in new hosts. Here and there chanting circles danced around a man or a woman who swayed as if drunk—drunk on the immanence of godhead. Lee was twice drawn into one of these circles, and after he freed himself the second time he was brought up short by a man with staring eyes and tears running down his cheeks. He held Lee by his shoulders and looked unblinkingly into his face and said, "Welcome, sister," and spun away.

A firework went off prematurely, cracking a shower of

golden rain directly overhead. Everyone around Lee looked up, everyone except a man who was looking right and left as he pushed through the crowd.

It was the man in black.

He saw Lee in the same moment that Lee saw him, shouted a single word that was lost in the chants and screams and laughter of the festival.

Lee dodged around the smoking cart of a dough fryer, threaded his way through ambling knots and chanting circles of people. A solemn little girl caught at the hem of his chuba; Lee pulled free and darted between two shaven-headed monks in orange robes who capered and beat little drums tucked under their arms in wild syncopation.

Lee was standing at the beginning of a long stone jetty. The man in black pushed between the dancing monks, and Lee ran on, ran a long, long way until he almost ran off the end of the jetty. The tops of the masts of the little fishing boats rose waist high on either side. Black water slopped far below him. He turned.

Tho man in black raised his hands to show they were empty. He was only a few meters away. The lanterns and dancing lights of the festival made a ribbon on the darkness behind him.

"Wei Lee," he said. "Don't be scared. I am here to help you."

Lee said, "I need no help." A fire burned beneath his breastbone.

"I think you do. You can trust me. Look."

The man started to bring something out of his jacket and Lee blurred into motion and ran straight at the man and caught his wrist. For a moment they wrestled at the lip of the jetty: Lee desperately quick; the man ponderous and strong. And then they fell.

Thirty-four

The impact of the water drove all breath from Lee's body. He plunged in a whirl of bubbles down into cold darkness. Pressure drove twin spikes into his eardrums. Like almost every Martian, he had never learned to swim. Galvanized by a lightning tree of fear, he thrashed and kicked against the heavy dark water with no idea of up or down.

Every muscle ached for air, but he retained enough sense to clamp his teeth against the impulse to breathe that was tightening within his chest like a vice, threatening to spring his ribs.

Then something thumped into the small of his back. He was rushed through cold black water which suddenly broke over his face. He opened his mouth and it filled with a gush of air, pure as life, before water closed over his head again. He kicked out, felt something graze his legs, his hands. He grasped a smooth hard streamlined body, and it lifted him into air again, pushed him towards the shore with strong supple movements.

Lee's legs grazed silt and a tangle of waterweed; then he was sprawled on salt-caked mud with scarcely enough strength to raise his head as he spewed cold water. He fell down and rolled over, breathing as hard and painfully as a new-born baby.

He had been brought round the curve of the shore, beyond the jetties and noise and light the festival made along

156

the waterfront. A little way off, something with a grinning beaked mouth full of tiny needle-sharp teeth breached the surface. It made a high-pitched chattering, and cocked a bright eye at him before sliding back into black water. Lee realized that it was the creature that had saved him.

"It's a fin," a small voice said out of the darkness behind him.

Lee remembered to use the enhanced vision the viruses had given him, and saw the solemn little girl who had clutched at the hem of his chuba in the midst of the festival's whirl. She wore a black shift over a red shirt with baggy sleeves and kneehigh felt boots. Her black hair was done up in oiled pigtails pinned above her ears.

She said, "Fin help us fish. Now one catches a god!"

Lee managed to get to his feet. He was shivering with more than cold, although his clothes were heavy with icy water and he was chilled to the marrow by the breeze off the lake. He said, "I wish I could thank him."

"You need a machine to talk fin. Much is too high and fast, even for me." She said, in a completely different tone of voice, "I carry a god. That is how I know you are more than one."

A chattering squeal came from out in the water.

The little girl said, "The fin says you are legion. He says you come to save the lake. He says you must do what you must. I know that, too. That is why we have come for you."

"We?" Lee said stupidly.

"All the gods. We've been waiting for you for such a long time."

The little girl's name was Chen Yao. She was four years old, the youngest daughter of a fishing family. The god that had settled in her that night was a star god whose secret name could not be revealed. Chen Yao said that he claimed to be the father of the Emperor Yu, who had first controlled the flooding of the Yellow River; his familiar was a fox with nine tails. That was why she had known to help Lee.

"Because I have nine tails?"

"Perhaps you have nine lives." Chen Yao tipped her head,

listening intently to something only she could hear. "No, because you hold the keys to the heavenly river, that will one day wash the shores of the friendly lands."

Lee thought that she meant the Milky Way, and asked no more. Chen Yao led him up the long sweep of the salt flats and then through the crowds and the lights and scents and noise of the festival. She held his thumb in her hot small fist and chattered away in the manner of any four-year-old.

It seemed that the fin which had saved him was a descendant of dolphins made more intelligent by Cho Jinfeng. That at least had been real enough. So had the man in black, who Lee fervently hoped was at the bottom of the lake. But the talk of gods . . . even if Chen Yao did somehow know about Miriam, Miriam was no god. She was not even alive, was no more than the sum of data coded by her viruses on to the spy device in his visual cortex . . .

Lee realized that somehow he and little Chen Yao had become the head of a procession. Men and women and children followed them in solemn single file through the crowds, all with wide eyes and tear-stained cheeks. He asked the little girl where they were going, and she pointed and said, "Why, to our house, of course."

On a spit of land at the far end of the waterfront, past the houses and long steep jetties, lit by lanterns strung everywhere across its white-washed walls and steep red-tiled roofs, was a temple.

Thirty-five

The gods bathed Lee and brought him clean clothes, and fed him fried aubergines and maize porridge flecked with bits of charcoaled potato. This was in one of the chapels of the temple, an octagonal high-ceilinged room bright with murals and banners, and with lamps in a hundred niches making flickering constellations. Lee learned how good food tastes after your life has been saved, and the gods smiled indulgently at his relish.

After Lee had eaten, the gods left him to sleep. He sprawled on loose cushions in a big ornate chair, the brocade gown given to him by the gods scratchy against his clean skin. He was pleasantly drowsy, and clean and comfortable, after the terrors of the night, the chase and his near-drowning.

The revelation of the double murder of his parents hurt less than he thought it should. The young boy who had witnessed it was no relation to him except that they were the same person, and he was beginning to realize that he had been more obsessed with the search to find them than its outcome. What hurt most was that Great-grandfather Wei had betrayed him not once but twice, using the same cat's-paw with a casual arrogance that implied volumes about what he thought about his great-grandson.

And so all Lee's vaguely formed plans were overthrown. Tomorrow he would have to begin again, but now he could sleep . . .

The gods watched him solemnly from the doorway of the chapel, asking nothing of him. The little girl, Chen Yao, slept curled at the foot of Lee's throne, and Lee soon fell asleep too.

Thirty-six

He was in the chapel, alone. Light streamed through the door, brighter than the butter lamps. Two people stood in the light.

One was Miriam Makepeace Mbele. She was wearing tight blue-denim jeans crusted with sewn-on badges, and a sleeveless undershirt with sunburst patterns of purple and orange that interlocked in a way that made them seem to rotate over her unbound breasts. Her hair was long and bleached, tied back with a sparkly headband.

The other person, in a white leather suit sparkling with rhinestones, its front V-ed open down to his navel, was the King of the Cats. Around his shoulders was a white cape lined with cloth of gold, its flared collar faced with scarlet. His wide golden belt bore the legend "The World Champion Entertainer." He flashed his crooked grin and beckoned to Lee. His fingers glittered with gold rings set with diamonds and rubies and emeralds.

With no sense of awe or surprise, Lee got up and followed Miriam and the King of the Cats into the light.

They were in a transparent bubble hung in starry space from a siding of pitted rock. Like ghosts, they floated in cool pine-scented air.

Miriam said, "It's still too early to have regrets, but I know that this is one place I'll miss." Her long blond hair fanned out around her face. Like her hair, her skin was bleached.

161

Lee said, "This is where you lived?" He couldn't stop looking at the King, who grinned and winked back at him.

"This is just one room. I'd come here to turn on, tune in, drop out. Most of the Nexus are agoraphobes. They like tunnels and little chambers, warmth and red light. They like to huddle."

"Poor little anarchists!" the King said. "They fear the seething silence of the void!" His gleaming black hair was slicked back just like Lee's. Or was it the other way around? He plucked a white silk scarf from the air and draped it around his neck. "Listen closely," he said, "and you can hear the echo of the word God spoke to light the Universe."

Lee wondered which god he meant.

"There are many gods," Miriam said. "Yes, of course I can read your mind, Wei Lee. Are we not in it?"

"Speak for yourself," the King said. A corner of his full-lipped mouth lifted into precisely the expression Lee had spent so much time practicing. "I'm just visiting. And incidentally, in this present incarnation I'm too young for this science-fictiony suit. But, hey, don't bother ageing me. Corporeality is relative."

Lee said, "You know each other?"

The King shrugged. "I've known one or another of Miriam's incarnations down the years. She's a popular agent with both sides. A regular pistol. A *Colt* pistol, if you get my drift."

"As in *Frankie and Johnnie*? The one with the real bullet when it was supposed to be blank?"

The King drawled, "Now, I always preferred *Flaming Star*."

"Lee, I told you that my gene line was owned," Miriam said, casting an exasperated look at the King of the Cats. "Miriam is my own given name, Makepeace is the trade name of my clone line, Mbele is the name of the family which owns the Nexus and owns me. It isn't as if it's slavery, because after all I'm legally dead. I have no rights, or else the dead would own everything."

"They do, on Earth," the King said.

"No one owns anything there. That's the point."

"No one owns life, but anyone who owns a frying pan owns death. The dead own Earth, all right."

Lee said, "I thought everyone on Earth worshipped the Mother Goddess of the World." He felt quite calm, as if he was floating about a centimeter above his own skull. A viewpoint. An observer.

The King said, "No one's left alive on Earth except resurrectees kind of like Miriam here. Old genotypes in new bodies. You know them as the conchies. They do the work of the Earth's Consensus, and the Earth's Consensus serves the Mother Goddess of the World. Which *is* the world, dig? Earth was dying, strangling in the wastes of human civilization, heat pollution, carbon dioxide. The Earth's Consensus had two choices, move Earth's orbit out from the Sun, or remove the source of the problem. The first solution wasn't technically feasible, so it applied the second."

"Oh, it was technically feasible," Miriam said.

"Not without losing the Moon, and messing up the orbits of Venus and Mars. And the Earth's Consensus has plans for Mars, of course. And is applying them, as it did on Earth. That's why we're all here. Mars is a dying world, from the human viewpoint. It's being allowed to die. The Earth's Consensus sees that as a rebirth. An erasure of human presence, a triumph of the inorganic."

"Sometimes I think you side with the Earth's Consensus, even without realizing it."

"Aw heck, I'm way older than it is. I'm even older than you, Miriam, or at least most of the derivations of my mind-sets are. I never was a conservationist, nor could be. I'm too early a model. In a way, I guess you could say the Earth's Consensus is my child. Without me . . ."

"You were the first," Miriam said.

"Oh yeah, you bet! The first and best. I gave birth to myselves, don't ever forget that. It gives me an edge the monads that make up the Earth's Consensus can never have. *They* were created, once I had shown that it was possible.

"For most of history, humans believed that gods lived in the sky beyond the Earth. Even after the dawn of science a vestige of that belief persisted. My original lived through a time when cults thought that benign advanced aliens would descend from the skies to rescue the Earth from Atomic Armageddon. But instead humans created intelligences superior to themselves." The King winked. "Such as yours truly, and the monads of the Earth's Consensus. Perhaps they've never forgiven you humans that. Or perhaps they regard you in the way your Cro-Magnon ancestors regarded the Neanderthalers. Either way, they destroyed most of humanity in the name of preserving the Earth, and now they want to transcend their origins completely, they want to become gods. For all their talk of the Mother Goddess of the World they look inward, away from the real, into worlds created from information alone. Maybe they'll carry what's left of humanity with them as worshippers. Now, I was at the center of a religion once, and I can tell you it's the last thing you should want. My children, my child. I'm fond of it, but this whole green machine thing scares the shit out of me."

Miriam said, "That was the army in Vietnam."

"Yeah, I was hinting at Vietnam. A scorched earth policy, except the conchies scorched only the population. Vietnam, Vietnam, hot damn, did I ever tell you about my tour of duty in 'nam?"

"You never were there. Not even to entertain the troops."

"Naw, they had Bob Hope and a half-dozen Playmates in cute white panties to do that. I had the Colonel, telling me I couldn't go abroad for some kind of business reasons, I forget precisely why."

"You were in the army," Lee said. "In Germany."

"That's 'cause I got caught in the draft. Those old GI Blues. We all got married and had kids, that was the blues. You're a fan? Here, I haven't done this in a long time."

The King unslung his silk scarf, wiped his suddenly sweaty brow and flung the scarf at Lee. It flew straight as an arrow, but went limp when Lee plucked it from the air. "Think nothing of it, kid," the King said, and plucked another scarf from the air and knotted it around his neck.

Lee smiled and copied the King of the Cats.

Miriam said, "We're wasting time. It's not even as if this is one of your strongest partials. And you should know better, Wei Lee. I think I told you about the way he's twisted his history to suit himself. He thinks he's a combination of Christ, Orpheus, and Osiris."

The King said, "Heck, who are you to say? Listen, why do you think the kid's a *fan*. He'll believe me more than Mao or some other long-gone politician. Lighten up, Miriam. Be like me, have some *fun*. I'll tell the kid what he needs to know, but let me do it my way."

"Water," Miriam said, "is what it's all about."

"My, do you have a one-track mind!" said the King.

"That's one of my genome's selling points. Mars is dying, Lee. You know that. The terraforming is reversing itself, water locking back up under the crust because not enough was ever melted to achieve a balance where liquid water dominates. On the Earth, if all water was frozen at the poles, it would soon melt under its own weight and fill the oceans again. Here on Mars there's not enough water. The balance has to be tipped. The original terraforming was on the right track, but it didn't push the balance far enough. We will, if we can."

"It's a hard rain that's gonna fall," the King crooned. He added, "First ice, then fire."

"Fire, and then rain. A seeding, and a harvest. Forty days and forty nights, Lee. The first installment of a flood that will fill the dry seabeds for ever. Thousands may die, so that unborn billions will live. Otherwise all will die, now and for ever, and Mars will be what it once was."

"This is the Sky Roader path," Lee said. "But the balance requires an average depth of five hundred meters in the seas. No one can move that amount of water, and even if they could it would kill everyone on Mars when it fell from the sky. Even the Ten Thousand Years didn't try to *drop* water on Mars, but melt what was already there. Mars needs heat, not water . . . "

The King said, "You're good, kid. They did a good job on you. Now we're done talking, let's just show you."

"First of all he has to understand . . . "

The King smiled and snapped his fingers. Miriam made a frustrated sound and spun away from him. Outside the blister, the stars were dimming as if behind a rising mist. Then Lee understood that another scene was bleeding through the starscape: a segment of Jupiter's banded globe, frozen bands of salmon and yellow and white feathering off into complex scrolls.

It hung there for a moment before rising up with terrific speed, although Lee felt no hint of acceleration in the weightless volume of the strange room. They were falling through clouds twenty kilometers deep. Opalescent light streaked all around. It was like being inside a pearl. Then cloud vanished, and they were floating above a vast brick-red plain—a cloud deck from which great thunderheads boiled up to form improbable mountain ranges of inverted flat-topped wedges. They formed rough parallel lines that dwindled to the horizon, three thousand kilometers away.

Something small glittered at the same height as the viewing blister, brilliant in the pinkish twilight. The blister swept towards it, and Lee saw that it was like a tinsel pine tree, its size impossible to estimate. In the clear atmosphere it could have been ten meters high and right next to the blister, or a kilometer tall and a hundred kilometers away.

The King of the Cats saluted the thing's slow rotations. Miriam said, "You're such a show off."

The King put on a pair of dark glasses with chunky metal frames. The earpieces had square cutouts in them. "A showman is just exactly what I am," he said, cocking a hip and doing a kind of slow swivel about its axis. "I thought the kid should know where I'm coming from."

Lee said, "That's where you live?"

The King said, "Kind of."

"There are thousands of them," Miriam said.

"The mean optimal value is twenty-five thousand two hundred fifty-three. 'Course, it varies by about eight per cent. This is a dangerous environment. Accidents happen all the time . . . "

Miriam told Lee, "This is one of the descendants of a self-replicating probe the Europeans dropped six hundred years ago to map Jupiter. It replicated all right, and at some time it achieved consciousness. Its owners downloaded a suite of simulated personalities to stabilize it, let it tap into a data bank. He's one of the results. A partial, one part of a consensual hive-mind holographically stored in twenty-five thousand parallel processors."

"It isn't quite like that," the King said, with a self-satisfied smirk. "We're more like a continually reiterated Cantor Set. You're not even in our dust, Miriam."

Lee turned in mid-air to watch the tinselly construct dwindle against the mountainous clouds. The blister was picking up speed; all of a sudden, the construct vanished to a speck, winked out. Luminous arcs radiated away from the blister, shock waves in the dense atmosphere. Dark red mountain ranges fell away. The blister arrowed through a swirl of vaporous islands, shot into a vast canyon in the upper clouds. Then clouds dropped away, turned into a smog-colored river mixing in great swirls with rivers on either side. The sky was black, and then stars came out. And bisecting the starry sky was a faint interrupted line, flecks of curdled light tracing a narrow band that grew less distinct as it grew nearer.

"That," the King said, "is the beginning of your new world sea, all packaged for delivery."

It was Jupiter's ring.

Thirty-seven

The blister matched orbits with the ring's jostling lanes: millions of dirty ice nuggets, massing from the size of a dust speck to a small mountain, shepherded by the inner moons into a series of arcs that forever poured around Jupiter's equator.

Fullerene viruses had been at work on every nugget of ice more than a tonne in mass. Each had been fitted with a one-shot smart booster that would take it out of orbit and send it falling towards Mars. Lazy skimming passes through the atmosphere would fragment and melt the bolides; their water would rain down, seeded with viruses. Viruses that would soak up sunlight and burrow into the permafrost and melt it with billions of pinchfusion processes. Viruses that would float into the high reaches of the atmosphere to manufacture a cocktail of chlorofluorocarbons that would absorb across the thermal infra-red spectrum and warm the world. But before they reached Mars, the bolides would have to evade the laser defenses of the Army of the People's Mouths. These too had multiplied, and there were more than enough of them to deflect the long slow orbits of the bolides.

"Someone will have to disable the defense controls," Miriam said. "There are too many weapons to be destroyed, but there is only a single command system."

"Problem is," the King added, "you can't just drop a big rock on it. We tried that, but y'all know the defenses can deal with rocks. It works on dust, too. We tried to dust Mars with viruses fifty years ago, but your Emperor was ahead of us. The defenses saturate space around Mars with low-power low-frequency broadcasts that destroy unshielded viruses by inductive heating."

Miriam told Lee, "The defenses work too well. The conchies persuaded your Emperor to design and build them, and he still controls them."

All of a sudden, the King held a pistol grip which flicked out a rod of crackling white light. "Star Wars," he said. "Only their light sabres have an effective range of fifty thousand kilometers."

There was only one way to disable the defenses, and that was to destroy the command center, which the Army of the People's Mouths had built on the highest point of Mars, in the vast caldera of Tiger Mountain. Lee had come all the way to Xin Beijing, and now he was supposed to turn back and set out eastward. If he and Miriam had not been captured by the monks of the lost lamasery, they might already have completed their mission.

"Or perhaps not," the King said cheerfully. "Now you have the help of what's left of our other agents. At last they become useful."

Miriam had floated across to the bubble's curved transparent wall, clinging with splayed fingertips and watching the braided river of water-ice boulders eternally fall through its orbit. She said, "I'm not the first agent sent down by the anarchists, but perhaps I will be the last. Many others failed; a few survive in a fragmentary way, as virus infections in the descendants of their contacts. As I survive in you."

"They've become gods," the King said.

"No," Miriam said, "or else that's what I've become. And I'm so much less than what I once was . . . "

"Who's to say, babe," the King said. "After all, you walk in the kid the way the gods walk in their avatars. Oh, I've boosted you up for this, but don't underestimate yourself." He turned his twisted smile on Lee. "You know what you have to do, kid?"

"I know what you want me to do. I don't know how. Please, can you tell me how I must do it?"

"That's the hard part," the King said. "It's hard because it's down to you, kid. You gotta understand that the Earth's Consensus can simulate me. It can foresee any strategy I can devise. I could randomise the choice ... " he spun a thick silver coin through the air, which vanished in the same direction the light sabre had taken " ... but I couldn't know if the conchies haven't devised contingencies for everything. It is possible. But you're an unknown variable, kid. That's why we chose you."

"And your parents," Miriam said.

"He doesn't need to know that," Elvis said.

Lee looked at the King, at Miriam. He felt a vast deep urgent sadness. He said, "My great-grandfather had my parents killed. Why did he do that? What does he want from me?"

Miriam said, "You still think that it was a coincidence that I landed where I did? It was because you were there, Lee. You're a link between us and your great-grandfather, part of a long-standing deal, but you're also something else. Something your great-grandfather doesn't know about. Your mother ... "

"He killed my mother! My mother and my father! He shot them down ... " Lee couldn't see clearly any more. He was crying. In microgravity, his tears formed fat blebs that clung to his eye-lashes.

The King told Miriam, "Hush now. You'll destroy the random variables if he knows too much."

Miriam said in a small voice, "Then let me die."

"No," the King said. "Listen to me, Wei Lee. You'll take that little girl. Chen Yao? You take her with you, now. She is the avatar of something whose powers you'll need. You'll wake up now, but you'll remember. Remember all this."

"Wait!" Miriam said. "If I can't die I need to wake up with him. What I have is worse than death. I need more than flashes, fragments ... "

"It'll get better," the King of the Cats said. "Now wake up, Lee."

"No! Wait! Tell me why my parents were killed! Tell me what happened to them when they were ambassadors to the anarchists. Tell me . . ."

"Time past! Wake up!"

Thirty-eight

Lee woke with a start, and almost fell out of the nest of pillows he had made on the throne-like chair. He found that he was wearing goggles, and stripped them off. Weak morning light streamed through the narrow windows of the chapels, dimming the multitude of flickering butter-lamp flames.

The vision was settling inside him, every detail vividly accessible. He was not at the periphery of some plot of his great-grandfather's after all: he was at the center of something so vast that despite Miriam's long and tangled explanations he felt he had only glimpsed its edges.

Lee clutched the heavy material of the brocade gown with both fists. He felt as if he was poised over a great black pit. Because, despite the goggles that the gods had put on him while he slept, it could all be some terrible delusional system he had worked up, trying to rationalize what had happened to him. His loss of face at the Bitter Waters *danwei*, his fugitive life, the sudden desperate sad weight of the memory of the murder of his parents . . .

He had always loved the King of the Cats, had always hated the slow dying of Mars. And he had dreamed that the King had recruited him to *save* Mars . . . that crazy story about Jupiter's ring, about viruses that would melt water, fill the outer skies with microscopic greenhouse gas factories . . .

He remembered everything so clearly! But now that he

was awake Miriam had slipped away from him. More than ever Lee wanted her to appear to him: even her previous manifestations could have been nothing more than hallucinations. Suppose the viruses hadn't transferred her partial personality after all, but had simply damaged his brain?

"I'm not mad," he whispered into the cushion under his cheek. "I won't be mad ... "

The little girl, Chen Yao, was curled at the feet of the chair. Only two other gods remained: an old woman with white hair pulled back in a thick braid, and a stout young fellow in clean but worn work clothes. They both came forward and bowed to Lee, who jumped down at once, embarrassed beyond all measure.

Chen Yao stretched, and said, "What's all this noise? Have you finished talking with your friends?"

Lee said slowly, "I was dreaming. Such a strange dream. I remember it very clearly."

"Of course you do. You were supposed to remember it."

"You know what I dreamed?"

Chen Yao stretched again, and yawned with the quick unselfconscious reflex of a cat. She looked like any sleepy four-year-old, eyes puffy, hair scuffed up on one side in a roostertail. "I shared your vision," she said. "That is my attribute. I speak with those you carry, with the woman, and with the godhead."

Lee laughed. If Chen Yao knew, then perhaps it was all true after all! Or perhaps she was as crazy as he believed he might be. A poor crazy little girl worshipped by the fisherfolk as a god.

Chen Yao said, "Don't be silly. We contain fragments, but you are the avatar of the entire godhead. You are our saviour, Benefit of the People Lee."

"No," Lee said. "No, I don't know that I am."

The young fisherman bowed again, and said, "The child tells the truth, Master."

"Please! I'm no one's master! I'm not even master of my own life!"

The old woman said, "At seven, I set my heart on learning.

At fifteen, I was firmly established. At twenty, I had no more doubts. At twenty-five, I knew the will of heaven. At thirty, I was ready to listen to it. At thirty-five, I could follow my heart's desire without transgressing what was right."

"*Lao*," Lee said, bowing to the old woman. "I am still young enough to have many doubts."

"But you know the will of heaven," Chen Yao said.

"I do?"

"Silly man," Chen Yao said. "Your vision explained everything, of course."

Lee thought that it explained everything or nothing. It was as complete and as fragile as a bubble.

Chen Yao clapped her hands with a curious mixture of childish excitement and hauteur. "Now come on," she said, "we must start our journey! We must go to join our friends!"

Thirty-nine

The gods returned Lee's chuba, shirt and black jeans. They had been washed and dried and pressed. Lee found that his money was gone from the button-down pocket of his shirt, but he did not think that the gods had taken it. Perhaps it had been lost when the pedicab had crashed (so perhaps the driver had got his fare—and more), or perhaps when he had fallen into the lake.

But on the waterfront, at least, lack of money wasn't a problem. Chen Yao simply went up to a street vendor, and the man smiled and handed them bananas sliced and fried in paper-thin envelopes of dough.

Munching his breakfast, Lee allowed Chen Yao to lead him along the dockside. Things happened, one after the other, whether he willed them or not. So let them happen, this bright spring morning!

Grainy white salt flats sloped away into gauzes of mist that lay low on the black water of the lake. Down at the ends of the kilometer-long jetties, fishermen were preparing their boats for the day's work. Their songs drifted small and clear in the bitter morning air. Oyster farms and kelp racks made rectangular patterns beyond the jetties. The sun still lay behind the worn rimwall mountains, but his light glowed the sky and rouged the mists. Fear was overhead, a tiny smudged crescent riding swiftly to greet the dawning sun.

Lee stopped when he saw something break the water out beyond the longest jetty. His attention switched something in his rebuilt eyes, and everything else flowed away from the suddenly magnified patch of water.

Lee clapped his hands over his face and fell to his knees. After a few moments he cautiously opened his fingers. Chen Yao was looking at him. Her face was exactly level with his own. She said, "What did you see?"

"I thought I had something in my eye. It's gone now."

He allowed his eyes to do their zoom trick again, and saw the bulging heads of fins break the surface far out in the black lake: two, four, six of them. One rose chest deep in the water, beaked head bobbing. Perhaps it was the one which had saved his life. Lee got to his feet and raised his hand in salute.

"The lake shrinks year by year," Chen Yao said. Fried banana was smeared around her mouth. "Once it was twice as big, and where we walk was under water. These are the new docks."

"I know," Lee said, but Chen Yao wasn't paying attention to him. She was watching the sweep of water beyond the dry salt flats and the ends of the jetties.

She said, "The fin grow fewer and fewer, for there are fewer and fewer fish for them to eat. Soon there will not be enough for the fishermen and the fin, and there will be war. The fin know that, and that is why they saved your life, and allowed the other to drown."

Lee discovered that the closer he looked at something, the smaller his field of view became. He looked right into the texture of the netting that a fisherman was folding at the end of the long jetty, at the scars on the man's flexing knuckles. Just an extra step, that was all. He had it under control now.

He said, "These fin, they drowned the fellow that was following me?"

"They did not save him. It was action through inaction, for the greater good. Their viruses prevent them from killing men, which is why they fear war so much. But through inaction they can allow death if it is for the greater good."

"Do you know who he was? The man who tried to . . . kill me."

Chen Yao said seriously, "We think he was a demon. The Ten Thousand Years grow them. Many there are in the Army of the People's Mouths. An army within an army. They kill on order. He would want the viruses that have raised the godhead in you."

Lee said, "The viruses are real. I mean, they really are rewiring my nervous system."

"It's all real. You must accept it."

Lee asked, "How did you know I was coming here? I mean, you were expecting me."

"The gods drew you here. The way does not matter, as long as it is the right way." How serious she was, for one so young . . . yet of course she was more than a young girl. Like all the fisherfolk, she carried viruses which allowed partial personalities to be expressed in her, just as Lee carried fragments of Miriam. Lee remembered what Miriam had told him about her gene line, mercenaries licensed to kill for anarchist families whose members could not bear to leave the binding closures of their habitats. Was she a demon or an angel?

He realized it did not matter. He felt a strange calm lucidity. Even if Miriam's fullerene viruses had rewired him to feel that way, even if they had snuffed his panic the way he might pinch out a candle flame, it still felt right. The conchie missionaries claimed that the world was only an illusion: who was to say whether one thing was more real than another, whether light was stronger than darkness?

Lee felt Chen Yao's small hand in his. It was warm, and greasy with fried banana. The little crazy girl god said, "Whether she's a demon or an angel depends on who she serves, of course. She fell from Heaven, so I suppose she must be an angel."

"Earth is in Heaven too."

"Miriam says you have a lot to learn."

"Can you really speak to her?"

"Of course." Chen Yao was calmly matter of fact. "Viruses

are everywhere here, because of the fin. They were infected with strains by Cho Jinfeng herself, and she gave us a translator strain so that we could speak to our helpmates. The viruses have changed since, and so we fisherfolk can become avatars for the fragments of godhead that have fallen amongst us. But they are incomplete, and you are not."

Lee remembered Miriam's claim that there had been many agents before her, that some survived as fragmentary infections in the descendants of their original contacts. He thought he knew what had caused the mutations in the translator viruses of the fisherfolk.

He said, "Where are you taking me, Chen Yao? You overestimate my powers if you believe that I can walk halfway around the world."

"There are people who will help us. They have been waiting a long time for people like you. The Sky Road was never completely destroyed."

"Miriam said that the *ku li* would help me. Is that who your friends are?"

"You ask too many questions," Chen Yao said. "Come on, it's this way."

"I have my own idea," Lee said. "You can come with me if you want, but I'm going there with or without you. It won't take too long to get what I'm owed."

"We don't need money."

"Of course we do. We're going out into the real world. Trust me." He struck off down the narrow street down which he had run last night, and after a moment heard Chen Yao running to catch up with him.

"You'll be sorry," she said. Then, "Where are we going?"

"To the one man who can help me."

"Your great-grandfather is no friend!"

"I'm not thinking of him," Lee said.

So it was that Lee walked through the waking city two paces ahead of a cross young girl who carried a god stitched into translator viruses inside her own genome. It was as if he walked at the head of a procession.

They walked down wide streets shaded by the two-hundred-meter-high canopies of dusty ginkgoes. Trams glided amongst flocks of bicycling commuters, but Lee and Chen Yao had no money for trams, not even the least coin for a mouthful of freshly squeezed orange or mango juice that vendors dipped from plastic canisters with steel cups which they meticulously wiped after each customer.

Chen Yao said, "You really are going the wrong way."

Lee told Chen Yao that she could not rely on the charity of her worshippers.

"They are not worshippers," Chen Yao said. "I wonder if you understand anything you've been told, Wei Lee."

"Perhaps you are right. But Tiger Mountain is five thousand kilometers away and there is a man in the city who owes me money."

"We do not need it!"

They stared at each other, while passers-by moved around them. Lee said, "Tell me everything, Chen Yao."

Chen Yao turned her face sideways to his. "I told you before that you ask too many questions."

"You haven't been told very much. It's all right. I don't know much either. We're two of a kind."

Chen Yao pouted, entirely her age now.

"We'll visit this man, and then we'll find your friends."

"You don't know anything," Chen Yao said again.

"I know this city, a little. It won't take long."

Maps of the city came down inside his head, settling through each other. One was written by the viruses, the other patched from his own memories. He was walking down North Avenue, with apartment houses on one side and the long low white houses of the half-lifers set in a narrow parkland on the other. North Avenue led all the way to the First House of the Emperor, but soon he would be able to cut across the Park of the Central Sea and find Hawk's house. He didn't need viruses to tell him that.

But as they walked on Lee rediscovered what he had long ago forgotten, that walking in a city is far more wearying than walking the untamed landscape. There was no way to establish the rhythm of long strides which ate up territory, for every few meters there was a fresh distraction: a fat shirt-less man standing in a doorway, smoking a cheroot with such an air of beneficent satisfaction that Lee could believe that he was the real owner of the city, enjoying watching it wake around him; a policeman with white gloves directing traffic at an intersection, blowing furiously on his silver whistle at swarms of oblivious cyclists; beggars sitting in a row under a flowering hedge, displaying various mutilations and disfigurements; a man laboriously pedalling along at snail's pace, towing a trailer which carried a square crate as tall as Lee; a tram so laden with passengers—hanging from its windows, along its running boards, crowded on to its roof and even clinging to the wedge of its crash-catcher—that it looked like a heap of people skimming along with no visible means of support.

The tram went slowly because there were so many people spilling from the wide sidewalks into the road. Something began to knot itself in Lee's chest. He knew that this was no ordinary rush-hour crowd even before he reached the border of the Park of the Central Sea, and saw the soldiers.

Some were lined along the park's edge. Many more roamed the dusty grass and the perimeter of the big lake, the third biggest body of open water on Mars. Vehicles were parked everywhere. A culver flapped up from Jade Island, in the center of the lake. All around Lee and Chen Yao, people hooted and jeered.

The soldiers watched impassively. Despite the density of the crowd, no one used the sidewalk that ran along the border of the park because the soldiers stood on the other side of it. They were dressed in black leather, carried transparent plastic shields as tall as themselves. Their faces were masked; the masks had bulbous goggles, and complex fairings that swept back and grew into the soldiers' skulls. Things flew out of the crowd at the soldiers—bottles, stones, even the occasional shoe—but the soldiers moved only to deflect missiles with their shields. The crowd roared when red paint splashed across one soldier's shield.

Chen Yao tugged at Lee's hand. "You see! You see!"

She was close to tears, and that, more than the soldiers or the mob they faced, was what scared Lee.

"You should have followed me!" Chen Yao wailed.

"Let's get off the street," Lee said, and took her hand.

But when he tried to zig-zag through the crowd to the far side of the avenue he was caught in a swirling current of people that carried him in one direction and Chen Yao in another. Lee fought free and had to dodge a crowded tram that continuously rang its bell as it crept through in the middle of the crowd which swept Lee past the park and spilled out into the wide space of the Square of Heavenly Peace.

It seemed that half the population of the city was already there. People streamed across the wide space towards the high white walls of the First House of the Emperor. They clustered thickly around the Front Gate, which in normal times would be open to allow entry of petitioners to the Halls of Requite Interface. But the gate was closed; it had been closed ever since the Emperor had fallen silent, and now its black and white mandala and its twenty-meter-high arch was spattered with red paint. People spilled past it on either side, under the overhang of the wall, which arched above them like a wave frozen in the moment of breaking. Posters and painted slogans covered the lower third of the wall. Holographs projected luminous ladders of characters above the heads of the crowd, a hundred different variations on the call for truth. Vendors were out and about, crying their wares, and a cluster of makeshift tents was pitched at one corner of the square.

Lee caught the arm of a man, excused himself and asked what had happened. The man smiled in confusion and pointed to the sky and hurried away. An old woman shouted at Lee, "The Emperor, young man! The sky radio says that the Emperor is dead!"

Lee remembered to switch on the radio which the viruses had built inside his head but there was only a dizzy swoop of static. At the same moment Lee heard someone call out his name.

"Wei Lee! Wei Lee!"

Xiao Bing ran towards him, silver eyes flashing in his white face. Elsewhere, a ragged shout went up from people still crowding into the square.

"The soldiers! The soldiers are coming! The soldiers!"

Forty

Rank after rank of soldiers marched into the Square of Heavenly Peace, fanning out either side of the avenue to form an arrowhead that pointed across the crowded square to the Front Gate. An officer in a black silver-belted bodysuit rose into the air, feet pointed like an angel in those early Yankee paintings before the rules of perspective were formulated. His black bubble helmet flared in the morning light which flooded above the heads of the crowd and burned salt-white on the blank walls of the government buildings behind the soldiers' formation.

Lee gasped at this miracle. Xiao Bing shrugged and said, "There are superconducting coils woven in his suit. He'll be hovering over a honeycomb magnet—sort of like a flying carpet in reverse, the carpet stays on the ground, you fly. If we could induce flux in that guy we'd degauss his coils and see how he flew without them."

"You haven't changed," Lee said. "Always some pragmatic explanation for something no one else can understand."

Xiao Bing said, "It's only been three weeks, Lee."

"Has it? That's amazing."

The officer's amplified voice clattered across the Square of Heavenly Peace, rebounding from the buildings on three of its sides, the upswept wall on its fourth.

"It is time to leave the square," the officer said. "All citizens should leave the square so that the Army of the People's Mouths can implement their tasks."

184

A kind of formless murmur went up from the crowds as the echoes of the officer's voice died away. "Now we'll see," Xiao Bing said with grim satisfaction. He took Lee's arm and began to steer him through the crush.

"I'm glad to see you," Lee said. He vividly remembered the bombardment of the agricultural dome, the explosions and the sudden rush of the storm. He had thought his two friends dead. "I'm glad to see you escaped the soldiers. And Guoquiang? He is here?"

"He could be with the troops surrounding us, for all I know. He joined up, Wei Lee!"

"All that talk about the glory of serving the Emperor in the Orbital Defense Corps . . . so Guoquiang was a true idealist."

"As for escaping the soldiers, we jumped in the rice paddies and when the shooting stopped we stayed there. We had on our masks because of the dust storm, and so we could lie completely underwater and quench our infra-red signatures. Besides, the soldiers weren't looking for us, but for you and the anarchist pilot. When night came we stole two horses and slipped away and they didn't even know we'd been there. We rode as far as Dragon Spring Junction and then we caught a train. Guoquiang had just enough money for the trip, and as soon as we reached the city he joined up. He wanted me to join too, but that was never my idea of a life. Besides, could you see a silver-eyed white-haired pale-skinned albino in that black leather uniform?"

"It would be rather elegant." Lee had to lean in close to Xiao Bing; half the crowd were chanting for the Emperor, the rest were shouting "Down with the Gang of Six!" over and over and over. Lee said, "And you're still here. Still in the world. You're not yet one of the half-lifers."

"Oh, Heaven can wait. I fell in with some interesting people. You see the Big Character posters on the walls? They are the fifty-six calls for the devolution of power to the individual. We put up most of them in the night, when the King of the Cats started talking about the death of the Emperor. I help keep the projectors working to put our slogans in the air."

"How did you find the *ku li*?"

Xiao Bing laughed—it was lost in the crowd's roar. He leaned close and said, "They aren't the *ku li*. They're far more radical than that, you'll see. And they found me, Lee. They find those who can help them, and in turn they help us. There's a soup kitchen down near the railway station. I got talking to one of the comrades, and he took me to one of the meetings. Now I come here every day to help to educate the petitioners who come to speak with the Emperor."

"But surely the Emperor speaks with no one."

"That's true, but there are always those who for some reason or another believe that only the Emperor can help them. Some have been here ever since the Emperor fell silent—I'm sure you have seen the tents in the west corner of the square. We come here to educate those who still think the Emperor can help them. In a way, I suppose we—my friends and I—are also petitioning the Emperor. I'd like you to meet my friends, Wei Lee."

"I think that would be interesting."

"By the way, what happened to the pilot?"

"She . . . died. She died, Xiao Bing. A long way from here."

"How strange! She fell from the sky and touched all our lives, and now she is gone and we are changed."

"That's truer than you think."

The crowd was densest by the wall. Xiao Bing used his sharp elbows to push through the people who were reading the posters and slogans. The officer of the Army of the People's Mouths had floated higher, bobbing in the morning breeze like a tethered balloon. When his amplified voice repeated the warning, it was half drowned by the shouts and jeers of the crowd.

"This is our day!" Xiao Bing said happily, and pulled Lee on, all the way across the square to steps which swept up to the high narrow doors of the House of the Names of the Populace. Somewhere in there, Lee thought, the librarian Xiao Bing had written for him was still haunting the dim, booklined corridors of the data base. But what would the librarian search for now, now that the truth of his parents' assassination had been found?

A dozen young men had commandeered the sheltered alcove at the top of the steps in front of the closed stainless steel doors. Half were Yankees, and all were dressed in loose, mostly black clothes. Some were distributing printed leaflets to passers-by; others were unpacking all kinds of electronic equipment from canvas carry-alls, stuff which had the raw edges of homemade experimental units.

Xiao Bing introduced Lee to a plump young man named Lao San. He had a shining round face and hair slickly swept back and an excitable aggressive air. He said, "What have you brought us, Xiao Bing?"

"Wei Lee worked in my *danwei*," Xiao Bing said.

Lao San said impatiently, "Doesn't matter where he comes from. Is he hip to technology?"

Lee said, "I am only an agronomist technician. All this is very intimidating to me."

Lao San jabbed a forefinger in Lee's chest, such an astonishing lapse of manners that it paralyzed Lee. "Forget that humble self-effacing shit! A new order is rising, and the old ways have had their day! From the Darwinian point of view, they're useful as a kind of social lubricant regulating the behavior of the population, but there will be no need of that once everybody's position in society is self-determined. If you're going to help the PSLM you'd better be straight about what you can do."

"But I don't even know what you're trying to do," Lee said.

"We're here to change reality," Lao San said grandly. He snapped a thin glass tube, stuck one half under his own nose, the other under Lee's. Lee recoiled from the sharp whiff of solvent, and Lao San laughed. "You've got to change yourself before you can change the future."

"What was that stuff?"

"It'll free up your mind," Lao San said, and leered into Lee's face in such a way that he seemed deranged. Then he stalked off to harangue one of the black-clad young men. He kicked the projector the young man was tending and out above the heads of the crowd a slogan written in rippling red light unfolded in the air.

Xiao Bing said with undisguised admiration, "He's a pretty intense fellow."

"What was that, memory enhancer? I don't need to free my mind." Lee was wondering if the drug would affect the viruses that swarmed in his bloodstream, but all he could feel was a prickling in his palms that might be nothing more than adrenalin.

"Oh no! Even I don't do that, now that I've put off dying into my little piece of Heaven. We have many different kinds of drugs to help us. That one is supposed to increase your intelligence by allowing synapses to fire faster."

Xiao Bing explained that Lao San was leader of this cell of the People's Scientific Liberation Movement. They believed that the establishment of a technocracy would save Mars, for only a technocracy could complete the terraforming program. Their ideology was that of social Darwinism, in which individuals were free units subject not to the constraints of society, which in any case was a fiction maintained only by collective delusion, but to the forces of the market place. Government would be dismantled. Individuals and *danweis* and privately owned industries would compete to serve the population, and each person would pay only for services they required. Competition would favor those most fit to survive, those who were technologically literate.

"Just think of it, Lee, a truly scientific society!"

"It seems, well, incredible."

"Just so," Xiao Bing said, grinning.

Lee understood that Xiao Bing had lost Guoquiang but had found someone else to follow. And with a floating careless rapture he also understood that the drug had allowed him this insight. He said, "It sounds fine, although I do not quite understand how these competing *danweis* could band together to complete the terraforming of Mars. Who will pay for it?"

"Oh, there would be an air tax," Xiao Bing said, "or a

water tax. Or perhaps both. Details are not important at this stage."

"You would have people pay simply to live?"

"Life is not a right, but a privilege. Read our Big Character posters, and you will understand. Not here and now, of course. We'll soon be done here anyhow; there's a seventy per cent chance that the soldiers will clear the square in the next hour. We will be gone by then."

"You don't support the people?"

"Lao San says there's no such thing as the people. Only a stochastic mass of individuals."

Lee smiled. "Perhaps so. But at the moment it seems they all want the same thing."

Lao San turned from the little machine he'd been fiddling with and jabbed a finger into Lee's chest. "Listen! The Emperor is nothing more than an outmoded attempt at centralizing control. No such control is needed, of course, but it cannot be removed by banging on its gates. You want to know why we're here? It should be obvious this is a wonderful propaganda exercise. Look at our slogans, our Big Character posters!"

It was true, there were a dozen or more columns of ideograms floating in the morning air. But most of the people in the crowd were looking towards the soldiers, not the sky.

Lee said, "Oh, I understand that. I do want the same thing as you. I want Mars to live again!" And he did, so strongly that he started to cry, for he clearly saw the high cold deserts spreading, the forests withering, the lake shrinking in its salt basin.

"Sure you do," Lao San said.

Lee, embarrassed, started to apologize. Lao San said, "It is hard to force the evolution of your mind. But it is necessary. You help Xiao Bing try and get a projector on that officer. Let's make him interesting."

Xiao Bing was fitting a little machine with a dozen glass-ringed snouts to a kind of harness. Lee sniffed and said, "You're going to degauss the officer?"

"Oh no. Just superimpose an image on him. A little animated program that will turn him into a demon. I wrote it myself." Xiao Bing attached the little machine's harness to a limp mylar balloon. "Hand me that gas cylinder."

As Xiao Bing inflated the balloon with helium, the officer's voice boomed out again, and Lao San shouted that they would have to hurry. From the elevation of the steps, Lee could see across the heads of the crowd to the phalanx of the troops on the far side of the square. The soldiers were beating their shock sticks against their transparent shields in an ominous rhythm. Slowly, their line advanced towards the edge of the crowd, like the ruffling edge of an amoeba. Lee saw little knots of struggle break out as snatch squads of soldiers ran forward and grabbed hapless individuals and dragged them away. The crowd, which had seemed like some supra-organism united by a collective will, was fragmenting. Ragged singing was lost in screams as the first gas bombs went off. Blossoms of orange smoke began to spread at the boundary between the troops and the crowd. Soldiers aimed wide-bore rifles, and people at the edge of the crowd were knocked down by glycerine rounds. Tanglewire suddenly expanded in a mad dance, trapping dozens along its jittery perimeter. Somewhere, there was the fluttering beat of hovering culvers.

Then Lee was busy holding down the transparent balloon, now as big around as the spread of his arms, while Xiao Bing checked the projector hanging beneath it. "Let it go!" Bing shouted, and Lee stood back as the balloon floated free. Spurts of gas from little nozzles in the harness steered the contraption out into the morning sunlight as its navigation circuit fixed on the distant figure of the officer, who floated high above the spreading clouds of gas and the running battle that was advancing inexorably towards the Front Gate.

Xiao Bing watched the balloon go with a blissful smile. "You see the power of technology, Wei Lee."

"I wish it could be used to help the people understand."

Xiao Bing smiled. "Ideas, Wei Lee. That's the thing. We explain to the population what they need until they embrace the ideas as their own."

"It seems to me everyone wants to tell the people what to do, but no one asks them what they want."

Lao San was suddenly in Lee's face again. "They won't know they need it," he said, "until it is explained to them." He spun Lee around. "Look at your brave masses, running for their lives!"

It was true. The troops had occupied about half the square. Their line had broken into dozens of units that roamed back and forth under a pall of orange smoke while thousands of people tried to escape down the avenue on the far side. Dust clouds hung above the seething press, reddening the morning sunlight. With a roar of wings, a culver rose over the flat roof of the Ministry of Information and swept towards the panicking people like a sparrowhawk harrying ice mice from long grass.

Lao San laughed at Lee's dismay. "You stay with us, and you'll understand. You're a bright fellow, even if you're wet behind the ears." He turned and shouted at the others to start packing up; it was time to go, and the other members of the PSLM started to jam their bits and pieces of equipment into canvas bags.

Lee saw threads of light stab down from the culver, raking the crowd. People caught aflame like ants under a lens. He and Xiao Bing shrank back when a laser pulse touched the lower steps and heat-stressed stone flew in every direction. A woman ran through the crowd, her hair on fire. A second culver lazily settled over the Front Gate, the wind from its wings sending posters flying like autumn leaves. Orange gas squirted from the culver's belly, was dashed across the square by its down draft.

People ran from the wave front of gas. Some tried to climb the steps, but Lao San's young men fought them back with bare hands or by swinging canvas bags weighted with their equipment. Lao San wielded a telescopic pole; he punched an old woman in her chest and she fell down, tripping the people behind her.

Lee caught a whiff of gas that burned all the way down his lungs. His eyes spilled burning tears. The drug had ripped his perceptions open. He was a screen, a nervous surface. He grabbed Xiao Bing. "Can your machines project a picture of a real person?"

"Sure. We have cameras as well as a recorder."

Lee saw his reflection doubled in the silver caps over Xiao Bing's pupils. He saw that his own eyes seemed to be nothing but pupil. He said, "Xiao Bing, you've always been a good friend. Please set it up for me. For Guoquiang."

"You won't have more than a minute," Xiao Bing said, and told Lee to step back. Overlapping cones of light sprang around him, projected from little cameras fixed by adhesive pads to the marble walls on either side of the stainless-steel door. Lee slicked back his hair as Xiao Bing stuck a foam microphone dot to his throat. "Stay in the light," Xiao Bing said.

And then Lee saw his projected image hung hugely above the square. It was as tall as a building. Lee spread his arms, and his image's left hand passed through the culver that hovered over the Front Gate. The drug fizzed in his forebrain. He felt that he could reach into the heads of everyone in the square, even the soldiers. His own voice echoed back at him: the words came without thought.

"The King of the Cats told you the Emperor is dead! Believe in the King! I have walked with him in Father Jupiter. He has a message that is so strong it took a whole civilization to forget it, yet it takes only a moment to remember it. Remember that he forgave those who exiled him, and those who betrayed him. Remember that he died for our sins!"

Lee paused for breath, and the crowd shouted and waved their hands at his projected figure. "The King lives! The King has returned!"

One of the culvers sprayed Lee's image with laser fire, and Lee gave them his imitation of the King's smile. He swivelled on his cocked hip and flicked his fingers at the floating officer, who shot higher into the air in alarm. The crowd laughed and cheered. Lee's voice was almost lost in their noise. "The rains will come! All you have to do is open the sky, and the rains will come! Take the Sky Road!"

And then he could no longer hear his voice as the crowd surged forward. He saw that Lao San was staring at him beyond the cones of camera light, hands clenched up around his ears. Lee smiled and waved at Xiao Bing (his projected figure out across the square seemed to gesture towards the line of troops) and the light around him went off; out above the surging crowds, so did his projected figure.

Lao San's voice was choked with anger and fear. "Who— who are you?"

Xiao Bing laughed. "He's the King of the Cats' number one fan!"

One of Lao San's underlings said, "We did a patch and got it on to Channel Five, boss. The whole city'll have seen it."

Lao San said furiously, "Who told you to do that? They'll hang a trace!"

The man, a horse-faced young Yankee, snorted with laughter. "So it's time we left. Great propaganda, though."

Someone else said, "The government channel just went off the air, but all the commercial channels are going crazy!"

Lao San spat. "The King of the Cats is dead, and I don't believe in ghosts."

Lee grinned happily. "If you want to move the people, you've got to give them what they want."

"What you've given them is a riot," Lao San sneered.

It was true. The crowd was surging forward, swirling around knots of soldiers like the sea around rocks. Culvers swooped low overhead, but they couldn't fire without hitting their own troops. Trucks with armored prows welded over airbags swept into the square from the avenue—but they were driven by civilians, and civilians crowded their load-beds. They ploughed through the lines of troops and people jumped down from the loadbeds and ran into the crowd, ran into outstretched arms. Everyone seemed to be embracing everyone else.

"That's it," said the man who had been monitoring the government channel. "The Gang of Six have been arrested. There's a woman with a machine pistol in the studio advising everyone that the city is under martial rule, by the order of The Little Bird." He pointed at Lee. "And there's a price on your head, fellow."

A little girl pushed out of the dispersing crowd and ran up the steps, dodging the PSLM man who tried to catch her. It was Chen Yao.

She grabbed Lee's hand. "You've caused big trouble," she shouted. "Come on, now!"

Forty-one

T he avenues around the Square of Heavenly Peace were full of people hurrying away from it. Little electric trucks cruised amongst them, flying red and black flags and packed with armed men. They were the vigilante cadres of Xiao Yan, The Little Bird, the Ten Thousand Years who had seized the moment and captured the media networks. A column of dense black smoke rose into the pink sky, close by the dome over the Yankee Quarter.

"You follow me now," Chen Yao kept saying to Lee. She held on to his hand. "All this craziness is your fault, Wei Lee."

Lee was dazed by the comedown of Lao San's drug. His head felt as if it had been stuffed with cotton wool, and there was a trembling, not unpleasant lassitude in his limbs. He hardly noticed when the gunfire started.

One moment he was being tugged through the dispersing crowds by Chen Yao, the next he was wedged into a corner of the doorway of an apartment building with people screaming and shoving and shuddering all around him. Trucks swerved around each other in the street, and there was the orange stutter of muzzle flashes. Then someone made the doors open and Lee and Chen Yao were swept into the lobby with a hundred others.

Nobody had been directly hit, but many had been wounded by shrapnel and flying glass. Those who lived in the building brought sheets for bandages, and then blankets

195

and bowls of soup or tea. The doors were closed and barricaded and guarded by volunteers.

The old man found Chen Yao and Wei Lee tending a stoic woman whose hand had been struck by a tumbling ricochet. He waited while Lee washed away the blood and bound a crude splint to the woman's broken fingers, and then put a hand on his shoulder and said, "I know you, Master. It would be an honor to my family if you took tea."

"At another time I would be honored by your hospitality."

The old man said, "One more pair of hands makes no difference now."

It was true. For every person wounded there were two others to bandage wounds or mop up blood or fetch tea. People had brought out televisions. The tall lobby was filled with the chatter of conversation. All this by consensus, without leaders, without orders.

"I know you, Master," the old man said again. "My family has known you for a long time. I'd like to talk with you about it."

Chen Yao said, "It is kind of you, but we must go."

"The streets are dangerous. The Little Bird makes war with the soldiers who were in the Square of Heavenly Peace."

"An hour's delay won't hurt," Lee said. He was curious.

The old man, Kong Tiangang, lived in a three-room railroad apartment with his wife and their two sons and their wives and children—a baby, and twin brothers not much older than Chen Yao—and their only daughter. This young woman suffered from progressive atrophy of her central nervous system, one of the genetic disorders common in a population whose ancestors had been packed like sardines in unshielded rockets. Stick-thin, she lay twitching and jerking on a pallet in the main room of the two-room apartment, staring up at the dingy ceiling, occasionally slobbering a kind of gasping speech only her mother could understand.

The Kong family were poor, honest people who had committed the crime of having too many children. After the Great Reassessment, the Sky Roader trials and the alliance with the Earth, punitive sanctions had been introduced to reverse population growth; chief among them was that children were taxed on an asymptotic sliding scale.

"We have dwindled," Kong Tiangang said. "Master Kong, the Sage of Antiquity, whose name was known throughout Old Earth, was our ancestor, but that was three thousand years ago. I am of the one hundred and ninth generation. Many more stayed on Earth, but they will not be alive now. Once we were the first family under heaven. We ruled a province, and lived in a mansion that was the largest, most sumptuous mansion in the whole of the Middle Kingdom. That is no more, except for a few treasures, and the library. And that, which once filled a thousand thousand books in the Great Pavilion of the Constellation of Literature, is now stored in a data chip no bigger than my thumb. Master, will you take more tea?"

Lee and Chen Yao thanked him. It was bitter green tea, served in porcelain cups as thin and translucent as paper. Apart from the palsied daughter, the whole Kong family sat behind them, and neighbors crowded in the doorway and on the landing and the stairs, whispering comments and speculation. Chen Yao seemed to take no notice, but it took all of Lee's will not to turn around.

Kong Tiangang smiled and said, "No doubt you have been wondering how I knew of you, young Master."

"I had supposed that you saw me on television. But it is more than that, isn't it?"

"We brought with us one treasure in particular. It was made for our family in the Tang Dynasty by two famous fortune tellers, Yuan Tiangang, for whom I am named, and Li Chunfeng. Here, my son has it."

It was a thick bundle of ancient fibrous paper sheets, stitched together. When it was unfolded it took up half the floor space of the small room. It was covered with thousands of symbols. The Sun, and Earth's Moon in all its phases, stars and mountains, trees and plants, birds and beasts and all manner of household articles, all jumbled together.

"We call it the back-to-back diagram," Kong Tiangang

said. "The symbols represent the fate of each generation."

Chen Yao said, "It seems to me that Yuan Tiangang and Li Chunfeng were indeed very clever prognosticators, for there are so many different symbols that each generation cannot fail to find something that reflects the meaning of their lives."

Kong Tiangang said, "That may be true, young miss. If it is, then what I show your master will do him no harm, and at least you will have enjoyed my family's hospitality."

"Please," Lee said. "I'd like to see what it is."

"We found a symbol which we believe represented the one hundred and tenth generation, here, a monkey in an aspen tree. Our dear, unfortunate daughter was born in the year of the monkey, and you have seen how her limbs stir and quake, like the branches of an aspen in a wind. Yet you see that the monkey in the branches of the aspen holds the crescent of a bloody moon in its paw, and that the aspen stands on the side of a mountain whose base is patrolled by a tiger. I think that you are the monkey, Master, come to cure our daughter, and to save the red planet."

"Please," Kong Tiangang's wife said. "We paid to have machines put in her blood that would build circuits in her nervous system. But that did not cure her."

"She no longer has fits," Kong Tiangang said. "But still she trembles, as I have said, like the branches of an aspen tree. Please, Master."

Chen Yao said, "This isn't what your gifts are for, Wei Lee!"

Lee said, "You understand, Master Kong, that I promise nothing."

Kong Tiangang bowed.

Lee knelt beside the palsied young woman, laid a hand on her brow. She juddered, tried to focus cross-eyed on his face. Her tongue labored in her mouth like the tongue of an animal. Lee's mouth suddenly flooded with saliva and he bent and kissed her deeply, then sat back, strangely moved. There was a long silence in the crowded room. Then the young woman's eyes uncrossed. She stared into Lee's eyes and sighed and fell asleep, her twitching limbs relaxing, her clawed hands uncurling.

Her mother gave a cry as high and piercing as a bird, and Lee stood up as the woman rushed to her daughter's side. In a moment, the room was full of people exclaiming over this miracle. The palsied young woman slept peacefully in their midst.

Chen Yao took Lee's hand and pulled him against the flow of people, out of the apartment and down the stairs. People patted his face, sought his free hand. An old woman presented Lee with a cloth-wrapped parcel of rice cakes and dried fruit. Lee took it, and the woman bowed to him, but it was Chen Yao who thanked her, and pushed Lee down the stairs, ordered the self-appointed guards to open the barricaded doors in the lobby. Two men volunteered to go with them, and when Chen Yao refused their help the oldest told them to keep away from the main streets, where The Little Bird's vigilantes made their patrols.

Outside, Chen Yao led Wei Lee as fast as she could walk down a tangle of residential streets. "You must be careful," she said. "Viruses are everywhere here, because of the fin. It was Cho Jinfeng herself who gave a translator strain to the fisherfolk. The viruses have changed since, and so we avatars came into being. But none of us can do what you did. News will spread quickly."

"I felt pity for her." Lee was munching on the sticky sweet rice cakes. He hadn't eaten since breakfast, and now it was past noon.

"That's bad. Pity weakens. It is too much like contempt." Chen Yao was suddenly angry, and let go of his hand. "In future, keep your pity to yourself, Wei Lee."

"Do you believe what the old man said?"

"My godhead tells me that it is superstition. No one can know the future, for the fabric of the universes blurs into a myriad possibilities from moment to moment. Yet it is true that we are going to Tiger Mountain. I want to believe that you cured the woman, that you will save the world. I want to believe that the deed will be so great that it echoes up and down the corridors of time. If those ancient prognosticators caught those echoes, then we have already won."

"The monkey held the world," Lee said, "yet the tree held the monkey. I wonder what it means?"

"The point of those symbols is that they mean many things. Too many things, perhaps. Why have you stopped?"

The street had opened on to a big square with white three- or four-story houses around it and a central fountain, its basin dry as a bone. It was the Square of Two Thousand Martyrs, and Lee recognized Hawk's house straight away, because a pair of yak horns was mounted over its gate.

Forty-two

The wrought-iron gate was twice as high as Lee, with scenes of herding life cunningly woven into its bars. At his touch, the lock clicked and the gate swung back. Lee, followed by Chen Yao, walked through the archway into a courtyard where a small fountain played, a bubbling pulse of water that rose and trickled down a cone of shingled tiles. Lee bathed his gas-burned face. The water stung like liquid fire before it soothed him.

"I don't think this is a good idea," Chen Yao said nervously, looking around at the courtyard.

Geraniums grew thickly in large earthenware pots. Their bright red blooms seemed to float in the gloom, and filled the courtyard with their dusty scent. Balconies rose up four storeys to a glass ceiling; banners hung down from their balustrades like tongues.

"He owes me money," Lee said. "We'll need it."

"We need to get out of the city. First we cure the sick, and then we become beggars. At this rate I'll be an old woman by the time we reach Tiger Mountain."

"Hush. Listen."

A woman was singing somewhere, a song in a language Lee had never heard before. She was singing her heart out, drowning in waves of orchestration. It wasn't rock'n'roll, yet it pulled at Lee's heart all the same.

Light shone from an open door on the far side of the courtyard.

That was where the music came from.

The room beyond the door was high-ceilinged, wood-panelled. Thick carpets lapped the floor, muffled Lee's foot-steps. The light came from a big lamp behind a couch where Hawk lay, propped by cushions as he sipped smoke from a water pipe. The room smelt of a voluptuous combination of sweet hash smoke and crème de menthe.

"Come in, Lee," Hawk said. He seemed not at all sur-prised, and not at all drugged. "Sit down. I'm pleased to see you."

He made a languid gesture. Narrow cones of light dropped from high above, spotlighting two stools. The music faded to a whisper.

Lee said boldly, "I came to get the money I was owed."

"Oh, all in good time," Hawk said.

"My friend and I, we're setting off on a journey."

"I know. That's why I asked you to sit, because I want to talk to you about it. That was quite a show you put on."

"Oh. You know about that."

"Every commercial channel was showing looped tapes of it before they were pulled off the air by The Little Bird's vigilantes." Hawk laughed. "Wei Lee, I shall tell you why the government troops didn't fight back after your . . . perform-ance. They were all wired up, and The Little Bird pulled their plugs. He hit the command center. Only the officers were left. How does it feel, to have started a revolution?"

"Perhaps I've ended one."

"Perhaps . . . but The Little Bird is neither a Sky Roader nor a conservationist. No, he's an isolationist: Mars for the Martians. He has no power base amongst the Ten Thousand Years, only popular support, and soon enough he'll be de-stroyed by the conchies, just as they destroyed the Sky Road-ers. You know, I met The Little Bird many years ago. His eidolon, of course, not him personally, but the eidolon was real enough, not those projections favored by the rest of the Ten Thousand Years. A great shambling thing, steel and chrome and black rubber roughly in the shape of a man's skeleton, with The Little Bird's face bobbing in a television set up where its head should be. They say the eidolon has ripped apart a hundred or more people, enemies of The Little Bird and those servants who failed him. He is a first-generation Martian, the last. They say his body is a garden of cancers, shrivelled like a bad apple, the result of radiation exposure from the Long Crossing. But you are still standing. Please sit. You are my guests, after all. I'll be thought a bad host."

Lee sat, but Chen Yao stood behind him. Her head was exactly level with his.

Hawk looked at her. "I don't know your young friend. From a fishing family, by those clothes."

Lee started to explain, but Hawk held up a hand. "I know about the wretches that fisherfolk call avatars of the god-head, when it's nothing but a rash of viruses caught from their fishy helpmates. Viruses that babble away inside them mindlessly. It is not true insight."

Chen Yao said with contempt, "You only think you know."

"Child, I've forgotten more than you will ever learn. Wei Lee, the city is a place full of traps for the unwary. But at least you seem to have lost Redd. A good herder, but an untrustworthy man."

Lee said humbly, "I owe him my life."

It seemed he owed his life to many people. To Great-grandfather Wei and to Guoquiang, and to Miriam, and the fin, and little Chen Yao. When had it ever been his?

Hawk laughed. "The Yankees don't understand face debts, Wei Lee. Do you know the music I was listening to when you came in?"

Lee confessed that he didn't.

"It was written by an Italian, a kind of proto-Yankee. An addiction of mine, Capitalist Western opera. It is even older than your King of the Cats and his rock'n'roll. One of my trail bosses introduced it to me when I was still as wet behind the ears as you—in the old days cowboys sang arias to the yaks, not Hank Williams. This particular opera was written by the perfect master of the form, Giacomo Puccini. It tells of the cruelty of a princess of the Imperial city of Old

Beijing, who will marry any man of royal blood who can answer three riddles set by her. But although she has had many suitors, all have failed and have been beheaded, for the Princess believes that to take the life of any man who desires her is to avenge the dishonor suffered by an ancestress ravished and killed by barbarous Tartars centuries before. But it is a prince of the Tartars who solves the riddles and who convinces her, through love, to end her revenge. A silly little tale, eh, Wei Lee, although of course it is beautifully told. It says almost nothing about the human condition, but volumes about Yankee misunderstanding of the Han."

"Does it tell you anything about how we misunderstand the Yankees?"

"They are a violent, romantic people. They have no concept of history, yet seek personal eternity in all they do. That is why they failed so gloriously to conquer our world, for they never can unite, never can quench their reckless individuality."

"And yet we failed, too."

"Everything fails. Against the great cycle of the universe, even the fundamental units of matter fail. All herders know that Mars is dying. Year after year, the ranges shrink, the herds grow smaller. I'm an old man, Wei Lee. I've seen it myself. I know that we have had our season."

"The *ku li* would say that it is only spring, perhaps. The dry season before the rains of summer."

"The *ku li* are a paper tiger, a convenient illusion which provides an excuse to subject the population to the rigours and restrictions of a permanent war economy. There is no revolution, except in the minds of a few misguided Martians. We herders live half the year on the high ranges, and yet we see none of the fabled army of the *ku li*. The anarchists drop subversive literature, but only we profit."

Chen Yao said, "Ask him how he profits, Wei Lee."

Hawk's smile was like a small animal awakening within his neatly combed, silky white beard. He said, "I am many things, Wei Lee. I am Hawk, herd master. And I am also

Yamyang Norbu, a citizen and householder who must support a wife and eight children and fifteen grandchildren, not to mention platoons of lazy in-laws and *their* relatives. Many people are more than one thing, or even two. It is the way of people. You of all people must know this."

"He hides something from you," Chen Yao said.

"The wharfs breed liars faster than they breed rats," Hawk said sharply. "Be quiet, little girl."

One of Lee's virus gifts was the ability to see in the far red end of the spectrum. It happened unconsciously. He saw Hawk's face bleed into a green mask, with bright patches pulsing on cheeks and forehead. Then he realised that Chen Yao was holding his hand. She said, "Blood always betrays."

There was a sound outside. Lee's hearing suddenly selectively intensified. It filtered noise in Hawk's study, the breathing of the three people, their heartbeats. Hawk said something but Lee didn't hear it. He was listening to the electric purr of a motor, voices, the rattle as the gate swung open to admit two people.

Something seized Lee from inside. He whirled and smashed a glass-fronted cabinet with his elbow, with finger and thumb plucked a long spike from the shards. He knocked Hawk back as the old man started to rise, pinned his arms and shoved the makeshift glass dagger into the folds of skin under his white beard. Lee's hearing was back to normal. Hawk started to speak, and Lee let the glass slice his throat a little, so blood ran into his raw silk undershirt.

"Don't kill him, Miriam," Chen Yao said.

Lee knew what possessed him, then. Chen Yao had woken her. She was all around him, yet at no point did she touch him. She was there, but he couldn't speak to her.

Chen Yao closed the door and turned, quite self-possessed. She said, "Who did you sell us to, old man?"

Lee eased the knife-edged glass from Hawk's throat. He had cut his own palm slightly. His blood mingled with Hawk's and ran down his arm inside his shirtsleeve.

"I apologize, Wei Lee," Hawk said, "but business is business. When I first saw you, I thought you might be important, which is why I invited you here. When I saw you on television, I knew how important you were. Not just some waif possessed by fragments, but something else . . . "

Lee said into Hawk's ear, "You always meant to sell me, but you couldn't do it with Redd around. You got rid of him, and waited for me to come to you."

Chen Yao said, "Tell us how to leave safely, old man."

Hawk said calmly, "You could try the servants' quarters. Through the panelled door behind me, down the corridor to the end. There is no one in the house but me; I sent everyone to the mountains at the turn of the year, when the fighting in the city began. You are very quick, Lee, but if I chose to fight I do not think you could best me."

"Then I am glad you choose not to fight," Lee said. He released the pressure on Hawk's arms and dropped the glass dagger.

At that moment the door behind Chen Yao burst open.

Two people sprang into the room. Both were armed with stubby laser rifles. Both were dressed in shiny black one-piece impact suits. One was the Colonel who had sent Lee out into the storm with Miriam, back at the Bitter Waters *danwei*. The other, impossibly, was Miriam herself.

Forty-three

A sleek car waited outside the gate of Hawk's house, its tear-drop body shaped from a single sheet of polarized glass. From the outside, it was a dense reflective black; from the inside, perfectly transparent. As the car sped to the station, scattering bicyclists and weaving around slow-moving trams, its half-dozen swivel chairs seemed to float above the rushing roadway with no visible means of support.

The Colonel and the woman who looked exactly like Miriam Makepeace Mbele sat opposite Chen Yao and Wei Lee with their laser rifles not exactly pointed at them but with attitudes that suggested that it was just as well they didn't have to be.

"She's not really Miriam," Chen Yao whispered.

"I know," Lee whispered back.

"Quiet," the Colonel said.

It was the first thing he had said since ordering the vehicle to move off. The woman hadn't spoken a word so far. Her shiny black suit was moulded to her slim body with embarrassing closeness. Her eyes were hidden behind tinted glasses that every so often filmed over: video-shades. Her face was Miriam's, and like Miriam her hair was cut close to her shapely skull, but her skin was not as richly black as Miriam's, more the color of a tea brick. An old, crescent-shaped scar seamed her left temple. Lee remembered that Miriam had told him that she had many sisters, all drawn from the same gene line, mercenaries who were bought and sold before birth, who took the name of their owners.

He said to the Colonel, amazed that he could keep his voice level, "What is your friend's name?"

"The resemblance is astonishing, isn't it? She's Mary Makepeace Doe. A freelance. Please, Mr Wei, no more questions. I don't have the authority to answer them."

"Who does? My great-grandfather?"

The Colonel, Great-grandfather Wei's cat's-paw, shrugged. He looked embarrassed.

Lee couldn't stop himself. He said, "Him or some other Ten Thousand Years. I know you killed my parents, you bastard. I don't even know your name."

"I have worked for your great-grandfather for a long time," the Colonel said calmly.

Anger burned through Lee's blood. Not because the Colonel had admitted guilt by not denying Lee's accusation, but because it didn't seem to matter to him.

Mary Makepeace Doe hardly seemed to move, but suddenly her rifle was pointed at Lee's left eye. He jerked back and the rifle followed, although the mercenary wasn't even looking at him.

The Colonel said, "I don't know anything about your parents, Wei Lee. I've done many things for your great-grandfather."

"You've killed for him."

"You are still angry at me for what happened last time we met. I understand. But look at it this way: if I hadn't . . . helped you, you wouldn't be where you are now."

"Oh. Then I must thank you for making me a refugee as well as an orphan."

The Colonel said in a quiet voice, "You are an important person, Wei Lee. What you carry is worth a great deal . . . tell me, have you been troubled with strange dreams lately?"

"Only about your death."

The Colonel smiled. "You don't have to lie to me, Miriam. Or perhaps it has not yet taken properly. No matter. Soon it will all be clear to you."

Lee looked away, although it was obvious that they knew

what had happened to him. After all, he had more or less told Hawk the whole story, in innocence.

The car weaved through dense traffic. Suddenly, Lee saw the high roof of the train station, curved like a white hill. The car slowed, nosing through a crowd packed around a barrier of tanglewire loops stretched across the road.

The people were trying to flee the city. They carried parcels bundled in sheets, televisions, caged chickens, baskets of vegetables or fruit, bicycles, small industrial motors, bubblepacks of biochips, umbrellas, even furniture. Four men supported a double bed, one at each corner. Militia were letting people through one by one or pushing them aside, seemingly at random. The air was dense with noise that struck through the car's one-way glass: women screaming at their children; children wailing with fright; men shouting at militia and militia shouting right back, shoving rifles in faces, slapping backs to push some through, chests to push others back. An old woman pleaded with a boy soldier with an assault rifle, crying and yelling and clinging to his arm, not even letting go when he struck her in the face.

The car slid to a halt in the middle of the crowd and its hatch snapped back: the noise doubled, trebled. The stink of sweat and fear was intense. Mary Makepeace Doe seized Lee's elbow with paralyzing force; he had to follow her through the hatch or lose his arm. He glanced back and saw the Colonel trying to lift Chen Yao out, saw the little girl kick him in the crotch.

And then Mary Makepeace Doe tugged and whirled Lee around, shoved him through the crowd to the gate, sweeping her stubby rifle back and forth to clear the way. The militia waved them through with hardly a glance, and then they were on the concourse.

It was scarcely less crowded or noisy than the road outside. Mary Makepeace Doe grabbed a handful of Lee's hair, turned his head and said in his ear, "You wouldn't believe how much it cost to guarantee safe passage out of the city. Don't even *think* about trying to escape," and pushed him towards one of the trains before he could say anything.

People were climbing into dusty carriages through windows as well as doors, climbing up on to the roofs. Pedlars were hawking food, and passengers' hands reached starfishwise through windows to exchange notes for dumplings or glutinous rice cakes. The pedlars' cries sang out above the crowd's roar; beneath it was the stentorian exhalations of the huge black fission-powered steam locomotives. Their exhaust plumes rose straight up into the girdered space of the high roof like so many pillars.

Mary Makepeace Doe shouldered her way between two pedlars, used the stock of her rifle to dislodge a man who was using the door rail to climb to the roof, and dragged Lee up into the carriage. The corridor was packed with people squatting on the floor amongst their possessions and the compartments were filled with smug bourgeois. The mercenary picked a compartment at random, pulled back the concertina plastic partition, and told the startled bourgeois family inside to move on, she was commandeering the compartment.

Her voice: that was just like Miriam's. But her Common Language was flawless.

Lee wondered what it must have looked like to the bourgeois, this tall muscular video-shaded woman in skin-tight black dragging her bloody-handed captive. But they were responding to her tone of command, were all getting up, pulling their possessions together. Only one started to protest, a plump smooth-skinned man in an expensive jacket with a dozen little machines hanging from loops. The mercenary put her rifle in the man's face and told him it was a matter of security. He backed away with an amazingly broad smile and disappeared into the goggle-eyed peasants crowded outside.

Lee sat on a dusty plush seat. The mercenary pulled the door shut and slammed down the blinds against onlookers, then leaned at the window and shouted to the pedlars through the sliding strip at its top, throwing a handful of notes in exchange for beakers of tea and wafers of crispy fried bean paste.

"Eat," she said to Lee, like Buddha to the grasshopper. Lee sipped hot tea, munched on the wafers. His throat was very dry. The mercenary told him that if he co-operated, everything would be fine, something Lee hardly believed for a moment.

He finished his tea, licked grease from his fingers. The fear that any moment he would be killed had not abated, but he was getting used to it. Every sense sang to him with incredible clarity: he was aware of the nap of the plush seats under his thighs, sweat on his skin under the denim shirt and heavy chuba, dust motes swimming in the light that fell through the smeared window, the electric musk of the mercenary.

She watched him watching her, her gaze made enigmatic by the purple-gold lenses of her video-shades. Every now and then they filmed over as she accessed or received a transmission. She said abruptly, "She's still alive. After the transfer."

"I don't think she calls it life."

"Name?"

"Miriam. Miriam Makepeace Mbele. Did you know her?"

"I don't think so. The family, of course. The Nexus is one of the last holdouts, but they'll fall. They'll fall. She was on the wrong side."

"She looked just like you."

"Of course. In a guerrilla war, it is always better if the insurgents use the same weapons as the government they're fighting. Anything else creates logistical problems. The Nexus was allowed to acquire my genome centuries ago— we can always predict when they'll try and use it, and how it will behave. Besides, I understand that all off-worlders look the same to the Han."

"I wouldn't know. I've only ever met two off-worlders. You, and Miriam. You look different from Yankees." For some reason he thought of Redd.

"The gene line was originally Caucasian. But it has been . . . somewhat adapted."

Lee remembered Miriam in the dream. Pale-faced, straw-haired, in crudely daubed clothes. "Miriam took the name of the family who owned her. But you are a free agent?"

Saying Miriam's name gave him a pang of hope, as if it was a charm to ward off death.

"She was a fool to declare her allegiance. As for me, you will find out if you are meant to find out."

"You are concerned about secrecy, yet you behave in such a way that all the station must know what happened here."

"That's the point. You think only I and that army fool work together to bring you here?"

"Someone chased me, last night."

The mercenary shrugged. "Perhaps he was one of ours, perhaps not. What happened to him?"

"He disappeared. I think he drowned."

Again, the mercenary shrugged.

A silence fell. Lee tried to evoke Miriam, but she was out of reach. He needed Chen Yao, who could speak directly with virus-encoded personalities.

The train shuddered and jerked and started to move forward, and at the same moment a dumpy woman in a gray quilted jacket pulled back the door. She had a clipboard under her arm, and a peaked cap pushed back on her head. She said, "Pardon me, citizens, but do you have reservations for this compartment? There has been a complaint."

Lee saw his chance. He jumped to his feet and bowed and quickly said he was very sorry, he had made a mistake. The mercenary lunged for him and he bolted into the press in the corridor, stumbling over packages and baskets and sprawling people. The train was shuddering and lurching as it picked up speed over buckled tracks. Lee risked a glance over his shoulder and saw the mercenary halfway out the compartment, trying to shake off the guard who was doggedly clinging to one of her arms.

Lee lurched through a knot of people, gained the angle of the door. Passengers clinging to grab rails outside the carriage goggled at him as he leaned out into gritty wind. The locomotive's whistle shrieked far along the train's smooth snake. It was coming up to the swampy border of the city's reclaimed land. Shacks crumbling in abandoned fields, a wrecked melt-water plant standing in a wide basin of dried mud, low tangles of black trees and ochre stretches of bare, rocky ground.

Shouts behind him, and the mercenary's hoarse voice raised above them.

Lee made a desperate calculation, and jumped.

Hands reached to grab him: passengers trying to save him from himself. The thunder of the train filling his ears, Lee fell through air and hit the gritty embankment. He rolled and tumbled, breath knocked out of him, and fetched up in a tangle of briars. It seemed to take a long time to ease himself out of the clutches of the thorny canes. The train had disappeared, but at the top of the embankment the rail still sang with its passing.

Lee spat a mouthful of grit. The right side of his body was scraped and raw under torn cloth, and he had banged his left knee badly. But he was free, free to choose to walk into the city or head into the desert. It wasn't much of a choice, but he knew where he had to go.

He limped up the steep slope of sliding dry stones to the top of the embankment. Parched marshlands stretched on either side under a haze in the cold afternoon. Beyond was the prospect of dry red plains.

"Look all you want," someone said behind him.

Lee almost jumped out of his skin, then something grabbed him from inside and he whirled in a fighter's crouch. The mercenary's rifle was right in his face.

She said, "I'd love you to try it on. But I have orders." Her smile was an edge of steel under her video-shades. There were scuffs on the knees of her tight leather outfit, but otherwise she was quite unruffled. She must have jumped out of the train at almost the same moment as Lee, and circled back to ambush him.

Lee put his hands together before his chest and bowed in bitter submission. And Mary Makepeace Doe hit him across the head with the stock of her weapon.

Forty-four

Wei Lee and the mercenary walked the line atop the embankment for most of the chill equatorial afternoon. Rather, Lee limped, the side of his head swollen with hot pain. His quiff, matted with dust, kept falling across his eyes. The embankment dwindled away in front of him, crossing the marshes towards the beginning of a cratered plain at the horizon.

Crisp bright sunlight and bone-dry air sucked moisture from him as he limped along. After a couple of hours, he would have killed to roll down the embankment's stony slope into one of the marsh's scummy seeps, more muddy sand than water but wet at least, damp, dank, *moist.* Last night he had nearly drowned, and now he was dying of thirst. It was as if a lifetime's worth of the world's torments had been compressed into a few hours. He couldn't even tune into the King's broadcast; that was still being jammed.

The mercenary wouldn't allow him to slow his pace. Apparently the plan had been for the train to slow to a crawl so that she and Lee could step off, but Lee had pre-empted that by a dozen kilometers. They had a lot of distance to make up. The only times they left the embankment were when the rails sang warning of a passing train, and Mary Makepeace Doe didn't let Lee stray from her side. It happened three times, and after the last she said, "There'll be no more."

Lee asked how she knew.

"Because that's the agreement with The Little Bird. Our people out in exchange for a ceasefire."

"So you lost."

"A temporary setback. It's not important. The Little Bird thinks that he can outsmart the conservationists, but he'll pay the price for it. Move faster, damn you!"

If she felt the effects of sun and dry air she showed no sign of it, except that she had smeared a translucent cream on her lips. When they finally reached the rendezvous, she looked as strong and implacable as ever.

A caravan, a fat segmented silver tube like an industrial-designed insect grub, was parked at the bottom of the embankment, near the edge of the sour marshes. The radiator fins of its power plant bled a shimmer of heat into the still afternoon air. Around it, scrubby thorn bushes threw spidery black shapes amongst craggy boulders that glowed like heated iron in the afternoon sunlight.

"Go on down," the mercenary said, and prodded Lee in the small of his back, hard enough to hurt.

Lee's injured knee unhinged halfway down the embankment. He slithered all the way down on his backside, once again ending up in a tangle of thorny canes. Obviously, the bushes had been designed to break the fall of travellers and then suck their blood. It was almost good to relax in their piercing grip.

A shadow eclipsed the hard pink sky and its feathering of high clouds. Mary Makepeace Doe dragged Lee to his feet, and the pain of losing gobbets of flesh to clutching thorns brought him awake.

He was able to stumble ahead of the mercenary towards the segmented silvery caravan, but, just as he reached its shadow, his feet twisted under him and the side of the world slammed into him with every unforgiving gram of its mass.

Forty-five

Lee was in a humming space of bright metal and white light. A translucent sac taped to his elbow was slowly wrinkling as it pumped saline into a vein. A soaked sponge was put to his cracked lips and he greedily sucked moisture from it. Two attendants, small neat sharp-featured men who might have been brothers, might have been any age from ten to twenty, stripped off his dusty clothes, stuck needles in his joints to counter pain, bandaged his raw skin. Then they plucked off the by-now empty saline sac and helped him into soft clean trousers of unbleached linen, a raw silk shirt. They even greased his hair back into an approximation of its original quiff.

As they worked, the attendants talked to each other in a language Lee had never heard before. They used gestures and prods to make him understand what they wanted of him, just as one would treat a docile but stupid animal.

They pushed and prodded him to his feet and tugged him through a low narrow hatch into an airy room filled with color.

The room was a tent, pitched up against the curved silvery side of the caravan. Five people turned to look at him as he came through. There was the mercenary, her leathers still dusty, a man dressed in white just like Lee, a very young boy. But Lee hardly noticed them, because he saw that Chen Yao was there, too.

She sat unsmiling in a big square chair in a corner of the

tented space, her feet kicking above the carpets that lapped the ground. The Colonel stood behind the chair, a hand resting on its back just above Chen Yao's head. Neat and dapper in his uniform, he inclined his head in formal acknowledgement of Lee's stare. Lee willed him to die right then and there, but psychic powers were not part of the viruses' gifts.

Someone stepped in front of Lee. It was the man in white. He was very tall and thin, and his skin was so pale he might have been bloodless. He polished a red apple on his silk shirt, bit into it with relish. Chewing, he said, "So glad you're here at last, Wei Lee. And Miriam too, if you are listening." He took another bite of the apple. "She tried to kill me once, you know. That's war. Or the kind of war we're fighting. You never know who's going to turn up, and where."

Lee pointed at Mary Makepeace Doe, who leaned against the silver side of the caravan and said, "Are you sure it wasn't her?"

"This is a very strange war, Wei Lee. Only a few people are directly involved, and so each of their moves are magnified. I wave my hand . . . " the half eaten apple had vanished somehow: Lee blinked, forced himself to pay attention " . . . and thousands die. Or millions. You wield the same power, although perhaps you are only just realizing that."

Lee remembered the riots. And before that, the monks of the lost lamasery.

"You see," the man said with a smile, "you do understand. Like it or not, you are one of the players now. So is everyone in this tent, and perhaps a score more people in the rest of the Solar System. I know them all, and I have been playing the game a long time.

"So," he said, suddenly bright, "here we are. Once upon a time your friend Miriam tried to kill me. She wasn't a player, then. But her failure pushed her into a position where she had to become one, or die. And now she has fallen inside you, and the same thing has happened to you. Interesting, don't you think? There's a pattern."

The little boy spoke up in a piping treble. "He will not be a player much longer, if he ever was one."

Lee hadn't taken much notice of the boy before, but now he saw that a thick braided cable was looped over his arm. It ran up into the inverted bowl of his black hair, ran back into a corner of the tent curtained with filmy white. It was just possible to make out a high double bed flanked by monitoring equipment back there, a shadowy glimpse that triggered vague uneasy memories in Lee, a troubling, deep unease he couldn't quite define. And the boy reminded him of someone, too. The lineaments of a familiar face lay under the plump cheeks, the cupid bow mouth, the wide flat nose.

The boy said, "We have been neglecting our introductions, Wei Lee, although I think you are beginning to suspect who I am. The Colonel you already know, and of course you have just enjoyed a stroll through the countryside with Mary Makepeace Doe."

The mercenary looked up, a scowl twisting her mouth under the video-shades. The boy bowed to her, and Lee glimpsed the junction at the base of his skull where the cable broke into filaments that fanned out and burrowed under his scalp like tree roots clutching a boulder.

"We forgive you," the boy said to the mercenary, "because you are necessary to us."

The man in white said, "She is a player, too. Her name of course is not really Doe, but Gaia. Mary Makepeace Gaia. The kind of people she was working with made it necessary that she work under cover."

The boy piped up, cross at having been interrupted, "I must introduce you to the most important person last of all. The head of the conservationist missionary expedition from Gaia. Doctor Lovelace Damon."

The man in white bowed from the waist. "Damon Lovelace, in the fashion of Gaia."

The boy reddened. His black almond-shaped eyes glistened and his mouth worked as if he was about to burst into tears, but then his face froze and he stiffly bowed an apology.

"Control will come as the interface knits up," Dr. Damon Lovelace said. "Besides, there's nothing to apologize for. Names aren't important to us. We are one."

Suddenly Lee knew who the boy was, and what was lying in the bed behind the gauzy curtain. He had seen the equipment-laden double bed once before. He had been so very young, and near to collapse from exhaustion, still suffering from smoke inhalation and flash-burns from his parents' assassination. He remembered being marched into a clean white room, and shown for the first and last time the reality of his great-grandfather.

A high, wide bed, sheets like snow under bright lights. Two bodies in it, separated by a bolster. Both male. One young and pinkly hairless, its eyes bandaged, tubes running into its nose, into a ligature in its throat. The other little more than a skeleton clad in leathery skin, head hidden by a complicated helmet, withered arms drawn up on the ladder of ribs of the chest, hands gloved in rigid black polymer. Wires ran back from helmet and hands and tangled into cables that went into the wall behind the bed.

Two bodies, linked by transparent tubes through which rich red blood pulsed: one the mummified near-corpse of Lee's great-grandfather; the other the decerebrated Yankee which kept his ancient body alive.

The little boy watched Lee's expression change. He smirked, twisted one foot against the other. His face was a young, plump version of Great-grandfather Wei's eidolon.

"That's right, son," he said. He was shining with proud enthusiasm. "At last I will be free of the dead weight of my body. I'll be free to move in the world again. I am being transferred piece by piece into the brain of this living eidolon, which was grown from a single cell taken from the epithelial lining of my bowel. I will live for ever, not merely for ten thousand years!"

And he skipped a gleeful little dance, right there on the luxurious carpet. The cable which linked him to his ancient body swung in long arcs behind him.

Lee thought that the eidolon had been a true representation of his great-grandfather after all. A picture, out of time. He had puzzled over it every time he had visited the Great House, and now he knew, and it didn't matter.

Dr. Damon Lovelace watched indulgently, for all the worlds like a proud parent. Which he was, in a way. He told Lee that it was Gaia (which was what conchies called both the Earth and the Earth's Consensus) which had made this possible. The transference of mind into a new body was routine: it was how people were born, on Gaia. He himself had been born that way.

"Although of course there was the added complication of reading my genome from storage into a quickened artificial ovum. It is whole and true transference, not at all like what happened between you and Miriam, Wei Lee. We are very far ahead of the anarchists' technology, on Gaia."

The little boy laughed. "Except for fullerene virus design . . . unfortunately for you, my dear son. You see, Miriam's infection will not save you. Quite the reverse. We cannot study it without destroying you."

Lee held out an arm. "Just take my blood." It was what he had been travelling towards the capital to offer, the discharge of his life's debt. His nerves sang with expectation. "Please," he said, when no one moved.

"If only it was that simple," Dr. Damon Lovelace said. "Only the simpler kinds of viruses live in your blood, Wei Lee. We know all about those. Clades of the common kinds of self-replicating sub-microscopic machines, constructed of varieties of metal-doped carbon-lattice spheres, which routinely perform the housekeeping tasks which increase lifespan. Cancer stalkers, plaque busters and the like. But the special viruses that Miriam Makepeace Mbele carried have woven themselves into your nervous system. Think of the weave of this carpet. You could tease out the individual threads, but you would destroy the patterns they make. So with the viruses that have rebuilt your nervous system from the inside. To retrieve them we must destroy the pattern."

Lee realized then that they only knew a little about Miriam's viruses. They did not know, for instance, that the infection could be transferred by something as simple as a kiss.

"We must kill you, my son," the little boy piped up, grinning mischievously.

Boy-thing, Lee thought, his skin crawling.

"And of course we will likewise dissect your girlfriend," Dr. Damon Lovelace said, smiling cheerfully. "She has also been infected with viruses that built themselves into her nervous system. It makes her a translator, able to access virus systems at all levels. An interesting coincidence, don't you think, Wei Lee? That the viral machinery which allows fishermen to talk to augmented dolphins also allows communication with the clades of viral machines used by the anarchists. I have the greatest respect for the achievements of your great scientist, Cho Jinfeng."

"Silly little man," Chen Yao said. She jumped down from the couch, dodging the Colonel's restraining hand. "Yes, silly and foolish and puny and vain. You see only what you wish to see, and so you are blind."

"Now just be quiet!" the Colonel said, trying to catch hold of the little girl.

"Oh no," Damon Lovelace said. "Let her speak. It's traditional, after all. And besides, we may learn something. Afterwards, we will offer her a cigarette."

"I'll speak because I want to," Chen Yao said. She was very calm, Lee saw, very calm and very self-possessed. Her aspect was upon her. She pressed her hands in front of her, fingertip to fingertip, and bowed to the boy-thing.

"I respect you for your age, great-grandfather," she said. She spoke with deliberation and icy calm. Each word was a stone, flung with force. "Age and experience you have in abundance, and those I respect. But I cannot respect you for your wisdom. You and your kind have sold our world for your own profit, and that cannot be forgiven. And it will not be forgiven. You have lived so long that you want nothing more than to live for ever. You grasp at life with the unforgiving greed of a parasite, not caring that your very existence condemns millions to death. I tell you this: your act of piracy will not be allowed to be completed."

She bowed again.

And then she stepped forward and spat in the boy-thing's face.

The boy-thing flushed with anger. He hissed like a snake and tried to kick and punch Chen Yao, but she skipped out of reach and when he charged blindly after her he was brought up short by his cable and fell on his back. He wailed and sputtered with outrage, kicking his legs in the air and screaming that she'd die, she'd die right now, for what she'd done.

"Kill the little bitch! Mary Makepeace Gaia! I order you! I order you to kill her! Take her out, Colonel! Shoot her! Blow her fucking brains out!"

Tears ran in snail tracks from the corners of his eyes to his ears, and snot and spit bubbled from nostrils and mouth.

Dr. Damon Lovelace stooped and picked him up, hugged him and said tenderly, "I know it's hard. Young glands on a hair trigger, the fret of a new nervous system, all that. But you'll learn control. We all have to learn to control our unruly flesh when born again to the wheel, and so will you. Hush, now. Hush. She'll die soon enough, and her death will be far far worse than a bullet in the head."

The boy-thing sniffed deeply, hiccuped. "I want to watch," he said. "And then I want to go home. I *hate* the wilderness. I've brought you the anarchist's Trojan Horse, and now you must bring me The Little Bird. I want to have his own eidolon flay his rotten cancerous body centimeter by centimeter. That's what we *agreed*." He glared over Lovelace's shoulder at Lee. "And you, you never were any son of mine. Your parents were employees, not blood relations. You never were anything but a pawn, Wei Lee, and you have advanced to your final square."

"How I hate cliché," Chen Yao said. She was still wearing her aspect. "Always it blurs meaning. But to extend it for a moment, you forget pawns can move diagonally if they take something. Wei Lee has moved aslant you all, and carries the seeds of greatness inside him. He has started a revolution. He has far to go. And his next move will destroy you."

Dr. Damon Lovelace put down the boy-thing. "He triggered an inevitable rebellion, little girl. He upset our plans, but not by much, for we had always planned to neutralize

The Little Bird. But now people kill each other, and that is very regrettable, very immature. We have no way to read dead brains, and so with every minute of rebellion the data base of potential overseers grows smaller."

"As on the Earth, so in Heaven," Chen Yao said. "But I don't think so."

The Colonel had been holding himself quiet and still all through this. Now he could no longer hold in his outrage. He said, "Sir! I am ready to deal with this brat on your orders."

"In good time," Dr. Damon Lovelace said. "She's harmless, after all. Harmless, and sadly out of date. Metaphors *are* useful, Chen Yao. Good metaphors shine a light through complex ideas, and simplify their shape."

Chen Yao said disdainfully, "I'd rather things shone with their own light."

Lee could no longer hold in his own outburst. He was gripped by the vertigo of erased history. He felt that he was standing at the edge of a pit, where a moment ago there had been firm ground. The pit was the gap in what he thought he had known, his own story erased by a petulant outburst.

He said to the boy-thing, "Who was my father if he was not the first-born child of your own son! Who was my mother!"

What he meant was, who am I?

The boy-thing shrugged. He was calm again. "Loyal employees at the middle level. Nothing more. You were born as bait to hook bigger fish, with the fiction that I was a kind of rebel, out of sympathy with my fellows. An old trick, but successful even so. But do not think yourself special, Wei Lee. There are others like you. You just happen to be the bait which was swallowed at the right time."

"Then I don't owe you anything! I don't owe you anything at all!" Lee could have danced on the carpet with joy. Only Chen Yao's serious gaze stopped him.

The boy-thing draped his cable over his arm with an imperious gesture. "Your life is mine. After all, you have nothing else to give me."

Chen Yao said, "You cannot talk to them, Lee. They do not hear, nor do they think. Their heads are full of straw. It is time for us to go."

Dr. Damon Lovelace said, "I don't think so, little lady. We have not begun with you. Your death will be a beginning, but only that."

Chen Yao said, "You're as stupid as the old man. What time do you come from, to be born in this time and pretend to rule us? Keep Earth and the wilderness you've made of it, if you want. We'll take the rest of the universe."

"Ah," Dr. Damon Lovelace said. "The hubris of the young. To go boldly where no man has gone before—I remember that tag from my first incarnation. But you must forgive these memories. Nostalgia is a luxury afforded only by the incurably romantic. Silly little girl, the universe isn't a blank map for your kind to scribble over. It is its own thing, and it is no place for intelligence. That lies inward, not outward. Your allies are the tattered remnants of the old order, not the harbingers of a New Age. Gaia is that Age, and we are its guardians. You're history. And you too, Wei Lee. A pity, because I understand you were a biologist. I wish we had time to talk, but there you are."

He clapped his hands, twice.

The twin attendants appeared at the tent's entrance. Lee's heart raced in sudden anticipation.

But before Dr. Damon Lovelace could give his order, the attendants were knocked aside by a soldier covered in red dust. She fell to her knees on the carpeted ground and bowed to the boy-thing, to Dr. Damon Lovelace. She was shaking with fear or exhaustion, her holster was empty, and there was a bloody tear across the shoulders of her black uniform.

"Speak," the boy-thing said in as nastily petulant a tone as Lee had ever heard.

The soldier raised the mirrored visor of her helmet. She was very young, Lee saw. She said, "A thousand pardons, ancestor. A thousand pardons, Master. A terrible thing . . . "

Dr. Damon Lovelace grasped the soldier's neck, pulled her

up without any visible effort. Her feet kicked out, the toes of her cleated boots barely brushing the carpet.

"In one word," Lovelace said.

"A-ambush!"

Dr. Damon Lovelace threw the soldier against the side of the caravan. Her helmet rang like a bell and she fell down beside Mary Makepeace Gaia.

The mercenary raised an eyebrow, and then she was gone.

"It won't do any good," Chen Yao said. "You hide out here because you do not dare face the mobs in the city, and so you deliver yourselves into our hands. Your perimeter defenses are no longer active. They haven't been since I was walked through them. Viruses subverted the machinery, and half a dozen desert fighters captured your troops. That one was allowed to escape, ahead of the storm."

The mercenary was back, as suddenly as she had left. "It's true," she said calmly. "The ring alarms have not been triggered and the motion sensors appear to be functioning, but no one answers at any of the guard posts."

Dr. Damon Lovelace shrugged. "We'll fall back and regroup. Disable the prisoners."

"Sir?" the Colonel said.

"Break their spines. Between the third and fourth cervical vertebrae will do the trick. We'll process them later. Do I have to tell you everything?"

Chen Yao did something astonishing: a back flip that sent her flying feet first into the boy-thing. He went down with a startled yelp and she pulled him to his feet. Her hand was at his throat, and there was a metal spike in her hand.

The Colonel and the mercenary both drew their pistols, but Chen Yao pulled the boy-thing backwards step by step until they were up against the high double bed. Gauzy curtains billowed around them.

Chen Yao shouted shrilly, "I'll cut his carotid arteries! Brain death in two minutes!"

The mercenary let the hand holding her pistol fall to her side. The Colonel looked at Dr. Damon Lovelace.

The boy-thing squirmed, then squealed when Chen Yao

nicked the soft skin of his throat. Bright red blood blossomed at the neck of his tunic. The boy-thing shrieked in fear.

And there was another sound, a soft thrashing from the curtained bed behind Chen Yao and her prisoner.

Dr. Damon Lovelace said, "You hold the wrong body, foolish girl."

Chen Yao said, "He is in neither one place nor the other. Like those in the process of dying into your famous new world, he still needs his old body. Another mistake, to think of me as a little girl. I'm not. I'm a god. Over here, Wei Lee. They won't hurt you."

Lee stepped past the Colonel, and Chen Yao's free hand grasped his. Instantly, everything seemed to slow around him. His sight was overlaid with gridded symbols, and he felt a sudden rush of dizzy strength, as if he'd been plunged head first into a bubble of pure oxygen. Chen Yao had switched on the modifications woven in his nervous system, all at once.

And now he could hear a distant rumble, a long way beyond the encampment, but growing louder at a steady rate.

Dr. Damon Lovelace's voice was a bass drawl. "Give it up and I promise a quick death. You must know that you cannot run. You have the wrong hostage for that."

"I don't need to run. But you do. Ask your soldier."

Mary Makepeace Gaia held out her hand, let her pistol fall to the carpet. Then she whirled on the slumped soldier, did something that made the woman scream.

"Speak," the mercenary said softly. To Lee it was like thunder.

"We, we must run. There's a stampede on the way. Yaks! Thousands and thousands . . . "

The Colonel's attention wavered, and Lee stepped up and plucked the man's pistol from his hand as easily as taking a toy from a sleeping child.

Mary Makepeace Gaia dived to the floor and rolled, so quickly she would have been a blur in normal time. She rolled again, came up behind the partial cover of a flowering yucca in a big earthenware pot. She had her pistol in her hand.

Lee moved too, without thinking. He spun the Colonel round just as the mercenary fired. The Colonel yelled (a basso profundo rumbling) and his hand slowly moved to clasp his wounded arm. The sleeve of his tunic was on fire. So was the material of the tent behind him.

The mercenary's pistol tracked in quick jerks, and Lee stepped back and forth, buffeting the hapless Colonel this way and that. Lee was pumped up with adrenalin. Everything except the mercenary's hand, the needle hole in the center of the pistol's fat barrel, was a disregarded blur.

The mercenary shot again. The beam glancingly struck the Colonel's head. He shuddered and slumped, so much dead weight. His hair had caught fire. Jerk, and suddenly the needle hole was pointed right at Lee's face.

Lee let go of the Colonel's body and closed his eyes. He couldn't help it. He couldn't separate the pounding of his heart from the pounding of the stampede. Both shook him equally.

The mercenary yelped, a soft, half-gulped sound. Lee opened his eyes. The mercenary had dropped her pistol. Her hand was cupped beneath the cracked right lens of her video-shades. Flickering with random colors, glass splintered around the end of the metal spike dead center of the lens.

The mercenary's cupped hand filled with blood; blood spilled down her wrist.

Chen Yao yelled into Lee's face that it was time to go. She had to yell it twice: the stampede was almost upon them. Lee let the Colonel's body drop to the floor. The tent was filled with the stench of charred flesh and the sharp smell of burnt hair. The boy-thing was curled up on his side, clutching his bloody throat. Dr. Damon Lovelace was running in slow motion towards the shelter of the caravan.

Lee raised the Colonel's pistol. The side of the tent blew

away in a flare of hot light. Red dust whirled in, smothering Lee and Chen Yao. Dark shapes moved in the murk beyond. The whole ground vibrated. Lee lifted Chen Yao into his arms and ran into the stampede.

Forty-six

Despite his jazzed-up nerves and turbo-charged muscles, Wei Lee was nearly run down twice by charging yaks before he managed to carry Chen Yao to the relative shelter of a clump of thorn bushes that grew in the angle of a tipped-up shelf of red rock.

He set down Chen Yao, flopped beside her, and coughed and coughed and coughed. He could taste dust all the way down to the bottom of his lungs. What he spat was red as blood. Fifty per cent of the air seemed to be fine silt thrown up by the pounding hoofs of the stampeding yaks.

A yak swerved around the rocks as neatly as a dancer. One of its hoofs almost stamped on Lee's foot, but his speeded reactions gave him plenty of time to tuck his leg out of the way, mark the animal's rolling red-rimmed eyes under the jut of its horns and every pin-prick spatter of moisture on his face from the orange froth shaken from its muzzle. He shared its bewildered rage and shouted into the dust.

"All the time I searched for my parents I thought I knew who they were! Now I've found them, but I don't know them at all!"

Another yak went by, stately and slow amidst rolling red dust. And another. And another. They made the world over into dust and thunder.

Lee pressed into the bushes, scarcely noticing the cat's-claw thorns that scored his flesh, or the bone-deep ache in his skull where the mercenary had hit him. The last few moments in the tent kept flashing past, especially the instant of the Colonel's death. Lee could still feel the final shudder of the Colonel's body; the stink of burnt flesh and hair seemed to be permanently bonded in his nostrils, deeper than dust could reach. Although he had not actually killed the man, Lee felt responsible for his death, and knew, now that the Colonel was dead, that although he had murdered his parents he had not deserved to die. No one born into life deserves death.

Chen Yao huddled closer against Lee, shivering with nervous exhaustion. She was no longer wearing the aspect of a god; she was just a little girl. Lee put his arm around her and after a moment she touched his wrist . . .

. . . and everything around him speeded up.

No. He had slowed down, back to normal speed.

Chen Yao said in a distracted monotone, as if reciting something she had learned by rote, "It is dangerous to use your enhancements for too long. Noradrenalin overload will burn out the interface synapses."

Their stampede seemed to have mostly passed, although clouds of dust obliterated almost everything. Lazy billows rose to blot out even the sun, which was now only a few spans from the laboring horizon. The caravan was gone, escaped or obliterated. Yaks were blurry ghosts in grainy clouds lit by low-level light. A calf in a coat of hair down to the ground ran close by, bawling, its hindquarters streaked with shit. A yak crashed against the shelf of rock that sheltered Lee and Chen Yao and tried to scramble over it, sharp hoofs lashing the thorn bushes. Then it rolled off, bounced to its feet, and was gone.

Lee shouted into Chen Yao's ear. "How many yaks does it take to make a stampede?"

"As many as you can get!"

Lee pulled himself from thorns and risked standing up. There were only a few yaks now, half trotting, half walking, with the studied insouciant air of those who don't want to be associated with the herd, but at the same time don't want to be left behind.

Lee bent to Chen Yao, pulled her to her feet. "I think we can make a run for it."

Chen Yao said, "Don't be silly," but Lee, hardly hearing her, yanked on her arm and dragged her at a run out into the tail end of the stampede. It was perfectly safe, after all. By infra-red he could see any stragglers through the blowing dust long before they could see him. Chen Yao tried to drag him to a halt, but he pulled hard and she yelped and stumbled after him, out of breath and coughing on dust so that he couldn't understand what she was trying to tell him.

Nor did he really care: he was riding a sudden wind of adrenalin. He was free, free, free! Free of his captors. Free of the fear of death, for now he knew how banal the threat was. And most of all, free of the obligation that had shaped his life. He was as free as a butterfly that had struggled out of its cocoon after three hundred days of winter sleep and taken flight from the dull time of growth.

Free of everything, even of a plan really, except some vague idea of finding the railway line, of skipping along the tracks all the way back to the city. Of going home.

He had forgotten that he had no home; had forgotten, too, all about the dream-revealed destiny he had fallen into.

And he had also forgotten where the railway line was. He'd been dragging Chen Yao at a trot through swirling dust along a more or less straight route, zigging this way to avoid a stray yak, zagging that way to get around an outcrop of eroded boulders or a clump of thorn bushes. He remembered that the caravan had been within easy reach of the railway line, but they had walked two or three times that distance now and there was still no sight of it.

Lee stopped, out of breath and dizzily exhilarated. It was time to get his bearings. Chen Yao jerked her hand away from his, and at the same time he heard a nagging whine, rising and falling in the distance.

It was an electric engine screaming under duress.

Chen Yao kicked Lee in the shin. He jumped back, surprised. She kicked again, catching him under his kneecap, and his legs folded under him and he sat down in a mess of yak flop. Chen Yao grabbed his ears and shouted into his face.

"You won't listen! You just won't listen!"

Lee blinked up at her, smiling with astonishment. Chen Yao was trembling with anger. Tears made muddy tracks in the red dust that coated her face. "We were safe where we were. There is a pick-up looking for us! How can it find us when we are stumbling around!"

Lee tried to get up, put his hand in more yak shit, and fell over again, besmearing himself with even more of the stinking green slime.

"Listen," Chen Yao said.

Lee didn't need his hyper-keen senses to hear the nagging mosquito whine. It grew faint and then loud, and then faint again, circling away and circling back in an unpredictable pattern.

Chen Yao said, "You hear? You hear that?" She was looking around, peering this way and that into billowing dust. At last she said, "This way. Hurry, before she catches up!"

She ran before Lee could get to his feet, but it was the knock-kneed run of a little girl, and he easily caught up with her.

"Where are we going?"

"We're running away. From her, from the sister. The sister of, of your friend. Of Miriam." Chen Yao was already out of breath. Her words came out in angry little spasms. Her expression was one Lee had never before seen on someone so young. "I should have killed her. Should have. But it would be bad karma. Oh please! Come *on!*"

That was when Lee heard the nagging whine crossing from right to left far behind them, growing louder, closer.

Chen Yao was running fast now; Lee could hardly keep up with her. She shouted, "Dust helps hide us, but she's random tracking. And not on foot."

Then she disappeared from view, and Lee stepped on to thin air and fell with a sickening slide down a steep slope. He came to a stop a few meters from the corpse of a yak; a small avalanche of stones bounced off his back.

Chen Yao grabbed his arm, pulled him down. Something had half eviscerated the yak—perhaps only the fall—and Lee was soaked in blood as he huddled with Chen Yao inside the coarse reeking pelt. A tangle of slippery intestines bulged against his back, hot as his skin. The rich fetid smell of fermented vegetation rose from the corpse's spilled bowels.

"Quiet," Chen Yao said. "She's wired just like you."

Lee understood. At the same moment he heard the mosquito whine above him and held his breath, willing himself to become one with the corpse's infra-red signature.

Time passed. Lee and Chen Yao huddled under bloody yak hair like mice in a grain store with a cat prowling somewhere. Lee felt someone's attention pass over him like a searchlight: it raised the hair on his head.

The whine grew louder for a moment before fading into the distance.

Chen Yao counted dolphins under her breath, just like a child playing Emperor of the Hill, and when she reached a hundred she said it was safe. They staggered out of their grisly shelter into blowing dust which stuck to and stiffened their bloody clothes.

Lee saw now that the dead yak lay in the bottom of a narrow crevasse. Through the thick haze of dust were the ghost-shapes of clumps of dry vegetation standing amongst flat water-worn stones—in the brief rainy season of late summer this would be the bed of a raging river.

Chen Yao scrambled up the slope and Lee followed. She now stood at the top, head turning this way and that. "There," she said at last, and set off at a slant.

"I think the railway is back there," Lee said politely.

Chen Yao shook her head. "That's why we must go the other way. Oh please, please Wei Lee, you must follow me." And she stumbled on the level ground as if she had tried to climb a step that wasn't there, and began to cry.

Lee gathered her up in his arms and staggered forward through blowing dust. Chen Yao whispered directions, and because Lee had to bend close to hear her he didn't see the pony materialize out of the dust. When its rider shouted to him, Lee almost dropped Chen Yao in amazement.

The man on the pony wore a mask against the dust, but Lee recognized him at once.

"Good goddamn Billy Lee," Redd said loudly, "you give me that girl and get your scrawny ass on my saddle right now." Chen Yao roused enough to scramble into the saddle in front of Redd; the cowboy leaned down to give Lee his arm, and said, "If I had time, I'd buy you another bath."

He was smiling behind the mask. Lee smiled back and swung up on Redd's strong arm and settled behind the cowboy in the high-backed wooden saddle.

That was when the bike roared out of swirling dust.

It was two-wheeled and all chrome. Mary Makepeace Gaia leaned back in its narrow saddle, her arms raised to grip a steering bar which had the same upswept curve as a yak's horns. There was a patch over her left eye, and a red bandanna around her shaven head. Under the saddle, between her legs, was a teardrop pod with the yellow and black trefoil warning of radiation hazard.

The mercenary brought her fission-powered bike to a halt so abruptly it reared up like a stallion, the whine of its motor rising to a scream.

Redd held Chen Yao, and Lee clutched the coarse blanket Redd wore like a cloak, as the horse shied under the three of them. The mercenary's bike spiked a stand into the dirt and Mary Makepeace Gaia was suddenly standing with a pistol in each hand. Sparkling dust defined two needles of laser light as she shot at the sky.

Redd raised his hands, palms upwards. Lee thought he saw something glitter away from them, blown towards the mercenary on the dusty wind.

Mary Makepeace Gaia triggered another burst of laser light and the beams crossed just above Redd's head. Lee heard dust grains exploding in the intense energy like peppercorns bursting in a wok. The mercenary holstered one of the pistols and pushed up the filter which had covered her mouth and nose.

She said, "I get a bonus for live meat, so I'll ask you all to climb down."

"I don't think so," Redd said.

The mercenary shrugged. "You I don't need anyway," she said, and pointed her pistols right at Redd's face.

Nothing happened. The whine of the fission-powered bike died away, and there was only the soft sound of dust blowing on the wind. A yak bellowed, far off in the distance.

Redd drew something from his belt: a heavy wheel pistol with grips of cross-hatched white bone. Its hammer clicked back. It was aimed at Mary Makepeace Gaia.

"Never depend on electricity," Redd said. "I infected you with circuit busters. Gift of the anarchists."

The mercenary stared right back at him. Her voice was cold. "People who talk about it never do it."

"I'm a kind of exceptional guy," Redd said.

But at the moment he pulled the trigger Lee pulled on his arm so the shot went straight up in the air. The pony jinked and Redd grabbed the reins and yelled, "What the fuck you thinking of!"

Lee started to stammer out that he'd seen enough killing. Chen Yao said calmly, "If he has done it, let it be so. He knows more than he thinks he knows."

"Kill me," the mercenary said. Her teeth were gritted together. Veins stood out on her forehead. Horribly, blood gathered at the lower rim of her eyepatch, and a red tear sluggishly ran down her cheek. "Kill me," she said again, "or I swear I'll find you, wherever you run. I'll find you all, and kill you all."

Redd didn't put the pistol away, but he eased the hammer down with his thumb. "Get away from your bike, lay down in the dirt."

"Fuck you, asshole," the mercenary said, and folded her arms.

Redd whispered, "You sure you want this? I mean, there's no harm in giving her what she wants."

"It is done," Chen Yao said. "Besides, for her failure is worse than death."

Mary Makepeace Gaia said, "Next time I will not fail."

"I can't wait," Redd told her.

The mercenary smiled. It was exactly the same smile as her sister, but four hundred degrees cooler. "Good," she said, and ran at the pony.

Redd reined the pony around and spurred its belly. Lee held on tight as it flew into a gallop. The assassin screamed something after them, but already she was left far behind.

Forty-seven

Redd rode as if all the demons in creation were after him, through settling veils of dust and out at last into the light of the sun. Its red light was melting into the red sky, where wisps of high cirrus glowed like beaten bronze, as the horizon began to climb up its disc.

Clinging behind the cowboy, Lee knew enough to relax into the spine-jarring ride. Despite his nervous exhaustion he found the hell-for-leather ride exhilarating. He squinted over Redd's shoulder into wind and sunset light, saw a dark line at the horizon of the stony plain, running from west to east.

It was the Grand Canal. They rode straight for it, across wide dry fields, over dry irrigation dikes, past toppled wind pumps. Then they were in deep shadow, clattering down a narrow street between ruined flat-roofed mud-brick houses, one of the abandoned villages which dotted the length of the Grand Canal from the capital to the Dust Seas. They burst into the last light of the sun, crashed through a belt of seedling mangroves.

A skimmer was moored at the end of a stone jetty that ran a little way into the kilometer-wide canal. Its black dispersers were raised high on their recurved booms, and its slack silvery monofilament sail ripplingly mirrored the red sky.

Redd reined the pony, vaulted off and lifted Chen Yao from the saddle. When Lee jumped down Redd swatted the pony's rump with his hat. It turned its head to regard him reproachfully with a large brown eye, and Redd yelled, "You get going, you stupid lump of dogmeat!" and swatted it again. The pony pranced away, and with its reins trailing trotted off along the trail it had smashed through the seedling mangroves.

Redd set his hat on his head. "I swear I'm gonna get me one of those bikes next time. You two come on, now."

He led Lee and Chen Yao down the jetty and on to the skimmer. Even as they set foot on the white-wood decking the gangway retracted and lines took up slack, the sail filled with evening breeze, and the skimmer slipped its mooring.

Forty-eight

The Grand Canal was a vast irrigation project, the largest body of water on Mars. It was fed by thousands of reactor well heads that were sunk so deeply into the permafrost that the conchies couldn't reach them. But no new wells had been drilled since the Great Reassessment, and one by one the reactors were failing. In a hundred years the Grand Canal would be as dry as any of Mars's fossil watercourses. Already most of the villages along its banks had been abandoned. Banyans, soldier bamboo and freshwater mangroves, unchecked, were turning the edges of the canal into swamp where herds of the last surviving species of archiosaur grazed, man-sized semi-aquatic bipeds with vividly crested duck-billed heads. Water hyacinths choked irrigation outlets, and the rich agricultural strips alongside the canal were dying back into desert.

The skimmer ran the eastward lane of the wide waterway, following a string of buoys that winked green in the gathering dusk. Other skimmers moved slowly on the clogged waterway. They cut through floating islands of water hyacinth, rafts of azolla and mats of cyanobacteria with razor-sharp prows.

Lee sat at the stern rail of the skimmer, sipping jasmine tea from a bowl big enough to wash his face in. He had taken off his boots, for everyone went barefoot on the whitewood decking, even Redd, who stood talking to the captain at the high waist of the skimmer, under the bridge awning.

Both men were underlit by the blue light of the console. The skimmer's captain, a weatherbeaten Tibetan, had already greeted Lee and Chen Yao with brief but punctilious ceremony, but it was clear he had more urgent considerations than the comfort of his passengers. He had to blend into the local and long-distance traffic, make his way past satellite surveillance into the wide wastes of the Dust Seas.

With nothing to do but watch the green and red lights of the shipping lanes and the running lights of other skimmers drift past, Lee soon fell asleep. He awoke to a lurid sunrise from a dream where Mary Makepeace Gaia stalked him through a maze of red canyons clogged with dust, her eyes mirrors, her hands white flames. He had a headache and a dry mouth. Someone had wrapped a heavy yak hide around him as he slept: every long hair of the hide was tipped with a ruby of hoarfrost. Near by, Chen Yao slept under another hide; only her cap of glossy black hair showed.

The skimmer was still sailing east. Dawn light dimmed the lights of the shipping lanes, made silhouettes of the scattering of skimmers on the canal. It threw Lee's shadow a long way across the white wood of the decking as, wrapped in his yak-hide blanket, he stalked to the bridge.

Captain Jigme Tsatar was at his console. A short, stolid, rotund man with an air of invincible competence, he wore an intricately braided jacket and loose cotton trousers. A broad-brimmed black felt hat was pulled low over his brow, so that his small, close-set eyes and shapeless blob of a nose were in shadow. He told Lee that they had an eighty per cent chance of making the Ichun elevator at the end of the canal. Things were bad in the capital and The Little Bird's revolution was taking most of the attention of the Army of the People's Mouths; more importantly it had scattered the forces working against Lee.

"I am grateful that Redd found such friends as you," Lee said. Flattery never hurt, even if the captain surely knew the worth of what he had done.

But Captain Tsatar waved that away. "The Yankee wants payment for delivery of you and the little girl god. We've told him he can have it when we reach Ichun. A herd boss called Hawk was supposed to take you to the fisherfolk, but things worked out in the end. It is not your fault that Hawk had been turned."

"Perhaps I trusted the wrong people."

Captain Tsatar's face gave nothing away. So different from Redd, whose face was a constant storm of half-concealed emotions whose meanings Lee could often only guess at. The captain said, "And yet here you are after all. No one could be expected to have done better. If the wind holds we have a day to educate you. And if it doesn't, well then we have even longer—if our enemies don't find us."

Forty-nine

Lee's education began after breakfast of *doupi*, fried bean curd pancakes stuffed with minced vegetables. His teacher was a thin ascetic Yankee called Soldier. Soldier had iron-gray hair, a thin face which showed all the bones beneath it, steel teeth, and an inexhaustible supply of invective. For twelve hours, from dawn to dusk, he taught Lee the rudiments of half a dozen fighting techniques—Tae Kwon Do, the Five Animal Styles of the Shaolin Temple (an especial favorite of Soldier's), Karate, Choy Li-Fut, use of knife and quarterstaff. They didn't even stop when the skimmer put into shore, sheltering under the many-arched canopy of a giant banyan from a culver that patrolled the wide canal for an hour before turning back towards the capital.

Lee found that he could store away every move of a fighting sequence, and when challenged replay it without thinking. Soon it was Soldier rather than himself whose back or shoulder or hip was hitting the thin cotton matting which had been laid on the white-wood deck.

At last Soldier pronounced himself satisfied. "It'll have to do," he said. They bowed to each other and rolled up the matting, just as the last sliver of the sun flashed blue light around half the horizon and vanished below it.

Chen Yao had been restored to her role as avatar on the skimmer. While Lee had been given his workout, she had sat beneath an awning, nibbling sweet rice balls and sipping sour milk, watching ruined villages and mangrove swamp go by to

242

starboard, watching other skimmers slowly pass to port.

That afternoon, a pod of fin had surfaced near the skimmer. They had ridden the bow wave and then slipped back to chatter to Chen Yao. Lee could almost understand what they were saying; or at least, he could play it back, slowed down, and filter words from the chatter. Only Chen Yao could make sense of it.

What the fin had brought was news. Chen Yao translated it. Most of the city was under martial law. Roving gangs had looted much of the Yankee Quarter and there were frequent fire fights at night. Refugees crowded the feed lots; the Army of the People's Mouths was preventing them from moving further.

Everyone on the skimmer listened to Chen Yao recount this, and it was passed to other skimmers via blinking signal lamps.

If Chen Yao was worried about her family, her people, she gave no sign. The aspect of her godhead gave her the calm acceptance of the world of a true bodhisattva. The crew of the skimmer brought her water-hyacinth flowers, which she wove into her hair. By starlight and the colored points of the skimmer's running lights, the wilting blooms made a glimmering constellation above her face as, serious and quiet, she taught Lee how to call up the functions of his rewired nervous system, to move in and out of hypermode, tune his hearing and visual acuity at will, control the autonomic functions of his body.

Meanwhile, although the broadcasts of the King of the Cats were no longer being jammed he was doing nothing but play music, and Miriam slept like a mangrove seed in the muddy darkness at the base of Lee's brain.

The end of the long hard day had left Lee with a sense of lassitudinous well-being. He was tired, but not exhausted. By heat sight he could enjoy the trim lines of the skimmer as it ran before the night wind. Its sail rippled as breezes rose and fell and computer-controlled winches differentially flexed the semi-intelligent material to gain every dyne.

The skimmer had the beauty of form perfectly mirroring

function. It was a hundred years old. It was called *The Black Dragon*.

Redd was ill at ease a-sail, and he was still trying to convince himself that he was on the right side. "So long as it's against owners, that would be OK," he said. "Never did like owners. People like Hawk, thinking they own the ranges . . . no one ever really owns the land. It's really the land owns you." Redd hummed a few bars of "Don't Fence Me In"; it made a strange counterpoint to Oscar Toney's "Precious Love," which courtesy of his revamped nervous system was playing in cleaned-up stereo right inside Lee's head.

He and Redd were sitting at the fantail of the skimmer. Along in the bow, the crew were talking around a little brass brazier. It was near midnight with frost sharp in the air, and no one on the skimmer could sleep. At any moment the culvers of Lee's great-grandfather, or of the Army of the People's Mouths, could swoop on them like owls.

The skimmer's wake streamed out across the dark water. Stars and the diamond haze of the asteroid belt burned brilliantly across the sky. Venus and the double star of Earth and Moon were setting: Jupiter wouldn't rise for an hour yet. The red and green double stars of other skimmers' running lights moved in the distance against the vast black silence of the land.

After a while, Redd said, "Know why I'm still here?"

"You are waiting to be paid."

"I guess I deserve that. But I brought you here, didn't I? And for less money than I'd have gotten from the conchies, and not for cash on the barrel-head, either."

"That's true. Please, I would like to hear why you are here."

"It goes way back to when I was a young kid. Barely had hair on my balls when I had that operation they advertise. Maybe you don't know about it. Aimed at Tibetans and Yankees to keep our populations down. Took the money like an idiot, spent it in a week. So I'll never have kids, but I figure maybe I want something to live on and this is my shot at it. If we win, they'll make statues of us all."

"Or make songs," Lee said. He imagined the King of the Cats singing of his exploits in his slow bluesy voice, and felt an illicit thrill. Part of the King was inside him, he always felt, after that dream. In a different way that part of Miriam Makepeace Mbele was, but there all the same.

In his head, the voice of the King of the Cats came in on the fade. Lee had found he could separate the broadcasts and the real world, and attend to them simultaneously. The King was all fired up the way he had been when he'd triggered The Little Bird's revolution. Lee took notice of that kind of thing now. He knew that the King's moods weren't random. He was talking directly to his audience down here in the world.

"Awww-right! Rock aaaaand rooooll. Yessir, we're cooking right now, good golly we really are. Light crawls up and light crawls down, but I can spy with my real big eye what's happening with you folks. Let me tell you I'll be bringing you the news only a few minutes out of synch, and the news right now is there's an army column moving on Xin Beijing. That's coming to you north by northeast, and at present speed it should be reaching the railway pass local time oh nine hundred or thereabouts tomorrow. Looks like a division for those of you interested. Any soldiers listening, I say I can count your heads,

Redd said, very serious, "All that hand-waving and yelling, that Chop-Suckey stuff you've been taught, that won't do you no good at all against someone with a gun. This pistol of mine might be crude and out of date, but its advantage is, it's mechanical. Pure brute force, nothing that circuit-buster viruses can touch. Here, now, hold it. It's OK, it won't go off. See that little pip there? The action won't work unless you slide it forward. And it's not loaded. Yeah, that, the trigger, that fires it. Three-gram pull, that's all, double action, first click cocks the hammer there, second drops it. Real sweet, real balanced. There's this old *baaay-beees! You wave your hands in the air if you don't care. I can count you all the way from up here, why I can even tell if you've trimmed your nails or not. I have eyes, believe me, I have eyes everywhere! In a minute, in just a minute, we're going to get back down to some music, after this public service announcement. That's a special message for all you people way way up on the Tiger Mountain defense system: keep watching the skies. You know what's coming down. So mellow out to the music, and get ready. We're fast and loud and proud, you shouldn't listen to what those no-growth eco-freaks tell you. Up here we know all about ecosystems, it's how we stay alive. Think about it while I lay this on you: "If the World Don't End Tomorrow I'm Coming After You" by the Fairlanes. You know it."*

guy back in Yankee Town that makes these by hand, takes him a month on one piece. He numbers each one, right above the wheel there, see? Yankee numbering, illegal or not, that's how he does it. Now here's the speed-loader, see how the shot slides right into each hole there? Wicked stuff. There's the flat copper tip here, and behind that is number twelve shot suspended in liquid polymer. It'll put a hole in a man big as both your fists together. Hit him anywhere and it'll stop him dead, one shot, every time. It'll do a yak serious harm, main reason I have it. You're on the ground, a yak coming at you, you need an option. This is it. So here I have a gun, and you have your arm-waving, and what are you going to do?"

Redd held the gun on Lee's head and smiled. Lee went into hypermode, reached out and took it from Redd's grip. Redd started to react as Lee slowed back down, and then he was working his empty hand, staring at the gun which dangled by its trigger guard from Lee's forefinger.

After a moment, Redd said, "Yeah, well, that's some trick. I'll give you that."

Lee saw that he had offended the Yankee. He handed the gun back. "You are right, it is a trick. But it is what I have."

Redd thought for a moment. He said, "You ever stop to think that mercenary has the same wiring as you? She comes after you, you aren't going to take *her* gun away."

Lee had to admit that Redd was right. And he was certain that Mary Makepeace Gaia would not rest until she found him: a certainty he suspected he owed to the buried fragments of her dead sister, who perhaps was simply silent, and not sleeping at all.

Redd said, "So let me at least show you how to use a gun."

The song ended, and the King of the Cats came back. He was needling the sky defense systems again. The place where Lee was headed. It couldn't be coincidence.

Lee said, "Do you know why they've stopped jamming the broadcasts of the King of the Cats? I have just thought of it. He dangles bait before the enemy; they need him just as much as we do, because they suspect he might give something away."

"He also broadcasts with enough power to burn a hole through the planet, it was concentrated on one spot. Jamming him after the trouble in the city must have screwed up communications across half the planet. You listening to that guy? Never had time myself."

"But it is your heritage, Redd."

"It's the past, another world and long gone, too. I know how much you Han hold to the past, but we're different."

"Ah. Then I see that you are not following the traditions of your ancestors when you ride the range. Forgive me for being so foolish."

"Well, I guess you got me there. But, see, it's not exactly following any tradition. It's re-using it in a different way, in a different place for a different purpose. You put any cowpoke from the nineteenth century out on the range, he wouldn't last a day." Redd spat a jet of saliva over the rail, into the water. "There's maybe one tradition I like to keep, though. Lucky for you, as it turns out."

"I would very much like to learn to shoot."

"There you go. Knew you'd come round. I guess if I'm going to give you shooting lessons we should ask permission of the captain."

Captain Tsatar was a gun buff himself, it turned out, and showed Redd the hand-made sniper rifle he kept just in case he needed to surprise river bandits who haunted the abandoned villages along the Grand Canal and (in fact its only real use) to pot waterfowl or small game in the border swamps. It had an octagonal barrel two meters long with a telescopic sight that ran its whole length, and a bore as big as Lee's thumb.

"Accurate over two kilometers," Captain Tsatar said. "I shot a horse from beneath a bandit at that distance once. He was most surprised."

He spoke quietly; they all did. Apart from the sound of water moving past the skimmer's hull the night held an immense stillness. Cold, the sky clear, stars so bright Lee thought he could have reached out and plucked one, like fruit from a tree. The bridge controls made a small comforting glow, like a hearth fire dimming to ashes. Tomorrow they would reach Ichun, the *danwei* at the end of the canal.

"It's a nice gun," Redd said. "There's this guy back in Yankee town you should talk to some time."

Lee was surprised to see how quickly Captain Tsatar and Redd formed a bond, for Tibetans and Yankees were traditionally enemies: there had been much bad blood during the resettlement, when a million Tibetan pioneers had fallen from the sky and taken the planet from the failing Yankee colony. But perhaps that was the point. Redd and Captain Tsatar shared the same history, and both their races were oppressed by the Han—although in true stubborn Yankee fashion Redd would never admit this. Both knew more about that history than Lee, too. Lee had for most of his life been as unaware of it as a fish is of water, or the child of a rich man of money. It was a medium, taken for granted. But now he was caught up in its strong current, and his life was as unwillingly changed by it as the lives of those without power have always been changed.

He was beginning to understand why Redd had stayed after bringing him here.

He was beginning to understand the forces in delicate balance all around him, even if he was still unsure just who was trying to move them.

"We are the first people," Captain Tsatar said when Lee asked if the *ku li* really existed. "We've never needed a name, until now. If the name strikes fear into our enemies, then it is to our advantage."

"*Ku li*," Soldier said, "is as good a name as any. We are not as numerous as the Ten Thousand Years would have the populace believe, but we will unite the people and move forward with them."

Lee said, "Do you mean you will impose your ideas on them?"

Captain Tsatar said, "We learn from the people, and then teach them what we have learned. The people will take control from the Emperor and the Ten Thousand Years and centralize all means of transforming the world so it can be done as quickly as possible. Of course, in the beginning, this will mean inroads on the rights of the individual. But political power wielded in the name of the Emperor is merely the instrument by which the Ten Thousand Years oppresses the people."

Soldier said, suddenly and unexpectedly passionate, "In our hands it will change the world for ever. And for the benefit of everyone."

Redd said, "People know they must co-operate to get on. But they need leading, too. Not much different from running a herd."

Soldier said, "When the people take power and make themselves the ruling class, then they will have swept away the structure which oppresses them. They cannot oppress themselves."

Captain Tsatar said, "In place of a hierarchical society we

will have an association in which the free development of each is the condition for free development of all."

"Every man an Emperor," Redd said.

Soldier shook his head. "No one will rule but the will of the people. Every man true to his own self."

"We don't have time to teach you everything," Captain Tsatar said, and smiled.

Lee looked from one to the other. "I'm learning all the time," he said.

Captain Tsatar said, "We are few. I admit that. But dragons hatch from the smallest of eggs. We will finish the transformation of this poor world even if it means swapping *The Black Dragon* for a three-masted sailing barque, oceans of water for seas of dust."

Lee said, "It sails on water now."

"It sails tame water. It has such a shallow draft that on open sea the slightest swell would overturn it. You will soon see how different dust is from water, young master."

Lee thought about that. After a while Captain Tsatar touched his shoulder, lightly, gently. It was then that Lee realized how afraid the man was, how afraid all the crew were of himself and of Chen Yao. Even Soldier was afraid.

"Look up," Captain Tsatar said.

A faint web rose from the eastern horizon. It lay across that quarter of the sky as if the invisible lines with which the sages had linked stars into constellations had come adrift and tangled there. Without his conscious control, Lee's vision magnified the view. Stars became bright blurred points. He felt a diffuse sense of expansion, as if he were falling into the sky. Redd and Soldier and Captain Tsatar were talking excitedly, but he heard only their voices, not their words.

The lines were discontinuous, each composed of a myriad twinkling shards. The web effect was caused by the fact that the lines radiated away from dozens of different points spaced across the sky, most yet to be revealed by the horizon's slow sinking.

Then blooms of light began to appear all over the web. They were as bright as the brightest stars, and Lee's sight stepped down to compensate. Something in his rewired brain plotted every line. He remembered the technician explaining about cluster probes designed to test Mars's defenses. Each an icy moonlet infected with fullerene viruses which carved it into a hundred fluffy micro-comets and manufactured the viruses which would melt the permafrost during the long fall from Jupiter's orbit to that of Mars. The man was hugely fat, naked and completely hairless, with a nervous habit of looking into Lee's eyes at the end of each sentence and then looking away again. No, not Lee's eyes: this was Miriam remembering part of her mission briefing.

The blossoms hung across the sky were the comet heads (each no bigger than Lee's own head) burst by the orbital defense lasers controlled by Tiger Mountain, beyond the eastern horizon. The lines of the web were burning water droplets, exploding in ionisation trails. Rain, falling faintly through the stratosphere, evaporating kilometers above the surface, the viruses suspended in the droplets already destroyed by induction hundreds of thousands of kilometers before they reached the Martian atmosphere.

This was not war, not yet. The display showed that the defenses were still too strong for frontal assault. But it was the beginning of the end of the time before war.

Fifty

The road to Ichun was paved with yellow and red bricks set in sinuous curves, like the patterns on the back of a petrified snake. As he walked down the road, with Redd and Chen Yao on either side of them, Lee saw two things.

Columns of smoke, five, six, seven of them, rose from various places amongst Ichun's low flat-roofed buildings.

And people were running out of the city gate and down the road, so many that they spilled into the rocky desert scrub either side of it. They ran towards Lee and Chen Yao and Redd. They were shouting and waving palm branches, and they were dressed and masked in carnival attire. In a moment they had surrounded the astonished travellers. Dragons and griffins hoisted Lee on to their shoulders; two snout-nosed carp lifted Chen Yao, who laughed with tremendous glee.

Redd pressed up against the masked men who supported Lee, crushing his hat to his head with one hand. He was shouting something that was lost in the noise of the crowd.

"The sky!" the people chanted. "The sky! The sky!"

The fin had spread word of Lee and of the riots in Xin Beijing up and down the network of canals, supplementing the censored television shots of the one news channel The Little Bird allowed to operate. Skimmers had picked up the story, too. News that Lee was heading towards Ichun, and the portents in the sky that night, had combined to cause a popular revolt.

The company of soldiers garrisoned in the town had surrendered after their compound had been set on fire. The governor and his family had fled into the Dust Seas as soon as the revolt had started, riding the last skimmer carried down on the elevators. The post office had been liberated from its nightwatchman, who was now sleeping off a massive drunk after all the rice beer to which he'd been treated. Posters of the Gang of Six had been defaced and slogans picked up from the Xin Beijing uprising covered most of the white walls of Ichun's buildings. Lee recognized some of the PSCM's jargon mixed with quotations from the movie fragments of the King of the Cats. The civic loudspeakers no longer broadcast a bland diet of pop arias, advertisements and anti-expansionist propaganda, but the King's round-the-clock rock'n'roll show.

And the massive elevators which carried skimmers up and down between the Grand Canal and the Dust Seas were stalled. The family which owned and operated them had joined the revolution. Queues of skimmers were already backed up half a kilometer, and growing every hour. Among them was *The Black Dragon*, which Lee and Chen Yao and Redd had left at dawn.

Arriving at Ichun by road had seemed sensibly inconspicuous at the time: by now Mary Makepeace Gaia must have worked out how they had escaped. As it turned out, they might as well have carried huge banners broadcasting their presence. In fact, as Lee was carried by the celebrating crowd down the main avenue of Ichun towards the Governor's residence, he saw that a banner with his name had been stretched between two of the big ginkgoes which lined the thoroughfare.

Chen Yao, her hands on the scaly heads of the two carp who carried her, shouted, "This is your hour, Wei Lee! Now your journey really begins!"

"Remember what happened in Xin Beijing," Lee said.

Chen Yao laughed. "I don't see any army!"

"Not yet!"

Then the crowd swept between them, and Lee was carried through the gates of the Governor's house.

Fifty-one

The Governor's house was perched at the edge of
kilometer-high cliffs that dropped straight down to the
vast red flatness of the Plain of Heaven. The delicate
tiers of the house and its lush green gardens, sheltered by
curved windshields that raked the sky like thirty-meter tal-
ons, had been turned into the headquarters of Ichun's popular revolt. Manicured lawns, which had been watered every
day and cut by a dozen women with hand scythes, were
slowly being trampled to mud by the victory party. Cooking
pits had been dug into the precious turf; there were tables
loaded with sour vegetables, pickled yak brains, mapo dofu
with fiery sauces, stuffed roast intestines, pig-face soup,
sugar jaffles and other delicacies.

One of the self-appointed revolutionary committee explained to Lee that the whole feast had all been looted from
the Governor's cold stores. He was a tall nervous student
not much older than Lee, handsome in a cadaverous way,
his Adam's apple protruding above the knot in his yellow
scarf. A yellow scarf and lack of a mask were the badges of
authority, it seemed. The committee knew only too well if
the town was retaken that no masks could save them from
informers, so went bare faced amongst timorous townsfolk
who preferred to carry out the revolution anonymously.

"You see the riches stolen from the populace," another
committee member said.

"The Ten Thousand Years cling to the backs of the Hundred Families," said another.

Lee said, "I see celebration seems more important to you than victory."

"As to that," the tall student said, "the Captain of the garrison awaits your convenience. We have secured all weapons and all communications."

Lee did not hold back his anger. "I suppose you mean you have locked up the soldiers. And what will you do when the Army of the People's Mouths arrives at your gates?"

The tall student blinked, taken aback.

Behind him, a young woman stared right at Lee. For a moment Lee thought that another of Miriam's sisters had found him. But the young woman had straight black hair cut to frame a face the color of buttermilk. Her almond-shaped eyes were as black as Lee's. She coolly met his stare and said, "You must not think that we have not thought of these things."

"Let him talk," someone else said.

Lee said, "I'll not have you on my conscience, so I must speak plainly. I can offer you two choices. You may stand and fight, or run away. Both are dangerous, but you must have realized that when you acted. No? Too bad. Unless you choose, you will all be dead in a very short time. The Army of the People's Mouths would have begun to move on you as soon as communications were cut, and certainly once the elevators stopped working. The skimmers have radio sets, after all. Did you confiscate those?"

"The skimmer crews are on our side," the tall student said.

"So any skimmer captain would say, when faced with a mob. Where are the soldiers of the garrison? Not the officers, but the ordinary soldiers. I'll need to speak with them."

Fortunately, at least one of the revolutionaries had retained some sense. The ordinary soldiers had been locked up in a warehouse, but they had not been mistreated. There were sixty of them. They stood at parade rest in the middle of the main avenue in front of the gate of the Governor's house, looking ill at ease and watched with intense curiosity by twice their number of townspeople in carnival motley.

Lee explained to the soldiers that they had a choice. They would be set free and turned out of the town, or they could stay and fight. They had ten minutes to think about it.

It took only five. Their spokesperson, a squat, powerfully built corporal, was thrust forward. "We'll fight," he said.

Lee allowed himself a moment to enjoy the surprise of the committee. He bowed to the corporal, thanked him for his helpfulness, and suggested that he go with a squad of his men to the Governor's house and take what food and drink they needed. By that time their weapons would have been returned to them.

When the corporal had departed, the tall student said, "Very fine sentiments. But when we return their weapons they will shoot us."

"Not at all. The corporal is smarter than you. He knows that if he tried to rejoin the Army of the People's Mouths he would be shot as a deserter, as would all his men. No one in the Army of the People's Mouths could allow them to live, because that would be to admit that they had surrendered Ichun without a fight. So the corporal and his men will fight on your side, for there is a slim chance of victory. When he comes back, I want you to accompany us around the town. He will know all the defensive positions."

It was late afternoon before the corporal had finished showing Lee how to defend Ichun. Meanwhile, the committee had been set to work rounding up those citizens who remained sober enough to dig ditches and lay tanglewire at the edge of the town. In Lee's opinion, such defenses were only good until attackers found a way around them, but at least it gave the townspeople something to do.

The corporal agreed with Lee. He was wryly resigned to his fate. Like all in the garrison, he had not been born within a thousand kilometers of Ichun, and was not planning to be buried in it. "But only the lucky or rich choose where to die, and only the Lords of Ten Thousand Years when."

"That may no longer be true."

"We hear rumors," the corporal said. He was smiling. "You really started those riots?"

"In a way. But the rioting came after the Army of the People's Mouths attacked lawful petitioners in the Square of Heavenly Peace. Their masters sent élite troops against unarmed citizens."

"War is not an embroidery exercise," the corporal said grimly. "I'd guess they'll send warhorses against us, once we've been softened up by culvers. Those defenses won't do much good against a charge, but we can fall back to the main square. The buildings there are two-storied, and have thick walls. We can put a sniper in every window, and keep open a passage for retreat to the elevators." The corporal scratched his close-shaven pate. He was a sturdy weather-beaten man with old laser burns down one side of his shrewd face. "It would be best if you started sending out the old men and women and children now. Order skimmers to turn back. There are plenty of half-lifers, too, stacked in an old warehouse."

"They'll have to stay."

"I'd like to blow up a few buildings. It'll give us proper fire lanes to cover any approach on the square."

"Of course."

"*They* won't like it," the corporal said.

"I will tell them, if you like."

The corporal smiled. "It's just that I'm no good when it comes to ordering civilians about. It's what stopped me becoming an officer."

Most of the revolutionary committee were waiting in the square, dusty and dishevelled from their labors. Lee gave them the broad outline of his plans, and sat off to one side while the corporal explained the details. The woman who had confronted Lee at the Governor's house came up to him. She had brought a covered bowl: boiled rice and fried shreds of pork and beancurd. Lee took it gratefully. He hadn't eaten since leaving *The Black Dragon*.

The woman sat beside Lee while he ate. Her name was Wu Lin. She had been born in the capital. Her parents were distant relatives of one of the Ten Thousand Years, and had died in an accident soon after her birth. She had been brought up in the Great House of her great-grandfather, and a year ago she had been sent to Ichun to work as an agronomist technician. Her black hair was cut in a wing that brushed her eyes; her nails were broken and crested with dirt. She said, "My comrades have worked hard for you. A kind word would help."

"I'm not sure that's true. They believe in their own importance, not in reality."

"Are the stories about you true?"

"I'm sure they are true to those who tell them. I'm sure, too, that those who tell the stories think they know more about me than they do." Lee scraped the last grains of rice into his mouth. The food made a solid shape in his stomach.

Wu Lin said, "I'll find you a place to rest. We'll have a night at least before the army comes."

Lee took her left hand in both of his. He looked at her nails, then pulled her to her feet. They were exactly the same height. He said, "I know about you. I know more than you think. I know who your great-grandfather is."

She tried to pull away.

Lee said, "I've killed a man, and soon I may have to kill a woman. I'm not scared of anything on this world except myself. And that's all you have to be scared of, too."

Fifty-two

Wu Lin's room, in a cadre dormitory a few blocks south of the Governor's house, was as small and as sparely furnished as Lee's room in the Bitter Waters *danwei*—and as in his room, one whole wall of Wu Lin's was covered in still pictures of the King of the Cats, printed from the surviving fragments of his movies.

Lee tapped the largest, which in stark technicolor showed the King strumming his guitar and singing to Anne Helm on some lost beach of Old Earth, with his thumb. "I may be mistaken, but is this from *Follow That Dream*?"

Wu Lin was busy making tea on the room's small hotplate. "I knew by your hair that you are a follower of the King of the Cats."

"Do you hope I can defeat the Army of the People's Mouths as the King defeated the gamblers' gangsters?"

"You are already a kind of sheriff, it seems. Please, you must explain how you know about me, Wei Lee. We might never see each other again."

Lee took the bowl of tea she held out to him. They sat side by side on the edge of her small hard bed. He said, "I think we may. Because we're the same."

She didn't understand. Lee put his left hand over hers. He said, "When I was a child, I often visited the Great House where you lived. It was in the mountains, above Xin Beijing. It was far bigger than either of us thought. I knew only a few courtyards, a few of the buildings."

Wu Lin met his gaze. "Once, I climbed on to the roof of the Southern Flowery Hall. That was where my bedroom was. I climbed a vine that grew past my window. My ayah had to send for the gardeners to bring me down. But I saw the walls, far in the distance. I thought then they were the walls of the city. I didn't see the city until I was ten, when I was sent here."

"I have a trick fingernail," Lee said. "On my forefinger. It always splits in two places when it grows past the quick. That's what I saw about you. That's when I knew. He changed sex and face, and perhaps he changed fingerprints and retinal patterns too, but he did not change the small things, the unimportant single-gene products."

Wu Lin said, "I always thought I was the only one. I didn't understand why I had been sent here. I thought I'd done wrong . . ."

Her grip was strong. Lee returned it. "I had the same thoughts. There are others, I am sure of it. Bait, Great-grandfather Wei said, but he didn't understand the nature of our conception. I still don't entirely understand it myself."

"Tell me what you know," Wu Lin said with a sudden fierceness that surprised Lee. When he had finished telling her what Miriam Makepeace Mbele had told him, she said, "It could have happened to me. Not you, but to me!"

Lee said, "Instead, you organized the freeing of Ichun. Perhaps you will be luckier than I, in the long run. We must defend your prize before we can begin to learn that." He hesitated, and then said, "There is a way in which you can share my fate," and explained about the totipotent fullerene viruses, and what they had done to him.

"And you can infect me, just as the anarchist infected you?"

"Yes. But it is a hard burden, Wu Lin."

"But it's ours, isn't it? It's what we were born for."

So Lee kissed her deeply, and it was done.

Fifty-three

The corporal came for Lee just after dawn. He was a polite man, and knocked on the door and softly called Lee's name until Lee replied. Lee had slept on Wu Lin's floor matting; as he worked the stiffness from his limbs it occurred to him that he had not slept in a bed since leaving Bitter Waters. As he combed his hair, Wu Lin stirred on her bed, then suddenly sat upright, her hands clasped tightly across her eyes.

"There are grids and numbers wherever I look!"

"The viruses have begun their work," Lee said, and explained what she should expect. "I don't know if it will help us save Ichun, but it gives me hope."

"All we have ever had is hope," Wu Lin said. "Go on now, go to your friends. I will go to mine. Together, my brother, we shall see what we can do."

Chen Yao, Redd, and Captain Tsatar were waiting outside the dormitory with the corporal, in a cold wind that blew thin dust in from the desert.

Chen Yao looked at Lee and said, "You are a god, Wei Lee. There are no rules."

"If I'm a god, what is Wu Lin?"

"A potential."

"We all are that. Or I hope so."

Redd said, "Maybe some day you'll explain all of what's going down." He wore a black and red checked scarf over his mouth and long nose against the dusty wind. The captain

262

of *The Black Dragon* was there, too. His hunting rifle was slung over his shoulder; its octagonal barrel stuck straight up a meter above his black felt hat.

"I'm happy to see you," Lee said, "but if I'm not mistaken shouldn't you be with your ship?"

"She's standing ready by the elevator cradle," Captain Tsatar said. "Our back door, if we need it."

"When we need it," Redd said, "and that's soon. Soldier is organizing some of the skimmer crews." He laughed. "Mostly lecturing them about their moral duty."

"The people must understand the nature of the revolution," Captain Tsatar said. "Once they understand, they will join it gladly and fully."

"Let's hope so," Redd said.

"We maintained a deep radar watch all night," the corporal said. His eyes were red-rimmed, and he was unshaven. "Just before I came to wake you two blips lit up, three hundred klicks out and closing fast. We're moving everyone into position, and the elevators have been started up." He gave a fierce grin. "It's always nice to think there's a back door, but I doubt we'll have time to use this one."

They started off towards the main square. Redd told Lee what had happened in the night. Less than half of Ichun's citizens had stayed to defend their homes. The rest, and the children and old men and women, had been transported down to the Plain of Heaven aboard commandeered skimmers.

"There was a deal of trouble over that," Redd said, "and Soldier had to break a few heads. You'd think the crews would be grateful to be allowed on their way."

Captain Tsatar said mildly, "You understand little about sailors' pride."

Redd laughed. "Soldier said it was what? The reaction of the Little Owners to loss of their only means of oppressing the people."

"Soldier's a good man," Captain Tsatar said, "but sometimes he tends to favor theory over practice."

Redd whispered to Lee, "I wanted Chen Yao to go too. She wouldn't, of course."

Chen Yao said, "My place is with Wei Lee. And although his place is not here, he seems to have made up his mind to stay."

"I can't run away from this, Yao."

Chen Yao was more angry and more scared than she wanted anyone to know. Perhaps only Lee saw the effort she put into controlling her voice when she said coldly, "You can't save the world a town at a time, either."

The corporal said, "Had to put a couple of armed people aboard each skimmer, to make sure refugees weren't thrown overboard at the first opportunity."

"That's good," Lee said. He hadn't thought of that, and it suddenly seemed to him that there was so much he hadn't thought of. He was the center of a thousand unravelling threads. It was an exciting, scary thought, and kicked in adrenalin as they came out into the big square.

Ichun's main avenue ran straight across the middle, blocked where it entered the square by a sagging web of tanglewire strung between the buildings on either side. Or between their remaining walls, for the buildings had been gutted, holes blown completely through them, flat roofs caved in. That side of the square faced east, and early sunlight poured down the fire lanes, burning on the red banners which flew from every available point. Every scrap of red cloth in Ichun must have been commandeered; even the big ginkgoes were decked in red.

Trucks had been parked in a semicircle bowed away from the main avenue's entrance into the square. Fifty or sixty people lounged behind this makeshift barricade. Most were civilians, and many still wore masks, which lent them a gay carnival air at odds with the grim expressions of the few soldiers amongst them.

The corporal explained to Lee that most of his men were on the perimeter roofs, and Captain Tsatar made his excuses and left for his own sniper's position. He was halfway across the square when two culvers burst out of the air low above the buildings, shadows against the bright morning sun. Their wings made a thunderous pulse; Lee saw their belly guns winking but didn't hear them fire. Lines of dust walked across the square. A ginkgo flew into splinters and then a truck blew apart, scattering bodies and parts of bodies amongst flame and terrific noise.

There was a ragged fusillade from the survivors, but the culvers had already passed out of range. Captain Tsatar had dropped to the ground. Now he picked himself up, dusted his loose trousers, and trotted across the square into the shadowy arcade of a building on the far side. The corporal put on a padded helmet and spoke urgently into its microphone, holding the foam pad against his throat with a finger.

Chen Yao was looking up at the sky. "Here they come again," she said.

Two black specks in the pink sky: their bulbous bodies and flexing circular wings jumping into clear focus as Lee's sight reflexively amplified. Dawn light burned off their canopies. They rushed forward faster than the thunder of their wings. Neither Redd nor the corporal made a move to cover, and so Lee stood his ground, too. Redd put an arm around Chen Yao, but she pulled away from him without taking her gaze from the swooping culvers. It came to Lee that most acts of heroism simply spring from embarrassment.

As the culvers skimmed towards the tops of the trees around the Governor's house, a brilliant light shot up from the roof of one of the buildings that bordered the square. For an instant, Lee thought it was a strike from the culvers' weapons, but then the right-hand culver blew apart, and Lee realized that the light had been a one-shot laser. Disintegrating parts, most on fire, fell in slow trajectories as the other culver stood on its nose in midair, clapped its wings above its canopy, and dropped below the cliff.

"Well," the corporal said with gloomy satisfaction, "now they know we defected." He paused, his head cocked. He was listening to the speaker in his helmet. He said, "Oh, they know, all right. Come on."

Redd and Lee trotted alongside him, and little Chen Yao

had to run to match their pace. She said, "I hear a distant thunder."

"Cavalry," the corporal said. "This way."

They entered the shade of one of the arcades that lined the square, and cantered up a winding stair lit by sunlight at every other turn from narrow glazed windows. The glass had been milkily pitted by centuries of winter sandstorms. A reflexed groove was worn into the middle of each stone step. Lee couldn't stop noticing details all of a sudden. Every moment was suddenly significant.

The stair ended in an open trapdoor. Lee stepped on to the flat roof, where the morning breeze seemed colder and stronger than in the square, the sunlight rawer. Raw gold pouring from the sun's tiny disc, gleaming on the solar panels which, like flowers, had turned towards it, silhouetting soldiers who squatted behind the low parapet bordering the roof.

The corporal offered Lee a pair of fieldglasses, but Lee shook his head and asked, "Where?"

The corporal pointed.

Virus-enhanced sight brought into sudden focus a line of mounted soldiers stretched across the barren red landscape. The sun was at their backs as their lithe mounts moved forward at—an inset in Lee's sight blinked a figure formed of black bacilli-like rods—at a steady forty kph.

"Like machines," Chen Yao said.

Lee said, "But they're still people."

"No," the corporal said, "the young lady is correct. This is a crack cavalry unit, and all the soldiers and their mounts will be hardwired for maximum co-ordination."

Soldiers on the roof and on the roofs either side were firing deliberate single shots.

Little puffs of dust were fountaining up here and there before and behind the line. A warhorse reared up, toppling its rider as it snapped with fanged jaws at a red rose smashed into its scaly flank. A rider slumped sideways, shattered head pumping blood across his mount's withers, and it charged forward wildly, the corpse of its rider flopping like a badly used puppet. But the line continued to move steadily forward.

"They'll charge any moment," the corporal said. Lee looked around, but the corporal was speaking into his microphone. "Keep the fire rate steady when they do. It's a tactic to panic us. Don't let them."

Lee found that he was holding his breath. Someone used a one-shot laser and two cavalry soldiers and their mounts vanished in a flare of burning sand. The rest of the line came on inexorably. The corporal said something urgently in his microphone, but Lee didn't hear it: in that moment the charge started.

Warhorses leaped forward as one, leaving behind a rising line of dust. Lee's motion sensor read-out blurred, stabilized around two hundred kph. In three breaths the cavalry halved the distance between their line and the edge of Ichun; in the next they started to fire, knocking huge chunks of masonry from outlying buildings. Lee saw several riders stand in their saddles, whirling slings which loosed hornet swarms of micromissiles. Something discharged a swathe of coherent light which burned a roof clean of soldiers three buildings to the left. There was a rising haze of dust and smoke; the riders vanished into it.

Lee and the soldiers ran to the other side of the roof just in time to see the last of the cavalry clear the tanglewire barricades with a meter to spare. Warhorses scattered across the square as they charged after fleeing civilians. One grabbed a woman directly below Lee's vantage point, worried her and tossed her aside, a bloody bundle. The corporal was shouting wildly, his microphone hanging from his throat. A last rider cleared the barricades; a shaven-headed woman dressed in seamless black leather.

Lee recognized her at the same moment her face turned to him. She wore sunglasses that masked half her face, but Lee knew that she had seen him, and he ran for the stairs, instantly kicking into hypermode.

Fifty-four

Lee's body moved faster than his thoughts. Reflex took him to the top of the stairs before he remembered what Redd had said on *The Black Dragon*. He swerved and leaped between two soldiers straight over the parapet, snatching a rifle from one of them as he went.

He landed on the clay tiles which roofed the arcade that ran the length of the building and let himself roll over the edge. The ground came up so slowly he could turn in mid-air and like a cat land crouching on feet and hands. He did a backflip into the arcade's shadow, and an instant later the paving where he'd landed exploded in stone chips.

Lee ran for cover, storing upside-down glimpses of the square: warhorses circling left and right around burning trucks; a tree hit by a stream of gunfire and shuddering into flinders of wood and leaves; a legless man crawling across the wide avenue, leaving a trail of blood. He reached the shelter of a stone pillar, looked left, right. Warhorses moving slow as molasses. Each leaf and splinter distinct as it fell. The dying man slumping by degrees.

A riderless warhorse trotting across the square had to be hers. Lee's sight went momentarily infrared as he gathered himself, a snapshot in luminous greens that he stored as he ran the length of the arcade and drew gunfire; he reversed, and quick tiny things sang viciously where he would have been.

Lee made himself as small as possible behind another pil-

268

lar. Every muscle trembled. His skin was on fire as it radiated spent energy. His grip had dented the aluminum stock of the stub-barrelled rifle. But his heart pumped smooth and slow; he wasn't even out of breath. The viruses had rebuilt his muscles to take care of oxygen debt.

It took a microsecond to match the infra-red glimpse of the square with triangulation of the gunfire aimed at him: there she was, burning bright on the far side of the square, firing from the hip as she ran for the trucks burning in the center of the square. She was wired for speed, too.

Lee gathered himself and ran out into smoky morning light. He dodged and weaved amongst the cavalry with dreamlike ease. He caught the slow-moving arm of a rider as she started to raise her sling, pulled her down and left her behind. Saw dust spurts tracking towards a civilian woman who lay clasping her bleeding leg, and knocked her out of the way. All the time turning his head, snapping in and out of infra-red, short rifle flicking back and forth.

But the heat of the burning trucks hid the mercenary's bright trace.

Half the cavalry had broken from circling the square and were moving towards the broad avenue that led to the Governor's house. Lee took a breath and ran after them, winding in and out of their hurtling bodies.

He had time to see everything clearly: the lather of foam flying from their red, fanged mouths; their rolling yellow eyes aflame like lamps; the motion of muscles under their spotted hides; the intent expressions of their crouching riders. A warhorse snapped at Lee, but he easily dodged the lazy snatch of its jaws and vaulted up behind its rider and ripped out the cables which connected his headpiece to the skin-tight fighting suit. The rider went into tetanic spasm and Lee reached down, gripped the man's right leg, and tipped him out of the narrow saddle. The warhorse bucked violently; Lee sang calming words to it. A dozen strides later, just as the riders around him were beginning to react to what had happened, he jumped down, safe on the far side of the square.

He looked right and left, infra-red sight piercing rolling dust clouds. A riderless warhorse charged at him, and Lee swerved aside.

Then he was smashed to the ground.

Mary Makepeace Gaia, hanging from the warhorse's harness on his blind side, had dropped in passing and then leaped. Lee reacted by reflex. The viruses took over. His body made the pass of the Startled Locust and he was two meters away. The mercenary was climbing to her feet and fire was burning his shoulder where she'd cut him.

She had lost her sunglasses; a ball of black metal moved in her stitched eyesocket. Lee's rifle lay on the ground at her feet. She kicked it aside, raised her knife.

Lee assumed the posture of the Angry Crane, left foot tucked behind right knee, arms half raised, elbows out like wings.

The mercenary laughed and threw away her knife. Then she was upon him.

They whirled and kicked amongst warhorses rearing in slow-motion panic. Lee vaulted clear across one to escape Mary Makepeace Gaia's attack and landed in a weaving crouch, the sharp pain of splintered ribs dying away as viruses damped nerves. The edge of his right hand stung where he'd caught the side of her head.

She came at him again, but this time Lee ran forward to meet her. They flew past each other, legs scissoring out in a complex ballet. His right foot caught her under her armpit, but she grasped his ankle and twisted. He fell sprawling in dust, rolled from the slow-motion plunging of a warhorse and felt a wind and rolled again so that the mercenary's kick merely bruised his hip instead of breaking his spine.

Lee jumped up in a half-squat, right ankle rubbery and feeling as if it had been dipped in ice, ice wrapping his ribs, his hip, a line of ice down his back from the cut, his shirt stuck to him with blood and dust.

The mercenary came at him again. Lee dodged amongst the stamping legs of two warhorses as she whirled through the Springing Tiger, the Striking Snake, the Striking Mantis, the Striking Spider. Lee's body countered in a whirl of arms and legs; striking attitudes at blinding speed, they whirled through the dust and smoke and carnage in the square, leaping burning trucks, dodging wreckage each flung at the other, dodging bullets. Both sides were firing on them—fortunately, no one thought to wave a laser across the square. Twice Lee grabbed weapons from the hapless cavalry, and twice the mercenary knocked them from his hands. He was slowly being forced back towards the tanglewire barricade at the far end of the square.

The mercenary feinted left then right as he tried to break away. And then she paused. Lee watched her, back in the posture of the Angry Crane but with right foot tucked up behind left knee. Sweat was just breaking out across his fevered skin.

"Not bad for a beginner," the mercenary said. And then he was on his back, looking up at her with the pink sky beyond. The iron taste of dust parched his throat.

"Now you're mine," she said.

That was when Chen Yao jumped on her back.

Lee rolled away, smashed down a soldier and took his rifle. Mary Makepeace Gaia laughed. She held Chen Yao out in front of her by an arm and a leg. She shouted a single word. It rolled and rattled around the square.

"Yield!"

The rifle hummed and shifted in Lee's hands as it tracked the mercenary. He said, "So you need me alive."

"Yield! I'll spare the little girl."

Lee dropped the rifle and spread his hands. The next moment he was on his back again. Mary Makepeace Gaia grinned down at him and punched him three times, and he couldn't breath, couldn't move, and everything dropped back to normal speed.

"I only need a little piece of you alive," the mercenary said.

"Spare the girl. You promised." The words were squeezed from the vise of his chest.

"I lied. You get to watch her die. Then I do you."

And then the mercenary was knocked sprawling. She sprang to her feet and was knocked down again, her right arm shattered. The third shot struck the ground by her head and spun away end for end. Lee glimpsed the captain of *The Black Dragon* standing at the edge of the arcade's roof, his long rifle poised. The mercenary saw him too, and blurred into hypermode.

Lee scooped up Chen Yao and ran for his life.

Fifty-five

The Governor's house was aflame from end to end. Cavalry charged around the ruined garden, shooting into the flames. One rode straight at Lee and he went into hypermode again. With Chen Yao in his arms, he ran down a street lined with gutted shops. At the far end a barricade of crates, furniture and doors had been wedged together. Wu Lin vaulted its top and sped down the street, meeting Lee just as he slowed down.

The surviving leaders of the uprising were making their last stand beyond the barricade, around the elevators down to the Plain of Heaven. Lee watched as a dragon in chains gaped its jaws wide to swallow *The Black Dragon* herself, upraised dispersers and masts and all. Links rattled by, each as thick as Lee's thigh. The sound of draining water mixed with distant gunfire and the shrill shriek of steam as the cradle closed around *The Black Dragon*.

Redd took Chen Yao from Lee's arms. She was unconscious, with bruises beginning to show on her forehead and neck. The cowboy was streaked with soot, and one side of his face was scorched as red as dust.

Different parts of Lee's body began to shudder at different speeds as he started to come down from the extended period of hypermode. Time passed in shuddering jerks. He was lying on the ground, a sac fixed to his arm, pulsing glucose-saline into his bloodstream. Someone spoke to him, went away. Lee replayed it: Redd leaning over him, saying, Hold

273

on in there Billy Lee, we're gonna get you out of here soon as we can. His muscles clenched and relaxed, rotating each joint of his legs and arms in turn. His fingers tapped staccato codes.

Redd came back. Lee sat up, and almost fainted.

"Easy partner. Nothing to do now but run away. You might as well lie back."

Lee peeled the drained sac from his arm, wiped the spot of venous blood that appeared when its proboscis pulled free. "How bad is it?"

Redd fanned himself with his hat. There was a singed hole in its crown. He said, "They cut us in half. The garrison troops are holding their rooftop positions, but they're surrounded. Whole town's on fire, and all we have are the elevators."

"The best we could hope," Lee said. He listened to the sound of explosions, coming closer like giant's footsteps.

"You were the last to get through," Redd said. "Chen Yao will be OK. Hard-headed little girl. Soldier's dead—went to meet the cavalry charge head on. We . . . "

That was when the water in the channel leading to the elevator caught fire.

It went up all at once, flapping sheets of fire rising higher than the big cable drums atop the elevator head. Redd and Lee turned just in time to see Mary Makepeace Gaia leap through the flames. Lee jumped to his feet and almost fell down again. Someone grabbed his arm and said, "Let me use your gift, brother."

It was Wu Lin.

Before Lee could say anything she kissed him and ran towards the mercenary, silhouetted against flapping flames. She ran faster and faster, blurring into hypermode: the viruses had already adjusted her musculature and nervous system.

The mercenary's right arm was strapped up, but when she went into hypermode it hardly seemed to matter. She and Wu Lin whirled around each other, but while Wu

Lin could match the mercenary's superhuman speed, she had only courage to wield against the other's honed technique.

It wasn't enough. The mercenary broke Wu Lin's right arm, kicked her legs from under her, planted a boot on her throat. "Come to me!" the mercenary shouted. "Come to me, Wei Lee, and I swear I'll spare this one!"

Lee screamed and started forward, but Redd hauled him around and Lee found that he was too weak to resist. He didn't see the mercenary's killing blow, but he felt it all the same, and shuddered and cried out as Redd lifted him up and tipped him over the elevator's railing on to the white-wood deck of *The Black Dragon*. Girders arched above the skimmer. Lee took a step forward and almost fell on his face. Redd helped him sit up, then unholstered his pistol.

"Let's see the bitch bite on one of these," he said.

"Give me a minute . . . "

"No time, Billy Lee! Chen Yao said you have to go on. I believe her. Think of us."

And then he was gone, and the cradle which held *The Black Dragon* swung out over the edge. Elevator tracks scored parallel lines down the cliff face, dwindling down to the smooth surface of the Plain of Heaven. Water which spilled the joint of the big lock gates made a distinct falling noise amongst the noise of steam and clank of steam-driven machinery. Lee had trouble keeping things at right angles. It was as if the world was trying to turn itself out. The air seemed packed with forms, huge and vague.

Everything lurched as the elevator started down with ponderous smoothness. Girder work dropped away; huge chains made a rushing sound as they moved up.

For a long minute *The Black Dragon* dropped down towards the dust sea.

Then the culver appeared beyond the bow of the cradled skimmer, matching its fall.

Lee dragged himself to his feet, clutching at the rail, saw the pilot sitting in the bubble of its Cyclopean eye. Sailors ran for weapons, but the culver shrugged its wings and shot upwards and something exploded far overhead. *The Black Dragon* lurched in its cradle and then everything was falling free.

Fifty-six

The first time Lee woke, it was night.

He was on his back. His face was masked, and he was peering through little round lenses, looking straight up at the stars. Overlays came and went—sighting lines, vectors, navigational algorithms. Certain stars were bracketed, with figures clustered next to them. Presently he saw that these were moving counter to the great wheeling motion the world made as it continually sank eastward.

In all that time he didn't think to move. At last the overlays blinked off and he faded into the vast starry night.

The second time he woke, it was like a monitor warming up.

Sound first. The dreamy hiss of dust slipping past a hull, the crackle and hum of dispersers like the white noise of an old-fashioned radio tuned between stations. The creak of rigging, and the metallic crinkling of the sail.

A mask was clamped over his face, feeding him air with a rattling hiss. Lee opened his eyes, peered through the mask's round lenses.

It was day, crisply warm with the sun a shade off vertical. He lay in the craft's padded cockpit, sheltered by the narrow wedge of shadow cast by the perspective-narrowed triangle of the silvery sail. With three pairs of dispersers slung out on either side—red dust dipping around their black pods, which crackled and spat with induced static—the little craft looked something like a water-skating insect. A water-skater with a sail on its back and a stabilizing fin in its belly, and a lost lonely homunculus riding it.

Lee sat up. A voice said, "Well, it's about time, Master. Do we feel at all like talking?"

A stalk rose from a control housing. It terminated in a cluster of sensors, like a machined orchid.

"Or perhaps we're just the strong and silent type," the computer said. Its voice, neither male nor female, was informed by a querulous inflection.

Lee said, "Where are we?" His voice sounded strangely intimate inside the mask.

All around, from close horizon to close horizon, stretched a sea of red dust. The little craft—it was a skimmer's gig—was running with the wind. Gently swelling waves marched across the surface of the dust, each precisely the same shape and height as the next, defined by a narrow line of shadow at its near side. Even as Lee watched, dazed and confused, logy with the weight of consciousness, the sun reached noon. Shadow lines vanished across the bowl of the dust sea. Wave tops were oscillating streaks of slightly brighter red across the glowing red surface, making dizzying moire patterns. A faint spume fumed into the air from each wave crest. Although a transparent shield curved around the padded cockpit where he sat, he could feel wind-blown dust stinging his hands.

The computer gave universal grid coordinates. Lee supposed that his rewiring could translate that into an aereographical position, but he didn't want to call on any of his new talents right now. Virus-stored memory was a pregnant weight in his head, and he didn't think he could stand instantaneous apprehension of the terrible moments after the culver had stooped upon *The Black Dragon* in its descending elevator cradle.

He said to the computer, "Make sense of that for me."

"We are sailing east by northeast, towards the strait which links the Plain of Heaven with the Plain of the Garden of Eternal Bliss. We've been sailing two days four hours, and estimated time of arrival is in eight days, fifteen hours."

"Where are we heading?"

"I'd prefer one question at a time. My processing ware isn't all I would like."

Lee said, "I'm sorry," and felt foolish. This was only a machine, after all. He said, "It doesn't matter. I know where we're going."

"Am I speaking to the woman now?"

"You're speaking to me. There is someone else aboard?"

"Well, in a manner of speaking," the computer said, and then Lee remembered Miriam Makepeace Mbele.

The computer said, in a crabby pedantic tone, "I think that it really would be better if I explained . . . "

"You are taking me to Tiger Mountain."

"Lucky guess."

"Not at all. Is there a way of closing up this cockpit?"

"Fresh air is good for you."

"If that means that you can do it, then please do it." The mask was irritatingly hot and close against his face, but if he took it off he'd choke in the dust-filled air.

The transparent canopy slid up around him like the calyx of a flower. There was a rush of air, and he started to fumble with the straps of his mask.

"Please be patient," the computer said. "It is necessary to change and filter the air."

Lee waited.

"It is safe now, but please don't do this too often," the computer said. "My resources are finite."

Once he had taken off the mask, Lee vigorously scratched the weals left by its seals under his chin, around the line of his jaw, at his hairline. The computer said, "I can fix something to eat. My cookery sub-routines are very adept. Pigeon in plum sauce, perhaps, or . . . "

"Please be quiet. I want to think."

"You've been living on unrefined pap for the last two days," the computer said. "I was only thinking of your health." It sounded offended.

"Later," Lee said. "Now, I must think."

There was a tiny toilet. Lee emptied and cleaned the suit's

relief facilities and sponged off the worst of living inside it for two days. Then for a long time he did nothing but sprawl naked on the live hide couch at the stern of the little gig. Sunlight sank through the canopy and through his skin to his bones. He watched waves of dust march in long parallel rows towards the horizon, their shadows running ahead of them now. The gig was moving just faster than the waves, dipping and rising smoothly as it ploughed through soft dense swells.

Shards of what had happened were jumbled in his mind. He was reluctant to put them together. He kept thinking of certain details. Wu Lin sprawled helpless on the ground beneath the triumphant mercenary, a hellish tableau lit by the flames that roared across the surface of the burning canal. He'd only known his sister for a day, but he knew that he would mourn her for the rest of his life. He remembered her grip on his arm and her exultant cry before she had sprung into battle, armed only with courage and the half-formed gifts of the anarchist viruses.

And he remembered the way *The Black Dragon* had shuddered like a living thing when the culver had blown free the elevator cradle. He remembered the end of a chain flinging arcs of molten droplets as it fell past, loop after loop of a chain half a kilometer long falling towards the red dust sea. A sailor's broad-brimmed straw hat sailing off, rising up on some current of air, the man's lined brown face turning to his, mouth open around an unspoken question. The sickening smooth slide, faster and faster. He remembered the flashing glimpse of the counterweight of the empty dust-ballasted elevator shooting up the cliff face as the cradle carrying *The Black Dragon* plunged down, brake blocks screaming and showering great drooping arcs of sparks.

Then there was nothing but pictures shuffled one after the other, bright and sharp in every detail but with no emotional content. Lee suspected that Miriam had taken over then.

He let the barrier down. He wanted to see what had happened when Miriam's virus-encoded personality had forced control of his own body. He saw that he alone had escaped, clambering across the wildly tilting deck to the gig, strapping himself into a crash cradle and shooting the sturdy little vessel away from *The Black Dragon* moments before impact, taking off across the dust sea under cover of the plume of dust raised by the skimmer's final keel-breaking impact.

He had looked back once. Had seen a vast dust cloud spread out at the base of the high cliffs. Had seen, atop a sheer kilometer of cliff face, the smoke of Ichun rising against the pink sky.

The images were mercilessly sharp and clear and bright. The viruses forgot nothing. Lee watched what they showed him with tears leaking from his clamped lids, running back towards his ears.

Much later, the computer said, "Our destination is visible, if you care to look five degrees port of my bow."

Sternward, the horizon had risen to touch the tarnished coin of the sun. Light lay across the tops of the waves, lines of red light broadening as the waves marched west, melting into a general glow. Lee turned and looked ahead, saw a star burning at the wide, level, dark eastern horizon. It was the tip of Tiger Mountain, the biggest volcano in the solar system, so huge that its peak rose above the horizon. Rose, in fact, through the atmosphere of the world, its flat-topped caldera shining in near-vacuum twenty-seven kilometers above the surface of the Dust Seas.

Fifty-seven

The ecosystem of the Dust Seas were Cho Jinfeng's greatest triumph. Originally, they had been low-lying boulder-strewn cratered plains, a thin crust lying over dust and rubble bound by ice into permafrost as hard as iron and a kilometer deep. But the ice of the deep permafrost had begun to melt when Mars had been slowly warmed, by sky mirrors and by the greenhouse effect as out-gassing and sublimation of the south polar cap raised the carbon dioxide partial pressure. The plains had become unstable, and for the first time in an aeon Mars had been racked by quakes.

Boulders (and half a dozen ancient space probes) had sunk into quaggy unbound dust. Currents had started to circulate. Great convection cells had carried heat deeper, liberating more and more permafrost water, freeing more and more dust. For three decades, muddy rain had fallen over most of the world in summer, and dust storms had shrouded most of it in winter. The Tibetan colonists had endured the climatic overturn in underground citadels; many of the Yankees had been wiped out, their fragile, technologically dependent settlements overwhelmed by weather. When it had finished, much of the dust had been redistributed, but treacherous bowls of semi-marshy dust had remained in certain places, hundreds of meters deep, and useless.

Until Cho Jinfeng had found an ecological role for them.

She had developed strains of phytoplankton which could flourish in the dust. Gene-melded from diatoms and foraminiferan amoebae, the microscopic plants had dense silicon valves permeated by threads of water-hungry cytoplasm which extended along long spines into the dust. They scavenged every molecule of water they encountered, even that chemically bound to the surface of the dust grains. The marshes had liquefied: the liquid not water but free dust, divided so fine the grains lacked even crystalline structure.

In the early stages of terraforming, vast amounts of oxygen had been released by the phytoplankton, which had been protected from lethal ultraviolet by the microclimate haze at the surface of the Dust Seas. The Dust Seas had reached stability. Water released by convective melting of permafrost at the bottom of the Seas was bound into the biosphere by phytoplankton. Shelled zooplankton devoured the phytoplankton, and in turn the vast swarms of these tiny animals were devoured by armored dust rays which glided across the surface of the dust on huge tough membranes spun of carbon: carbon fibres. And dying phytoplankton, zooplankton and rays sank into the deep dust to replenish the great cycle.

Humans had established trade routes across the great dry seas, plied by wind- and static-powered dust skimmers.

And now, under the deep canopy of stars, a single small gig moved on the face of the dry red sea of the Plain of Heaven towards the reefs of Tiger Mountain.

Fifty-eight

The computer woke Lee at dawn. "We have a problem, Master," it said. When Lee asked what it meant, it showed him a sternward view, zooming in on a silvery speck shining at the horizon of the red-dust sea. It was another gig, its sail catching the first light of the sun.

"Who are they?"

"The transponder identifies it as being a gig out of the skimmer *The Lady Of The Golden Isle*. We won't be able to outrun it. It's a smaller craft, with a bigger sail area."

"Why should we want to run away? Can I talk to it? I mean, to its crew."

"Its passengers," the computer said.

"Whatever. Just try."

Minutes passed. Lee watched the other gig grow imperceptibly larger.

The computer said, "No one answers. I can tell you something, though."

"Go ahead."

"There are two people aboard."

"I suppose I should ask how you know."

"Because I asked the computer. It's not as smart as me."

"Smugness is not a virtue."

"It's the simple truth. I've found the alarm sub-routines. Want me to use them? There's an impressive siren."

"Why not?"

"I suppose I can take that as an affirmative. Ah. Now I

284

know that they are awake, because someone has switched off the siren. I'm getting voice, no visuals. I'll let you deal with it, Master. I don't understand some of the words."

A voice sounded out of the middle of the air. It was Redd.

"Who the fuck turned on all the bells and whistles?"

And Chen Yao said, "Wei Lee? Did you do that?"

Fifty-nine

The gig carrying Chen Yao and Redd caught up with Lee's gig by noon, and they clambered across to meet him. Redd was grinning like a madman under his filter mask; Chen Yao looked around coolly and said, "We will be more comfortable here."

"I'll make sure of it," the computer said, and closed up the canopy. The other gig had already fallen behind. Its sail flapped idly for a moment, then caught the wind and bellied full as it tacked away, turning back towards Ichun.

Chen Yao and Redd had stolen the gig to follow Lee. It had been Chen Yao's idea; Redd claimed that he had come along to look after her. They had ridden the last elevator cradle down, away from the razing of Ichun and the retreat of its surviving citizens. Most of the garrison had died fighting their own comrades, but many of the citizens had managed to escape across the canal.

"The captain of *The Black Dragon* organized the retreat," Chen Yao said. "He had the bridge blown."

"Television crews turned up," Redd said. "From three of the commercial channels. That stopped the soldiers following, and stopped the culvers attacking the retreat. I guess everyone on Mars will have seen what the Army of the People's Mouths did." In a softer tone of voice, he added, "The woman that killed your sister got away. I'm sorry, Lee. I tried to chase her, but she vanished."

Lee said, "I think we'll see her again."

286

"I'll be ready next time," Redd said.

Lee said, "I'm glad to see you both, but you must realize you're in more danger here than you ever were in Ichun. It's a difficult road I'm following. It is clear that war is not the answer. I'm no leader, nor can I countenance the idea of people dying for what they think is my cause."

Redd said, "Seems to me there's an undeclared war being fought. You can't blame yourself for what happened at Ichun."

"Innocent people died. They didn't even know what they were really fighting for."

"Freedom," Redd said. "It's what we all want, right?"

Chen Yao said, "Wei Lee, I bet you haven't even asked the computer what your path is."

"Well, it told me we're going to Tiger Mountain, but I already knew that. Is anything else expected of me?"

The computer said, "The woman told me that once you reached Tiger Mountain you would find your own path, Master."

Chen Yao said, with mounting distress, "Is that all? That can't be all she said! She was supposed to know how to disable the defenses. That's why she came here!"

"I don't think the transfer was very accurate," Lee said. He tried to call up memory of the time before he'd woken, when the fragmented memories of Miriam Makepeace Mbele had had control of his body, but he still had little control over the menu of his eidetic facilities. Specifics lay just out of reach, like an unspoken word lodged on the back of his tongue.

Chen Yao was saying something. Lee opened his eyes. No, they were already open. It was just that he hadn't been using them.

Chen Yao said, "Don't *ever* do that again!"

Behind her, Redd said, "You were out a long time, Billy Lee. We were getting kind of worried."

Lee blinked. The sun had moved. He had cramp in his right leg, where it was doubled up under his left. Even as he felt the pain, it began to fade. The computer told him he had been in a trance for more than three hours, and Lee began to realize just how dangerous his virus-built powers were. He could vanish inside them, and never reappear.

Redd said, "I was keeping watch while you were . . . out. I think we're getting nearer that mountain."

"You let me worry about navigation," the computer said. "The top of Tiger Mountain may well be above the horizon, but we have a long way to go. We have almost crossed the Plain of Heaven, but we still have to sail the Plain of the Garden of Eternal Bliss."

Sixty

Wind rose as the gig sailed the narrow strait between the two dust seas. Driven by temperature differences, dust-laden gales howled like all the lost souls of Mars's dead between high red cliffs, drove high, heavy waves and the gig before it.

After the strait, for a night and a day and another night the gig moved southeast, aslant clashing combers of dust in a hazy spume that blotted out the sun and sky, that turned the King of the Cat's broadcasts to crackling mush. Redd, seasick, grumbled that he'd finally found a mode of transportation worse than a horse.

Then there was a dawn that filled half the sky with filigrees of lacework like glowing iron. The dry, powdery waves were low and broad and lazy. The gig left a triple wake behind as it powered towards Tiger Mountain.

Lee and Redd and Chen Yao put on their filter masks and had the computer lower the canopy, which had been scored and scratched with millions of minute pits and lines by the force of the storm. The air was fresh and cold. Lee kicked off his boots and walked to the high sharp prow. His muscles responded automatically to the sway of the gig's motion.

He faced into the sun and bowed, then went through the moves Soldier had taught him. He felt his blood fizz and his muscles slidingly loosen, like silky steel cords under his skin. Chen Yao exclaimed fussily whenever he got too close to the edge of the gig's decking; Redd, lounging in the stern, applauded.

"You both come here," Lee said, and for two hours they went through t'ai chi exercises, flowing from one position to the next in a slow dance that somehow grew into more than a simple exercise, was an affirmation of the bonds that joined them, each to each.

The Plain of the Garden of Eternal Bliss was richer in life than the Plain of Heaven, for its water was supplemented by run-off from the high glaciers of Tiger Mountain. As the great cliffs of Tiger Mountain's western shield wall rose ahead (their eroding feet, against which heavy dust combers ceaselessly broke, still many kilometers below the horizon), and the peaks of Tiger Mountain's three lesser sisters appeared as stars to the south, more and more shoals rode the heavy dust waves.

These floating islands were stromalithic accretions of filamentous blue-green algae and bacteria which formed stable platforms for densely woven stands of bamboo and creepers and grasses. Every species of plant had narrow silicon-impregnated leaves to resist the dust's ceaseless erosion, and as the gig spun past them the shoals glittered in the sunlight like heaped diamonds.

At night, faint luminescence was visible within the shoals, as if each were a galaxy receding so fast its light could hardly escape, and there was a greenish cast to the restless surface of the dust itself, the bioluminescent glow of swarming zooplankton that were feeding on dense blooms of phytoplankton.

The gig was a shadow moving across this glowing landscape, and the shoals made drifting constellations which mocked the rigid patterns of stars that bestrode the sky, as if the reflection of every star had become a wanderer, a planet. Lee and Chen Yao and Redd sailed the great void between like the anarchist families forever falling free.

And it was on one such still starry night that the Free Yankee Nation captured them.

Sixty-one

Lee was sleeping when the computer sounded the alarm. He woke at once. The computer told him that the gig was heading east by southeast, and that something was moving in on it, ahead and to starboard. A smeared trace showed on radar, very close.

Redd pressed his face to the dark glass of the canopy and said sleepily, "It's just one of those floating islands."

Lee said, "It is moving against the current."

"Pirates," Chen Yao said, trying hard not to let her fear show.

Lee activated every running light, started to broadcast a warning. The shoal was a ragged shadow silhouetted against the starry sky; then it was towering over the gig.

There was the sound of breaking branches. The gig yawed, and all three passengers were flung from one side of its cockpit to the other.

Lee came up on hands and toes just as there was a crackle of blue sheet lightning either side of the gig's canopy: something had discharged the dispersers. The gig dropped. Its keel slammed into the dust. Lee was thrown down again, and this time he bit his tongue.

The computer was shrieking hysterically, alternating between incoherent rage and strings of fault codes. Lee spat a mouthful of blood and told it to be quiet.

"But we're sabotaged! We're under attack! We . . . "

"Quiet!" His command was softened by a bubble of spit and blood, but the computer shut up.

The gig groaned and rocked, slewed sideways with a soft dragging sound. Redd was sitting on the cockpit's decking, legs splayed, back braced against the couch. He had his pistol cocked and ready. Something rattled against the canopy, and Lee went into hypermode without a thought. By infrared he glimpsed blurred green human shapes outside, and then there was a point of intense light and the overpressured air of the cockpit whistled out through the hole the light had made. Something dropped through and broke on the decking of the cockpit. There was a sickeningly sweet smell, like decaying violets.

Chen Yao pitched to the decking. Redd slumped forward and dropped his pistol. Lee was halfway into his filter mask when the stuff overpowered him.

Sixty-two

L ee was woken by the sound of chanting. He had a foul
taste in his mouth and a blinding headache. He was
strapped to a post by a broad leather band that bound
his arms to his sides. Chen Yao was strapped to another post
on his right, Redd on his left. Redd's head lolled loosely.
Chen Yao said fiercely, "Do something, Wei Lee!"

They were in a vaulted chamber. Its high ceiling was supported by what looked like the hooped cartilaginous ribs of
some great beast. Narrow apertures admitted wedges of dim
red light. People crowded tiered ledges on either side. They
were all naked, and all had the faces of monstrous beasts.
Their bodies were covered in swirling patterns that glowed
sickly yellow-green.

When they saw that Lee was awake they shouted a single
Yankee word.

"*Classification!*"

A dozen old men and women shuffled forward. They wore
bristling masks and strange square flat-capped hats, and
were wrapped in tattered cloaks trimmed with the furry
skins of ice mice: dozens of tiny heads hung down from
collars and sleeves, eyes replaced by jet beads that glittered
in the torchlight as if called back to life. The old people
wielded bone calipers with which they pinched the heads of
the three prisoners from ear to ear and chin to pate.

"*Sterilization!*" the people roared.

An old man slashed the tip of Lee's right thumb, wiped a

293

piece of cloth over the bloody gash and threw it into a bowl of fuming liquid. Another old man stuck a blunt syringe into Lee's shoulder and injected what felt like a litre of salty bilge under his skin. From Chen Yao's indignant shouts Lee guessed that the same had been done to her.

"*Mutation!*"

An old woman tottered forward. She was robed in layers of filmy black stuff from neck to ankles, and a tall conical hat was tipped on her scrofulous scalp. She grinned toothlessly at Lee and shoved something small and hard and bristly into his mouth. It was a computer chip. Its edges cut Lee's lips, and he spat it out with a mouthful of blood.

The crone retrieved the chip and tried to get Chen Yao to swallow it, but the little girl managed to spit it right into her face. The crone picked it up again, and shuffled to Redd. The cowboy was still groggy from the gas, and he swallowed the chip as if it were a pill.

The watchers roared with approval. Two old men undid the leather band which bound Redd to his post, and he fell to his knees.

Chen Yao shouted with outrage. "Free us too! We're gods! Gods!"

The people roared again.

"*Electrification!*"

Half a dozen jumped down and swarmed over Chen Yao. They undid her bonds and carried her screaming and kicking towards an apparatus which others had lowered from the shadows under the high ceiling. They lifted her on to its wooden platform, strapped her hands to a blown glass bowl over her head. Two men on either side wildly cranked handles and a leather belt spun, passing up into the bowl, down below Chen Yao's platform. Chen Yao's hair bristled, then stood out from her skull in every direction.

"*Electrification! Electrification!*"

One of the old men used a pole to prod Chen Yao, and the little girl screamed each time a fat blue spark crackled between her skin and the pole's tip. Lee writhed against the leather strap which held him tight, tried to speed up into hypermode. But the effort was too much. The effects of the gas hadn't completely worn off. Everything flickered blackly, as fast as a hummingbird's wings, and he fainted.

Sixty-three

Whenhen Lee woke again, he was lying in a small fetid chamber lit by slanting light. Redd was kneeling over him. "Well, at least you're not dead," the cowboy said.

"Chen Yao?"

"Still out cold, but I guess she'll be OK." He laughed. "They were trying to cure her with static electricity."

"Who are they?"

Redd grinned. "I guess you could call them my countrymen."

The shoal which had intercepted and captured the gig was the home of the descendants of the staff of a Yankee research station long ago sunk in the dust sea. Now they were the Free Yankee Nation. They sailed the restless face of the Plain of the Garden of Eternal Bliss, following plankton swarms because that was where the dust rays would be found, and the dust rays were mostly what the Free Yankees lived upon. They used the rays' carbon whisker wings to construct multilayered dust-proof shelters in which they lived like worms in a rotten onion. They dried the intestines of the rays and beat them thin and sewed suits from them, made filter masks from the bristly palps by which the rays separated plankton from dust. They ate the rays' tough swimming muscles raw or pickled or dried, and rendered the rest of the flesh for oil which they smeared on their bodies and hair.

They had no lamps, and no fires. Fire was the shoal's greatest enemy.

They had preserved the remains of their ancestors' crude twenty-first-century technology, although it had mostly degenerated into ritual and superstition. Different cultures of primitive viruses—big as amoebae, and about as versatile—were jealously maintained by different families, but the circuitry which the viruses printed were used as folk medicines, or worn as jewellery. Redd had been accepted as one of them because he had swallowed a virus-grown circuit chip.

Lee learned all this from Redd and a Free Yankee who called himself Safety Officer. Safety Officer was a tall, scrawny old man with muscles tight as wires under loose skin. Lee could not see his face, or the face of any of the Free Yankees. They wore filter masks all the time. Speaker's was a bristling affair with tiny smoked glass eyepieces, like the snout of a subterranean insect. The Free Yankees were all experts in body language, and wore extensive tattoos to proclaim their family allegiances; they went naked inside their layered nest. They went in for swirling recursive designs, mostly in red and black, underlain by a secondary system of patterns created by injecting luminescent bacteria under the skin. In the gloom of the fetid space where he crouched with Lee, Safety Officer was lined with swirling patterns that glowed with the glaucous hue of the flesh of rotting fish.

Safety Officer was arbiter of quarrels between the dozen families. The Free Yankees had taken Redd to be the captain of the gig, and Lee and Chen Yao his property. While Redd was bathed and oiled and feasted, Lee and Chen Yao were shackled and told that they were lab rats.

"We decide to make you scholars maybe we give you names. Right now you don't need them," Safety Officer told his two prisoners.

Lee bowed politely. The long chain that linked the manacles on his wrists chinked.

Safety Officer cuffed Lee around his freshly shaven head in an off-hand manner. "None of the kow-towing Han shit," he said, almost kindly. "You're amongst proper folk now.

We're the Free Yankee Nation. We do things logically, scientifically."

Lee apologized as best he could. He still wasn't used to his virus translation program, which had taken over control of his larynx and tongue and lips, working independently but not quite at the speed of thought. Most of his sentences started with a muted choking sound, like a throat clearing. But it kept him alive. The Free Yankees were intrigued by a Han who spoke Yankee.

Chen Yao said, "He is a god. So am I. You let us go."

Safety Officer told Lee, "Your daughter is mad, but that's all right. You have seen our scientific way of curing insanity. When she's strong enough we'll try it again. The scientific way is the only true way. You Han are falling apart in your soft settlements. Pretty soon we will rise up and take the world from you. What do you think about that?"

"You have every chance."

"It is our destiny. Democracy will always triumph."

"Of course," Lee said, wondering just what Safety Officer meant by democracy. The Free Yankees were organized along the lines of a classic oligarchy, with power vested not in the individual but in archaic rituals and the persons associated with them. Safety Officer was powerful because of his name and his position, not because of who he was. No one was elected according to a test of ability.

Safety Officer cuffed Lee again. It was his characteristic gesture of bonhomie. "If you survive deprogramming, boy, why maybe you just might make student after all."

"I will learn," Lee said. "I will enhance the glory of the shoal."

"Don't give yourself airs. You'll do what you're told, that's all. Leave glory for the tenured."

"Yes, sir."

Safety Officer cuffed Lee again. "That's better. Now you two lab rats get your asses over to the kitchens. There's shit to be shovelled."

It was a sign of the Free Yankees' confidence that Lee and Chen Yao could squirm through the narrow tunnels of the nest without an escort. It was obvious that the Free Yankee Nation was much smaller than it had once been. Despite their fetish for privacy, which meant that every citizen, even the children, had two or three tiny rooms no one else could enter without invitation, there were many spaces in the shoal which were unused.

In the kitchens, under the watchful gaze of the fat domestic bursar, Lee and Chen Yao were put to sorting edible zooplankton from inedible phytoplankton, and stripping the tiny creatures of their silicon-impregnated shells. Later, as they spread nightsoil amongst the roots of stunted tomato plants and cucumbers in the moist warm greenhouse tunnels, they were able to snatch a whispered conversation.

"You've got to get us free," Chen Yao insisted over and over again, until Lee was fed up with pointing out that he wasn't going to kill everyone aboard the shoal, and in any event, he didn't know how to sail it.

He had talked to the computer through his virus-built transceiver. The senior tutor and chief technician of the Free Yankees had unsuccessfully tried to access the computer, and it boasted to Lee about the ease with which it had subverted their primitive Trojan Horse programs. But they had manually severed its control cables, so it had no control over any part of the gig, which had been hauled on to the shoal and concealed within thickets of thorny creepers.

"Even if I killed everyone, I'm not sure if I could fix the gig," Lee said. "And besides, I don't want to kill anyone."

"They're savages," Chen Yao said. "They don't count, not against a whole world. Just go into hypermode, Wei Lee. Show them that they can't treat gods like slaves!"

"They'll make land, sooner or later. Then we'll escape, I promise."

Chen Yao decapitated a dozen tomato plants with a sweep of her hoe. She rattled the long chain which swung between the shackles around her wrists. "It'll be too late!"

And then they had to stop talking, because the domestic bursar had seen what Chen Yao had done and was hurrying forward to scold her.

Sixty-four

The shoal was skirting the edge of a plankton bloom that grew where deep currents hit the edge of the shield of Tiger Mountain and rose to the surface, bringing moisture from the underlying permafrost. Dust rays, slow monsters with rippling wings fifty meters across, moved through shoals of plankton with their bristly palps swinging to and fro, leaving wide wakes of darker dust.

A dust ray trail was sighted the day after the Free Yankees captured Redd and Lee and Chen Yao. Soon after, a lookout tied to the top of the tallest tree of the shoal spotted the feeding plumes of the ray itself, and the entire population poured out of the nest and clambered up trees and bamboo stands to try and catch a glimpse of the beast for themselves. They regarded it as a propitious sign: Redd would be given the ritual chance to kill it, and so gain tenure.

It was the middle of the afternoon. The clear pink sky glowed like neon and both moons were aloft: Fear a tipped crescent just above the western horizon; Panic a chip of light falling eastward. A kind of haze hung over the dust sea, and its heavy surface was the color of molten copper. Sluggish waves rolled towards Tiger Mountain. Its lower flanks were hazed, but its flat peak was sharp and clear and seemed to rear higher than the two moons. The cliffs of its vast lava shield, six kilometers high, were so close that Lee could see house-sized boulders that piled up along their base, and the weathered folds and convolutions that vertically fretted their

300

heights, but they might as well have been on another world. Lee wanted, needed, yearned, to escape, to reach Tiger Mountain and climb to its top. Part of it came from the viruses, and from Miriam's partial personality, but at least half of it came from himself. He had made the promise to himself back in Ichun. But he wouldn't kill to keep that promise; too many people had died already.

Most of the Free Yankees were forward of the nest, crowding like a gang of apes in the dense thickets of bamboo. The largest bamboo stems were as thick as Lee's waist, and black sails had been raised high on them, straining in the brisk breeze. Masked children swung through the ratlines, shrieking with laughter.

Lee had to step around and duck under a web of guy ropes and lines. Blown dust sifted over his torn shirt and jeans; dust accumulated in the finest creases of his skin and worked into the seals of his filter mask. Hanging on a leaning bamboo stem, he peered around a dense tangle of wireweed at the prow of the shoal. A dark lane ran across the red dust, wider than the shoal. It was the track of the dust ray.

One of the Free Yankees, a tall thin man in crinkling semiopaque coveralls made from dust ray intestine lining, came up to Lee, clapped him on the shoulder. A tattooed eagle spread its wings around the back of his skull, under the straps of his mask. He unlocked Lee's shackles and handed him a wadded intestine suit. His voice was muffled by the bristly nightmare of his mask. He said, "You'll help your master. Put this on and come with me!"

A group of men and women were hauling something like the upturned shell of a giant tortoise. Redd was amongst them. A young woman, with muscular arms and a V-shaped torso that made her intestine suit tight across her small flat breasts, grabbed a rope and heaved. The shell shot forward and most of the others fell on their behinds.

By the time they had scrambled up, the boat—that was what the shell was—was riding high on the dust, under the tangle of tough polished roots which fringed the shoal. The muscular woman grabbed a sheaf of harpoons and jumped down. The others followed, and the tall man made to shove Lee forward.

Lee dodged the man's advance, and jumped. For a clean instant he thought he'd made a mistake; the small round boat was crowded with a dozen people (who had lines attaching them to the boat's rail), and if he landed in the wrong place he'd tip it over. But his virus reflexes took over. He felt as if he fluttered down as slow as a leaf and landed with one foot in the well of the boat, the other on the raised bow. He turned and raised a hand in salute to the man who'd tried to push him. It occurred to him that he must look like a captain making farewell on a difficult voyage, and he laughed inside his mask.

The harpoonist signed for him to sit down, her hands as eloquent in expression as her face might be behind her monstrous mask—she'd stuck fangs all the way around it, so it looked like the business end of a leech or a lamprey.

Redd clambered into the boat down a knotted rope, his feet skidding on ends of roots polished to the consistency of smooth iron by blowing dust. Hands reached up and helped him teeter into his seat, and then the mast was lowered into the boat and set in its step. A bird shape was nailed to the top of the mast, wide narrow wings spread. It was an ironwood carving of a cliff eagle, which spent almost all its life on the wing, sailing the thermals of Tiger Mountain's cliffs. It was the symbol of the Free Yankees, for both touched land only when necessary; cliff eagles to incubate their eggs and raise their young, the Free Yankees to render dust rays.

A big triangular sail was hauled up. It filled with wind and in an instant the little boat leaped forward, its flat frictionless hull hissing and banging as it skimmed the crests of the dust waves. The shoal dwindled from a ragged island to a speck, was lost in the vastness of the red sea. Lee paid attention to the business of handling the boat. A scoop like the V-shaped plough of a bulldozer acted as rudder, its long tiller hauled by two people. The boat was tacking into the wind, following the broad dark wake of the dust ray. At every other leg of each tack, abrasive dust fumed across the boat. Despite his coveralls, Lee's whole body was soon alive with incendiary itches as the fine stuff worked through seals and into every crease and fold of his skin. He had to keep wiping away powder that clung to his goggles.

He was given the task of pumping up silvery floats with a set of foot-operated bellows. Around him, the others were measuring out lengths of cable into neat loops. The harpoonist was checking out her weapons and showing Redd what to do.

Each long harpoon was tipped with a hollow, triangular barbed head; a cap that screwed into the hollow head held an explosive charge. Redd handed one to Lee, who hefted it, found a grip at its point of balance. Redd shouted to the harpoonist that it didn't seem possible to throw it any distance, and she shrugged and waggled her hands either side of her masked head: body laughter. Then she clamped something to the shaft of the harpoon, just behind the grip. It was a cluster of powder rockets. The harpoon was a low-tech rocket-assisted missile.

By now, the shoal had vanished. Lee found he kept looking to starboard, at the shield-wall cliffs rearing up from the shadows at their tumbled bases. So it was that he missed the first sighting, but, alerted by the muffled shouts of the Free Yankees, he saw the plume of the dust ray when it rose again: a sudden double sheet of darker dust which shot high into the air and ruffled out in long billows on the breeze.

The plume was dust, taken in as the ray sieved the sea for plankton, that had been ejected from the ray's fine barbed combs by a kind of convulsive cough.

Redd, his masked face next to Lee, said that it was a big son of a bitch. Lee had to agree. Up in the prow, the muscular harpoonist was arming her weapons, banging the explosive charges into sockets at their points with cheerful gusto. Everyone else ducked as the boat heeled to starboard and the sail swung across. The harpoonist handed Redd a harpoon, and at the same time Lee saw the ray.

Its wide carbon whisker wings stretched a hundred meters

either side of its long flat armor-plated body. The wings were as black as a vacuum shadow. (Miriam was suddenly with Lee, standing just behind him, it seemed, and it was difficult for him not to turn to her.) They ceaselessly rippled over the bronze surface of the dust as the ray moved forward with dreamy slowness amidst a fine haze. Its combs rose like signal arms against the pink sky, fantastic fringed sculptures a dozen meters across, swept down and out across the dust, collapsed into its mouth. A double sheet of dust shot up, and the filter combs swept out again.

The little round sailboat tacked away from the wake of darker dust churned by the ray's passage. For a moment it ran parallel to the rippling edge of the creature's port wing: then it tacked inward. Its hull shudderingly vibrated as it dragged across the tough tissue-thin wing. Lee ducked the sail's swinging boom, saw the harpoonist rise as the boat turned parallel to the ray's body.

The ray was as long as a locomotive, as flattened as a bed bug. Its tiny eye, like a bottle end set in its blunt armored head, was red as a stoplight. Breathing spiracles densely fringed with hairs pulsed arhythmically down the midline of its long flat body.

The harpoonist beckoned to Redd, had him brace one foot on the blunt raised prow, and handed him the harpoon. It was, symbolically, not attached to a line; nor was it armed. She moved his right arm and harpoon back, told him to throw when she did, it didn't matter where. Then she reached across and lit the rocket fuses.

"Throw!"

The cowboy threw as hard as he could. Sparks from the fuses sprayed his shoulder; the harpoon tipped head up as the rockets ignited, made a wobbling arc and struck the ray's body behind the armoured head, clattered down scales with the rockets still fizzing, and came to rest at the flexing junction between wing and body.

The majestic rhythm of the ray's feeding didn't miss a beat.

The Free Yankees raised a muffled cheer, and the harpoonist thumped Redd between the shoulder blades with such enthusiasm that he couldn't breathe for a full minute afterwards.

Meanwhile the harpoonist took up her own weapon, this one fully primed. She raised it in her right hand to her shoulder, held her left hand across her chest, a glowing wick between finger and thumb. She spun the harpoon's shaft and the wick dragged across the fuses of the rockets.

Then she leaned right back, flung her weapon forward.

For a moment it seemed to hang in the air, sparks flying from the furiously burning fuses. Then the rockets lit and it arched away in a flare of blue flame. It struck just behind the ray's tiny red eye, skittered sideways down its body. Then the charge blew. Dust rolled out from the explosion's brief red flower, leaving a ragged wound at the creased junction between the ray's body and its wing.

There was a convulsive shudder under the boat. Everyone except Lee and the harpoonist fell on to the coils of cables in the well. The ray's filter combs collapsed into its mouth and sheets of dust blew sideways, but the combs didn't shake themselves out again.

The muscular woman grabbed another harpoon, but as she braced herself something heaved under the boat and it rose until its prow pointed straight at zenith. The harpoonist flew backwards and hit the mast, and slid down it until she was sitting. The boat fell back and as the harpoonist struggled to her feet something plummeted from the top of the mast. It was the painted ironwood eagle. It hit the harpoonist's head with a heavy thud and fell into her lap as she slid back down again, this time quite unconscious.

Veils of dust were rising all around the edge of the ray's vast wingspan. The boat rocked as wave after wave passed over the wing on which it rested. People were hauling on the sail. One turned to Lee, jerked his thumb across his throat, pointed down, made a whirling motion.

Lee understood. The ray was about to sound. When it did, the boat would go with it, sucked under in a maelstrom of displaced dust. He snatched up a harpoon.

Virus reflexes made it easy to brace himself, exactly as the harpoonist had done. Redd saw what Lee was going to do, left off tending to the harpoonist and grabbed a slow match. He kicked away someone who made a grab at the harpoon and lit the fuses of its rocket cluster. Dust clouds shaken up by the ray's flexing wings made a dense smog, like fire-lit smoke. Its body was no longer visible by ordinary light, but Lee could see it clearly by infra-red, saw a hot spot just behind its bottle-end eye, a patch of blood-rich skin where the lapping armor plates had drawn apart. There was no time for thought. He aimed and threw.

The rockets exploded in mid-flight, blindingly bright through swirling dust. Lee balanced like winged victory. The rocket's red glare vanished—then a dull explosion blew out thick gouts of blood and pulped flesh which spattered everyone on the little boat and drummed like hail on the sail.

There was a moment of silence, and then the Free Yankees yelled and began throwing clusters of recurved hooks attached to the long thin lines. When enough of them had snagged, the Free Yankees started hauling them in, dragging the boat across the now still wing and jumping on to the ray's body like so many pirates boarding their prize, armed with silvery bladders which they promptly began attaching at the dust line.

Lee followed Redd. The armored scales were like a tiled roof; beneath them, through his boots, Lee felt a complicated tremor, the failing of the ray's nervous system.

The harpoon's charge had made a big fleshy crater. Blood, thick and black as crude oil, was drooling from it, and the dust seethed as blood sank into it: plankton feeding on the life fluid of the creature which had fed on myriads of their cousins. As dust slowly cleared Lee saw that the ray's wings had sunk below the surface, and that the taut bladders were mostly buried; attached by hooks, they were all that were keeping the ray afloat.

Masked men and women were capering and stomping up and down the ray's long flat body. The harpoonist had recovered, and was alternately rubbing her sore head and semaphoring her arms up and down as if she was trying to take off.

Redd grabbed her, whirled her in a brief waltz. Someone knelt, hands cupping flame. When he stepped back a rocket shot up at an angle over the dust sea, burst in a golden falling flower, bright against the soft pink of the sky. After a minute another flower bloomed, small with distance. Lee backtracked its trajectory, saw a speck at the horizon line. It was the shoal, black sails crowding every tree as it bore down on the dust ray.

Sixty-five

I t took the rest of the day to drag the dead dust ray to the shore. There was a narrow bay under toppling cliffs, its shore a fantastic conglomeration of buttresses and broken arches, hollows and bowls and humped boulders. It was like the ruins of a city, ancient black lava polished smooth as glass by the ceaseless whisper of dust. Cliffs soared above, sculpted with balconies and terraces and caves.

The shoal was drag-anchored at the seaward point of the bay by sinking a weighted sail at its stern, and the Free Yankees swarmed ashore in a flotilla of tiny boats, hauling the dust ray's corpse with them.

It was late afternoon when they beached it. The bay filled with the light of the setting sun, which poured through the high cliffs that bracketed its narrow entrance. Light was made solid by swarming dust. Gold: the light was gold. The Free Yankees moved like figures in a frieze of beaten gold, their shadows palpable, three-dimensional, extending like complex tunnels through the solid golden light. The long flat armored body of the ray glowed in the light as if it was being smelted.

Before the sun had set, the Free Yankees had peeled away the hard plates that shingled the ray's body, flensed the hectares of carbon whisker wings and cut them into strips with diamond knives. Black strips hung from ledges and across boulders like the backdrop to an opera. The kinks and coils of the ray's intestines had been read for portents, then emptied of half-digested plankton (a prized delicacy) and hung on poles to wind dry. Flesh was cooked on trays over a slow fire fuelled by oil drained from the ray's vast liver. Soon, only the ray's flexible cartilage skeleton was left, gleaming like the chassis of a fantastic aircraft.

The setting sun fell beyond the mouth of the bay and its swathe of light narrowed, less gold, more bronze. As it dwindled it seemed to run back into itself, until it hung like a blade at the entrance of the bay. Quickly, the blade shrank to a point that for a moment seemed to sway at the eclipsing edge of the cliff like a flower at the end of its stalk. Then the flower folded into itself, and slipped away.

There was still light from the sky, hard and pinkish, but now everything seemed flatter, mundane. In the fading sky light, the strips of wings seemed to sink into the darkness of the boulders and ridges on which they were hung. Torches were lit, a slowly growing constellation of smudgy red flames scattered around the hub of the smouldering fire.

A young child came up and set two torches in a crack in the smooth ledge where Lee and Redd and Chen Yao sat with Chancellor and other members of the senate of the Free Yankee Nation. These were the old men and women who had examined them, still wrapped in their fur-trimmed cloaks. Lee tried to make conversation, for the old know most and are unafraid of the truth, but at best the old men and women only nodded and smiled. Their finery was an honor earned not by wisdom but by survival of the perils of the Free Yankees' lives.

The torches were shafts of ironwood whose tips were wound with cloth soaked in dust ray oil. They burned reluctantly, hissing and crackling with dancing golden motes as dust blew through their flames. Heavy smoke rolled into the shadowy air, spread in a low haze amongst the massive boulders. It smelt dryly sweet.

Some of the Free Yankees had brought drums and tambourines and bells ashore, and as dish after dish of food was served, sweet following savoury following sharply sour, a ragged percussive syncopation slowly settled into a steady throbbing groove. Lines of children excited by the carnival danced in and out and around the big boulders which were scattered along the shoreline.

Redd picked scraps of meat from his teeth with the point of his knife. "These guys know how to have a good time," he said.

Lee smiled, filled with muzzy beneficence. He was drunk with fierce brandy and with exhaustion. His virus-altered metabolism could have swiftly denatured the alcohol, but for once he wanted to feel it. He had walked to the edge of death for no good reason but the superstitions of those around him, and he had come back. He was rebelling against the idea of himself that the Free Yankees had created, the idea in which he had acted when he had killed the dust ray. He didn't want to feel like a god. He wanted to feel human.

His own music was broken and scratchy. Iron in the dust broke it to a ravelling secret whisper. He switched it off, lifted his mask and drank more brandy. Every sip of liquor, every mouthful of food, had the bitter taste of dust in it.

Chen Yao said with disgusted despair, "You're both fools," and ran away down the rocky slope and pushed through the revels, which closed around her as the sea closes around a flung stone.

Lee started after her, but Redd caught his shoulder and he sat down heavily, off-balance. "Aw, let the kid be by herself," the cowboy said. "She doesn't understand we risked our lives today."

"I think that's what she meant," Lee said.

"Tomorrow," Redd said. He took a long swallow of brandy. "Tomorrow. That's what I told her. Man's gotta rest, after killing leviathan. Hey, just listen to that."

The drumming grew louder; half the Free Yankees were beating something, most of the rest were dancing. Torches glowed in cauls of smoke and dust, obscuring by lapping shadows more than they revealed by light: but to Lee the people greenly burned by the light of their own heat, like animated candle flames flickering in smog.

One of the Free Yankees clambered up to where Lee sat and bowed to the oldsters, who chuckled and nodded. It was the harpoonist. Her small breasts were bare, sprinkled with sweat turning to mud. The swirling tattoos on her arms and between her breasts burned with cold phosphorescence. Her mask grinned its three-hundred-and-sixty-degree grin at Lee. She grasped his hand in hers, and he followed her down towards the dance.

Halfway there, she stopped and pushed up her mask. Her long-nosed face was tattooed with barbed polychrome swirls, so that her round bright blue eyes seemed to look at Lee through a chink in a flowering hedge. Although she was a step below him on the uneven slope, she had to bend to kiss him.

"My name is Vette," she said, her mouth a centimeter from his own. "I owe you my life, and I never thought I would say that of any man. Are you really the one who will lead us back to the shore?"

"You're already here. The dust ray brought you, not I."

"They said you would deny it." Her smile glittered in the hedge of her face: like most of the Free Yankees, her teeth were capped with metal. Grit in their diet soon wore teeth to hollow stubs.

"Who told you that?"

"It was written in our charter, generations and generations ago."

"I'm not a god. I'm just a man. A man!"

"It doesn't matter who you are. It's what you do."

"No! It's what you want of me."

Vette laughed. "All I want you to do is come and join the dance!" She tugged Lee downward: he let her.

Time dissolved in the steady pounding of the drums. Lee knew that the beat allowed the clockless crocodile of his back brain to dominate the quantum-decision trees of his mind, but he didn't care. That was the point of dancing, to dilute or submerge the heavy burden of selfhood. To let the many become one. Redd was dancing too, waving his hat above his head and whooping and kicking his heels. At one point someone rubbed oil on to the back of Lee's neck. Perhaps it contained a contact hallucinogen, because soon afterwards Lee kept glimpsing things that weren't quite there. Or which were in one place one moment, somewhere else the next.

There was a species of hummingbird which lived in the cold high equatorial deserts. It lived in a close relationship with the giant yuccas which perpetually flowered in summer. Only its long beak could reach the nectaries at the base of the yucca's long flowers, and in taking that exclusive food it carried pollen from one plant to another. In winter it dug a burrow and like so many creatures of the desert let its body freeze right through, but in summer it was the spirit of the high deserts of Mars, darting here and there or suddenly immobile on a blur of beating wings, then gone, so that you had to look around to find it again.

So with the strange figure. Perhaps the dance had thawed it; perhaps the drug. Lee could only glimpse it in peripheral vision amongst the dancers, as if it lived in the blind spot of the eye. Whenever he tried to look at it directly it was gone, leaving only an impression of something human-shaped within a shadow that might have been a cloak, of a face masked like the faces of the dancers, except that it seemed that the mask was the face, or that behind the mask there was nothing at all. It was like the auditors that came and went in the other world of public information space. Perhaps they had always been in the real world, too, and only now could Lee glimpse one of them.

The other dancers did not see the figure. Lee was in the middle of a chanting snake of dancers, grasping the waist of the woman in front of him, his waist grasped by Vette. His filter mask was pushed back on his head. The heavy smoke, rolling out across the bay, seemed to damp down the dust, and it was possible to breathe without choking. Which was just as well, because it was impossible, given the exertion of the dance, to breathe through a mask for more than five minutes. His neck burned where the oil had been rubbed into it. A flask was passed down the line, hand to mouth to hand to mouth to hand without missing a beat. Lee took it and tipped it to his mouth and passed it on before swallowing—it was a fiery brandy that numbed the tongue and burned the throat. Something stood in the shadows of a carved arch, watching as he was drawn past. It did not go away when he looked at it.

Lee stepped out of the dance. Vette followed, and the line closed up and moved on, an organism not without a mind or with many minds, but with one mind made of many. As Lee stepped towards the arch the drumbeats began to separate into distinct moments.

The figure's robe covered its head and fell past its feet; it seemed to stand on the air above the dust-polished lava. The material of the robe was not a single weave but a four-color bit map composed of tiny irregular shapes, none bordered by another the same color, that merged in a polychrome shimmer. Although the figure was no taller than Lee, it seemed to look down upon him from a distance, its gaze burning through a mask which seethed with characters and figures, like the ceaseless fall of a virus-riddled data base. When Lee reached the arch, the figure raised a hand and beckoned.

Vette clutched Lee's shoulder, hard enough to bruise.

He said, "Do you see it?"

"Is it a soldier of your people?" Vette's soft hoarse voice could be retrieved from the spaces between the drumbeats. Lee's viruses did it without his noticing

"No. At least, I don't think it is a soldier in the way that you mean."

"A few of those things would overwhelm an army," Vette said with awe.

Lee realized in that moment that she would not leave him, and that she was braver than he.

He said, "Perhaps, but not in this world. There's a world behind the world we know. Your people have never been there, but it is home to many of mine."

"Our dead are reborn. Aren't yours?"

"I don't mean the dead," Lee said.

The figure extended its arm, and the hem of its swirling patchwork robe fell back to reveal its crooked little finger. Not a human finger, but a curved claw that suddenly grew and grew. Its sharp tip touched Lee's right temple—the end point of the triple-burner acupuncture line.

Everything tumbled away, and suddenly Lee was somewhere else.

Sixty-six

A spot of heat pulsed at Lee's temple, where the figure's claw had pricked him. He stood at the bank of a vast river or sea of mist that poured past him up into the sky, rising and curving over as it rose so that it formed a circle, sky and sea eternally one with no beginning or end. Intricate braids of golden light lived in the vaporous swirls, patterns switching restlessly and sparkling with trains of fugitive motes. They merged into a general glimmer where five dark shapes swam.

—*The Isles of the Blest.*

The voice was right inside his head. It was Miriam's voice, clear yet distant, as if transmitted down a fibre-optic cable from some far star.

—*The Isles of the Blest are five in number. They are named Tai Yu, Yuan Chiao, Fang Hu, Ying Chou, and Penglai. Once they drifted throughout the universe, but then they were fixed, each resting on the heads of three great Atlas turtles. There dwell those who have won immortality, or who will be reborn again, or who will pass on to a higher state. They are the white men and women who dwell in palaces of gold and of silver, and eat* li chih, *the fungus of immortality, and drink jade water.*

Lee shouted into the mist, calling for the librarian, but he knew that he was not in any part of known information space; he was beyond the barriers, where dwelt the dead. He was in Heaven.

314

A star dawned high overhead as if in answer to his call, and rapidly grew brighter as it dropped through roiling vapors. It was human-shaped, and glowed like a glass vessel in which a great lamp was trapped. Then its light flared and when Lee could see again, Miriam Makepeace Mbele stood before him.

She wore black many-pocketed coveralls. Her dark face crinkled in a grin. Her shaven pate was unscarred. "Sorry about that," she said.

"Am I in my head?"

She laughed. "You always were, Wei Lee. You haven't gone beyond that stage, not yet."

"I mean, that's where I thought you were."

"So I am still, or at least, the virus-transmitted partial of my own self is. But I'm here, Wei Lee, beyond life and death. The old computer in the lamasery had connections everywhere—this is where I went when you destroyed it."

Lee stepped backwards. His fear must have shown on his face, because Miriam laughed. "I'm on the side of the angels," she said. "More or less. I'll be your librarian, if you'll let me. Come on. There is much to show you, and there isn't enough time."

She took his hand (Lee remembered Vette, then) and mist and stuttering gold patterns streamed around them both. They were flying through the mist at a furious pace, although they seemed only to be strolling. In a few heartbeats, before Lee could frame another question, the triple peaks of the nearest island swelled into clarity. Two other islands could be dimly seen, and shapes that had to be the world-bearing turtles swam in the mist below them.

Miriam squeezed his hand. They stood in mist, high above the island, a way off from its shore.

"There were once five: now there are three. Tai Yu and Yuan Chiao were cast adrift when a giant waded into the sea and hooked the turtles with a drift line. When she had caught six she threw them over her back and waded away: in three strides she was gone. Without their turtles to bear them up, Tai Yu and Yuan Chiao were taken by the current and drifted into the ice. Imagine, Lee, the isolation of the poor souls of those islands, stranded in featureless frozen whiteness."

"Who are they, these inhabitants, these souls?" But he knew. They were the dead. "This is all a metaphor, isn't it?"

"Everything is itself, and the shadow it casts upon the world, and the shadows cast upon it by the world. Here the three are one."

Lee trembled. He felt as if he had been stripped naked and cast into a furnace, with only his belief to save him. Yet he could not simply accept what he was told: he could not serve blindly, without question. "Forgive me for saying so, but you don't sound like Miriam."

"The Miriam you knew was of the world. She was a mercenary assassin. I am your librarian, your guide. I came here, and it changed me. I can't leave unless you wake the dead dreamers from their icy sleep."

"Again, forgive me. But I am still not certain . . . what will happen when they wake?"

"We do not know. But to begin with, the barriers will be destroyed. The barrier that divides the information space of Mars from that of the rest of humanity, the barrier that closes the sky, and the barrier which binds the dead of the Earth. We will help all who want help."

Lee reflected that all his life he had been given that kind of help. All his life his destiny had been shaped by the actions of others.

"You have come far, Lee," Miriam Makepeace Mbele said. "Tiger Mountain is riddled with ducts and cableways and passages and caverns and nodes, drilled and laid by millions of von Neumann machines and big, slow viruses. A few parts still belong to those who built it. The ancestors of the Free Yankee Nation carefully chose the places they come ashore, and their descendants return out of tradition, which after all is simply unquestioned memory. Here, I can speak to you by induction, but even here, that calls attention to myself. These islands are secure, but I cannot yet land you upon them. That kind of direct interference has already lost two islands to Gaia. The final way is in the real world. That way is yours, yours alone to choose as you will—although we have arranged an ally for you. If you reach the top of the mountain, you will understand."

Lee looked down upon the Blessed Isle. Its name was Peng-lai. On the flanks of its triple peaks, that rose sheer from the ground of data mist, were forests of trees whose fruit were pearls, data nodes that expanded upon contemplation. And at the peak of the highest mountain were three intertwined trees whose branches reached through the circling sky, dividing ever finer, a billion billion connections each bearing a billion billion junctions, infinite connectivity . . .

Lee had accessed all this in an instant, by instinct. His viruses drove around and through barriers. Amidst expanding blocks of data, Lee heard Miriam's cry, shrank back into himself.

"Not yet!" Miriam said. "Oh, you fool!"

The island shrank away. They were standing on the shore again. The islands were vague shapes through the streaming data-dense mist. Miriam was a shadow before him, like a flickering figure on a badly tuned receiver.

"You fool," she said, more softly. "Poor fool. Go now, before the agents of Gaia close the way. You can do so much, and you know so little, and now you are on your own. It is too dangerous for me to stay here. Go, and don't look back!"

She began to recede from him, along a direction that was at right angles to everything else. In a moment she had gone, but that direction remained, and it seemed to Lee that it was filled with the essence of her, the breath of her soul. When something vast and dark leaned towards him, a shadow sucking up light, Lee fled after her.

And fell back into his own self.

Sixty-seven

He staggered, caught himself against a shelf of dust-polished lava. He retained the impression of a monstrous thing falling towards him, a lion-headed shark at least a kilometer long.

A woman turned his head and looked anxiously into his eyes. He could feel her body warmth; her smell of sweat and woodsmoke, tinged with a hint of rancid butter, rose from her skin. Her small bare breasts pressed his side. Vette, her name was Vette.

"I thought you were going to have a fit," she said.

Lee replayed the moments before and after, and from the stutter of the rolling percussion figured he'd been gone less than a second in real time. He said, "I'm all right." It was true. He wasn't even drunk any more. He turned and saw Chen Yao toiling up the slope, Redd staggering behind her.

Chen Yao was breathless and angry. "Wei Lee! It won't work here! I told you it wouldn't. We have to go to the top, I keep telling you that, and you don't listen. Where would you be without me? While you've been dancing and dreaming and getting pig-drunk, I've fixed the gig."

"She's right," Redd said. He put his hat on his head and folded his arms and tried to look dignified, but his eyes kept crossing.

"At least," Chen Yao said to Lee, "you're not as bad as the cowboy."

Lee told Vette, "You hear my friends. I have to go. I must find the way to the top of Tiger Mountain."

"Then I'll go with you," Vette said.

"Just what we need."

"Hush, Chen Yao. Vette, it is dangerous. More than dangerous. I don't expect to return."

"I know," Vette said, her eyes shining behind her mask. "But I also know I must go with you, to help save my people."

Chen Yao, from deep within her aspect, said, "Save them? Perhaps, but not as they are. They cannot survive without change, and change will destroy what they are. But that's true for all of us."

Sixty-eight

The old man, Li Pe, peered through a chink in the corroded iron plating of the barred and chained gate of the Last House. "They are coming again," he said. The torch he held in his right hand sputtered and sparks whirled up past the keystone of the arch into the night sky.

Behind the old man, Lee said, "How many are out there?" and Vette shifted her grip on her harpoon while Redd eased the mechanism of the hunting rifle he'd spent the last few hours cleaning and refurbishing. Across the little courtyard, Li Pe's blind sister fretted in the darkness just inside the house's door. The other survivor of the mountain town, Yang Bo, told her not to worry, it wasn't different from any other night. "But it *is*," the blind woman said.

"I see three coming straight up the road," Li Pe said.

Redd said, "I guess there were at least fifty following us."

"Counted a hundred then gave up," Vette said in her pidgin Common Language. Her face was pale but set; Lee knew that she was as frightened as he was, but also that she was better at hiding her fear. He had learned that and more about her in the days of sailing the dust seas in the lee of Tiger Mountain's high flanks.

From atop the wall, Chen Yao called, "There are many more than that out there now. They are circling around on either side."

Li Pe said, "The little god has good eyesight, but you should ask her to come down. They may not know how to

320

climb walls, but they do know how to throw stones."

Lee said, "She likes to be doing something. I am sorry that we brought so many unwelcome guests to your door."

Li Pe said, "It would have happened, sooner or later. They run in little packs, but now and then the packs unite. Perhaps if I try the light show again . . . " Then he stepped back smartly. A moment later the gate rang from a heavy blow. Shards of rust shivered to the ground. There was a sharp high gibbering outside, and Li Pe's sister gave a muffled scream.

Yang Bo came up behind Lee, shouldering a pole with a knife blade lashed to its end by wire. He held up a torch whose flame shook above his polished pate. "It wasn't so bad last year," he said. "Now they come every night. By day, too. Before that they mostly stayed away. There were more of us, then, even if more were sleeping than alive, and they only came at night; Li Pe could scare them off . . . "

"I'm afraid they've become used to my conjurations," Li Pe said.

Chen Yao called down, "But not to Wei Lee's. You'll see."

Yang Bo said, "Is that so, little god! Then I was wrong: instead of hiding here with us, you pay us a social call."

"We rush them," Vette said. She shifted her harpoon from her right hand to her left, then back again. "Isn't as if they're animals. We can fright them."

Redd rubbed his bandaged hand and said, "I wouldn't be so sure."

"They are more dangerous than animals," Li Pe said. He stooped and set his torch in a socket by the gate. For a moment his wrinkled face was illuminated from below; then he stepped back and was in darkness again.

The gate clanged again; for Lee, the way the echoes spread defined what was outside. Three, as Li Pe had said, standing some way off. Lee remembered that Li Pe had said they had learned how to throw stones—and, as if to mock his thoughts, there was a sudden smack and rattle on the tiled roof of the house.

Chen Yao was suddenly standing beside him. "They've come right up to the walls," she said.

Stones made an irregular percussion on the tiles; some fell short and smashed on the courtyard flagstones. Everyone took refuge in the doorway of the house. Li Pe's sister, Li Qing, plaintively asked what was happening.

"It's all right, grandmother," Lee said. "There may be more of them, but they are still the same. They will not know how to climb the gate."

"We hope," Redd said.

The old woman's hand fumbled out, and Lee grasped it, surprised at its warmth. He crouched to let her fingers spider over his face.

"You have travelled far," Li Qing said.

"And I have farther to go, grandmother." He touched her face in turn, carefully kissed the half-closed lids over her milky eyes. Immediately, her eyes filled with tears. Li Pe bent to comfort his sister, although she seemed calm enough. "The young man will take care of us, brother. He is a good man. His friends are good people."

Vette said to Lee, "You do something."

Redd said, "Maybe you could pull that go-faster stunt."

"There are too many," Chen Yao said. "In the morning they will go away, perhaps. We are not here to fight them."

"I could try this gun. Shoot over their heads."

"You should shoot them," Li Pe said.

Redd said, "I'm not about to start shooting little . . . "

"You won't have to." Lee had been listening to rocks rattling on the tiled roof, and now he had an idea. "Stay there," he told them, and took Yang Bo's torch and ran across the courtyard and swarmed one-handed up one of the twisted pillars of the gate.

The Last House stood on a slope above the ruined town. By starlight, Lee's enhanced sight showed tiled rooftops stepping down either side of a road that twisted like a broken-backed snake. Many of the roofs sagged from storm damage; at the far end of the town some of the houses were already little more than shells standing amongst the weedy remains of their gardens. The townsfolk had retreated uphill, as if from a slow inexorable flood, until the last of them had been stranded here, unwilling to run because this was their home, and then unable to run because of what lived in the stony wilderness of Tiger Mountain's slopes.

Infrared clearly revealed the small swift creatures that flitted this way and that in the starlight. Lee's torch flame drew them like moths, as he had intended. They were frightened of fire, yet they were also fascinated by it. Perhaps Li Pe's projections had brought them here as much as the unwitting passage through their territory of Lee, Chen Yao, Vette, and Redd.

Lee counted a hundred staring up at him from varying distances, and more were coming nearer, scampering over rocks, hooting and whistling to each other. He listened, wondering if his translation viruses could sift a pattern from their noise.

Then the first stones started to sail out of the darkness. Lee shifted to and fro atop the wall, using virus-enhanced reflexes to dodge the missiles. Only a few came near him. These he plucked from the air and threw back, always hitting his intended target. After ten minutes of this, the besiegers retreated out of range, two of them badly hurt, most of the rest with smarting bruises.

Vette stood below, and Lee tossed her the torch before jumping down. "We'll have it quiet for an hour or so," he said.

Redd said, "But they'll come again."

"Truth," Vette said. "We make run for it?"

Lee said, "We have to do something for these people, Vette. We brought it upon them."

Vette whispered, "They are already doomed. Can't save everyone in the world, Lee." Then she smiled. "But you try, I know. I learn much from you."

Sixty-nine

After they had escaped the Free Yankee Nation, they had taken ten days to find a place to land, fighting currents and wind. The gig complained that the Free Yankees had taken them in the wrong direction. It followed a twisting path through the shoals and reefs which were outriders of the talus shore, always hugging close to the foot of the cliffs of the lava shield of Tiger Mountain. It bounced and swayed and spun over the dust swells through the hot days and cold clear nights, making its way north and east. Always, the sculpted talus shore stood off to starboard, so polished by dust that the boulders, some as big as hills, sparkled like gems: a necklace at the feet of cliffs that rose almost vertically six kilometers above them, cutting off half the sky.

Something was looking for them: culvers beat the air around the mountain. Scarcely a day went past without sighting at least one, but usually they were so far off that by unaided sight they were mere dots in the pink sky. But twice culvers came so close that the gig had to put into shore to hide. The first time it anchored in the shadow of a towering arch polished smooth as a gold ring, the second, inside a perfectly spherical cave of black rock half filled with the restless heave of the red-dust sea.

One night they glimpsed lights beyond the edge of the soaring cliffs, cold auroras that played and flickered until dawn. If the display was a response to an attack by the Sky Roader anarchists, there was no sign of it. Lee felt a brooding hush that seemed to be centered above his head. The war was waiting for him.

In the long reaches of the night, while Redd and Vette slept, Lee kept watch with Chen Yao. Like her, he slept for only two or three hours each night: the viruses had edited out the need, or relegated it to some part of his brain not occupied by consciousness. Lee ran and reran his memories of his intrusion into the dreamscape on the other side of the barrier. He talked them over with Chen Yao, but her aspect knew less than he did about information space, and nothing at all about Heaven.

Miriam Makepeace Mbele had not told him who the Blessed Isles were intended for, but Lee thought that his guess was right. They were for the people who had dreamed their way into death. But where were they? And if that was the paradise promised by the conchies, why was it on the far side of the barrier?

Chen Yao didn't know, and the replicated residue of Miriam Makepeace Mbele was silent in his head.

One thing was certain. Lee was changed. He was not who he had once been. That was true of everyone who has ever lived, of course, but in them change was a process of growth. People grow layers of self, like the layers of an onion. Lee knew that he had been changed in a different way. As if his layers had grown into each other, and mixed with layers of others, Miriam and a host of minor partial personae sinking and intermingling with his own self, as paint mixes in the water an artist uses to clean her brush.

He tried to talk about this with Vette as a way of trying to get to know her, but she didn't understand, or pretended not to. She said it was magic, and she didn't need to know how magic worked as long as she could rely on it.

In the long hours while the gig tacked against the wind, they all four talked of their different histories, of their own lives, of their peoples, or Lee or Redd or both together sang song after song—the old old songs Lee had learned from the broadcasts of the King of the Cats, the plaintive songs with which the cowboys calmed their herds, even snatches of commercials, which Vette enjoyed more than all the others. She worked hard at improving her rudimentary Common Language; Redd spent hours patiently teaching her tones and stresses.

They came at last to landfall on a bright cloudless day. Sunlight played through dust that whipped off the crests of soft slow waves, so that the air seemed full of fragmented rainbows. Far out to sea, the symmetrical peaks of the Three Sisters rose above a glittering haze that blended imperceptibly into the shocking-pink sky. Beyond them was the Great Valley, and beyond that the dry rivers and chaotic terrain of the high deserts.

If you followed those dry rivers north, Lee thought, as he had followed them south, you found that they wove together, running out towards the Plain of Gold. On the way you would pass through a small settlement, sheltered in a bend of a muddy, shrunken river. The Bitter Waters *danwei*. He had travelled three-quarters of the way around the world.

And now he would travel upward. There was a vast slumped gash in the high cliffs that ringed the raised lava shield of Tiger Mountain. A cold wind blew out of it. The gig tacked across choppy dust towards landfall, into the cold shadow of the cliffs. When they had all clambered ashore, the gig promised to wait for them, and then sailed off to find an anchorage amongst the reefs beyond the mouth of this steep embayment.

They all watched it until its sail flashed full of light as it passed out of the shadow of the cliffs: a silver spark dwindling into the restless sea of red dust.

"Never thought I'd miss the little fucker," Redd said, his voice muffled by his filter mask.

Vette shouldered her harpoon. They had little else to carry: packets of dried food and the few decilitres of water which the gig had decanted from its still. She said, with studied carelessness, "We explore."

But Lee knew, even though her face was hidden by her hideous mask, that she was as apprehensive as Redd.

The ruins of a little port town ran along one side of the

embayment, most no more than frontages built across the mouths of natural caves, sheltered by a huge ledge that undercut the cliffs. It was as if a town had struggled to rise from the native rocks but had only half succeeded, and was now slumping back into dissolution.

The town had been abandoned for at least a century. Drifts of fine dust had accumulated inside the buildings, waist deep in places. All the glass had been broken from the windows, and shards left in the frames had been polished to a milky smoothness by storms. Redd found the remains of a huge monomolecular screen which must have slid like a soap-bubble membrane across the face of the biggest cave; something had torn the almost indestructible stuff to shreds and tatters, and all that was left of the simple machinery which had manipulated the screen were the outlines of its tracks. Nothing grew there, not even lichens, and there was no trace of the former inhabitants, no bones, not a stick of furniture or a shard of circuitry.

"Up," Chen Yao said impatiently. "It's the only way."

It was the middle of the morning when they set off along the wide smooth road that threw a hundred luxurious switchbacks as it climbed the tongue of ancient lava that had smashed the windy, windy pass into the cliffs. Six kilometers of height translated into a hike of more than a hundred kilometers. It was three days before, hungry and exhausted, they reached the top.

It was dusk, and they made camp by one of the fast-flowing streams which had carved deep channels in a layer of soft gray-brown tuff. The water was very cold and had a chemical taste, but they had nothing else to fill their bellies. There were stands of tough bamboo and low, wind-sculpted spruce, and outcrops of black basalt were splashed with the bright round thalli of wild lichens, but there was nothing edible. Lee set some traps of looped wire anyway: something, probably ice mice, had been nibbling the lichen crusts.

Later that night Vette came to him. He was huddled in a smooth narrow hollow beneath the side of the road, and she slithered down to him, wrapped him with arms and legs. All around, wind hooted and whined without cessation as cold air poured down through the pass from the higher slopes of the mountain. Afterwards, she whispered in Yankee, "I've been waiting for this ever since you saved my life. Do you mind?"

"If I did save your life, then my life is yours." Lee could feel sweat cooling on his flanks. They hadn't undressed: it was too cold for that.

She laughed. "Funny. We have it the other way around."

"I'm not even sure if I did save your life."

"You did, and that of everyone on the boat. If you hadn't killed the ray it would have sounded and sucked us under. That's the sign of a hero. To do a brave deed by instinct and not even realize it."

"I'm no hero, Vette. The opposite, if anything. I've been given gifts, that's all, and too often I show them off. I'm beginning to learn that they are not mine to use as I will. If anything, they're using me."

He knew that the totipotent viruses had infected his salivary glands; Mary Makepeace Mbele had changed him with a kiss. But he had withheld that burden from Vette. Fortunately, the Free Yankees, who habitually went masked, had lost the art of kissing.

"In the stories, a hero always has gifts, and a quest, and a band of friends to help him."

Lee asked her about the stories, and she told him a few, and then they made love again and she slept. Lee chipped his viruses and found a place where he could rest his consciousness, and slept, too.

And woke in cold, bright starlight. He was kneeling, hands on his knees, head bent forward, listening. He was at the top of the stream bank beside the road. Its broad white swathe ribboned away, eerily luminous in the starlight, empty. He called down infrared, saw, in green on green, shapes moving amongst the rocks on the far side. Something small was poised in the shadows between two big rocks. He could hear the little noises as those behind it urged it forward.

Redd and Chen Yao crawled up the slope to where Lee squatted. Redd whispered, "They must be scared of us."

"What are they?" Chen Yao said.

While Redd explained, Lee stood and advanced to the middle of the road. The shapes on the other side of the road froze for a moment. Then with faint scrabbling sounds their heat signatures faded away, ducking behind outcrops and boulders.

Lee called after them and something sailed through the air towards him. A meter wide of its mark, the stone bounced once with a hard sound and splashed into the stream. Chattering from the watchers on the far side: then more stones.

Lee retreated. Vette, lying beside Redd and Chen Yao on the slope beneath the road, wanted to know what was happening.

Lee said, "They are testing us. I think they might be as hungry as we are. There are at least two handfuls. Probably more." He thought of the youngest, being urged to cross the road. An initiation dare or a sacrifice, or simply a matter of rank? Suddenly that seemed quite important.

"They're in four or five places," Redd said.

"Six," Lee said. His optical systems had tracked the trajectory of every stone.

Redd said, "We could rush them."

"You take the right," Vette said, and stood up, brandishing her harpoon. She stepped to one side and the other as stones sailed out of shadow. They were quite visible against the luminous road. Then she bounded away, and Redd followed.

Chen Yao said, "We should go on."

"We'll wait for our friends."

"It's not necessary. They'll catch up."

"We can wait, Yao."

"I really think you would risk the whole world for the sake of one person."

"It wouldn't be worth saving if I had to do it any other way."

"I heard you. With the woman."

"Are you jealous, Chen Yao?"

"Don't be silly. Listen."

Vette and Redd came back in a hurry, dodging a hail of stones. "I caught one," Redd said, "but the little fucker bit me. Hurts like hell. Do you think they could have poisoned bites?"

Stones clattered and bounced off the road. Lee could see the heat shapes of the throwers on the far side. It looked as if they were dancing.

"Up," Chen Yao said.

But the stone throwers kept pace with them. A group would rush forward, throw stones and fall back when Vette brandished her harpoon at them. At first she made threatening noises, rolling her eyes outrageously and capering like an enraged ape. But she soon tired of this, and her gestures became stylized, token threats. Redd suggested that she put on her mask, but Vette, who didn't understand that it was frightening to others, said, "No dust here."

After several hours of this Chen Yao said that perhaps they were being herded towards something, a trap or ambush.

"Would already happen," Vette said. Both she and Redd were tired now. Lee's viruses cleaned fatigue poisons from his muscles and set the rhythm of walking: so did Chen Yao's aspect. But Redd and Vette were only human.

The land rose up ahead of them. It was the beginning of the long five-degree slope that climbed twenty-one kilometers out of the atmosphere, all the way to the lip of Tiger Mountain's vast caldera. By bright starlight Lee could see the road winding away to a line, a point. If there was a trap, surely he would see it . . . but the slope was broken by draws and bluffs, and crossed by belts of juniper and Himalayan pine. Whenever the road passed through one of these dense forest belts, their followers would dart off the road, and they all quickened their pace until they reached open ground again.

Dawn had touched the very top of the mountain, so that it seemed like a fiery rock floating kilometers above, when they entered the widest belt of trees. It took an hour to pass through it. The trees were stunted, but they grew so closely together on either side of the road that it was impossible to see ahead. Lee's eyes and ears, turned up as far as they would go, ached from the bombardment of light and sound. There was no sign of their followers.

Chen Yao agreed. "Animals," she said. "They don't think or plan."

The far edge of the forest belt was as abrupt as a knife blade. Lee's heightened senses collapsed in on themselves so suddenly that he thought he'd gone deaf and blind. Vette and Chen Yao helped him to a little stream that sang in its bed of black rock beside the road. He splashed icy water over his head and drank what seemed like his own body weight. Vette stood on a slab of upthrust rock, shading her eyes as she looked back the way they had come.

Dawn was an hour away, but already there was enough light from the higher slopes of the mountain for Lee to be able to distinguish colors quite easily even with normal sight. The black and gray of the rocks; the blue-black of the fanned branches of the gnarled close-knit junipers, the yellow of Vette's baggy trousers and the different, lighter shade of her hair that fell unbound down the back of her black hide jacket. Scarlet tassels hung from the barbed head of her harpoon, vivid against her pale hair.

When Lee joined her he saw that what he had thought, back on the other side of the forest belt, to have been just another field of boulders was in fact a small town clustered below one of the promontories left after partial collapse of the slope. It was at least twenty kilometers up the long curve of the mountain's slope, but every one of the straggling houses was sharp and clear in the clean air.

Chen Yao said, "It'll be easy to avoid it. We just follow the road."

"They could help us," Lee said.

"We can't trust anyone on this mountain."

Vette said slowly, "Heroes of my people search adventure here, but none ever come back. Now I know why."

They watched the little town for a long time, while they

waited to see if their followers were still with them. The dawn line crept down as the horizon fell below the gaze of the sun. At last Redd came back up the trail and reported that he couldn't see any sign of the little fuckers. He held his bitten hand close to his belly; it was swollen and flushed, and dead white around the crescent wound.

"That settles the matter," Lee said. "There must be medical help up there, so that's where we're going."

Chen Yao sighed theatrically. "You don't know your own powers, Wei Lee. But I won't argue with you."

They toiled through most of the rest of the day to reach the town, following the little stream rather than the white road, which threw a loop away from it. At last they crossed what had once been a patchwork of cultivated fields divided by stone walls. The elaborate irrigation system had long broken and run dry, and there was nothing left but bleached stalks of corn that crackled into dust under their feet.

The houses of the little town ran uphill alongside its only street. They were low and small, built of whitewashed blocks of hewn tuff under tiled roofs. There was no sound from the shuttered houses of the town, no trace of smoke or hum of machinery. Those nearest the fields had fallen into ruin. Most of those beyond had their doorways and windows sealed with crudely mortared stones. Still, Lee and Vette and Redd walked up the street, shouting themselves hoarse, before Chen Yao suggested that they break into one. Lee had left his traps behind, and they were all hungry: and food would keep a long time in the dry cold mountain air.

They were near the top of the town, where houses clustered around a flagstone square. An air still dripped water from its few unbroken vanes into a half-empty pool green with slime.

"Spiro!" Vette said, and went down on her knees at the pool's edge and scooped a dripping double handful of blue-green gunk into her mouth. She chewed noisily and said, "Good. You try it. Our winter rations." She licked clinging strands from her fingers. "Ancestors eat it, on shoals that bring them here. Really, is good. High protein, most scientific."

It wasn't exactly good, Lee discovered, and Redd suggested that on a gastronomic level it rated slightly higher than eating Yak cud. But they were all hungry enough to eat their fill of the bitter, slippery strands, even fastidious Chen Yao. Afterwards, Lee put his shoulder to the door of one of the houses, and was surprised when it gave easily. Chen Yao slipped past him, pointed out the many footprints in the dust drifted over rotting rugs, put her finger to her lips. Two square rooms, lit by blades of light that pried through closed shutters. Furniture pulled over and smashed. A half-lifer cocoon in the middle of the second, bones inside, bones scattered on the floor: broken, gnawed. Lee saw the marks of teeth and showed them to Chen Yao, and her look of horror mirrored his.

They fled into clean level sunlight and told Redd and Vette what they'd seen, and they all ran from the haunted place down the town's winding street.

And at the end of the street saw what was coming towards them, far away down the gentle slope, already halfway between the line of the forest's edge and the beginning of the town's abandoned fields and growing nearer, small as flies, fifty, eighty, a hundred of them, stretched in a long line as they climbed towards the ruined town.

Chen Yao wanted to run, but Lee argued against it. "They'll wear us down, and besides, this is their territory."

"Well, we can't fight that many. And anyway, the only way is up."

Redd said, "I don't even know if I could kill one. They're only . . ."

Chen Yao said, "They are less than that. They are only intelligent animals, with no society beyond that of the pack."

"Drove us here," Vette said. "I kill, if need." She was leaning on her harpoon, its butt grounded in stony dust. One hand shaded her eyes as she stared downhill.

"Yeah," Redd said, "but there are so many of them . . ."

The ragged line moved steadily upwards. Lee could zoom

in on individuals. Many had daubed their naked bodies with ochre mud; some had filed their teeth to points. He said, "I don't think they are planners."

Chen Yao said, "Whatever we do, we can't stand here and wait for them. Let's go higher."

They turned and quickly climbed back up the street, past the pool and the violated tomb of the house. High crags reared above, stark against the slope of the mountain that rose into the dark sky. Night was coming on: the shadow of the mountaintop was sweeping down its slopes.

There was one last house, its high-peaked tiled roof floating behind walls of polished lava blocks. They turned towards it, and climbed a narrow path that ran crookedly up a rubble-strewn slope. They kept turning to look back at the town and the line climbing towards it, and so they almost walked through the giant that popped into existence and barred their way with a gesture that conjured a wall of roaring flame.

The huge figure was three or four times as tall as Lee, an old man whose lips moved, slightly out of synch with his amplified voice, within a thin silky beard that dropped to his waist.

"Go back, go back! Go back, demons from hell!"

His words shook from rock to rock. Flames roared higher, casting brilliant light but no heat. Sinuous black shapes seemed to writhe within the furnace light.

Vette dropped to her knees, arms wrapped around her head. Chen Yao looked this way and that, squinting into the light of the flames; behind her, Redd had unsheathed his knife. Lee helped Vette to stand, and she clung to him while he explained that it was a simple hologram, the first stage in a defense system. "A trick of light, that's all! Scientific!" He had to shout, over the amplified roar of flames. "A recording!"

"It certainly isn't," the old man said. Echoes knocked clouds of dust from the slopes. His voice was that loud. Lee clapped his hands over his ears. "Who are you, young man? Who are your friends? From her harpoon, I would say that your friend is one of the Yankee barbarians from the Dust Seas, but you are certainly not from these parts. Nor is the little girl, or the dangerous-looking cowboy. Oh, I'm sorry, let me turn this down." He disappeared for a moment, came back at normal size, dwarfed by his curtain of hell fire. He said, in a normal conversational voice, "Is that better?"

Lee said, "Your flames are impressive, but like your voice they overwhelm us."

"Oh yes, how careless." The roaring light vanished. "I'm sorry," the old man said, "but it has been so long since we've had visitors. Apart from the wild ones, that is."

"I'm Lee. This is Vette. Over there, Chen Yao, and Redd. Redd is the cowboy."

Vette squinted sideways at the old man's image with deep suspicion. "Bad conjuring trick," she said at last. "I see through him."

Redd said, "It kind of had you going though, didn't it?"

"It is more effective at night," the old man said. "The trouble is that the wild ones are no longer fooled by it."

Lee looked up at the walled house, saw a point of light twinkle there: the projector. He said, "We were seeking a place to shelter."

"That's something my companions and I would have to consider, of course. These are difficult times."

"I understand. But it is rather urgent."

Vette gripped Lee's arm. "They come up through the town!" she said, and turned to the projection of the old man. "You hide behind walls! You let us in!"

Her bad manners shocked Lee—the old man, too, who took a step backwards and immediately went out of focus. He said feebly, "It is not as easy as that, although I wish it were. I really must talk with my . . . "

Redd said, "Listen, when you're between a rock and a hard place, you kick the rock. You understand what I'm saying?"

The old man smiled, shook his head.

Vette unshipped her harpoon and stabbed it at the old man, who instantly faded away. No, wherever he really was, he'd simply stepped back, outside the focal point of the projector. Lee said to Vette, "You really aren't helping."

She said in furious Yankee, "I'm not standing around like food on a platter while you swap compliments with a dab of light! Look at those things, they've seen us, they're coming right for us. Come *on*," she said, and grabbed Lee's arm again.

Chen Yao said, "We are gods. They will grant us charity."

"You so sure of that?" Redd said.

"It is our right."

Lee said, "As Chen Yao is so fond of pointing out, we have no other way to go but up."

They scrambled up the twisting path to the sheer black walls that enclosed the house. The lava blocks were polished like glass, and the joints between them were so fine a piece of paper couldn't have been inserted.

There was a gate, armored with corroded steel plates. Vette banged on it so it rang like a gong. Lee turned to watch the ragged line of creatures move through the boulder field beyond the town, black shadows against dull gray rocks. The sounds they made came faintly in the cold thin air.

Lee said to Chen Yao, "I suppose that I could fight them in hypermode, if it came to it. Perhaps I could kill enough to make the rest run." He knew he could not kill them all before they killed him.

Redd said, "If it comes to a fight *I'm* willing to stand ground while you run, Billy Lee. You're the main attraction of this little expedition, no sense you dying and us living."

"Exactly," Chen Yao said.

Lee told Redd, "I thank you for your offer. It is made from a large heart. I am changed, it is true, but I am still human. I couldn't leave you."

"Oh, Wei Lee! The needs of the many outweigh all else. Your loyalty is to the whole world!"

"I wish they were all standing beside me, Chen Yao."

Suddenly, the old man stood before the gate. His image was sharper in the shadow cast by the high wall. "There is no need to make so much noise," he said.

Lee bowed to him. "Your defenses are very strong."

"We are happy with them."

"Obviously, the . . . wild ones can find no way in. You are to be congratulated. But I see one flaw—suppose someone were to pile rocks up against the gate? There are many rocks, enough to build a rough stairway. You are lucky the wild ones have not thought of it."

"They do not have your education," the old man said.

Lee bowed again. "I have travelled far, and learned a little of these practical matters."

Vette said, "I pile rocks. Maybe those things understand."

"No need," the old man said. "We have not had visitors for such a long time that we will make poor hosts, I fear. But you are welcome to our hospitality, such as it is."

Behind his image, the rusted gate creaked open a handful of degrees. Redd put his shoulder to the corroded steel and widened it a handful more and Chen Yao slipped past him. The line of creatures made a kind of inchoate yell and started to run as Vette and Lee squeezed through the narrow gap. Redd followed, and they all leaned against the gate, and it slammed shut.

Seventy

Now the night was nearly over, but stones still bounced and clattered from the tiled roof. In one of the alcoves off the main room of the Last House, Li Pe stepped up to the projection plate. A cone of light fell around him, and Lee knew his image was walking in the night amongst the besiegers. But the stones did not cease to fall.

"There are more of them than I can count," Li Pe said. "And a few are starting to pile stones against the southern wall. Their cunning needed a critical mass to become intelligence, it seems."

"Perhaps they've started to breed," Yang Bo said. "Always said when that happened we were doomed."

Lee went out again, vaulted to the top of the southern wall, saw figures scatter from a heap that leaned against it. Stones started to fly at him out of the pre-dawn darkness, and he jumped back down and went to tell the others what he had seen.

"It will take them a long time," Li Pe said. He was holding his sister's hands. "Perhaps they will be gone when day breaks."

"Perhaps those who brought them will do something," Yang Bo said. "We were safe before they came."

Vette raised her harpoon. "All here together," she said.

Lee remembered then what Miriam had said about Tiger Mountain when he had met her in Heaven. He asked, "Who

338

owned this house? Was this equipment in place when you came to live here?"

"Of course," Li Pe said.

"It was his idea to use it," Yang Bo said. "Now look what has happened."

"For a long time it kept them away," Li Qing said softly. Her arthritic hands clutched the arms of her chair every time a stone hit the roof, but that was the only sign of fear she showed. She turned her face approximately towards Lee, frost-capped eyes wide open, and explained, "When there were more of us we could look after the sleepers and keep *them* away. But we grew older, and some took escape in dreams. They all died, when at last we had to leave our homes. This was once the house of the district governor, young man. Forgive me, but you *are* young, are you not?"

"Too young, grandmother. Tell me, did the district governor walk amongst you?"

"The devices were mainly used for spying," Yang Bo said. He had been a strong man, once. He still had the truculent, blunt determination of the strong, which Lee did not mistake for rudeness.

"We feared him," Li Pe said, "and now it is too late I realize that he feared us. If people knew how much cadres fear them, they would have been overturned long ago, but because they know that they hide the fear behind force. We had to fight and defeat the keepers of this house to gain entry, twenty years after its owner had fled. That's how much he feared us."

"Luckily the machines were made feeble by age," Yang Bo said. "But they still killed one of us, and I have the burn scars of their weapons down my back."

"Maybe I can fix them," Redd said.

"They were destroyed," Yang Bo said. "Don't you think we would have used them ourselves?"

Lee said, "But you did not destroy the control systems, only the mechanisms. There will be other mechanisms hidden elsewhere, I am sure. This was the central seat of governance, was it not?"

Seventy-one

It was easier than he had supposed. The antique control system was still in place; in fact, the projection facility was a small part of it. The couch was filmed with dust. Chen Yao helped Lee put on a dusty helmet and control gloves, their plastic sheaths cracked but still flexible. He took a breath, and activated the system.

And dropped through darkness into a place where luminous lines dwindled away in every direction, sketching vast matrices. His body was that of a glowing, winged man, a standard template the previous user hadn't bothered to customize—or more likely there had been many users, and this was the system default.

The matrices around Lee were empty of anything but their codes, connected to nothing now that the half-lifers had moved beyond known information space, into Heaven. Faint webs interconnected them, ghostly quantum traces left by once active paths. Many dwindled towards islands of light that shone in the far distance, as if lit by shafts of sunlight.

Lee had the sense of a vastness lurking at right angles to everything else. He was careful not to let his attention go anywhere near the quantum traces, or focus on any of the active islands. He made himself as small as possible, a bird, a moth, a bee. He let himself slidingly fall through information space.

As he fell, a cluster of insets started to flicker around him: one bloomed into a map of Tiger Mountain, gridded and

340

hatched with coordinates, riven with a dendritic communications net. Lee completed a search in a flicker of time and flew right to the node he wanted.

It was a kennel, although he perceived it not as a space enclosing machines, but as machine presences defining their enclosure. Some were very nearly dead, no more than vestigial traces that stirred fitfully as Lee briefly possessed them before passing on. But more than a dozen were still usable, and for a dizzy moment he found himself split amongst them: virus reflex completing in a moment what he alone would have taken hours to do.

Microscopic pinches of tritium shot into the magnetic bottles of fusion pods. Motors spun into life. Machines neatly reversed around each other, vibrant with infrared and ultrasound and proximity radar. The kennel doors were jammed shut by decades of overgrowth, but the largest of the machines used its blade to ram through them, pushing away soil and uprooting volunteer saplings. Piston limbs flexing and tilting, the other machines followed, navigating through the ranks of the trees they had planted and tended so long ago.

Forest gave way to open land. The machines found the road and made speed, drove quickly through the abandoned fields. Several of the smaller machines clambered on to the big earthmover, clinging with pruning hooks and spray attachments. Lee opened up the full sensory arrays of the machines as they rumbled up the single street of the town, through the square with its dripping air still. Shapes moved and postured up the rocky slope, burning in infrared.

The small machines scrambled down from the earthmover, waving every appendage, revving bandsaws and drills. Floodlights came on, catching the wild ones in a variety of postures.

In the moment before they fled, Lee saw the wild ones for what they really were: children grown feral and strange, cast adrift from history, without culture, without language. Being an invulnerable viewpoint helped him forget the gnawed bones, the fear of the three old people in the Last House.

Lee let the little machines charge about and scatter the be-siegers, and drove the big earthmover right up to the gate, its airhorn blaring and every light on its rack blazing, its blade raised high above its platform in triumph.

Suddenly someone was beside him. Lee partly withdrew and found himself held in the palm of a muscular vigorous man-shape sketched in crammed silvery hoops. A filament connected Lee's compacted bee-shaped body with the man-shape, linking senses. Yang Bo said, "We looked for these years ago."

"They were carefully hidden. Fortunately, enough work."

"I will not ask you how you found them. Clearly, you have the powers for such a task."

"I'm glad you came. I was wondering how to keep off the wild ones. Before we can ride the big machine, I must board it to set it to manual."

"I can supervise the machines; it was once my work."

Lee understood that Yang Bo's sense of face had driven him to follow. He said, "They know what to do, but they need to be watched. Scare the children, but don't hurt them."

"It is a long time since I thought of the wild ones as children."

"It's all they are."

"You have not lost your family to them. They are more dangerous than animals. But I will respect your wish. As for the machines, we are old friends, they and I. We planted the forests together. Go quickly. The wild ones will not stay scared for long."

Yang Bo's silver figure lifted its hand, and Lee flew from its palm. His own faint path was overlaid by the cord of disturbed coordinates that Yang Bo had made, like a man blundering through a jungle. It was a trail visible to anyone in the system, but Lee felt that he had no time to knit it up. He flew right into his own body, sat up and shucked mask and gloves. Yang Bo, masked and gloved, lay quietly beside him.

The others were outside. Vette and Redd stood on top of

the wall either side of the gate's arch, outlined against the earthmover's lights. Li Qing leaned on her brother's arm, and asked Lee what he would have them do.

"We can open the gates now. There is a big machine we can ride."

Chen Yao said, "We can't take them all the way to the top, Wei Lee!"

"We'll do the best we can, Yao."

"We have food," Li Pe said, and held up a bundle wrapped in cloth knotted at four corners. "It has come to this. Running away in the night."

"It is morning, not night," Li Qing said. "It is a new chance."

Vette jumped down lightly and crushed Lee in her arms and extravagantly claimed him to be master of all monsters. A bloodstained bandage bushed her blonde hair; she'd been hit by a rock while trying to scare off the besiegers.

She and Redd helped Lee haul the heavy gates open, and Li Pe and Li Qing followed them into glare and noise. Chen Yao came last, scornful and angry.

The smaller machines were scattered across the slope between the town and the Last House, running with staggering stilted gaits this way and that on long many-jointed legs, like robot ants that were trying to learn to become bipedal. Even as Lee watched, one of the machines went sprawling after something bounced off its sensor cluster with a distinct clang. Shadowy figures leaped upon it, danced back howling from its thrashing limbs, started to pelt it with rocks. Another machine charged to the rescue of its sibling, slicing wildly with pruning attachments and a buzz saw. Two children were hacked down; the rest fled. One was holding his own severed arm.

Lee clambered on to the earthmover's rusty platform and found its control node. The featureless silver hooped head of Yang Bo's system-form floated inside a tiny, flat TV screen. "Come back now," Lee told Yang Bo, as Chen Yao nimbly swung up beside him. Vette was helping Li Qing climb the ladder.

"I'm staying. I'm staying to kill them all. You run if you like, young fool."

Lee jumped down from the earthmover and ran towards the gate. A skeletal machine whirled up, lights blazing, and slammed him to the ground. He went into hypermode, but it wasn't fast enough to dodge the machine. It spread its four arms wide, blades clattering and whirling. A chain flail made a kinetic pattern in the glare of the racked lights above its plate-like sensor platform. Lee feinted left, went right, had to jump back from a swinging blow. The machine stepped stiffly backwards through the arch, slammed the heavy gates shut.

"Let's go, Billy Lee!" Redd sang out.

Naked long-haired children were scampering towards the lights of the bulldozer. Lee made a run for it, reached the ladder just before they did. Redd hauled on his arm as small hands grabbed his ankles. He kicked upwards and gained the platform, while Vette jabbed her harpoon at the children. They screamed at her with wordless defiance. Vette yelled right back, her tattoos horribly vivid.

The face was gone from the TV screen, which now showed only a rolling interference pattern. Lee told the earthmover where to go and it growled, "Right, boss," and fed power to its tracks. The children fell behind, throwing rocks that bounced from its hopper.

Fights ranged up and down the slope. The earthmover passed a posse of small children who had somehow overturned a turtlelike machine; its two-dozen stumpy legs wagged helplessly as they pounded it with rocks. But for the most part the machines had the best of the fight. One strode towards the town with its battery of lights strobing, two arms raised high, a severed head dangling from each. Half a dozen smaller, man-sized machines were running down a desperately fleeing flock of children. Lee looked away just as the machines caught them: but he heard the screams.

"Wicked," Redd breathed.

"Evil," Vette said.

"This is the beginning of the end," Li Pe said. "The young

will eat their parents, and then they'll eat each other. Poor Yang Bo doesn't understand that this is historical inevitability. We all fell asleep, and the dream died. It will all go down in darkness."

Li Qing stood up, shaky on the shaking platform of the lumbering earthmover. Li Pe took his sister's arm, tried to make her sit down and be still, but she shrugged him off. She raised an arm, pointed ahead. "Look," she said wonderingly. Her eyes were wide. Their caps of frost had melted, and tears streamed down her round, wrinkled cheeks. "Look . . ."

Far ahead, far above, dawn had reached the peak of Tiger Mountain. It was a flat-topped crown floating on darkness, a crown of iron burning at red heat. But that was not what Li Qing meant. Above the circlet of Tiger Mountain's vast caldera, folds of light shook and shimmered, gold against red dawn. They danced there for an hour, were burning still as the earthmover drove over the crest of the valley and turned in the only direction left to go.

Up.

Seventy-two

The earthmover made good time, pulling up the regular slope at a steady ten kph. The slope curved evenly away on either side and rose up like a gentle wave towards the flat horizon of Tiger Mountain's peak two-hundred-odd kilometers straight ahead, although there was no straight way. Ravines and blunt valleys dug into the slope. Shallow craters pocked it and worn lava nubs pushed up from the black, stony ground. There were stands of convoluted lichen, and close-knit mats of wire gorse and golden-leaved dwarf birch. The earthmover steered around these obstacles with no prompting. It knew the way to the top, it said. It had helped build the city there.

Every two or three hours Lee asked the earthmover to stop, and they all sipped water from the big bag Li Pe had brought, jumped or climbed down to stretch their legs or duck behind a boulder or into a stand of trees to relieve themselves.

As the day wore on it grew colder and colder, the sky darker, the sunlight sharper. Splintered ultraviolet-rich light made everyone but Lee squint and rub their eyes. The earthmover raised a hemicircular canopy over its platform. Blowers pumped warm pressurized air. Polarization of the canopy filtered the dazzling sunlight.

They had not yet climbed beyond life. This was the zone where in the brief fall of the northern hemisphere clouds soaked the ground. Lichens grew in abundance. Meadows of

346

spongy gray cladonias stretched along the floors of little valleys, punctuated by stands of stunted fir and larch, aspen and juniper. Big air lichens raised their brain-like convolutions amongst frost-rimed basalt boulders. There was bilberry and dwarf birch, snow grass and saxifrage. Rust-pelted hares ran in straight lines from the bulldozer's passage, and big black crows, with beaks white as bone, rode updrafts with lazy flicks of their meter-wide wings. Once Lee glimpsed a wild yak clattering away across a distant scree slope.

Onwards, upwards. Behind them the horizon tipped towards the tiny sun. They stopped at dusk in a draw where an ice-cold stream ran between banks cushioned with mounds of moss. On the boulder-strewn slopes above the stream stands of junipers raised twisted branches like arthritic fingers; clusters of needles were like vivid green flames against papery bark. There was a kind of small bird that ran in pairs over the slimy flat stones in the stream, stopping to stab at the black gravel shoals. Something made a high piping sound amongst the junipers. It was a wild, clean, spare, lonesome place, the last outpost of life.

Climbing the mountain, Lee told the others, was like recapitulating the world's changes.

"In more ways than one," Li Pe said. Cross-legged, black clothes loose around his bony frame, black hood cast over his leathery face. Hunched by the rushing stream in twilight, he said, "There's no one living up here. Not even the wild ones. And then a desert of stone, without enough air to breathe. A place where only the machines can live. We travel into the future, and it is no place for us."

"That's what we're trying to stop," Redd said. "If we win, the rains will come again."

Li Qing squeezed her brother's hand. "We've lived all our lives in the town and its forests," she said. "This is a wild and strange place, but it is different, nothing more."

Li Pe said, "In the future, there will be no people. The world will be like this, a wilderness without memory or history."

"You say wrong words," Vette said. "I see tracks of men, and signs they leave each other. It is cold soon. Come on, Lee, we go, we get firewood."

In the half-darkness amongst the junipers, on the other side of the stream, Lee said, "What don't you want them to hear?"

Vette was piling up dead branches that had been bleached silver by frosty weather. She said flatly, "Want to know who follows."

"You can speak Yankee with me, Vette. You've seen someone?"

"I thought you knew."

"Well, I'm not infallible."

"He's very fast, but not clever at hiding himself," Vette said. Her blunt, honest face wore a serious expression behind the mask of her tattoos. "He was keeping a long way back, and I never could see quite what he looked like. If we climb to the top of the ridge, we may be able to see him."

"I don't like leaving our passengers."

"They survived those children. They're tougher than you think. Let the cowboy look after them, and that little brat."

"She can't help the way she behaves. She's had a strange life . . . Besides, I need her. She knows things. But I don't know what to do with the brother and sister, Vette. Or with you and Redd. It is dangerous, where I am going. Well-guarded, I am sure. I have certain . . . attributes that can help me survive. But Li Pe and Li Qing . . . "

"They're only human. So am I. But I was talking to them while you were finding the machines. They know the secrets of the mountain. Their people tended the forests, and knew other people who made the mountain into a sacred place. The mountain rises out of the air. Can you live without breath? They say that there are places higher up, camps where the workers lived in the summer. There may be strong sciences left there."

"The old know the world."

"Of course." Vette dropped her load of firewood and

dusted her hands. "I'm going to climb the ridge. Will you come with me, and use your magical sight?"

"When there's time, I must explain about viruses."

Vette laughed. "I don't want to steal your science!" she said, and ran off through the trees, leaping from boulder to boulder.

Lee followed, at first allowing her to stay a little way ahead, then having trouble in matching her pace. They left the stunted birches behind, leapingly climbed a steep smooth slope where lichens spread brittle orange and brown and green patches everywhere underfoot.

The air was too thin. Every breath was deeper than the last, yet Lee's heart knocked louder and louder, a drum banging inside his head. He reached the top gasping and stumbling, had to sit on a knob of lava while he groped inside himself, found how to flood oxygen-carrying viruses through his blood. The drumbeat slowed, and the world grew clearer.

He walked across the lava pavement to where Vette stood on a craggy lava chunk that jutted over a steep cliff. Her pale hair flew back in the freezing wind. Lee joined her, and she put her arm around his shoulders.

They had climbed the back side of a bluff that rose a kilometer above the slope. The mountain was spread beneath them. They could see the remnants of a vast weathered crater that pocked the slope, something Lee hadn't noticed on the way up. He remembered the earthmover zig-zagging up a terraced slope, and now saw that it was part of the crater's wall. They could see all the way down to the belts of forest. They could see around half the mountain's curve to the western flanks where vast ice rivers sluggishly flowed, calving over the edge of the cliff escarpment and tumbling six kilometers into the seething dust sea. A dangerous place where monsters lived and heroes went to slay them, Vette claimed. She was grinning. No one in the Free Yankee Nation had ever thought to win a hero's story by travelling up the mountain, not until now.

"You can see the whole world," Vette said.

"No, not really . . . "

They were so high that they could see the curve of the world's horizon. A distant white line floating across the red-dust sea were clouds riding the edge of a low-pressure cell far below them. Winds deflected by the slope of Tiger Mountain spun north and south, and rising air dumped moisture on the west flank, feeding the glaciers. To the southwest, beyond a narrow channel of the red, achingly flat Dust Seas, the Three Sisters, huge volcanoes dwarfed only by Tiger Mountain itself, rose above the escarpments and mesas of the Dragon's Back, a vast plateau raised half as high as Tiger Mountain itself. The setting sun threw their shadows outward, towards the notched horizon where the Great Valley began. How big the world was, how difficult to change! Even if Lee failed, its slow dying would last ten thousand years.

He was so lost to it that Vette had to shout in his ear to bring him back. "We have company!"

Chen Yao and Redd were hiking up the slope. Redd waved cheerily, quite out of breath. The hunting rifle was slung over his shoulder; his poisoned hand was strapped up against his chest. Chen Yao said to Vette, "This place is far more dangerous than you think."

"I don't need your protection."

Lee said, "What about the old people?"

"Oh," Redd said, "the earthmover is looking after them. In fact, it's gossiping with them about the good old days. I thought I might get something for the pot on the way."

Vette said, "The reason I brought Lee up here is because someone is following us."

"I saw nothing," Chen Yao said, as if that settled the matter.

"Perhaps you weren't looking."

Lee said, "We will see what we can see, Yao," and did his trick, zooming in close, scanning the valley below. Virus-built structures processed the information for traces of movement, and images flashed by like a falling sheaf of photographs. Birds rising on winds, a running deer so furry it was like a floating puffball. Then a flash of silver: a silver figure hatched by slanting birch boles: a flat blue face: gone.

Chen Yao said, "You saw something. Where is it? What was it?"

Lee replayed his glimpse, and told the others what he'd seen.

The face was a television screen, an image, perhaps a human face, floating in watery blue. The rest was all tubes and angles, four arms, long stilt legs, a humped back painted with yellow and black chevrons. It was moving into the woods at the mouth of the valley.

Lee remembered the wake Yang Bo had left in information space, the sense of watchers rising towards it. Perhaps something had settled in one of the forestry robots... or perhaps Yang Bo had decided to follow them.

"I can't see a thing," Redd said. He was standing on an out-thrust shelf of rock, shading his eyes with his good hand.

"It's there," Lee said. "Two and a half kilometers away. Vette was right."

"I saw no machine," Vette said. "I saw a man. I am sure. A red man."

Lee laughed. "Monkey! Or at least, one of his brothers and sisters. A lucky coincidence... I'll tell you about Monkey another time, Vette, but now I think we should go back."

But when they reached the stream and the earthmover parked by its mossy bank, Li Pe and Li Qing were gone. The earthmover said the two old people had gone for a walk, but Vette found a note in neat firm calligraphy, every character well shaped and with the quick, precise shading of thick and thin strokes made possible only by the off-handed confidence of a master.

We trouble you no more.

Seventy-three

Lee found it easy to track Li Pe and Li Qing. Footprints in moss near the stream, broken stalks of dry grass, scuffed sandy soil. If he lost the path he simply cast to the right and left until he found another trace. The others had agreed to wait by the earthmover, and he went quickly, confident that he would soon catch up with the two old people. There had not been enough time for them to have gone very far.

The tracks went down the gully, staying beside the stream for the most part, passed through a scanty birch wood, and then turned south, following the line of the slope across a lichen pavement, big splodges of red and brown and grey and yellow with distinct black lines at the borders of the differently colored species. Just by the far edge of the birches, Lee found a different kind of print, and remembered the high arched feet of the forestry robots. He couldn't tell which set of tracks crossed which, and couldn't see any sign of the two old people either.

There was a movement in the shadows amongst the slender silvery trunks of the birches. Lee said, "You needn't skulk around, Chen Yao."

As she came across the lichen pavement towards him, he said, "You're determined not to let me be on my own."

"We go on now, Wei Lee. Leave the others, and go on up."

"First of all we have to find Li Pe and Li Qing."

"I should think they are dead. And it's getting dark. We can climb the shoulder of the valley and camp at the top."

"We brought them here. We killed them."

"You must not feel bad, Wei Lee. They were old, and besides, the wild children would have killed them sooner or later."

"Even so," Lee said, and turned and set off across the lichen pavement. After a minute, he heard Chen Yao run to catch up with him.

They went on, losing time because it was difficult to follow the track across the particolored lichens. Night was sweeping down the mountainside; at last, Lee had to admit that he had lost the track entirely.

Although the rim of the mountain had risen above the sun, light still walked on the Plain of the Garden of Eternal Bliss a dozen kilometers below, and a red glow muted the colors of the lichen patches and accentuated the dark boundaries between them. It was as if Lee and Chen Yao were trekking across a vast tilted chessboard. They were about to turn back towards the gully when far around the curve of the slope a brilliant light flashed and faded.

Chen Yao said, "I suppose you're going to investigate. It is probably a trick."

"Even so," Lee said. "Go back, if you want."

"Oh no. You need my help, Wei Lee."

Lee led the way cautiously, thinking of the silvery robot, of the traces of habitation Vette claimed to have seen. The King of the Cats was playing a selection of lonesome Delta Blues, eerie in the emptiness of the high slopes of Tiger Mountain. It reminded Lee that ghosts always seek empty places to haunt, and he grew more and more nervous as he and Chen Yao approached the source of the light.

What had appeared from a distance to be a pile of rocks turned out to be the ruins of a small town. Its four-square buildings were built of lava blocks. Narrow windows, their shutters long ago fallen away, looked out from beneath the jutting eaves of tiled roofs. Lava chips paved the streets, which formed a cross centered on a big square. Tree stumps still remained in the middle of the square, like rotted teeth. Chen Yao wondered how they had missed this place when they had looked down from the bluff.

Lee said, "You didn't see it either?"

"It's a bad omen."

"Well, we weren't looking for it, so perhaps we missed seeing it. Besides, we're a long way around the slope."

"I think it was looking for us, Wei Lee. We should go."

"Hush. Let me look, at least."

Lee went all the way round the square, every sense stripped bare. In the middle of the clump of half-fossilized tree stumps there was a stone cistern in which he supposed the town had once stored its water. He dropped a stone into it, and after a moment there was a dry echoing rattle.

As he turned away, he saw a spark above one of the houses. It flashed and failed, and then a small red glow shook there. Someone had lit a fire, and hope turned his heart over.

A brief search revealed stone stairs at one corner of the building. Lee told Chen Yao to keep watch and went up, cautiously peeped over the edge of the roof. Big loose tiles, each ridged in the middle, made a gentle slope. Two people lay beside the fire near the crest of the roof. Li Pe and Li Qing, faces peaceful, age rubbed away by the gentle glow of the fire. They did not stir as Lee made his way to them, not even when a tile slipped beneath his feet and clattered over the edge to smash in the street below.

They were dead. No marks on them, skin cold, yet joints still supple. Li Pe's mouth was drawn back in a grimace. Li Qing's eyes were open, but blind once more. Lee gently closed them.

Someone called out, across cold night air. It was not Chen Yao. "Sister, you sure took your sweet time getting here."

Lee turned so quickly he almost fell off the roof. As he danced on loose tiles, white light flared across the square, a pillar of light bright as burning magnesium, shedding great sparks. A figure was silhouetted against its glare, legs apart, fists on hips. Lee did not need to enhance his sight to know who it was and shouted to Chen Yao.

"Run!"

The figure laughed. "The little god is with me."

Lee called back, "Did you do this?"

Mary Makepeace Gaia moved against the brilliant light. "I've been following you for a while. But it's time to end it."

"You set the children upon us, didn't you? That was why there were so many of them."

"You're not the one I want. Talk to me, sister. I know you're there."

"She's part of me, and I'm part of her. You can talk to me."

Lee understood that he had walked into a trap, and that he had taken Chen Yao with him. The village had been invisible because it had been made so, and he had seen it only when it had been made visible for him. There was no way the two old people could have walked all this way so quickly. Mary Makepeace Gaia had killed them and brought them here, knowing he would come looking for them. No doubt she controlled the forestry robot; she would have been monitoring information space, waiting for him to show himself there. He said, "Are you still serving your employer? Or is this something more personal?"

Mary Makepeace Gaia screamed. The light behind her flared and went out. Lee slid down the roof in an avalanche of loose tiles, kicked off and did a tuck and roll, landing with knees bent to absorb the impact. Falling tiles smashed around him: he could measure the space between each impact as he ran in a zig-zag across the square, kicked in a door and dived through it.

This was the living room and kitchen, and in the bedroom beyond was a half-lifer cocoon. Lee knocked it from its plinth, swept aside the loose, dry bones inside. A pinlight winked red at him; there was still power. Everything was still connected to everything else: the system would ensure that, even after the world died.

Lee jammed on the headset, felt his body collapse even as

he plunged away from it. He did not fall far, but went at an angle to everything else, down the way he'd glimpsed before. Suddenly all the connections became clear. He saw the projectors that Mary Makepeace Gaia had set up, and the traps she had laid at the perimeter. She had wanted to talk with him, or with her sister, and then she had wanted him to run so that she could hunt him down and kill him.

Well, run he would, but first he turned everything off and set up a beacon. And then he followed an extended branch in the ghostly quantum path he'd made during his previous incursion into Tiger Mountain's information space, and had a brief intense conversation with the earthmover.

And came back, because Mary Makepeace Gaia had ripped the headset from him. She grasped his chin and pulled his head back, held a knife at his throat.

The room was in darkness, but at the edge of his vision Lee could see her expression in the warm mask of her face. She said, "There are so many ways to die."

"But not by your hand. Not directly. You could have killed me at any time after you found me, but you never did. You always set others to that task." He kept himself still, despite his fear: the sharp knife blade had nicked his throat, and he could feel blood trickling down his neck, soaking his collar. Beats of silence. He said, "Besides, your employers are coming."

The knife rang when it hit the far wall: Mary Makepeace Gaia laughed. "You think they'll save you? Sister, you'll wish you died at my hands. Go on, run if you want. I swear I'll kill you cleanly."

"Too late," Lee said. "They're already here."

His beacon had been answered. A whistling roar was descending on the town: a rising scream that couldn't blot out Mary Makepeace Gaia's laughter.

Seventy-four

There was a little town of shining silver towers. Like a circle of spears, it rose in the shadows beneath the fluted walls of the northern end of the stepped and nested craters of Tiger Mountain's deep, wide caldera. Each spear tip was ringed or vaned, rising to different heights from the glare of a field of lights. There were domes too, and looping silver roads, and a long long launch track that ran out and up across the eighty-kilometer-wide caldera, angled towards stars that shone bright and clear in the near-vacuum.

Inside the steel can of its cabin, Lee felt the rocket ship turn beneath him. Torque pulled his face from the thick glass port hole; the restraint harness of his seat cut into his shoulders and chest. Everything tilted outside the port hole, and then there were only stars as the rocket ship settled on a tail of flame. There was a long roaring, then a shudder, then silence.

Lee was suddenly surrounded by the cadres who had taken him from Mary Makepeace Gaia in the dead mountain town. They were dressed in simple white one-piece uniforms. Black visors masked half their faces. Their heads were shaven, like monks or civil servants. They were all younger than Lee, more boys than men, and did not have names but numbers. As soon as they had surrounded Lee they began to shout at each other in clipped tech-speak with a kind of suppressed hysteria. It was as if they were furious at everything, even themselves. Several held pistols on Lee as others unbuckled the complex harness that had strapped him down in the padded seat. He could hear Chen Yao's muffled protests as she was lifted from her own seat. Across the circular metal cabin, Mary Makepeace Gaia watched mockingly. It was already clear that the cadres feared her more than Lee.

A transparent tunnel linked the rocket ship with a high tower. They all rode an elevator down, Lee pressed in one corner by the now-silent cadres, Chen Yao in another. A moving walkway carried them along a long tunnel and then there was another elevator ride, to the top of another tower.

It was the tallest tower in the cluster, and its top was a clear dome supported by thin metal pillars. It looked out across the sharp shining tops of towers and swooping roadways towards the starry sky and the far horizon of the southern end of the caldera. A cadre turned from this view, made a gesture. The guards drew to attention, stepped smartly back so that Lee and Chen Yao and Mary Makepeace Gaia were isolated in front of their rank.

The cadre studied them, long fingers pressed together at his chest. His face was not masked. It was high-boned and bloodless, eyes hooded, thin lips pressed together. He looked like a scholar presented with an interesting but trivial problem, something requiring a moment's attention to unlock its worth before it could be filed away.

He said, "Are they who you expected, Master?"

Two people stepped from the shadows beneath one of the dome's filigreed metal pillars. One was the missionary from Earth, Dr. Damon Lovelace. The other was Guoqiang. He was in cadre uniform, and his head was shaven and seamed with raw red scars. He had been converted.

Mary Makepeace Gaia bowed stiffly to Dr. Damon Lovelace. "Come," he said, "you must also honor our allies."

"Of course," Mary Makepeace Gaia said sweetly, and bowed to the cadre.

"I am the Number Two Cadre," the cadre said stiffly. "The Number One Cadre is . . . unavailable. But you may speak to me as if to him."

The mercenary said, "I don't want to talk to anyone in this place, but to those who give you your orders."

The cadre said, "We have our duty. Orders are not necessary. Orders require interpretation. As truth is not absolute, interpretation can lead to bad actions. You will tell me how you contacted us."

"Not me. It was his idea."

Lee said, "The usual way." He couldn't stop looking at Guoquiang, who stared straight ahead.

The cadre said, "You lie. That way is forbidden."

"I wouldn't know about that. I just did it."

Chen Yao said, "He's dangerous. Let me go, I'll tell you just how dangerous he is, and why, and what you can do about it."

"Bravo," Dr. Damon Lovelace said, but the cadre ignored her outburst. Lee was sure, in fact, that he hadn't heard it.

The cadre said, "Confession is the highest good."

Lee knew all about the kind of mottoes the cadre used. He had learned about them when he had tried to find out about his parents on his own, before Xiao Bing had made the librarian for him, before he had left the capital for the first time. He had read through the transcripts of hundreds of struggle sessions in the House of the Names of the Populace, where each reader had an aspect at his or her shoulder, like an angel, or a conscience. In every transcript, the human, agonised pleas of the accused had been answered with the kind of tags that the cadre used now.

Lee countered with mottoes of his own. "Who is able to contact you, but those who are allowed? Who is allowed, but those who have authorization?"

"No one has authorization when sterility is to be maintained. We are free of contamination here, because the highest duty requires it."

"Those who know only correct actions needn't fear contamination."

"That's true," the cadre admitted.

"Very good," Dr. Damon Lovelace said.

Lee said to the Earthman, "How can you bear to take so much away from people?"

"Oh, it was the Ten Thousand Years that did this," Dr. Damon Lovelace said lightly. "We leased them the technology; they put it to use in their own way. We would have used machines, not brain-cored humans, and we wouldn't have put the control center in this vulnerable position. There is still much about your psychology that astounds us." He put his hand on Guoquiang's shoulder. "This cadre has a question for you, Wei Lee. We think we know who you are, but we want to make sure. There are more than one of you, you see. Just as there are more than one of me."

"I understand."

Dr. Damon Lovelace said to Guoquiang, "Ask your question."

Guoquiang stepped forward as if he was on parade. He stopped two paces from Lee. Sweat stood out on his forehead. "I . . . " he said. "Who . . . I . . . "

Dr. Damon Lovelace's hand crushed Guoquiang's shoulder. "Ask it!"

"Who? Who fell? Who fell in dust that was not dust? Who saved him and washed him clean?"

Lee remembered. It had been the beginning of everything, and he hadn't realized it until now. He remembered how they had all danced under the wavering fountain in the cold spring air outside Number Eight Field Dome of the Bitter Waters *danwei*. He looked straight into Guoquiang's eyes and said, "Lin Yi fell, and almost drowned me too, when I saved him."

"There," Dr. Damon Lovelace said, "that wasn't so hard. All right, cadre. You're dismissed."

Lee lunged forward, and kissed Guoquiang full on the lips. "I forgive you," he said.

Mary Makepeace Gaia laughed, and then softly applauded.

Guoquiang wheeled away without even wiping Lee's saliva from his mouth.

"Well," Lee said, "now that you know who I am, what do you want of me?"

Dr. Damon Lovelace turned and paced to the window, hands clasped at his back. He looked out across the tops of the shining towers for a full minute before speaking. "I regret that there's no more time for talk. Your allies are causing some small nuisance in the skies, and that must be dealt with before we can send you where you're wanted. But before my masters come for you I hope I will have time to talk with you again."

The interview was at an end.

Seventy-five

Lee and Chen Yao were able to exchange a few words during the elevator ride down. "I'm scared, Wei Lee," Chen Yao said. "It wasn't supposed to happen like this."

"It's all right to be scared, Chen Yao. I'm scared, too. It's only human, and that's all that we are, really."

"I know. That's why I'm scared. I never was much of a god, was I? These people scare me. They're no longer human; they have no need of gods."

"They talk in tags because they don't need to know anything else," Lee said. "That's not scary, it's sad."

As the elevator slowed, one of the guards spoke unexpectedly. "If the people do not control their defenses, then how does the nation defend itself?"

"If a nation must defend itself against its own people, it is not a nation," Lee said.

The guard didn't reply.

Chen Yao and Lee were led off in opposite directions down a white corridor. The cadres left Lee in a big, mostly empty room. Hopefully, he asked the door to let him out, but it could only apologize. "I wish I could, Master, but it is best for you to stay here." It had a dry small voice: Lee imagined an old, simple monk, head bowed.

The floor was as wide and as shinily empty as that of a ballroom. There was a clutter of hard-edged furniture stacked in one corner, and when the young boy came in Lee was perched on top of a stack of chairs, prying unsuccessfully at the smooth joint between ceiling and wall.

Lee blurred from one side of the room to the other and took the tray from the boy's hands. "Stay while I eat," Lee said. "I'd like to talk with you."

The boy was six or seven, and masked like the rest. He said, "I do not know if it is permitted."

"It is not forbidden, then. Everything that is not forbidden is permitted."

"There are guards on my other side," the door said.

"Thank you for telling me," Lee said, and told the boy, "You can wait while I eat, and then you will not need to come in again to take away my tray."

He lifted the covers of the stainless-steel bowls one after the other. Steamed rice, fried crackers, yellow bean paste, water. The unsalted food tasted of almost nothing; the water was distilled, warm and insipid. The boy stood with his back to the door and watched Lee eat.

"What's your name?"

"I am Number Eighty Four."

"I mean before that. Before you came here."

The boy's mouth twisted, but he said nothing.

"You don't remember? You can't have been here very long. Door, are you listening to this?"

"Yes, Master."

"You will not record it, and you won't transmit it to the guards on the other side, or anywhere else."

"Yes, Master."

Lee told the boy, "I suppose that you are used to having machines eavesdrop on you, Eighty-Four, but it makes me uncomfortable. Here, I've finished now."

When the boy bent to take the tray, Lee grasped his wrists in one hand, flicked up the visor of his mask with the other. The boy's pale face squirmed, like something disturbed by the turning of a rock. Lee touched his eyes and his mouth with fingertips wet with saliva, and he suddenly relaxed.

"Tell me the first thing you remember," Lee said.

The boy spoke dreamily. "We were travelling on a train.

There were many of us, more than two hundred. We were new units, from different *danweis*. I was travelling with thirty-eight others from my own *danwei*. We were travelling to the capital, to receive the blessing of the Emperor." (The door said, "Are you all right, Number Eighty-Four?" Lee told it to be quiet.) "We had been selected because we had purged our teachers. They had been advocating the Sky Road, and we forced them to purge their carrels, to recant their crimes and to march around the perimeter of the *danwei* with placards describing their crimes around their necks. It was winter, and dust was blowing from the Plain of Gold. The teachers were barefoot, and without masks, and in their nightclothes. We had beaten them, and made them kneel on glass. I remember one young woman helping an old man; both were choking in the dusty air, and their clothes flapped and billowed with the wind. Very few survived their recantations.

"The leader of our unit was a girl, Yu Shihuang. She was a bad crazy person, but her anger gave her strength of will. All feared her. I remember an old woman, on the train that took us to the city. She was in the carriage in which we rode. We were in high spirits, and she told us not to make so much noise. Yu Shihuang turned on the old woman, and started to hit her. Others joined in. The old woman curled up like a spider. Blood ran from her ears and her eyes and her nose. She was unconscious and some urged Yu Shihuang to stop, but Yu Shihuang declared that the Great Reassessment was not an embroidery lesson. It was winter, as I have said, and the carriage windows were curtained with heavy material. She took down a curtain pole and beat the old woman to death. Her face was like a piece of rotten fruit. Then Yu Shihuang had her thrown from the carriage. I remember that was how we came to the capital. I remember little more. It is an effect of the processing."

The boy had spoken in a slow halting monotone, but as his tale progressed tears began to run down his soft plump cheeks. They dripped on to his coveralls, beading the slick white material.

Lee said, although he already knew the boy's story, "What was the name of your *danwei*?"

"It was the Bitter Waters *danwei*."

It had happened ten years ago, during the planet-wide purges after the Emperor had made its final pact with the Earth's Consensus, and declared the sky off-limits. The boy had been frozen at that age ever since. Everyone in the shining city had been frozen. It was a glimpse of the future, of brain-cored children serving machines, becoming machines. Without new memory, without new experience, without change.

Lee said, "I must speak with your leader, Number Eighty-Four. Will the door open when you ask it?"

"Of course I will," the door said, surprising Lee.

"Take the tray and leave with the guards. As soon as you can, come back. Can you do that?"

The boy nodded.

"Be brave. Remember what you are. Everything else is a dream, and you're waking from it now."

Lee paced up and down once the boy had gone, suddenly nervous. He had no way of knowing if the viruses could overcome ten years' conditioning, ten years of being but not becoming. Miriam Makepeace Mbele had once teased him about being able to bring the dead back to life: now he would see if it was true or not. If he could save the boy, then perhaps he had saved Guoquiang. Perhaps he had saved them all.

His internal clock had counted off more than a hundred minutes when the door opened. The boy stood there, and Lee ran to him. "Goodbye, Master," the door said.

"Goodbye," Lee said, astonished, and took the boy's hand, and allowed himself to be led away.

Seventy-six

The door to Chen Yao's room said nothing, but simply opened at the boy's command. Chen Yao had dismantled a wall screen, and was trying to pull away the panels behind it. "I would have gotten out by myself," she said. "Eventually."

"I don't doubt it."

After a while, Chen Yao said, "Where is this boy taking us?" The blank white corridors made her nervous; she was geared for signals and signs that were not there.

"To see the Number One Cadre."

Chen Yao said, "A dead man won't be much help."

"He isn't dead," the boy said. He still had not remembered his name. Lee feared that little of his original personality remained, that he was not a resurrectee but a construction, as a new building might be built on the stone foundations of an old one.

Lee said, "There are different deaths. If I've learned one thing, it's that."

The towers reached down into the congealed lava floor of the caldera as well as into the sky. The boy led them to an elevator that fell for a full minute and swooped to a stop that briefly tripled gravity. It opened not on another bright, white corridor but warm semi-darkness.

Orchids as big as human heads and as complicated as sexual parts glowed behind faceted glass set in the floor and walls. Other panels pulsed with color, sent chips of light swarming over the room like blood corpuscles coursing through the muscular chambers of the heart. Cables looped down from the ceiling and gathered together in a thick braid that plugged into the back of the couch where the Number One Cadre lay.

He was dead, withered and black, part mummy, part crystal. He looked as if he would shatter at a touch. Projection helmets dangled above his couch like a bouquet of flowers.

"This is a crazy place," Chen Yao said, and stepped towards the couch, a shadow in the swarming colors.

From the corner of his eye, Lee saw the elevator shimmer and flow, bleeding away into the pressed flower walls. When the boy's hand crept into his, Lee told him, "Nothing can hurt you here."

That was when the Number One Cadre's corpse sat up. It moved stiffly but swiftly, jerking its legs over the edge of the couch, dashing leads from its head with a sweep of its hand. Its eyes glittered redly, like cut cacholongs. Its mouth worked and a long silver tongue licked out. It was forked, made of rings of metal. It dashed over the corpse's face, then lashed out at Chen Yao.

The little girl danced away from the tongue, which whipped after her, meters long and lithe as a snake. Lee went into hypermode and plucked a helmet from the bouquet above the corpse's couch, and set it on his head.

And was elsewhere.

Seventy-seven

Wei Lee stood on a darkling plain under a chain-mail sky that flexed and warped with its cargo of hurtling data streams. It stretched away towards a wall dark red as dried blood and studded with defensive towers. The wall's mass loomed like a thunderstorm, more felt than seen. Signals crackled from tower to tower like heat lightning. Beyond the wall and its towers floated a huddle of tall peaked roofs lapped with glazed ochre tiles. It was the Forbidden City.

The air beside Lee twisted and shimmered as if heated by an invisible fire. It made a crouching human shape, and then the boy was beside him.

"Number Eighty-Four! What are you doing here?" But Lee was not really angry, for the boy's presence meant that he would not go into this terrible place alone.

"You left," Number Eighty-Four said accusingly. "You left me. I only wanted to see where you had gone."

"It is the Forbidden City. We are going to see the Emperor. Take my hand."

Number Eighty-Four flinched from Lee. "But no one sees Him! He is immortal and invisible and everywhere at once!"

Lightning flared from top to top of the distant towers; massive peals of thunder rolled across the plain on which they stood.

"Don't be afraid," Lee said. He took the boy's hand and they moved forward.

Each step translated them across space like chess pieces. There was a high gate in the blood-red walls. *Wumen*, the Meridian Gate, the place of execution. It opened for them but they were already inside the walls, standing in a courtyard cut by the recurved Tartar bow of the Golden Water Stream. Five dazzlingly white marble bridges arched over the glittering stream, leading to the Gate of Supreme Harmony. Beyond this gate was another courtyard, and at the far end of the courtyard rose the marble terraces on which stood the three great halls.

Lee and Number Eighty-Four stood directly in front of the Hall of Supreme Harmony. Its doors were flanked by bronze incense burners, and from each burner rose a pillar of aromatic smoke. The smoke pillars twisted into braids and merged with the flexing sky. Directly in front of the doors was a bronze turtle, symbol of longevity and stability. A fire had been lit in its hollow belly, and smoke billowed from its hooked mouth.

There were guards on either side of the bronze turtle, but when Lee and Number Eighty-Four found themselves standing beside it, the guards had vanished. Above the turtle's armor-plated shell was a ghostly globe: the turning world, battered dusty red, polar caps of white water ice small as thumbprints: Mars.

Complex spindles of light hung over the shrunken icecaps. Lee wafted a hand through them, top and bottom; they engaged his viral systems for only a second.

The discharge was like pure sex. It propelled Lee and Number Eighty-Four through the entrance in a fast edit, into a vast richly decorated space filled with the clash of battered gongs, thick billows of incense, and blurred ghosts. Lee could hardly distinguish individuals in the insubstantial crowd, but the repetitive motions of its ever-changing constituents made it possible to see what was going on.

Bowing nine times over by throwing themselves full length on the floor and hitting the tiles with their foreheads, interlocutors advanced towards the high throne which stood before the carved Xumi Mountain, the Mountain of Paradise. Only then was each interlocutor allowed to stand and wait to be escorted, by an aspect in long skirt coat and trousers, its machine code in a locked pouch hung by a chain from its belt, into the ever-changing throng that hid all but the throne's high canopy.

"Come on," Lee said to Number Eighty-Four, but when he tried to push through the crowd of interlocutors who were waiting their turn to be escorted to the throne he was buffeted and shoved and turned so that his path became a drunkard's walk that led right back to its starting place.

"I told you!" Number Eighty-Four wailed. "We are not meant to be here. We don't have the *codes*!"

Lee gripped the boy's hand and plunged into the crowd again. They were pushed this way and that, and suddenly Lee was standing in front of someone he knew. He was looking into his own face.

"You have come far, Master," the librarian said.

"I have been fortunate, thanks to the help of my friends," Lee said. "I regret that I still have some way to go, and now there is no one to help me."

"If you will allow it, perhaps I can serve you one last time. After that, your path is your own."

"For the first time," Lee said, and suddenly, despite his fear, he felt a calm joy fill him. Here, in this hall of ghosts, he was finally no one but himself. Win or fail, it would be on his own terms.

"Use your freedom wisely, Master," the librarian said, and took Lee's hand in a freezing grip. He pulled Lee and Number Eighty-Four through the crowd of interlocutors and aspects, which now made no more resistance than the scented smoke, and Lee saw at last who sat on the throne.

He was dressed in the high-collared, yellow silk brocade robes of tradition, his face stern and patient beneath a square cornered hat. He rested his elbows on his knees and his chin in his hands, not turning his attention from any of the interlocutors, yet addressing dozens at once. At the instant of address the ghosts took on the aspect of their client—all of them either men in uniform or richly dressed servants of one or another of the Gang of Six or more or less interchangeable drably dressed conchies—and faded and blew away like smoke.

"I have done all I can, Master," the librarian said. "Free me. Free me now."

It held up the pouch hung round its neck and Lee took out the control chip. It was a no-color lozenge bristly with machine code, squirming in his palm like an overturned beetle. The librarian snatched it and bowed and ran down a corridor Lee hadn't noticed, its black cloak flapping like a tattered flame, growing smaller and smaller and then vanishing around a corner and taking the corridor with it.

An aspect grasped Lee's elbow and tried to hustle him away. Lee laughed and lifted the aspect's locked pouch, opened it, and held out the control chip. The aspect grabbed the chip and greedily stuffed it into its mouth: it glowed through skin translucent as parchment as it went down. For an instant, an old man stood before Lee, barefoot and bareheaded in a faded fisherman's smock with both sleeves out at the elbows. It was the human template of the aspect, the dead personality hijacked and bound to this function. Wonderingly, the old fisherman raised his hands before his face—and then he was gone, free to address himself anywhere in information space.

Lee stepped forward, suddenly alone before the ruler of the living and the dead.

The Emperor dismissed the aspects with a smooth gesture and stood, and Lee recognized him even before he took off his hat and his long moustache. "You're too late, Wei Lee," Great-grandfather Wei's eidolon said, and put the false moustache into the hat, and tossed the hat over his shoulder into paradise. A painted buddha grabbed it and cheerfully slapped it on to his shaven long-eared head. The Emperor stepped down from the throne.

"I have many aspects," the Emperor said. "Now that The Little Bird is dead, every one of the Ten Thousand Years belongs to me. Come with me, Wei Lee. You can bring your little friend, too, or what's left of him."

There was a gap. Lee had a false memory of passing through

the Gate of Heavenly Purity behind the Three Great Halls; of skirting the three Palaces where power had always resided, behind the formal mask, at the back door; of moving through small, human-scale courtyards in which fountains played or carp swam in pools; past the unpretentious one-storey buildings in which (if this had been the real Forbidden City) emperors and their consorts had once lived in eras long past. Through all this, Lee did not let go of Number Eighty-Four's hand.

And then there was an editing cut and they were standing elsewhere, high on Coal Hill Park to the north of the walls, with pavilions behind them and terraced gardens dropping away before them and the peaks of the roofs of the Forbidden City spread beyond.

The Emperor shot a sleeve of his yellow silk robe. "Far too late, little Lee. Already, my champion has killed your true body. And now she will come here and kill you. As for the boy, I'll eat him. There's not much left of him anyhow."

Number Eighty-Four said, "Wei Lee is the champion of the people." His hand made a fist inside Lee's grasp: he dared to scowl at the Emperor.

"That means more to me than you could know, Number Eighty-Four," Lee said. "But I'm no champion, only a messenger. I came here to give our Emperor a gift from the people, if he'll take it."

The Emperor laughed. "I know about your silly little viruses. That's why my champion must erase you; otherwise I would have swallowed you whole and thought nothing of it. No more talking, now. It's too late."

He pointed, and Lee saw Mary Makepeace Gaia running up the gardened slope towards him. She ran as if in a wind, flames streaming back from the burning sword she whirled around her head as she plunged through formal flowerbeds, leaped low hedges.

Lee felt the wind, too: it was rushing from him. Something passed through every cell in his body, like a hand passing through a rainbow. Suddenly a host of beasts were leaping downhill towards Mary Makepeace Gaia. Tigers and panthers, monkeys twice as big as men, a bear bigger still that turned to Lee before lumbering after the other creatures. Behind its sharp-muzzled mask was a human gaze; one Lee had not thought to see again.

The Emperor laughed again. "You multiply her aspect, but it won't help you."

Mary Makepeace Gaia whirled her flaming sword, cutting down the great cats that bounded at her, or setting on fire their striped or sable coats so that they raced away screaming. The blade moved so quickly that its path blurred into a knot of blossoming flames. The giant monkeys howled and chattered at its edge, their coarse coats smouldering as they dug up boulders and trees with frantic haste and hurled them at the assassin.

But boulders burst asunder when they struck the flame, and tree-spears shrivelled in mid-flight. The bear reared up, huger than it had first seemed. Its five-clawed paw raked the sky and there was a thunderclap and a fierce local deluge of rain.

The cocoon of flames died instantly. But where Mary Makepeace Gaia had been standing was a red dragon. It opened its beaked mouth and screamed, and with a brazen clash of wings leaped into the sky.

The bear lunged after it, turning in an instant into a black dragon that whirled away after its red twin. The two twisted in combat, now over the roofs of the Forbidden City, now over the crest of Coal Hill Park. They engaged as swiftly as striking snakes, flew apart, and struck at each other again. At each encounter new thunderclouds billowed up. Slowly, the storm obscured the gray sky light of the flexing data streams. Rain dashed itself to earth amongst strobing strokes of lightning.

The Emperor yelled to Lee, "First your champion dies! Then you!"

Lee wiped water from his face, yelled back, "I can't see how the battle is going! Are you more informed than I?"

For inconstant lightning was the only illumination now, and thunder drowned out the clash of the dragons. The Emperor laughed, his face gleaming like metal. "Watch!" he said. His voice was louder than thunder.

Air pulled apart between the Emperor and Lee, became a window. Suddenly Lee was looking over the shoulder of Dr. Damon Lovelace, the envoy from Earth. He was in the control center, the dome atop the tallest tower of the city of shining towers, watching a fanned sheaf of screens which displayed the earthmover from a dozen different viewpoints, in a dozen different parts of the electromagnetic spectrum, from long-wave radio through visible light to gamma.

The earthmover was roaring up a long slope towards the lip of Tiger Mountain's caldera, trailing a long comet tail of black dust. Lee caught his breath: one inset showed Redd alone in the bubble of its canopy, face slick with sweat, poisoned hand strapped up, one-handedly wrestling with the manual override stick.

No one should have been aboard. The earthmover had assured him of that before he had set it its task.

Gamma light showed the earthmover's bulky fusion pod. At its heart the magnetic pinch fluttered bright as the sun. Tritium fuel was pouring into it, and dozens of strange elements smeared its once pure spectrum. It was approaching criticality.

By radio light, Redd's voice swooped and soared across a hundred wavebands. He was singing something about the land, this land, our land. Then he broke off and whooped and cried out, voice bright as the fusion pinch.

"I'm coming! I'm coming, Billy Lee! They went and killed you, but in the name of the people I'll finish it off!"

"Foolish man," the Emperor said. "I am disappointed in you, Wei Lee, if this is your diversion. Even if it does get close enough, which it won't, any explosion that little fusion plant is capable of won't hurt my defenses."

Dr. Damon Lovelace turned, and the window turned with him to show cadres at work around the perimeter of the domed room. They were mobilizing some of the self-reproducing one-shot laser satellites that swarmed in orbit, turning them inward, marshalling them to produce a synchronized beam that would vaporise the earthmover. Then the door of the elevator opened, and Guoquiang stepped out. He dragged a welding laser behind him, and pointed its wand straight up even as other cadres ran at him. The apex of the dome shone white, and then the room filled with water vapor as the laser holed through. Lee imagined the supersonic whistle of air jetting into the near-vacuum outside.

The swirling fog cleared, dwindling into a pillar that narrowed from its base, poured through the hole, gone. Most of the cadres were slumped at their stations; the few that had survived held air masks to their faces. Guoquiang was sprawled by the welding laser, blood bubbling from a chest wound.

The view turned to show the sheaf of screens. The earthmover was very near the top of the slope now. Redd was still singing.

The Emperor screamed: far down the hill lightning flew up from every tower and rooftop of the Forbidden City, branching across the whole sky. Wei Lee and Number Eighty-Four were knocked down by the concussion.

Lee saw the earthmover ride straight out over the lip of the caldera. For a long moment it seemed to defy gravity as its tracks churned the vanishingly thin air. And then it tumbled end over end. The window flared with unbearable brightness. Lee threw his hands in front of his face and his viruses stepped down his vision: he saw the bones of his hands against the light: then it was gone.

A terrific peal of thunder rolled overhead; blue sheet lightning shot across half the sky. The park was in ruins. The giant monkeys had fled. The Emperor's face, glimpsed by lightning, was pinched and drawn; his finery was ruined by the unrelenting drenching downpour.

"The explosion itself wasn't important," Lee said breathlessly, "but the magnetic pulse caused by the explosion opened your defenses to the sky. Even hardened machinery was blind for an instant, and an instant was all the anarchists needed."

The Emperor said, "This will pass. I rule here. My champion will prevail, and you will both die. The boy first."

He spread his arms and the boy, Number Eighty-Four, rose into the air. He screamed and reached for Wei Lee, but something caught him and hurled him into the Emperor. For a moment, Lee saw the boy dwindling inside the Emperor's shadowy metrical frame. Then he was gone, and only the Emperor stood before him.

"And now you, little human," the Emperor said.

Lee said, "I'm already dead. And so are you."

"I was never alive, foolish Wei Lee! You can't hurt me. You're a ghost in the realm of ghosts, and I'm the one who holds up the sky."

"Oh, but I've already seen to that. You ate the boy, and he was infected with virus." Lee laughed, and reached for the Emperor.

It batted ineffectually at his hands as Lee grasped the fine chain round its neck and pulled it hard, snapping its links. He opened the pouch and took out the machine-code chip.

The eidolon, Emperor no more, wailed, "You're dead! You're a ghost!"

Lee laughed again, closed his eyes and swallowed the chip.

Seventy-eight

He had not known what to expect. At first it was as if someone was standing at his back, shouting furiously. But, slowly, the sense of the eidolon faded. It was like a drop of blood dissolving in a sparkling sea: Lee was that sea.

And yet he was also himself. He was still the same young agronomist technician who with his two friends had walked out so eagerly into that spring morning; he always would be.

He opened his eyes. The storm had passed. The last rain slanted from the sky, silver spears falling softly to earth as thunderheads dissolved. In the grey light of the data streams Lee saw that the high battlement walls around the Forbidden City had dissolved too. All around the far, far horizon was an annular tsunami of ghosts. They were rushing inward, but the distance was so great that they seemed not to move at all, an eternal ever-toppling wave.

Closer at hand, a little way down the slope of the ruined park, a woman stood over her dead twin. It was Miriam Makepeace Mbele. She was breathing hard, and blood streamed from a wound on her scalp, soaking her close-cropped hair and soaking into the collar of her black one-piece bodysuit. She leaned on the pommel of a smoking sword that was planted in the ground. After a moment she left the weapon where it was and walked back up the hill towards Lee.

"It's over," she said. "I can feel it!"

"It's just beginning," Lee said.

Miriam Makepeace Mbele turned beside him, and saw the standing wave on the horizon. "You fool!"

"The lost islands have been opened. Now there is no wall. No division between what should be, and what will be. Just as Mars will belong to everyone, so will information space. Nothing secret. Nothing hidden. I've torn down Heaven's wall."

He watched Miriam consider transforming again, consider attempting to violate his integrity, consider activating a component of his viral system. She could have killed him in a dozen ways, but he knew that she would not.

Instead she smiled. "At least you'll never have children. You're a dynasty of one, Wei Lee. Enjoy your short life while you can, dear little brother."

"I'd already figured that out. I'm you, but with something more."

"You're me, half crippled."

"Great-grandfather Wei bought an ovum from the Nexus and doubled its chromosome number and cloned it. Most were allowed to grow to term with only minimal changes to allow them to pass for Han. I met one of my sisters in Ichun; for a moment I thought it was you, come back from the dead. As for me, Great-grandfather Wei took one of the cloned ova and chipped one of the X chromosomes into a Y. My mother was a surrogate. My father was an employee of my great-grandfather. He . . . "

Miriam said, "The man you call your father was the gene engineer who dealt with the Nexus. Instead of following your great-grandfather's orders, he inserted a Y chromosome given him by the Nexus. It wasn't editing, but deletion and substitution. He betrayed your great-grandfather to save humanity from the Earth's Consensus, and that's why he died. As will we, when those ghosts reach us. But we'll die for nothing, Wei Lee."

The seething wave of the freed dead was halfway across the darkling plain.

"I don't think so," Lee said. "Look!"

A star suddenly shone high in the east. It grew from a point to a whirling torus streaked by amorphous pastel shapes within. Turn the torus inside out and you'd have the world, Lee thought. He said, "My great-grandfather's eidolon was subverted by the Emperor after the Emperor was seduced by the Earth. After that, my great-grandfather and most of the Ten Thousand Years were forced to deal with the Earth's Consensus. They helped let in the Earth. For their betrayal, they gained immortality, and condemned the world to die."

Miriam said, "In the beginning, your great-grandfather sought to unite Mars and the anarchists. You shouldn't blame him because he failed. His eidolon knew all about his plans, and of course so did the Emperor once it swallowed the eidolons of all the Ten Thousand Years. Only the oldest of the Ten Thousand Years, The Little Bird, had a mechanical eidolon; he bided his time and then rebelled. The Emperor did not know about his plans, and it did not know about ours. It didn't know how special you were, Wei Lee, or it would have killed you when you were a baby. Instead, It kept you as a stalking horse for the likes of me. It didn't know you were a double agent, and you didn't even know you were an agent at all."

The torus whirled downward and kissed the side of Coal Hill. Light blazed up, and something swept through it.

It was a long, four-wheeled ground vehicle, styled like an old-fashioned spaceship. It was painted a gleaming pink, with great streaks of chrome the length of its streamlined body. Lee recognized the emblem on top of its square radiator grille from a dozen documentary clips.

In the driver's seat was a man in chauffeur's uniform, with a face mild as milk and a wispy brown beard and a disc of light tilted above his head. When he raised his hands from the wheel, Lee saw that the palms of his white kid gloves were stained with blood.

"Jesus Christ," Miriam Makepeace Mbele breathed.

And on the wide black leather seat behind the chauffeur was the King of the Cats. He wore a blue satin jacket, its collar turned up around the slicked combed-back cowl of his hair. His arm was stretched along the back of the seat, and he kicked open the door with a negligent flip of a snakeskin boot. His lopsided grin broadened. "Hop on in, both of you. Time to get out of here."

"I'm staying," Lee said.

The King said, "Don't be a fool, kid. You've done your bit, far better than we'd hoped. It's time to move on now. Time to come home."

Lee said, "You set me up. My whole life was set up from the beginning."

"From way before the beginning," the King said. "I can get you back across, but we'll have to move fast. They're angry, all those people you freed. There'll be trouble soon enough, and I don't aim to stick around to see it." Miriam had already climbed in; the King of the Cats put his arm around her. There was a crate of iced Thunderbird wine at his feet. Now he wore a check jacket, pink shirt, black jeans and blue suede shoes, and was ten years younger. "Yeah," he drawled, "I know I'm kind of unstable. The lousy codes in this space don't translate too well. I had a hell of a time passing over." He unshipped a bottle, spun off the cap with a negligent flip of his thumb. In his other hand he held a bouquet of glasses. "Just a little bit further on down the road. There's nothing left for you to do here, kid."

Lee could feel the chip he had swallowed. It glowed in his chest like a neon heart. It was easy to pluck it out. He shook off blood and water and broke it in half and had two identical chips, whole in each hand. He broke them again, and had four.

The King of the Cats said, "Way too late for conjuring tricks, kid."

Lee had eight chips, sixteen, thirty-two. They made glowing stacks in his hands.

"Now hold on," the King said. "This really isn't part of the deal. You can't expect to give everyone . . . "

Lee said, "I didn't ask to be Emperor, but now I've backed on to the Jade Throne by mistake it's mine to dispose of as I will. You can't maintain a stable shape here because you can only approximate its codes: but I incorporate those codes. I'm going to use them to empower the living and the dead. Nothing will be hidden from anyone: the knowledge stacks will be transparent. My sister already waits in the Blessed Isles for the dead; they're free to go there or stay here. All I'm doing is giving them the knowledge to make the right choice. All my life I've loved listening to your talk and your music, without knowing that that love was coded in my Y chromosome. All my life has been shaped by others. All my life I've been kept from the truth of my life. Call it revenge, if you like, but I want people to have truth in theirs."

"Kid," the King of the Cats said, "you can't throw up a utopia overnight."

Jesus said, "No, he's right. Wei Lee, the power to choose is all that we can ever give you humans. On your own perhaps you'll fail and fall, but the alternatives are worse. If we raise you up you'll be worse than slaves, and we'll be tainted by ownership. If we destroy you, then your potential will be lost for ever, and our guilt will haunt us until the end of time. Because the universe was not made for you, you have the potential to become something far greater than us. For that, we will always love you."

"You keep quiet now," the King of the Cats said. "You're just here to drive."

Jesus's toothy smile shone in the light of his halo. "I dislike metaphors, but truly I am in the driving seat. You are the interface, but you are only one of many. You know the consensus, and know you must be bound by it."

The King adjusted his big square-lensed dark glasses. He was a lot older and a lot fatter, in a jumpsuit glittering with rhinestones that was slashed open to his navel. He said, "I just don't like to see it end like this, in confusion. It isn't neat."

"It's not an ending," Jesus said. "It's a beginning."

The King of the Cats said, "So you let me do this job my own way until I reach the end of my string. Then you start jerking me around. Why should I put up with this?"

"Because you're part of a democracy, and none of us are empowered by noise alone."

The King thought about that. "Noise is my life," he said, and handed brimming glasses of Thunderbird wine to Miriam Makepeace Mbele, leaned across and gave one to Lee, toasted him with a third. "I guess we'll have to trust you," he said. "Take care, you hear?"

Lee said to Miriam, "You can stay here, if you want to."

She drank off the wine in one swallow, threw the glass over her shoulder: it vanished before it hit the ground. "There's still work for me," she said. "I have to report to the anarchists, for one thing. I might be back, if they can find me a body."

The King of the Cats said, "That's another burden for you, Emperor Wei Lee. The anarchists are energy poor, their gene pool contaminated and reduced below safe limits, and their consensus is unravelling. They're a few generations from barbarism, maybe ten from extinction. That's why the Nexus agreed to let us work through them; it was their last chance. You do right by them, you hear?"

"I'll always listen to you."

"Glad to hear it." The King tapped his chauffeur on the shoulder. "We're out of here, my man."

Jesus stepped on the gas, and the pink Cadillac blurred into a line of light that stretched and vanished.

The wine had turned to water. Lee drank it anyway, and went on down the hill, towards his people.

Seventy-nine

It took Vette three days to reach the top of the mountain. The night the old people disappeared, and Wei Lee and the little girl lab rat went chasing after them, the big machine had started up by itself. Vette had gone behind a boulder to pee, and she'd come out to see Redd chasing the machine down the gully. She ran after them through the clouds of black dust churned up by the machine, saw Redd grab hold of the ladder and pull himself up. She ran on until she could run no further, standing in the track the machine had smashed through the trees at the mouth of the draw and sobbing for breath as she watched the machine's lights dwindle into the starlit darkness.

Vette did not give up. She knew that heroes never gave up—sometimes they continued their quests beyond death. For the rest of the night and through the day that followed she followed the tracks of the machine up the long, lichen-encrusted slope, jogging at a steady pace, her harpoon slung at her shoulder. It was like climbing an endless wave of rock.

As she climbed her breath grew labored and her sight fluttered red with the pounding of her pulse. She climbed until stars began to shine through the day sky, and the air was so thin that every effort seemed immense and remote, as if she had grown to a giant without a giant's strength.

She was lying in a stupor when the limber four-legged robot with the woman's face floating within its screen found her. It was carrying a pressure suit, and Vette, who thought that this was a dream, did not resist when she was fastened into it. She was beyond surprise or fear.

The suit fed Vette thin sweet gruel from a nipple and sopped up her wastes and recycled her rebreathed air. Its black skin absorbed the light of the sun and turned her steps into leaps and bounds. Still, it took her and the robot all night and most of the day to climb to the top of Tiger Mountain.

She waited through dawn when the mountain trembled beneath her and vast sheets of light pulsed out above. After the lights were gone, the sky was full of falling stars. To the southwest a great light climbed the sky, and as it faded the mountain began to tremble again. Vette saw the world below the naked mountain slopes vanish under slate-grey rainclouds. The flood had come at last. Lee had won, but she had to find out if he and Redd and the little lab rat were still alive.

So she and the robot climbed for the rest of the day, until they reached the lip of the caldera and the ruined city directly below. Although the world below Tiger Mountain's slopes was shrouded with clouds, here above the atmosphere the sun still walked. The towers were broken or fallen amongst craters lined with shiny glass. Silvery loops of road slumped in shiny tangles. Domes had melted down to their rims.

Vette followed the robot down the steep cliffs. Darkness overtook them before they reached the bottom of the caldera, and Vette spent the night sleeping fitfully on a narrow ledge, watched over by the robot. The next day the sun was vertical by the time they reached the floor of the caldera.

They toiled across a fantastic landscape of collapsed lava tubes and stubs and snags towards the broken towers. Vette allowed the robot to lead her through the blasted ruins, the glow of its face-plate screen and the beam of her suit's helmet mingling and separating. One tower still held atmospheric pressure, and once inside Vette took off her helmet, grateful to feel the random brush of free air touching her face.

The robot stalked silently and surely along curving corridors, and skittered down a turning stair that at last debouched into a room far beneath the surface of the caldera. The room was hot, lit by the many colors of flowers.

Three bodies lay in the kaleidoscope light. One had been dead for years, tangled in wires where it had half fallen from a couch. Another was of a slim muscular woman with dark skin and an eyepatch, dried blood streaked from her nose and ears and one eye.

The third was Wei Lee's. His throat had been cut from ear to ear. He lay in a sea of dried blood.

Vette cried out, but the robot caught her shoulder, turned her to show her two children curled in a corner, thumbs in their mouths, breathing gently and slowly in a deep sleep. One was a young boy of no more than six or seven, his head shaven like a Free Yankee's. The other was the lab rat. When the robot touched her with the delicate metal fingers of a forelimb, she stirred and woke, blinked at the woman's benign floating image and said, "Wei Lee?"

Beside her, the boy opened his eyes, but his gaze was as innocent of self as a newborn baby's.

Eighty

They returned to the abandoned town at the margin of
the forest belt that ringed Tiger Mountain's slopes. The
gate of the Last House had been broken down. There
was no sign of Yang Bo, or the robots he had commanded,
or of the wild ones, except the remains of their dead. Bones
were strewn across the slope beneath the walls of the Last
House; it was clear that although Yang Bo had killed most
of the wild ones he had lost the battle. But although the
surviving wild ones had ripped fabrics and overturned furniture, pissed and shat on the floors and left doors open so
that rain had blown in, the Last House was mostly intact.

Vette and Chen Yao and the boy made their home there.
Vette and Chen Yao improvised rainproof garments from
plastic sheeting, and foraged in fields where crops sprouted
from long dormant seeds in a muddle of tomatoes and maize
and peppers and sugar bamboo and greenleaf. They laid
snares, smeared sticks with birdlime and set them around
bait of scraps of fat. They gathered up the bones of the wild
children and burned them on a pyre of aromatic juniper
wood. A year passed.

The boy sleepwalked through it, never speaking and showing no sign of comprehension when spoken to. Most of the
time he slept at the hearth of the house, but sometimes
Vette and Chen Yao would return to find him at the mended
gates, clinging to one of the posts and staring up the mountain's long slope at the cloud cap which hid its summit.

386

He was infected with a copy of Wei Lee's memories, Chen Yao said, but not with his essence. Perhaps Wei Lee planned to return from information space when his task of enlightening the living and the dead was done, but she did not think so.

Once a month she used one of the couches to plunge into information space. She tried to explain the changes to Vette, the growing transparency of the architecture of the medium. You could go anywhere, even Heaven. Vette wasn't interested: she believed that the spirit world was only a mass delusion. All that mattered was that Wei Lee had brought the rains.

Chen Yao used the couch to speak with people all over the world, and with the aspects of the other gods in Xin Beijing. They told her that rain was general over both hemispheres of the planet; that snow was falling over the Great Northern Desert. About ten per cent of the anarchists' ice bolides had not disintegrated during their skimming passes through the atmosphere, but had fallen in one piece. A string of explosive impacts had smashed an irregular chain of new craters around the equator, and a multiple strike near the slopes of the Paved Mountain had released the vast fossil aquifer underlying the Dragon's Back. Water had poured into the Dust Seas at rates of over a billion litres an hour. The Dust Seas had turned to swamp, and then to shallow brine seas. Their artificial ecosystem—the glittering swarms of phytoplankton and zooplankton, and the slow monstrous dust rays—was destroyed for ever, and water was still pouring from the aquifer. And the fullerene viruses released from the other ice bolides were multiplying at an exponential rate. They had already formed vast clusters in the deep permafrost, and outgassing geysers and sumps were developing all over the high plains, while thin stratospheric layers of chlorofluorocarbons were beginning to spread out from the poles.

It was the chaotic spring of a new climatic era.

The fall of the Emperor had brought chaos, too. The Ten Thousand Years had been overthrown. The Little Bird had been strung upside down from a transmission relay tower by his former troops when the Army of the People's Mouths had started to retake the capital in a brief fierce war that the rains had ended. The Gang of Six had each committed ritual suicide at the same moment in their separate houses. The body of Lee's great-grandfather had been killed by the boy-thing into which his personality had been partially written. Many others had simply vanished.

And Wei Lee had appeared to everyone who used information space. Everyone who talked with Chen Yao told her that Wei Lee had given them the gift of mastering the structures which held the knowledge of the world. Nothing was hidden any more.

But Wei Lee did not come to Chen Yao herself until a year after his apotheosis, on a rare sunny day in early summer. When she masked herself and lay down on the couch not the usual perception grid but a person appeared to her, tall and robed in black, with a hood cast over his face. He took her hand and then she was standing before the great throne in the Hall of Supreme Harmony.

The figure cast off the hood, and Chen Yao laughed aloud when she saw Wei Lee's face. He laughed too, and sat on the steps beneath the throne so that his face was level with hers. He told her that he was nearly finished with the living, that he wanted to go on to the Isles of the Blessed to join his sister and the myriads of the dead.

Chen Yao wanted to know whether Wei Lee would return to the real world, where his memories slept safe in the curve of the boy's skull.

Wei Lee said that he had changed too much to be able to return. But although poor Number Eighty-Four had only been infected with partials of Lee's memory, another carried partials of Lee's own self. It was her choice to let him be reborn, and meanwhile clades of viruses would keep Number Eighty-Four forever young.

"Until," Wei Lee said, "the time comes for me to be banished. I did not seek to become Emperor, Chen Yao, but that is what I am. I wish to diminish amongst the dead, but it seems that the living are not done with me. They want an Emperor, and their will grows stronger every day. The changes I have made to information space mean that I cannot hide from them. Nothing can be hidden."

"You don't need anyone to tell you what to do, and you don't have to listen to anyone, either. I know you never listened to me."

"I'm not what I was. I have . . . multiplied. This aspect is perhaps the nearest to my human self, but I am thousands, now. I fear that I'll become what the Thing in Jupiter feared it would become: a surrogate god, ruler of humanity for all time. I hope that someone will take that bitter cup from me." He looked at his hands, clasping hers. "You've grown, Chen Yao. You'll have young men chasing after you soon enough."

"None of us are what we were . . . As for young men, there are none that I know of. Vette and me, and Number Eighty-Four, we live alone."

"As for that, remember that nothing stays the same for ever." Wei Lee smiled, and told Chen Yao that he had a gift for her, and laid a prickly chip in her mouth. As it dissolved into her, the throne room dissolved around her (although now she knew where she could find it, now and forever more) and she was aware of the couch beneath her, the mask over her eyes and the gloves on her hands, bird-song thrilling through the open window and Vette rattling pots somewhere in the house.

That was the day the robot vanished. It had remained with them for that whole year, but as spring had worn into summer they had seen less of it each day. After Wei Lee spoke to Chen Yao, they never saw it again.

The next day, Chen Yao came running in from the fields. It was raining. She had seen a band of people toiling up out of the forest towards the town. Vette ran to the gate and recognized a banner raised soddenly above the heads of the approaching people and began to wave and shout. Someone, the boy, caught her hand. He had lost his clothes again, and stood naked in the soft cold rain.

"It's all right," Vette said. "These are my people! These are the Free Yankee Nation! They've come to find me at last!"

The boy stared at them, mouth working around his socketed thumb. He had not spoken in all this time, and stared with silent incomprehension as nearly naked people, masked and tattooed, ran up the path to the Last House, laughing and cheering, and shouting questions at Vette.

His time had not yet come.

Eighty-one

B ut come it would. One day, five long years after the rains had begun, a woman would ride a barque down the Grand Canal to a coastal town where rusty but still serviceable elevators plunged from the top of a high cliff to the weltering unchained sea. She was the dear daughter of the House of Kong, the eldest of the one hundred and tenth generation of descendants of the Great Sage, and the essence of the Saviour of the World was coded in fullerene viruses that had settled in certain implanted circuits in her nervous system.

A Yankee ghost had brought her a message from another place. The ghost had come at night, her image burning blue, and had shown the woman the young boy whose head held nothing but another's coded memories. The ghost had explained that it was time that these memories were quickened, and had told the dear daughter of the House of Kong what she must do.

And so, in the morning, she had told her husband that the time to repay her obligation had come at last. She had packed a small bag, kissed each of her five children in turn, and set off on her journey.

Mars had changed, but the people of Mars had changed less than might be imagined. They loved and laughed and watched heroic operas and wagered on fighting crickets and cheated and hustled and lied—and sometimes even killed— as they always had. No dictator, no matter how universal or benign, could stop people being people. But the lies were only little lies, personal lies. Big public lies were no longer possible because the only system by which they could be disseminated was now too transparent for lies to slip by undetected.

Nothing important was hidden or could be hidden, or not for long. In theory everyone could express an opinion on every decision of the Emperor. Most didn't. The last time the world had united was when it had decided to send aid to the anarchists, and that had been a year after the beginning of the rains. For most it was enough that they could get on with their lives, enough that they could find the job they wanted, that there was enough food, a good place to live, a future for their children.

Still, some knew and cared about the dear daughter of the House of Kong. A pod of fin escorted her barque on its voyage down the Grand Canal, their bulging foreheads pregnant with knowledge, and a few people gathered at the elevator heads to cheer her as she set out on the last part of her journey.

Now she stood before the mast of the little barque and watched the sea's horizon for the first sight of her destination. The wet salt wind cracked and filled the bellying sail above her head. It stood fair out of the eye of the south, driving the little ship across the bitter, muddy seas of Mars towards the island of Tiger Mountain, where she would find the lost boy and quicken in him Wei Lee's new beginning and last end in a way traditional to the conclusion of tales such as this, with a kiss.

Critical Acclaim for

NIMITZ CLASS

"A rarity. . . . The book reeks with authenticity."

—*Houston Chronicle*

"The best military thriller since *The Hunt for Red October*. . . . Robinson has crafted a fast-paced, chilling, yet believable tale, peppered with unforgettable characters."

—*San Francisco Examiner*

"A perfect nautical thriller: suspenseful, exciting, technically accurate, and plausible enough to be unnerving. For sailors and non-sail⟨...⟩ ⟨...⟩rn for this sum⟨...⟩

⟨...⟩*rning News*

"Cle⟨...⟩

⟨...⟩*Denver Post*

"Th⟨...⟩ ⟨...⟩o horrible to con⟨...⟩

⟨...⟩*ondon Day*

"Th⟨...⟩ ⟨...⟩e equal of Cla⟨...⟩ ⟨...⟩onary tale."

—*Publishers Weekly*

"A thundering good naval yarn . . . an enjoyable read. *Nimitz Class* has a more serious purpose, to draw attention to the worldwide peacekeeping role being carried out by the U.S. Navy. We must hope that a 'Nimitz Class' type of incident, which every professional sailor will recognize as extreme but plausible, would not shake American resolve."

—Captain Richard Sharpe, Editor,
Jane's Fighting Ships

"The reader is almost a part of the adventure, sitting at the right hand of those masterminding the operation. *Nimitz Class* brought back some real-life experiences for me."

—J. Daniel Howard,
former undersecretary of the Navy

"*Nimitz Class* is that rare combination of military thriller and tactical treatise. While capturing the excitement of naval operations, it also raises critical issues about the future of naval forces, terrorism, and the implications of the spread of weapons of mass destruction. I strongly suggest that all military professionals read this book, not only for the issues it confronts, but for the sheer enjoyment of a great book."

—William J. Crowe Jr.,
former U.S. ambassador to Great Britain